THE SOFT SIDE

THE SOFT SIDE

BY

HENRY JAMES

Short Story Index Reprint Series

BOOKS FOR LIBRARIES PRESS

FREEPORT, NEW YORK

First Published 1900
Reprinted 1970

INTERNATIONAL STANDARD BOOK NUMBER:
0-8369-3722-8

LIBRARY OF CONGRESS CATALOG CARD NUMBER:
77-140330

PRINTED IN THE UNITED STATES OF AMERICA

CONTENTS

THE GREAT GOOD PLACE

I

GEORGE DANE had waked up to a bright new day, the face of nature well washed by last night's downpour and shining as with high spirits, good resolutions, lively intentions — the great glare of recommencement, in short, fixed in his patch of sky. He had sat up late to finish work — arrears overwhelming; then at last had gone to bed with the pile but little reduced. He was now to return to it after the pause of the night; but he could only look at it, for the time, over the bristling hedge of letters planted by the early postman an hour before and already, on the customary table by the chimney-piece, formally rounded and squared by his systematic servant. It was something too merciless, the domestic perfection of Brown. There were newspapers on another table, ranged with the same rigour of custom, newspapers too many — what could any creature want of so much news? — and each with its hand on the neck of the other, so that the row of their bodiless heads was like a series of decapitations. Other journals, other periodicals of every sort, folded and in wrappers, made a huddled mound that had been growing for several days and of which he had been wearily, helplessly aware. There were new books, also in wrappers as well as disenveloped and dropped again — books from publishers, books from authors, books from friends, books from enemies, books from his own bookseller, who took, it sometimes struck him, inconceivable things for granted. He touched nothing, approached nothing, only turned a heavy eye over the work, as it were, of the night — the fact, in his high, wide-windowed

room, where the hard light of duty could penetrate every
corner, of the unashamed admonition of the day. It was the
old rising tide, and it rose and rose even under a minute's
watching. It had been up to his shoulders last night — it
was up to his chin now.

Nothing had passed while he slept — everything had stayed;
nothing, that he could yet feel, had died — many things had
been born. To let them alone, these things, the new things,
let them utterly alone and see if that, by chance, wouldn't
somehow prove the best way to deal with them : this fancy
brushed his face for a moment as a possible solution, just
giving it, as many a time before, a cool wave of air. Then he
knew again as well as ever that leaving was difficult, leaving
impossible — that the only remedy, the true, soft, effacing
sponge, would be to *be* left, to be forgotten. There was no
footing on which a man who had ever liked life — liked it,
at any rate, as *he* had — could now escape from it. He must
reap as he had sown. It was a thing of meshes; he had
simply gone to sleep under the net and had simply waked
up there. The net was too fine; the cords crossed each other
at spots so near together, making at each a little tight, hard
knot that tired fingers, this morning, were too limp and too
tender to touch. Our poor friend's touched nothing — only
stole significantly into his pockets as he wandered over to
the window and faintly gasped at the energy of nature. What
was most overwhelming was that she herself was so ready.
She had soothed him rather, the night before, in the small
hours by the lamp. From behind the drawn curtain of his
study the rain had been audible and in a manner merciful;
washing the window in a steady flood, it had seemed the
right thing, the retarding, interrupting thing, the thing that,
if it would only last, might clear the ground by floating out to
a boundless sea the innumerable objects among which his feet
stumbled and strayed. He had positively laid down his pen
as on a sense of friendly pressure from it. The kind, full

swash had been on the glass when he turned out his lamp; he had left his phrase unfinished and his papers lying quite as if for the flood to bear them away on its bosom. But there still, on the table, were the bare bones of the sentence —and not all of those; the single thing borne away and that he could never recover was the missing half that might have paired with it and begotten a figure.

Yet he could at last only turn back from the window; the world was everywhere, without and within, and, with the great staring egotism of its health and strength, was not to be trusted for tact or delicacy. He faced about precisely to meet his servant and the absurd solemnity of two telegrams on a tray. Brown ought to have kicked them into the room — then he himself might have kicked them out.

'And you told me to remind you, sir——'

George Dane was at last angry. 'Remind me of nothing!'

'But you insisted, sir, that I was to insist!'

He turned away in despair, speaking with a pathetic quaver at absurd variance with his words : 'If you insist, Brown, I'll kill you!' He found himself anew at the window, whence, looking down from his fourth floor, he could see the vast neighbourhood, under the trumpet-blare of the sky, beginning to rush about. There was a silence, but he knew Brown had not left him — knew exactly how straight and serious and stupid and faithful he stood there. After a minute he heard him again.

'It's only because, sir, you know, sir, you can't remember——'

At this Dane did flash round; it was more than at such a moment he could bear. 'Can't remember, Brown? I can't forget. That's what's the matter with me.'

Brown looked at him with the advantage of eighteen years of consistency. 'I'm afraid you're not well, sir.'

Brown's master thought. 'It's a shocking thing to say, but I wish to Heaven I weren't! It would be perhaps an excuse.'

Brown's blankness spread like the desert. 'To put them off?'

'Ah!' The sound was a groan; the plural pronoun, *any* pronoun, so mistimed. 'Who is it?'

'Those ladies you spoke of — to lunch.'

'Oh!' The poor man dropped into the nearest chair and stared awhile at the carpet. It was very complicated.

'How many will there be, sir?' Brown asked.

'Fifty!'

'Fifty, sir?'

Our friend, from his chair, looked vaguely about; under his hand were the telegrams, still unopened, one of which he now tore asunder. '"Do hope you sweetly won't mind, to-day, 1.30, my bringing poor dear Lady Mullet, who is so awfully bent,"' he read to his companion.

His companion weighed it. 'How many does *she* make, sir?'

'Poor dear Lady Mullet? I haven't the least idea.'

'Is she — a — deformed, sir?' Brown inquired, as if in this case she might make more.

His master wondered, then saw he figured some personal curvature. 'No; she's only bent on coming!' Dane opened the other telegram and again read out: '"So sorry it's at eleventh hour impossible, and count on you here, as very greatest favour, at two sharp instead."'

'How many does *that* make?' Brown imperturbably continued.

Dane crumpled up the two missives and walked with them to the waste-paper basket, into which he thoughtfully dropped them. 'I can't say. You must do it all yourself. I shan't be there.'

It was only on this that Brown showed an expression. 'You'll go instead ——'

'I'll go instead!' Dane raved.

Brown, however, had had occasion to show before that *he* would never desert their post. 'Isn't that rather sacrificing the three?' Between respect and reproach he paused.

'*Are* there three?'

'I lay for four in all.'

His master had, at any rate, caught his thought. 'Sacrificing the three to the one, you mean? Oh, I'm not going to *her!*'

Brown's famous 'thoroughness'—his great virtue—had never been so dreadful. 'Then where *are* you going?'

Dane sat down to his table and stared at his ragged phrase. '"There is a happy land—far, far away!"' He chanted it like a sick child and knew that for a minute Brown never moved. During this minute he felt between his shoulders the gimlet of criticism.

'Are you quite sure you're all right?'

'It's my certainty that overwhelms me, Brown. Look about you and judge. Could anything be more "right," in the view of the envious world, than everything that surrounds us here; that immense array of letters, notes, circulars; that pile of printers' proofs, magazines, and books; these perpetual telegrams, these impending guests; this retarded, unfinished, and interminable work? What could a man want more?'

'Do you mean there's too much, sir?'—Brown had sometimes these flashes.

'There's too much. There's too much. But *you* can't help it, Brown.'

'No, sir,' Brown assented. 'Can't *you?*'

'I'm thinking—I must see. There are hours——!' Yes, there were hours, and this was one of them: he jerked himself up for another turn in his labyrinth, but still not touching, not even again meeting, his interlocutor's eye. If he was a genius for any one he was a genius for Brown; but it was terrible what that meant, being a genius for Brown. There had been times when he had done full justice to the way it kept him up; now, however, it was almost the worst of the avalanche. 'Don't trouble about me,' he went on insincerely, and looking askance through his window again at the bright and beautiful world. 'Perhaps it will rain—that *may* not be over. I do love the rain,' he weakly pursued. 'Perhaps, better still, it will snow.'

Brown now had indeed a perceptible expression, and the expression was fear. 'Snow, sir — the end of May?' Without pressing this point he looked at his watch. 'You'll feel better when you've had breakfast.'

'I dare say,' said Dane, whom breakfast struck in fact as a pleasant alternative to opening letters. 'I'll come in immediately.'

'But without waiting —— ?'

'Waiting for what?'

Brown had at last, under his apprehension, his first lapse from logic, which he betrayed by hesitating in the evident hope that his companion would, by a flash of remembrance, relieve him of an invidious duty. But the only flashes now were the good man's own. 'You say you can't forget, sir; but you do forget —— '

'Is it anything very horrible?' Dane broke in.

Brown hung fire. 'Only the gentleman you told me you had asked —— '

Dane again took him up; horrible or not, it came back — indeed its mere coming back classed it. 'To breakfast to-day? It *was* to-day; I see.' It came back, yes, came back; the appointment with the young man — he supposed him young — and whose letter, the letter about — what was it? — had struck him. 'Yes, yes; wait, wait.'

'Perhaps he'll do you good, sir,' Brown suggested.

'Sure to — sure to. All right!' Whatever he might do, he would at least prevent some other doing: that was present to our friend as, on the vibration of the electric bell at the door of the flat, Brown moved away. Two things, in the short interval that followed, were present to Dane: his having utterly forgotten the connection, the whence, whither, and why of his guest; and his continued disposition not to touch — no, not with the finger. Ah, if he might *never* again touch!

All the unbroken seals and neglected appeals lay there while, for a pause that he couldn't measure, he stood before the chimney-piece with his hands still in his pockets. He heard a brief exchange of words in the hall, but never afterward recovered the time taken by Brown to reappear, to precede and announce another person — a person whose name, somehow, failed to reach Dane's ear. Brown went off again to serve breakfast, leaving host and guest confronted. The duration of this first stage also, later on, defied measurement; but that little mattered, for in the train of what happened came promptly the second, the third, the fourth, the rich succession of the others. Yet what happened was but that Dane took his hand from his pocket, held it straight out, and felt it taken. Thus indeed, if he had wanted never again to touch, it was already done.

II

He might have been a week in the place — the scene of his new consciousness — before he spoke at all. The occasion of it then was that one of the quiet figures he had been idly watching drew at last nearer, and showed him a face that was the highest expression — to his pleased but as yet slightly confused perception — of the general charm. What *was* the general charm? He couldn't, for that matter, easily have phrased it; it was such an abyss of negatives, such an absence of everything. The oddity was that, after a minute, he was struck as by the reflection of his own very image in this first interlocutor seated with him, on the easy bench, under the high, clear portico and above the wide, far-reaching garden, where the things that most showed in the greenness were the surface of still water and the white note of old statues. The absence of everything was, in the aspect of the Brother who had thus informally joined him — a man of his own age, tired, distinguished, modest, kind — really, as he could soon see, but the absence of what he didn't want. He didn't want, for the time, anything but just to *be* there, to stay in the bath. He was in the bath yet, the broad, deep bath of stillness. They sat in it together now, with the water up to their chins. He had not had to talk, he had not had to think, he had scarce even had to feel. He had been sunk that way before, sunk — when and where ? — in another flood; only a flood of rushing waters, in which bumping and gasping were all. This was a current so slow and so tepid that one floated practically without motion and without chill. The break of silence was not immediate, though Dane seemed indeed to feel it begin before a sound passed. It could pass quite sufficiently without words that he and his mate were Brothers, and what that meant.

Dane wondered, but with no want of ease — for want of ease was impossible — if his friend found in *him* the same likeness, the proof of peace, the gage of what the place could do. The long afternoon crept to its end; the shadows fell further and the sky glowed deeper; but nothing changed — nothing *could* change — in the element itself. It was a conscious security. It was wonderful! Dane had lived into it, but he was still immensely aware. He would have been sorry to lose that, for just this fact, as yet, the blessed fact of consciousness, seemed the greatest thing of all. Its only fault was that, being in itself such an occupation, so fine an unrest in the heart of gratitude, the life of the day all went to it. But what even then was the harm ? He had come only to come, to take what he found. This was the part where the great cloister, inclosed externally on three sides and probably the largest, lightest, fairest effect, to his charmed sense, that human hands could ever have expressed in dimensions of length and breadth, opened to the south its splendid fourth quarter, turned to the great view an outer gallery that combined with the rest of the portico to form a high, dry loggia, such as he a little pretended to himself he had, in Italy, in old days, seen in old cities, old convents, old villas. This recall of the disposition of some great abode of an Order, some mild Monte Cassino, some Grande Chartreuse more accessible, was his main term of comparison; but he knew he had really never anywhere beheld anything at once so calculated and so generous.

Three impressions in particular had been with him all the week, and he could only recognise in silence their happy effect on his nerves. How it was all managed he couldn't have told —he had been content moreover till now with his ignorance of cause and pretext; but whenever he chose to listen with a certain intentness he made out, as from a distance, the sound of slow, sweet bells. How could they be so far and yet so audible? How could they be so near and yet so faint? How, above all, could they, in such an arrest of life, be, to *time* things, so frequent? The very essence of the bliss of Dane's whole change had been precisely that there was nothing now to time. It was the same with the slow footsteps that always, within earshot, to the vague attention, marked the space and the leisure, seemed, in long, cool arcades, lightly to fall and perpetually to recede. This was the second impression, and it melted into the third, as, for that matter, every form of softness, in the great good place, was but a further turn, without jerk or gap, of the endless roll of serenity. The quiet footsteps were quiet figures; the quiet figures that, to the eye, kept the picture human and brought its perfection within reach. This perfection, he felt on the bench by his friend, was now more in reach than ever. His friend at last turned to him a look different from the looks of friends in London clubs.

'The thing was to find it out!'

It was extraordinary how this remark fitted into his thought. 'Ah, wasn't it? And when I think,' said Dane, 'of all the people who haven't and who never will!' He sighed over these unfortunates with a tenderness that, in its degree, was practically new to him, feeling, too, how well his companion would know the people he meant. He only meant some, but

they were all who would want it; though of these, no doubt —
well, for reasons, for things that, in the world, he had observed
— there would never be too many. Not all perhaps who wanted
would really find; but none at least would find who didn't
really want. And then what the need would have to have
been first! What it at first had to be for himself! He felt
afresh, in the light of his companion's face, what it might still
be even when deeply satisfied, as well as what communication
was established by the mere mutual knowledge of it.

'Every man must arrive by himself and on his own feet —
isn't that so? We're brothers here for the time, as in a great
monastery, and we immediately think of each other and recognise each other as such; but we must have first got here as
we can, and we meet after long journeys by complicated ways.
Moreover we meet — don't we? — with closed eyes.'

'Ah, don't speak as if we were dead!' Dane laughed.

'I shan't mind death if it's like this,' his friend replied.

It was too obvious, as Dane gazed before him, that one
wouldn't; but after a moment he asked, with the first articu-
lation, as yet, of his most elementary wonder: 'Where is
it?'

'I shouldn't be surprised if it were much nearer than one
ever suspected.'

'Nearer town, do you mean?'

'Nearer everything — nearer every one.'

George Dane thought. 'Somewhere, for instance, down in
Surrey?'

His Brother met him on this with a shade of reluctance.
'Why should we call it names? It must have a climate, you
see.'

'Yes,' Dane happily mused; 'without that——!' All it so
securely did have overwhelmed him again, and he couldn't
help breaking out: '*What* is it?'

'Oh, it's positively a part of our ease and our rest and our
change, I think, that we don't at all know and that we may

really call it, for that matter, anything in the world we like —
the thing, for instance, we love it most for being.'

'I know what *I* call it,' said Dane after a moment. Then as
his friend listened with interest: 'Just simply "The Great
Good Place."'

'I see — what can you say more? I've put it to myself
perhaps a little differently.' They sat there as innocently as
small boys confiding to each other the names of toy animals.
'The Great Want Met.'

'Ah, yes, that's it!'

'Isn't it enough for us that it's a place carried on, for our
benefit, so admirably that we strain our ears in vain for a creak
of the machinery? Isn't it enough for us that it's simply a
thorough hit?'

'Ah, a hit!' Dane benignantly murmured.

'It does for us what it pretends to do,' his companion went
on; 'the mystery isn't deeper than that. The thing is probably simple enough in fact, and on a thoroughly practical basis;
only it has had its origin in a splendid thought, in a real stroke
of genius.'

'Yes,' Dane exclaimed, 'in a sense — on somebody or other's
part — so exquisitely personal!'

'Precisely — it rests, like all good things, on experience.
The "great want" comes home — that's the great thing it
does! On the day it came home to the right mind this dear
place was constituted. It always, moreover, in the long run,
has been met — it always must be. How can it not require to
be, more and more, as pressure of every sort grows?'

Dane, with his hands folded in his lap, took in these words
of wisdom. 'Pressure of every sort *is* growing!' he placidly
observed.

'I see well enough what that fact has done to *you*,' his
Brother returned.

Dane smiled. 'I couldn't have borne it longer. I don't
know what would have become of me.'

'I know what would have become of *me*.'

'Well, it's the same thing.'

'Yes,' said Dane's companion, 'it's doubtless the same thing.' On which they sat in silence a little, seeming pleasantly to follow, in the view of the green garden, the vague movements of the monster — madness, surrender, collapse — they had escaped. Their bench was like a box at the opera. 'And I may perfectly, you know,' the Brother pursued, 'have seen you before. I may even have known you well. We don't know.'

They looked at each other again serenely enough, and at last Dane said: 'No, we don't know.'

'That's what I meant by our coming with our eyes closed. Yes — there's something out. There's a gap — a link missing, the great hiatus!' the Brother laughed. 'It's as simple a story as the old, old rupture — the break that lucky Catholics have always been able to make, that they are still, with their innumerable religious houses, able to make, by going into "retreat." I don't speak of the pious exercises; I speak only of the material simplification. I don't speak of the putting off of one's self; I speak only — if one has a self worth sixpence — of the getting it back. The place, the time, the way, were for those of the old persuasion, always there — are indeed practically there for them as much as ever. They can always get off — the blessed houses receive. So it was high time that we — we of the great Protestant peoples, still more, if possible, in the sensitive individual case, overscored and overwhelmed, still more congested with mere quantity and prostituted, through our "enterprise," to mere profanity — should learn how to get off, should find somewhere *our* retreat and remedy. There was such a huge chance for it!'

Dane laid his hand on his companion's arm. 'It's charming, how, when we speak for ourselves, we speak for each other. That was exactly what I said!' He had fallen to recalling from over the gulf the last occasion.

The Brother, as if it would do them both good, only desired to draw him out. 'What you said ——?'

'To *him* — that morning.' Dane caught a far bell again and heard a slow footstep. A quiet figure passed somewhere — neither of them turned to look. What was, little by little, more present to him was the perfect taste. It was supreme — it was everywhere. 'I just dropped my burden — and he received it.'

'And was it very great?'

'Oh, such a load!' Dane laughed.

'Trouble, sorrow, doubt?'

'Oh, no; worse than that!'

'Worse?'

'"Success" — the vulgarest kind!' And Dane laughed again.

'Ah, I know that, too! No one in future, as things are going, will be able to face success.'

'Without something of this sort — never. The better it is the worse — the greater the deadlier. But my one pain here,' Dane continued, 'is in thinking of my poor friend.'

'The person to whom you've already alluded?'

'My substitute in the world. Such an unutterable benefactor. He turned up that morning when everything had somehow got on my nerves, when the whole great globe indeed, nerves, or no nerves, seemed to have squeezed itself into my study. It wasn't a question of nerves, it was a mere question of the displacement of everything — of submersion by our eternal too much. I didn't know *où donner de la tête* — I couldn't have gone a step further.'

The intelligence with which the Brother listened kept them as children feeding from the same bowl. 'And then you got the tip?'

'I got the tip!' Dane happily sighed.

'Well, we all get it. But I dare say differently.'

'Then how did *you* ——?'

The Brother hesitated, smiling. 'You tell me first.'

III

'WELL,' said George Dane, 'it was a young man I had never seen — a man, at any rate, much younger than myself — who had written to me and sent me some article, some book. I read the stuff, was much struck with it, told him so and thanked him — on which, of course, I heard from him again. He asked me things — his questions were interesting; but to save time and writing I said to him: "Come to see me — we can talk a little; but all I can give you is half an hour at breakfast." He turned up at the hour on a day when, more than ever in my life before, I seemed, as it happened, in the endless press and stress, to have lost possession of my soul and to be surrounded only with the affairs of other people and the irrelevant, destructive, brutalising sides of life. It made me literally ill — made me feel as I had never felt that if I should once really, for an hour, lose hold of the thing itself, the thing I was trying for, I should never recover it again. The wild waters would close over me, and I should drop straight to the bottom where the vanquished dead lie.'

'I follow you every step of your way,' said the friendly Brother. 'The wild waters, you mean, of our horrible time.'

'Of our horrible time — precisely. Not, of course — as we sometimes dream — of any other.'

'Yes, any other is only a dream. We really know none but our own.'

'No, thank God — that's enough,' Dane said. 'Well, my young man turned up, and I hadn't been a minute in his presence before making out that practically it would be in him somehow or other to help me. He came to me with envy, envy extravagant — really passionate. I was, heaven save us, the great "success" for him; he himself was broken and beaten. How can I say what passed between us? — it was so strange, so swift, so much a matter, from one to the other, of

instant perception and agreement. He was so clever and
haggard and hungry!'

'Hungry?' the Brother asked.

'I don't mean for bread, though he had none too much, I
think, even of that.   I mean for — well, what *I* had and what
I was a monument of to him as I stood there up to my neck
in preposterous evidence.   He, poor chap, had been for ten
years serenading closed windows and had never yet caused a
shutter to show that it stirred.   My dim blind was the first
to be raised an inch; my reading of his book, my impression
of it, my note and my invitation, formed literally the only
response ever dropped into his dark street.   He saw in my
littered room, my shattered day, my bored face and spoiled
temper — it's embarrassing, but I must tell you — the very
blaze of my glory.   And he saw in the blaze of my glory —
deluded innocent! — what he had yearned for in vain.'

'What he had yearned for was to *be* you,' said the Brother.
Then he added: 'I see where you're coming out.'

'At my saying to him by the end of five minutes: "My
dear fellow, I wish you'd just try it — wish you'd, for a while,
just *be* me!"   You go straight to the mark, and that was
exactly what occurred — extraordinary though it was that we
should both have understood.   I saw what he could give, and
he did too.   He saw moreover what I could take; in fact what
he saw was wonderful.'

'He must be very remarkable!' the Brother laughed.

'There's no doubt of it whatever — far more remarkable
than I.   That's just the reason why what I put to him in
joke — with a fantastic, desperate irony — became, on his
hands, with his vision of his chance, the blessed guarantee
of my sitting on this spot in your company.   "Oh, if I could
just shift it all — make it straight over for an hour to other
shoulders!   If there only *were* a pair!" — that's the way I
put it to him.   And then at something in his face, "Would
you, by a miracle, undertake it?" I asked,   I let him know all

it meant — how it meant that he should at that very moment
step in.   It meant that he should finish my work and open my
letters and keep my engagements and be subject, for better or
worse, to my contacts and complications.   It meant that he
should live with my life, and think with my brain, and write
with my hand, and speak with my voice.   It meant, above all,
that I should get off.   He accepted with magnificence — rose
to it like a hero.   Only he said : " What will become of
you ? " '

'There was the hitch ! ' the Brother admitted.

'Ah, but only for a minute.   He came to my help again,'
Dane pursued, ' when he saw I couldn't quite meet that, could
at least only say that I wanted to think, wanted to cease,
wanted to do the thing itself — the thing I was trying for,
miserable me, and that thing only — and therefore wanted
first of all really to *see* it again, planted out, crowded out,
frozen out as it now so long had been.   " I know what you
want," he after a moment quietly remarked to me.   "Ah,
what I want doesn't exist ! "   " I know what you want," he
repeated.   At that I began to believe him.'

'Had you any idea yourself ? ' the Brother asked.

'Oh, yes,' said Dane, ' and it was just my idea that made me
despair.   There it was as sharp as possible in my imagination
and my longing — there it was so utterly *not* in fact.   We
were sitting together on my sofa as we waited for breakfast.
He presently laid his hand on my knee — showed me a face
that the sudden great light in it had made, for me, indescribably beautiful.   " It exists — it exists," he at last said.   And
so, I remember, we sat awhile and looked at each other, with
the final effect of my finding that I absolutely believed him.
I remember we weren't at all solemn — we smiled with the
joy of discoverers.   He was as glad as I — he was tremendously glad.   That came out in the whole manner of his reply
to the appeal that broke from me : " Where is it, then, in
God's name ?   Tell me without delay where it is ! " '

The Brother had attended with a sympathy! 'He gave you the address?'

'He was thinking it out—feeling for it, catching it. He has a wonderful head of his own and must be making of the whole thing, while we sit here gossiping, something much better than ever *I* did. The mere sight of his face, the sense of his hand on my knee, made me, after a little, feel that he not only knew what I wanted, but was getting nearer to it than I could have got in ten years. He suddenly sprang up and went over to my study-table — sat straight down there as if to write me my passport. Then it was — at the mere sight of his back, which was turned to me — that I felt the spell work. I simply sat and watched him with the queerest, deepest, sweetest sense in the world — the sense of an ache that had stopped. All life was lifted; I myself at least was somehow off the ground. He was already where I had been.'

'And where were you?' the Brother amusedly inquired.

'Just on the sofa always, leaning back on the cushion and feeling a delicious ease. He was already me.'

'And who were you?' the Brother continued.

'Nobody. That was the fun.'

'That *is* the fun,' said the Brother, with a sigh like soft music.

Dane echoed the sigh, and, as nobody talking with nobody, they sat there together still and watched the sweet wide picture darken into tepid night.

IV

At the end of three weeks — so far as time was distinct — Dane began to feel there was something he had recovered. It was the thing they never named — partly for want of the need and partly for lack of the word; for what indeed was the description that would cover it all? The only real need was to know it, to see it, in silence. Dane had a private, practical

c

sign for it, which, however, he had appropriated by theft —
'the vision and the faculty divine.' That, doubtless, was a
flattering phrase for his idea of his genius; the genius, at all
events, was what he had been in danger of losing and had at
last held by a thread that might at any moment have broken.
The change was that, little by little, his hold had grown firmer,
so that he drew in the line — more and more each day — with
a pull that he was delighted to find it would bear. The mere
dream-sweetness of the place was superseded; it was more and
more a world of reason and order, of sensible, visible arrangement. It ceased to be strange — it was high, triumphant
clearness. He cultivated, however, but vaguely, the question
of where he was, finding it near enough the mark to be almost
sure that if he was not in Kent he was probably in Hampshire.
He paid for everything but that—that wasn't one of the items.
Payment, he had soon learned, was definite; it consisted of
sovereigns and shillings — just like those of the world he had
left, only parted with more ecstatically — that he put, in his
room, in a designated place and that were taken away in his
absence by one of the unobtrusive, effaced agents — shadows
projected on the hours like the noiseless march of the sundial
— that were always at work. The institution had sides that
had their recalls, and a pleased, resigned perception of these
things was at once the effect and the cause of its grace.

Dane picked out of his dim past a dozen halting similes.
The sacred, silent convent was one; another was the bright
country-house. He did the place no outrage to liken it to an
hotel; he permitted himself on occasion to trace its resemblance to a club. Such images, however, but flickered and
went out — they lasted only long enough to light up the difference. An hotel without noise, a club without newspapers —
when he turned his face to what it was 'without' the view
opened wide. The only approach to a real analogy was in
himself and his companions. They were brothers, guests,
members; they were even, if one liked — and they didn't in

the least mind what they were called — 'regular boarders.' It was not they who made the conditions, it was the conditions that made them. These conditions found themselves accepted, clearly, with an appreciation, with a rapture, it was rather to be called, that had to do — as the very air that pervaded them and the force that sustained — with their quiet and noble assurance. They combined to form the large, simple idea of a general refuge — an image of embracing arms, of liberal accommodation. What was the effect, really, but the poetisation by perfect taste of a type common enough? There was no daily miracle; the perfect taste, with the aid of space, did the trick. What underlay and overhung it all, better yet, Dane mused, was some original inspiration, but confirmed, unquenched, some happy thought of an individual breast. It had been born somehow and somewhere — it had had to insist on being — the blessed conception. The author might remain in the obscure, for that was part of the perfection: personal service so hushed and regulated that you scarce caught it in the act and only knew it by its results. Yet the wise mind was everywhere — the whole thing, infallibly, centred, at the core, in a consciousness. And what a consciousness it had been, Dane thought, a consciousness how like his own! The wise mind had felt, the wise mind had suffered; then, for all the worried company of minds, the wise mind had seen a chance. Of the creation thus arrived at you could none the less never have said if it were the last echo of the old or the sharpest note of the modern.

Dane again and again, among the far bells and the soft footfalls, in cool cloister and warm garden, found himself wanting not to know more and yet liking not to know less. It was part of the general beauty that there was no personal publicity, much less any personal success. Those things were in the world — in what he had left; there was no vulgarity here of credit or claim or fame. The real exquisite was to be without the complication of an identity, and the greatest

boon of all, doubtless, the solid security, the clear confidence
one could feel in the keeping of the contract. That was what
had been most in the wise mind — the importance of the
absolute sense, on the part of its beneficiaries, that what was
offered was guaranteed. They had no concern but to pay —
the wise mind knew what they paid for. It was present to
Dane each hour that he could never be overcharged. Oh, the
deep, deep bath, the soft, cool plash in the stillness! — this,
time after time, as if under regular treatment, a sublimated
German 'cure,' was the vivid name for his luxury. The inner
life woke up again, and it was the inner life, for people of his
generation, victims of the modern madness, mere maniacal
extension and motion, that was returning health. He had
talked of independence and written of it, but what a cold, flat
word it had been! This was the wordless fact itself — the
uncontested possession of the long, sweet, stupid day. The
fragrance of flowers just wandered through the void, and the
quiet recurrence of delicate, plain fare in a high, clean refec-
tory where the soundless, simple service was the triumph of
art. That, as he analysed, remained the constant explanation:
all the sweetness and serenity were created, calculated things.
He analysed, however, but in a desultory way and with a
positive delight in the residuum of mystery that made for the
great artist in the background the innermost shrine of the
idol of a temple; there were odd moments for it, mild meditations when, in the broad cloister of peace or some garden-
nook where the air was light, a special glimpse of beauty or
reminder of felicity seemed, in passing, to hover and linger.
In the mere ecstasy of change that had at first possessed him
he had not discriminated — had only let himself sink, as I
have mentioned, down to hushed depths. Then had come the
slow, soft stages of intelligence and notation, more marked
and more fruitful perhaps after that long talk with his mild
mate in the twilight, and seeming to wind up the process by
putting the key into his hand. This key, pure gold, was

simply the cancelled list. Slowly and blissfully he read into the general wealth of his comfort all the particular absences of which it was composed. One by one he touched, as it were, all the things it was such rapture to be without.

It was the paradise of his own room that was most indebted to them — a great square, fair chamber, all beautified with omissions, from which, high up, he looked over a long valley to a far horizon, and in which he was vaguely and pleasantly reminded of some old Italian picture, some Carpaccio or some early Tuscan, the representation of a world without newspapers and letters, without telegrams and photographs, without the dreadful, fatal too much. There, for a blessing, he *could* read and write; there, above all, he could do nothing — he could live. And there were all sorts of freedoms — always, for the occasion, the particular right one. He could bring a book from the library — he could bring two, he could bring three. An effect produced by the charming place was that, for some reason, he never wanted to bring more. The library was a benediction — high and clear and plain, like everything else, but with something, in all its arched amplitude, unconfused and brave and gay. He should never forget, he knew, the throb of immediate perception with which he first stood there, a single glance round sufficing so to show him that it would give him what for years he had desired. He had not had detachment, but there was detachment here — the sense of a great silver bowl from which he could ladle up the melted hours. He strolled about from wall to wall, too pleasantly in tune on that occasion to sit down punctually or to choose; only recognising from shelf to shelf every dear old book that he had had to put off or never returned to; every deep, distinct voice of another time that, in the hubbub of the world, he had had to take for lost and unheard. He came back, of course, soon, came back every day; enjoyed there, of all the rare, strange moments, those that were at once most quickened and most caught — moments in which every apprehension counted

double and every act of the mind was a lover's embrace. It
was the quarter he perhaps, as the days went on, liked best
though indeed it only shared with the rest of the place, with
every aspect to which his face happened to be turned, the
power to remind him of the masterly general control.

There were times when he looked up from his book to lose
himself in the mere tone of the picture that never failed at
any moment or at any angle. The picture was always there,
yet was made up of things common enough. It was in the
way an open window in a broad recess let in the pleasant
morning; in the way the dry air pricked into faint freshness
the gilt of old bindings; in the way an empty chair beside a
table unlittered showed a volume just laid down; in the way
a happy Brother — as detached as one's self and with his innocent back presented — lingered before a shelf with the slow
sound of turned pages. It was a part of the whole impression
that, by some extraordinary law, one's vision seemed less
from the facts than the facts from one's vision; that the elements were determined at the moment by the moment's need or
the moment's sympathy. What most prompted this reflection
was the degree in which, after a while, Dane had a consciousness of company. After that talk with the good Brother on the
bench there were other good Brothers in other places — always
in cloister or garden some figure that stopped if he himself
stopped and with which a greeting became, in the easiest way
in the world, a sign of the diffused amenity. Always, always,
however, in all contacts, was the balm of a happy ignorance.
What he had felt the first time recurred: the friend was
always new and yet at the same time — it was amusing, not
disturbing — suggested the possibility that he might be but
an old one altered. That was only delightful — as positively
delightful in the particular, the actual conditions as it might
have been the reverse in the conditions abolished. These
others, the abolished, came back to Dane at last so easily that
he could exactly measure each difference, but with what he

had finally been hustled on to hate in them robbed of its terror in consequence of something that had happened. What had happened was that in tranquil walks and talks the deep spell had worked and he had got his soul again. He had drawn in by this time, with his lightened hand, the whole of the long line, and that fact just dangled at the end. He could put his other hand on it, he could unhook it, he was once more in possession. This, as it befell, was exactly what he supposed he must have said to a comrade beside whom, one afternoon in the cloister, he found himself measuring steps.

'Oh, it's come — comes of itself, doesn't it, thank goodness? — just by the simple fact of finding room and time!'

The comrade was possibly a novice or in a different stage from his own; there was at any rate a vague envy in the recognition that shone out of the fatigued, yet freshened face. 'It has come to *you* then? — you've got what you wanted?' That was the gossip and interchange that could pass to and fro. Dane, years before, had gone in for three months of hydropathy, and there was a droll echo, in this scene, of the old questions of the water-cure, the questions asked in the periodical pursuit of the 'reaction' — the ailment, the progress of each, the action of the skin and the state of the appetite. Such memories worked in now — all familiar reference, all easy play of mind; and among them our friends, round and round, fraternised ever so softly, until, suddenly stopping short, Dane, with a hand on his companion's arm, broke into the happiest laugh he had yet sounded.

V

'Why, it's raining!' And he stood and looked at the splash of the shower and the shine of the wet leaves. It was one of the summer sprinkles that bring out sweet smells.

'Yes — but why not?' his mate demanded.

'Well — because it's so charming. It's so exactly right.'

'But everything *is*. Isn't that just why we're here?'

'Just exactly,' Dane said; 'only I've been living in the beguiled supposition that we've somehow or other a climate.'

'So have I; so, I dare say, has every one. Isn't that the blessed moral? — that we live in beguiled suppositions. They come so easily here, and nothing contradicts them.' The good Brother looked placidly forth — Dane could identify his phase. 'A climate doesn't consist in its never raining, does it?'

'No, I dare say not. But somehow the good I've got has been half the great, easy absence of all that friction of which the question of weather mostly forms a part — has been indeed largely the great, easy, perpetual air-bath.'

'Ah, yes — that's not a delusion; but perhaps the sense comes a little from our breathing an emptier medium. There are fewer things *in* it! Leave people alone, at all events, and the air is what they take to. Into the closed and the stuffy they have to be driven. I've had, too, — I think we must all have, — a fond sense of the south.'

'But imagine it,' said Dane, laughing, 'in the beloved British islands and so near as we are to Bradford!'

His friend was ready enough to imagine. 'To Bradford?' he asked, quite unperturbed. 'How near?'

Dane's gaiety grew. 'Oh, it doesn't matter!'

His friend, quite unmystified, accepted it. 'There are things to puzzle out — otherwise it would be dull. It seems to me one can puzzle them.'

'It's because we're so well disposed,' Dane said.

'Precisely — we find good in everything.'

'In everything,' Dane went on. 'The conditions settle that — they determine us.'

They resumed their stroll, which evidently represented on the good Brother's part infinite agreement. 'Aren't they probably in fact very simple?' he presently inquired. 'Isn't simplification the secret?'

'Yes, but applied with a tact!'

'There it is. The thing's so perfect that it's open to as many interpretations as any other great work — a poem of Goethe, a dialogue of Plato, a symphony of Beethoven.'

'It simply stands quiet, you mean,' said Dane, 'and lets us call it names ? '

'Yes, but all such loving ones. We're "staying" with some one — some delicious host or hostess who never shows.'

'It's liberty-hall — absolutely,' Dane assented.

'Yes — or a convalescent home.'

To this, however, Dane demurred. 'Ah, that, it seems to me, scarcely puts it. You weren't *ill* — were you ? I'm very sure *I* really wasn't. I was only, as the world goes, too "beastly well" !'

The good Brother wondered. 'But if we couldn't keep it up —— ? '

'We couldn't keep it *down* — that was all the matter !'

'I see — I see.' The good Brother sighed contentedly; after which he brought out again with kindly humour: 'It's a sort of kindergarten !'

'The next thing you'll be saying that we're babes at the breast !'

'Of some great mild, invisible mother who stretches away into space and whose lap is the whole valley —— ? '

'And her bosom' — Dane completed the figure — 'the noble eminence of our hill ? That will do; anything will do that covers the essential fact.'

'And what do you call the essential fact ? '

'Why, that — as in old days on Swiss lake-sides — we're *en pension*.'

The good Brother took this gently up. 'I remember — I remember: seven francs a day without wine ! But, alas, it's more than seven francs here.'

'Yes, it's considerably more,' Dane had to confess. 'Perhaps it isn't particularly cheap.'

'Yet should you call it particularly dear ? ' his friend after a moment inquired.

George Dane had to think. 'How do I know, after all? What practice has one ever had in estimating the inestimable? Particular cheapness certainly isn't the note that we feel struck all round; but don't we fall naturally into the view that there *must* be a price to anything so awfully sane?'

The good Brother in his turn reflected. 'We fall into the view that it must pay — that it does pay.'

'Oh, yes; it does pay!' Dane eagerly echoed. 'If it didn't it wouldn't last. It has *got* to last, of course!' he declared.

'So that we can come back?'

'Yes — think of knowing that we shall be able to!'

They pulled up again at this and, facing each other, thought of it, or at any rate pretended to; for what was really in their eyes was the dread of a loss of the clue. 'Oh, when we want it again we shall find it,' said the good Brother. 'If the place really pays, it will keep on.'

'Yes, that's the beauty; that it isn't, thank heaven, carried on only for love.'

'No doubt, no doubt; and yet, thank heaven, there's love in it too.' They had lingered as if, in the mild, moist air, they were charmed with the patter of the rain and the way the garden drank it. After a little, however, it did look rather as if they were trying to talk each other out of a faint, small fear. They saw the increasing rage of life and the recurrent need, and they wondered proportionately whether to return to the front when their hour should sharply strike would be the end of the dream. Was this a threshold perhaps, after all, that could only be crossed one way? They must return to the front sooner or later — that was certain: for each his hour would strike. The flower would have been gathered and the trick played — the sands, in short, would have run.

There, in its place, *was* life — with all its rage; the vague unrest of the need for action knew it again, the stir of the faculty that had been refreshed and reconsecrated. They seemed each, thus confronted, to close their eyes a moment for dizziness; then they were again at peace, and the Brother's confidence rang out. 'Oh, we shall meet!'

'Here, do you mean?'

'Yes — and I dare say in the world too.'

'But we shan't recognise or know,' said Dane.

'In the world, do you mean?'

'Neither in the world nor here.'

'Not a bit — not the least little bit, you think?'

Dane turned it over. 'Well, so it is that it seems to me all best to hang together. But we shall see.'

His friend happily concurred. 'We shall see.' And at this, for farewell, the Brother held out his hand.

'You're going?' Dane asked.

'No, but I thought *you* were.'

It was odd, but at this Dane's hour seemed to strike — his consciousness to crystallise. 'Well, I am. I've got it. You stay?' he went on.

'A little longer.'

Dane hesitated. 'You haven't yet got it?'

'Not altogether — but I think it's coming.'

'Good!' Dane kept his hand, giving it a final shake, and at that moment the sun glimmered again through the shower, but with the rain still falling on the hither side of it and seeming to patter even more in the brightness. 'Hallo — how charming!'

The Brother looked a moment from under the high arch — then again turned his face to our friend. He gave this time his longest, happiest sigh. 'Oh, it's all right!'

But why was it, Dane after a moment found himself wondering, that in the act of separation his own hand was so long retained? Why but through a queer phenomenon of change, on the spot, in his companion's face — change that gave it another, but an increasing and above all a much more familiar identity, an identity not beautiful, but more and more distinct, an identity with that of his servant, with the most conspicuous, the physiognomic seat of the public propriety of Brown? To this anomaly his eyes slowly opened; it was not his good Brother, it was verily Brown who possessed his hand. If his eyes had to open, it was because they had been closed and because Brown appeared to think he had better wake up. So much as this Dane took in, but the effect of his taking it was a relapse into darkness, a recontraction of the lids just prolonged enough to give Brown time, on a second thought, to withdraw his touch and move softly away. Dane's next consciousness was that of the desire to make sure he *was* away, and this desire had somehow the result of dissipating the obscurity. The obscurity was completely gone by the time he had made out that the back of a person writing at his study-table was presented to him. He recognised a portion of a figure that he had somewhere described to somebody — the intent shoulders of the unsuccessful young man who had come that bad morning to breakfast. It was strange, he at last reflected, but the young man was still there. How long had he stayed — days, weeks, months? He was exactly in the position in which Dane had last seen him. Everything — stranger still — was exactly in that position; everything, at least, but the light of the window, which came in from another quarter and showed a different hour. It wasn't after breakfast now: it was after — well, what? He suppressed a gasp — it was after everything. And yet — quite literally — there were but two other differences. One of these was that if he was still on the sofa he was now lying down; the other was the patter on the glass that showed him how the rain — the great rain of the night — had come back. It was the rain of the night, yet when had he last heard it? But two minutes before? Then how many were there before the young man at the table, who seemed intensely occupied, found a moment to look round at him and, on meeting his open eyes, get up and draw near?

'You've slept all day,' said the young man.

'All day?'

The young man looked at his watch. 'From ten to six. You were extraordinarily tired. I just, after a bit, let you alone, and you were soon off.' Yes, that was it; he had been 'off' — off, off, off. He began to fit it together; while he had been off the young man had been on. But there were still some few confusions; Dane lay looking up. 'Everything's done,' the young man continued.

'Everything?'

'Everything.'

Dane tried to take it all in, but was embarrassed and could only say weakly and quite apart from the matter: 'I've been so happy!'

'So have I,' said the young man. He positively looked so; seeing which George Dane wondered afresh, and then, in his wonder, read it indeed quite as another face, quite, in a puzzling way, as another person's. Every one was a little some one else. While he asked himself who else then the young man was, this benefactor, struck by his appealing stare, broke again into perfect cheer. 'It's all right!' That answered Dane's question; the face was the face turned to him by the good Brother there in the portico while they listened together to the rustle of the shower. It was all queer, but all pleasant and all distinct, so distinct that the last words in his ear — the same from both quarters — appeared the effect of a single voice. Dane rose and looked about his room, which seemed disincumbered, different, twice as large. It *was* all right.

'EUROPE'

I

'OUR feeling is, you know, that Becky *should* go.' That earnest little remark comes back to me, even after long years, as the first note of something that began, for my observation, the day I went with my sister-in-law to take leave of her good friends. It is a memory of the American time, which revives so at present — under some touch that doesn't signify — that it rounds itself off as an anecdote. That walk to say good-bye was the beginning; and the end, so far as I was concerned with it, was not till long after; yet even the end also appears to me now as of the old days. I went, in those days, on occasion, to see my sister-in-law, in whose affairs, on my brother's death, I had had to take a helpful hand. I continued to go, indeed, after these little matters were straightened out, for the pleasure, periodically, of the impression — the change to the almost pastoral sweetness of the good Boston suburb from the loud, longitudinal New York. It was another world, with other manners, a different tone, a different taste; a savour nowhere so mild, yet so distinct, as in the square white house — with the pair of elms, like gigantic wheat-sheaves in front, the rustic orchard not far behind, the old-fashioned door-lights, the big blue and white jars in the porch, the straight, bricked walk from the high gate — that enshrined the extraordinary merit of Mrs. Rimmle and her three daughters.

These ladies were so much of the place and the place so much of themselves that, from the first of their being revealed to me, I felt that nothing else at Brookbridge much mattered. They were what, for me, at any rate, Brookbridge had most to give: I mean in the way of what it was naturally strongest in, the thing that we called in New York the New England expression, the air of Puritanism reclaimed and refined. The Rimmles had brought it down to a wonderful delicacy. They struck me even then — all four almost equally — as very ancient and very earnest, and I think theirs must have been the house, in all the world, in which 'culture' first came to the aid of morning calls. The head of the family was the widow of a great public character — as public characters were understood at Brookbridge — whose speeches on anniversaries formed a part of the body of national eloquence spouted in the New England schools by little boys covetous of the most marked, though perhaps the easiest, distinction. He was reported to have been celebrated, and in such fine declamatory connections that he seemed to gesticulate even from the tomb. He was understood to have made, in his wife's company, the tour of Europe at a date not immensely removed from that of the battle of Waterloo. What was the age, then, of the bland, firm, antique Mrs. Rimmle at the period of her being first revealed to me? That is a point I am not in a position to determine — I remember mainly that I was young enough to regard her as having reached the limit. And yet the limit for Mrs. Rimmle must have been prodigiously extended; the scale of its extension is, in fact, the very moral of this reminiscence. She was old, and her daughters were old, but I was destined to know them all as older. It was only by comparison and habit that — however much I recede — Rebecca, Maria, and Jane were the 'young ladies.'

I think it was felt that, though their mother's life, after thirty years of widowhood, had had a grand backward stretch, her blandness and firmness — and this in spite of her extreme physical frailty — would be proof against any surrender not overwhelmingly justified by time. It had appeared, years before, at a crisis of which the waves had not even yet quite subsided, a surrender not justified by anything, that she should go, with her daughters, to Europe for her health. Her health was supposed to require constant support; but when it had at that period tried conclusions with the idea of Europe, it was not the idea of Europe that had been insidious enough to prevail. She had not gone, and Becky, Maria, and Jane had not gone, and this was long ago. They still merely floated in the air of the visit achieved, with such introductions and such acclamations, in the early part of the century; they still, with fond glances at the sunny parlour-walls, only referred, in conversation, to divers pictorial and other reminders of it. The Miss Rimmles had quite been brought up on it, but Becky, as the most literary, had most mastered the subject. There were framed letters — tributes to their eminent father — suspended among the mementos, and of two or three of these, the most foreign and complimentary, Becky had executed translations that figured beside the text. She knew already, through this and other illumination, so much about Europe that it was hard to believe, for her, in that limit of adventure which consisted only of her having been twice to Philadelphia. The others had not been to Philadelphia, but there was a legend that Jane had been to Saratoga. Becky was a short, stout, fair person with round, serious eyes, a high forehead, the sweetest, neatest enunciation, and a miniature of her father — 'done in Rome' — worn as a breastpin. She had written the life, she had edited the speeches, of the original of this ornament, and now at last, beyond the seas, she was really to tread in his footsteps.

Fine old Mrs. Rimmle, in the sunny parlour and with a certain austerity of cap and chair — though with a gay new 'front' that looked like rusty brown plush — had had so unusually good a winter that the question of her sparing two members of her family for an absence had been threshed as fine, I could feel, as even under that Puritan roof any case of conscience had ever been threshed. They were to make their dash while the coast, as it were, was clear, and each of the

daughters had tried — heroically, angelically, and for the sake
of each of her sisters — not to be one of the two. What I
encountered that first time was an opportunity to concur with
enthusiasm in the general idea that Becky's wonderful preparation would be wasted if she were the one to stay with their
mother. They talked of Becky's preparation — they had a
sly, old-maidish humour that was as mild as milk — as if it
were some mixture, for application somewhere, that she kept
in a precious bottle. It had been settled, at all events, that,
armed with this concoction and borne aloft by their introductions, she and Jane were to start. They were wonderful on
their introductions, which proceeded naturally from their
mother and were addressed to the charming families that, in
vague generations, had so admired vague Mr. Rimmle. Jane,
I found at Brookbridge, had to be described, for want of other
description, as the pretty one, but it would not have served to
identify her unless you had seen the others. *Her* preparation
was only this figment of her prettiness — only, that is, unless
one took into account something that, on the spot, I silently
divined: the lifelong, secret, passionate ache of her little
rebellious desire. They were all growing old in the yearning
to go, but Jane's yearning was the sharpest. She struggled
with it as people at Brookbridge mostly struggled with what
they liked, but fate, by threatening to prevent what she *dis*-
liked, and what was therefore duty — which was to stay at
home instead of Maria — had bewildered her, I judged, not a
little. It was she who, in the words I have quoted, mentioned
to me Becky's case and Becky's affinity as the clearest of all.
Her mother, moreover, on the general subject, had still more
to say.

'I positively desire, I really quite insist that they shall go,'
the old lady explained to us from her stiff chair. 'We've
talked about it so often, and they've had from me so clear an
account — I've amused them again and again with it — of what
is to be seen and enjoyed. If they've had hitherto too many

D

duties to leave, the time seems to have come to recognise that there are also many duties to *seek*. Wherever we go we find them — I always remind the girls of that. There's a duty that calls them to those wonderful countries, just as it called, at the right time, their father and myself — if it be only that of laying up for the years to come the same store of remarkable impressions, the same wealth of knowledge and food for conversation as, since my return, I have found myself so happy to possess.' Mrs. Rimmle spoke of her return as of something of the year before last, but the future of her daughters was, somehow, by a different law, to be on the scale of great vistas, of endless aftertastes. I think that, without my being quite ready to say it, even this first impression of her was somewhat upsetting; there was a large, placid perversity, a grim secrecy of intention, in her estimate of the ages.

'Well, I'm so glad you don't delay it longer,' I said to Miss Becky before we withdrew. 'And whoever should go,' I continued in the spirit of the sympathy with which the good sisters had already inspired me, 'I quite feel, with your family, you know, that *you* should. But of course I hold that every one should.' I suppose I wished to attenuate my solemnity; there was something in it, however, that I couldn't help. It must have been a faint foreknowledge.

'Have you been a great deal yourself?' Miss Jane, I remember, inquired.

'Not so much but that I hope to go a good deal more. So perhaps we shall meet,' I encouragingly suggested.

I recall something — something in the nature of susceptibility to encouragement — that this brought into the more expressive brown eyes to which Miss Jane mainly owed it that she was the pretty one. 'Where, do you think?'

I tried to think. 'Well, on the Italian lakes — Como, Bellagio, Lugano.' I liked to say the names to them.

'"Sublime, but neither bleak nor bare — nor misty are the

mountains there!"' Miss Jane softly breathed, while her sister
looked at her as if her familiarity with the poetry of the subject made her the most interesting feature of the scene she
evoked.

But Miss Becky presently turned to me. 'Do you know
everything——?'

'Everything?'

'In Europe.'

'Oh, yes,' I laughed, 'and one or two things even in
America.'

The sisters seemed to me furtively to look at each other.
'Well, you'll have to be quick—to meet *us*,' Miss Jane
resumed.

'But surely when you're once there you'll stay on.'

'Stay on?'—they murmured it simultaneously and with the
oddest vibration of dread as well as of desire. It was as if
they had been in the presence of a danger and yet wished me,
who 'knew everything,' to torment them with still more of it.

Well, I did my best. 'I mean it will never do to cut it
short.'

'No, that's just what I keep saying,' said brilliant Jane.
'It would be better, in that case, not to go.'

'Oh, don't talk about not going—at this time!' It was
none of my business, but I felt shocked and impatient.

'No, not at *this* time!' broke in Miss Maria, who, very red
in the face, had joined us. Poor Miss Maria was known as
the flushed one; but she was not flushed—she only had an
unfortunate surface. The third day after this was to see them
embark.

Miss Becky, however, desired as little as any one to be in
any way extravagant. 'It's only the thought of our mother,'
she explained.

I looked a moment at the old lady, with whom my sister-
in-law was engaged. 'Well—your mother's magnificent.'

'*Isn't* she magnificent?'—they eagerly took it up.

She *was* — I could reiterate it with sincerity, though I perhaps mentally drew the line when Miss Maria again risked, as a fresh ejaculation: 'I think she's better than Europe!'

'Maria!' they both, at this, exclaimed with a strange emphasis; it was as if they feared she had suddenly turned cynical over the deep domestic drama of their casting of lots. The innocent laugh with which she answered them gave the measure of her cynicism.

We separated at last, and my eyes met Mrs. Rimmle's as I held for an instant her aged hand. It was doubtless only my fancy that her calm, cold look quietly accused me of something. Of what *could* it accuse me? Only, I thought, of thinking.

II

I LEFT Brookbridge the next day, and for some time after that had no occasion to hear from my kinswoman; but when she finally wrote there was a passage in her letter that affected me more than all the rest. 'Do you know the poor Rimmles never, after all, "went"? The old lady, at the eleventh hour, broke down; everything broke down, and all of *them* on top of it, so that the dear things are with us still. Mrs. Rimmle, the night after our call, had, in the most unexpected manner, a turn for the worse — something in the nature (though they're rather mysterious about it) of a seizure; Becky and Jane felt it — dear, devoted, stupid angels that they are — heartless to leave her at such a moment, and Europe's indefinitely postponed. However, they think they're still going — or *think* they think it — when she's better. They also think — or think they think — that she *will* be better. I certainly pray she may.' So did I — quite fervently. I was conscious of a real pang — I didn't know how much they had made me care.

Late that winter my sister-in-law spent a week in New

York; when almost my first inquiry on meeting her was about the health of Mrs. Rimmle.

'Oh, she's rather bad — she really is, you know. It's not surprising that at her age she should be infirm.'

'Then what the deuce *is* her age?'

'I can't tell you to a year — but she's immensely old.'

'That of course I saw,' I replied — 'unless you literally mean so old that the records have been lost.'

My sister-in-law thought. 'Well, I believe she wasn't positively young when she married. She lost three or four children before these women were born.'

We surveyed together a little, on this, the 'dark backward.' 'And they were born, I gather, *after* the famous tour? Well, then, as the famous tour was in a manner to celebrate — wasn't it? — the restoration of the Bourbons — ' I considered, I gasped. 'My dear child, what on earth do you make her out?'

My relative, with her Brookbridge habit, transferred her share of the question to the moral plane — turned it forth to wander, by implication at least, in the sandy desert of responsibility. 'Well, you know, we all immensely admire her.'

'You can't admire her more than I do. She's awful.'

My interlocutress looked at me with a certain fear. 'She's *really* ill.'

'Too ill to get better?'

'Oh, no — we hope not. Because then they'll be able to go.'

'And *will* they go, if she should?'

'Oh, the moment they should be quite satisfied. I mean *really*,' she added.

I'm afraid I laughed at her — the Brookbridge 'really' was a thing so by itself. 'But if she shouldn't get better?' I went on.

'Oh, don't speak of it! They want so to go.'

'It's a pity they're so infernally good,' I mused.

'No — don't say that. It's what keeps them up.'

'Yes, but isn't it what keeps *her* up too?'

My visitor looked grave. 'Would you like them to kill her?'

I don't know that I was then prepared to say I should — though I believe I came very near it. But later on I burst all bounds, for the subject grew and grew. I went again before the good sisters ever did — I mean I went to Europe. I think I went twice, with a brief interval, before my fate again brought round for me a couple of days at Brookbridge. I had been there repeatedly, in the previous time, without making the acquaintance of the Rimmles; but now that I had had the revelation I couldn't have it too much, and the first request I preferred was to be taken again to see them. I remember well indeed the scruple I felt — the real delicacy — about betraying that *I* had, in the pride of my power, since our other meeting, stood, as their phrase went, among romantic scenes; but they were themselves the first to speak of it, and what, moreover, came home to me was that the coming and going of their friends in general — Brookbridge itself having even at that period one foot in Europe — was such as to place constantly before them the pleasure that was only postponed. They were thrown back, after all, on what the situation, under a final analysis, had most to give — the sense that, as every one kindly said to them and they kindly said to every one, Europe would keep. Every one felt for them so deeply that their own kindness in alleviating every one's feeling was really what came out most. Mrs. Rimmle was still in her stiff chair and in the sunny parlour, but if *she* made no scruple of introducing the Italian lakes my heart sank to observe that she dealt with them, as a topic, not in the least in the leave-taking manner in which Falstaff babbled of green fields.

I am not sure that, after this, my pretexts for a day or two with my sister-in-law were not apt to be a mere cover for another glimpse of these particulars: I at any rate never went to Brookbridge without an irrepressible eagerness for our customary call. A long time seems to me thus to have passed, with glimpses and lapses, considerable impatience and still more pity. Our visits indeed grew shorter, for, as my companion said, they were more and more of a strain. It finally struck me that the good sisters even shrank from me a little, as from one who penetrated their consciousness in spite of himself. It was as if they knew where I thought they ought to be, and were moved to deprecate at last, by a systematic silence on the subject of that hemisphere, the criminality I fain would fix on them. They were full instead — as with the instinct of throwing dust in my eyes — of little pathetic hypocrisies about Brookbridge interests and delights. I dare say that as time went on my deeper sense of their situation came practically to rest on my companion's report of it. I think I recollect, at all events, every word we ever exchanged about them, even if I have lost the thread of the special occasions. The impression they made on me after each interval always broke out with extravagance as I walked away with her.

'*She* may be as old as she likes — I don't care. It's the fearful age the "girls" are reaching that constitutes the scandal. One shouldn't pry into such matters, I know; but the years and the chances are really going. They're all growing old together — it will presently be too late; and their mother meanwhile perches over them like a vulture — what shall I call it? — calculating. Is she waiting for them successively to drop off? She'll survive them each and all. There's something too remorseless in it.'

'Yes; but what do you want her to do? If the poor thing *can't* die, she can't. Do you want her to take poison or to open a blood-vessel? I dare say she would prefer to go.'

'I beg your pardon,' I must have replied; 'you daren't say anything of the sort. If she would prefer to go she *would* go. She would feel the propriety, the decency, the necessity of going. She just prefers *not* to go. She prefers to stay and keep up the tension, and her calling them "girls" and talking of the good time they'll still have is the mere conscious mischief of a subtle old witch. They won't have *any* time — there isn't any time to have! I mean there's, on her own part, no real loss of measure or of perspective in it. She *knows* she's a hundred and ten, and takes a cruel pride in it.'

My sister-in-law differed with me about this; she held that the old woman's attitude was an honest one and that her magnificent vitality, so great in spite of her infirmities, made it inevitable she should attribute youth to persons who had come into the world so much later. 'Then suppose she should die?' — so my fellow-student of the case always put it to me.

'Do you mean while her daughters are away? There's not the least fear of that — not even if at the very moment of their departure she should be *in extremis*. They would find her all right on their return.'

'But think how they would feel not to have been with her!'

'That's only, I repeat, on the unsound assumption. If they would only go to-morrow — literally make a good rush for it — they'll be with her when they come back. That will give them plenty of time.' I'm afraid I even heartlessly added that if she *should*, against every probability, pass away in their absence, they wouldn't have to come back at all — which would be just the compensation proper to their long privation. And then Maria would come out to join the two others, and they would be — though but for the too scanty remnant of their career — as merry as the day is long.

I remained ready, somehow, pending the fulfilment of that vision, to sacrifice Maria; it was only over the urgency of the case for the others respectively that I found myself balancing. Sometimes it was for Becky I thought the tragedy deepest — sometimes, and in quite a different manner, I thought it most dire for Jane. It was Jane, after all, who had most sense of life. I seemed in fact dimly to descry in Jane a sense — as yet undescried by herself or by any one — of all sorts of queer things. Why didn't *she* go? I used desperately to ask; why didn't she make a bold personal dash for it, strike up a partnership with some one or other of the travelling spinsters in whom Brookbridge more and more abounded? Well, there came a flash for me at a particular point of the grey middle desert: my correspondent was able to let me know that poor Jane at last *had* sailed. She had gone of a sudden — I liked my sister-in-law's view of suddenness — with the kind Hathaways, who had made an irresistible grab at her and lifted her off her feet. They were going for the summer and for Mr. Hathaway's health, so that the opportunity was perfect, and it was impossible not to be glad that something very like physical force had finally prevailed. This was the general feeling at Brookbridge, and I might imagine what Brookbridge had been brought to from the fact that, at the very moment she was hustled off, the doctor, called to her mother at the peep of dawn, had considered that *he* at least must stay. There had been real alarm — greater than ever before; it actually did seem as if this time the end had come. But it was Becky, strange to say, who, though fully recognising the nature of the crisis, had kept the situation in hand and insisted upon action. This, I remember, brought back to me a discomfort with which I had been familiar from the first. One of the two had sailed, and I was sorry it was not the other. But if it had been the other I should have been equally sorry.

I saw with my eyes, that very autumn, what a fool Jane would have been if she had again backed out. Her mother had of course survived the peril of which I had heard, profiting by it indeed as she had profited by every other; she was sufficiently better again to have come down stairs. It was there that, as usual, I found her, but with a difference of effect produced somehow by the absence of one of the girls. It was as if, for the others, though they had not gone to Europe, Europe had come to them: Jane's letters had been so frequent and so beyond even what could have been hoped. It was the first time, however, that I perceived on the old woman's part a certain failure of lucidity. Jane's flight was, clearly, the great fact with her, but she spoke of it as if the fruit had now been plucked and the parenthesis closed. I don't know what sinking sense of still further physical duration I gathered, as a menace, from this first hint of her confusion of mind.

'My daughter has been; my daughter has been ——' She kept saying it, but didn't say where; that seemed unnecessary, and she only repeated the words to her visitors with a face that was all puckers and yet now, save in so far as it expressed an ineffaceable complacency, all blankness. I think she wanted us a little to know that she had not stood in the way. It added to something — I scarce knew what — that I found myself desiring to extract privately from Becky. As our visit was to be of the shortest my opportunity — for one of the young ladies always came to the door with us — was at hand. Mrs. Rimmle, as we took leave, again sounded her phrase, but she added this time: 'I'm so glad she's going to have always ——'

I knew so well what she meant that, as she again dropped, looking at me queerly and becoming momentarily dim, I could help her out. 'Going to have what *you* have?'

'Yes, yes — my privilege. Wonderful experience,' she mumbled. She bowed to me a little as if I would understand. 'She has things to tell.'

I turned, slightly at a loss, to Becky. 'She has then already arrived?'

Becky was at that moment looking a little strangely at her mother, who answered my question. 'She reached New York this morning — she comes on to-day.'

'Oh, then ——!' But I let the matter pass as I met Becky's eye — I saw there was a hitch somewhere. It was not she but Maria who came out with us; on which I cleared up the question of their sister's reappearance.

'Oh, no, not to-night,' Maria smiled; 'that's only the way

mother puts it. We shall see her about the end of November — the Hathaways are so indulgent. They kindly extend their tour.'

'For *her* sake? How sweet of them!' my sister-in-law exclaimed.

I can see our friend's plain, mild old face take on a deeper mildness, even though a higher colour, in the light of the open door. 'Yes, it's for Jane they prolong it. And do you know what they write?' She gave us time, but it was too great a responsibility to guess. 'Why, that it has brought her out.'

'Oh, I knew it *would!*' my companion sympathetically sighed.

Maria put it more strongly still. 'They say we wouldn't know her.'

This sounded a little awful, but it was, after all, what I had expected.

III

My correspondent in Brookbridge came to me that Christmas, with my niece, to spend a week; and the arrangement had of course been prefaced by an exchange of letters, the first of which from my sister-in-law scarce took space for acceptance of my invitation before going on to say: 'The Hathaways are back — but without Miss Jane!' She presented in a few words the situation thus created at Brookbridge, but was not yet, I gathered, fully in possession of the other one — the situation created in 'Europe' by the presence there of that lady. The two together, at any rate, demanded, I quickly felt, all my attention, and perhaps my impatience to receive my relative was a little sharpened by my desire for the whole story. I had it at last, by the Christmas fire, and I may say without reserve that it gave me all I could have hoped for. I listened eagerly, after which I produced the comment: 'Then she simply refused——'

'To budge from Florence? Simply. She had it out there

with the poor Hathaways, who felt responsible for her safety, pledged to restore her to her mother's, to her sisters' hands, and showed herself in a light, they mention under their breath, that made their dear old hair stand on end. Do you know what, when they first got back, they said of her — at least it was *his* phrase — to two or three people ? '

I thought a moment. 'That she had "tasted blood"?'

My visitor fairly admired me. 'How clever of you to guess! It's exactly what he did say. She appeared — she continues to appear, it seems — in a new character.'

I wondered a little. 'But that's exactly — don't you remember? — what Miss Maria reported to us from them; that we "wouldn't know her."'

My sister-in-law perfectly remembered. 'Oh, yes — she broke out from the first. But when they left her she was worse.'

'Worse?'

'Well, different — different from anything she ever *had* been, or — for that matter — had had a chance to be.' My interlocutress hung fire a moment, but presently faced me. 'Rather strange and free and obstreperous.'

'Obstreperous?' I wondered again.

'Peculiarly so, I inferred, on the question of not coming away. She wouldn't hear of it, and, when they spoke of her mother, said she had given her mother up. She had thought she should like Europe, but didn't know she should like it so much. They had been fools to bring her if they expected to take her away. She was going to see what she could — she hadn't yet seen half. The end of it was, at any rate, that they had to leave her alone.'

I seemed to see it all — to see even the scared Hathaways. 'So she *is* alone?'

'She told them, poor thing, it appears, and in a tone they'll never forget, that she was, at all events, quite old enough to be. She cried — she quite went on — over not having come sooner. That's why the only way for her,' my companion mused, '*is*, I suppose, to stay. They wanted to put her with some people or other — to find some American family. But she says she's on her own feet.'

'And she's still in Florence?'

'No — I believe she was to travel. She's bent on the East.'

I burst out laughing. 'Magnificent Jane! It's most interesting. Only I feel that I distinctly *should* "know" her. To my sense, always, I must tell you, she had it in her.'

My relative was silent a little. 'So it now appears Becky always felt.'

'And yet pushed her off? Magnificent Becky!'

My companion met my eyes a moment. 'You don't know the queerest part. I mean the way it has *most* brought her out.'

I turned it over; I felt I should like to know — to that degree indeed that, oddly enough, I jocosely disguised my eagerness. 'You don't mean she has taken to drink?'

My visitor hesitated. 'She has taken to flirting.'

I expressed disappointment. 'Oh, she took to *that* long ago. Yes,' I declared at my kinswoman's stare, 'she positively flirted — with *me!*'

The stare perhaps sharpened. 'Then you flirted with *her?*'

'How else could I have been as sure as I wanted to be? But has she means?'

'Means to flirt?' — my friend looked an instant as if she spoke literally. 'I don't understand about the means — though of course they have something. But I have my impression,' she went on. 'I think that Becky ——' It seemed almost too grave to say.

But *I* had no doubts. 'That Becky's backing her?'

She brought it out. 'Financing her.'

'Stupendous Becky! So that morally then ——'

'Becky's quite in sympathy. But isn't it too odd?' my sister-in-law asked.

'Not in the least. Didn't we know, as regards Jane, that Europe was to bring her out? Well, it has also brought out Rebecca.'

'It has indeed!' my companion indulgently sighed. 'So what would it do if she were there?'

'I should like immensely to see. And we *shall* see.'

'Why, do you believe she'll still go?'

'Certainly. She *must*.'

But my friend shook it off. 'She won't.'

'She shall!' I retorted with a laugh. But the next moment I said: 'And what does the old woman say?'

'To Jane's behaviour? Not a word — never speaks of it. She talks now much less than she used — only seems to wait. But it's my belief she thinks.'

'And — do you mean — knows?'

'Yes, knows that she's abandoned. In her silence there she takes it in.'

'It's her way of making Jane pay?' At this, somehow, I felt more serious. 'Oh, dear, dear — she'll disinherit her!'

When, in the following June, I went on to return my sister-in-law's visit the first object that met my eyes in her little white parlour was a figure that, to my stupefaction, presented itself for the moment as that of Mrs. Rimmle. I had gone to my room after arriving, and, on dressing, had come down: the apparition I speak of had arisen in the interval. Its ambiguous character lasted, however, but a second or two — I had taken Becky for her mother because I knew no one but her mother of that extreme age. Becky's age was quite startling; it had made a great stride, though, strangely enough, irrecoverably seated as she now was in it, she had a wizened brightness that I had scarcely yet seen in her. I remember indulging on this occasion in two silent observations: one to the effect that I had not hitherto been conscious of her full resemblance to the old lady, and the other to the effect that, as I had said to my sister-in-law at Christmas, 'Europe,' even as reaching her only through Jane's sensibilities, had really at last brought her out. She was in fact 'out' in a manner of which this encounter offered to my eyes a unique example: it was the single hour, often as I had been at Brookbridge, of my meeting her elsewhere than in her mother's drawing-room. I surmise that, besides being adjusted to her more marked time of life, the garments she wore abroad, and in particular her little plain bonnet, presented points of resemblance to the close sable sheath and the quaint old headgear that, in the white house behind the elms, I had from far back associated with the eternal image in the stiff chair. Of course I immediately spoke of Jane, showing an interest and asking for news; on which she answered me with a smile, but not at all as I had expected.

'*Those* are not really the things you want to know — where she is, whom she's with, how she manages and where she's going next — oh, no!' And the admirable woman gave a laugh that was somehow both light and sad — sad, in particular, with a strange, long weariness. 'What you do want to know is when she's coming back.'

I shook my head very kindly, but out of a wealth of experience that, I flattered myself, was equal to Miss Becky's. 'I do know it. Never.'

Miss Becky, at this, exchanged with me a long, deep look. 'Never.'

We had, in silence, a little luminous talk about it, in the course of which she seemed to tell me the most interesting things. 'And how's your mother?' I then inquired.

She hesitated, but finally spoke with the same serenity. 'My mother's all right. You see, she's not alive.'

'Oh, Becky!' my sister-in-law pleadingly interjected.

But Becky only addressed herself to me. 'Come and see if she is. *I* think she isn't — but Maria perhaps isn't so clear. Come, at all events, and judge and tell me.'

It was a new note, and I was a little bewildered. 'Ah, but I'm not a doctor!'

'No, thank God — you're not. That's why I ask you.' And now she said good-bye.

I kept her hand a moment. '*You're* more alive than ever!'

'I'm very tired.' She took it with the same smile, but for Becky it was much to say.

IV

NOT alive,' the next day, was certainly what Mrs. Rimmle looked when, coming in according to my promise, I found her, with Miss Maria, in her usual place. Though shrunken and diminished she still occupied her high-backed chair with a visible theory of erectness, and her intensely aged face — combined with something dauntless that belonged to her very presence and that was effective even in this extremity — might have been that of some centenarian sovereign, of indistinguishable sex, brought forth to be shown to the people as a disproof of the rumour of extinction. Mummified and open-eyed she looked at me, but I had no impression that she made me out. I had come this time without my sister-in-law, who had frankly pleaded to me — which also, for a daughter of Brookbridge, was saying much — that the house had grown too painful. Poor Miss Maria excused Miss Becky on the score of her not being well — and that, it struck me, was saying most of all. The absence of the others gave the occasion a different note; but I talked with Miss Maria for five minutes and perceived that — save for her saying, of her own movement, anything about Jane — she now spoke as if her mother had lost hearing or sense, or both, alluding freely and distinctly, though indeed favourably, to her condition. 'She has expected your visit and she much enjoys it,' my interlocutress said, while the old woman, soundless and motionless, simply fixed me without expression. Of course there was little to keep me; but I became aware, as I rose to go, that there was more than I had supposed. On my approaching her to take leave Mrs. Rimmle gave signs of consciousness.

'Have you heard about Jane?'

I hesitated, feeling a responsibility, and appealed for direction to Maria's face. But Maria's face was troubled, was turned altogether to her mother's. 'About her life in Europe?' I then rather helplessly asked.

The old woman fronted me, on this, in a manner that made me feel silly. 'Her life?'—and her voice, with this second effort, came out stronger. 'Her death, if you please.'

'Her death?' I echoed, before I could stop myself, with the accent of deprecation.

Miss Maria uttered a vague sound of pain, and I felt her turn away, but the marvel of her mother's little unquenched spark still held me. 'Jane's dead. We've heard,' said Mrs. Rimmle. 'We've heard from — where is it we've heard from?' She had quite revived — she appealed to her daughter.

The poor old girl, crimson, rallied to her duty. 'From Europe.'

Mrs. Rimmle made at us both a little grim inclination of the head. 'From Europe.' I responded, in silence, with a deflection from every rigour, and, still holding me, she went on : 'And now Rebecca's going.'

She had gathered by this time such emphasis to say it that again, before I could help myself, I vibrated in reply. 'To Europe — now?' It was as if for an instant she had made me believe it.

She only stared at me, however, from her wizened mask; then her eyes followed my companion. 'Has she gone?'

'Not yet, mother.' Maria tried to treat it as a joke, but her smile was embarrassed and dim.

'Then where is she?'

'She's lying down.'

E

The old woman kept up her hard, queer gaze, but directing it, after a minute, to me. 'She's going.'

'Oh, some day!' I foolishly laughed; and on this I got to the door, where I separated from my younger hostess, who came no further. Only, as I held the door open, she said to me under cover of it and very quietly:

'It's poor mother's idea.'

I saw — it was her idea. Mine was — for some time after this, even after I had returned to New York and to my usual occupations — that I should never again see Becky. I had seen her for the last time, I believed, under my sister-in-law's roof, and in the autumn it was given to me to hear from that fellow-admirer that she had succumbed at last to the situation. The day of the call I have just described had been a date in the process of her slow shrinkage — it was literally the first time she had, as they said at Brookbridge, given up. She had been ill for years, but the other state of health in the contemplation of which she had spent so much of her life had left her, till too late, no margin for meeting it. The encounter, at last, came simply in the form of the discovery that it *was* too late; on which, naturally, she had given up more and more. I had heard indeed, all summer, by letter, how Brookbridge had watched her do so; whereby the end found me in a manner prepared. Yet in spite of my preparation there remained with me a soreness, and when I was next — it was some six months later — on the scene of her martyrdom I replied, I fear, with an almost rabid negative to the question put to me in due course by my kinswoman. 'Call on them? Never again!'

I went, none the less, the very next day. Everything was the same in the sunny parlour — everything that most mattered, I mean: the immemorial mummy in the high chair and the tributes, in the little frames on the walls, to the celebrity of its late husband. Only Maria Rimmle was different: if Becky, on my last seeing her, had looked as old as her mother,

Maria — save that she moved about — looked older.   I remember that she moved about, but I scarce remember what she said; and indeed what was there to say?   When I risked a question, however, she had a reply.

'But *now* at least ——— ? ' I tried to put it to her suggestively. At first she was vague. ' " Now ? " '

'Won't Miss Jane come back ? '

Oh, the headshake she gave me!   'Never.'   It positively pictured to me, for the instant, a well-preserved woman, a sort of rich, ripe *seconde jeunesse* by the Arno.

'Then that's only to make more sure of your finally joining her.'

Maria Rimmle repeated her headshake.   'Never.'

We stood so, a moment, bleakly face to face; I could think of no attenuation that would be particularly happy.   But while I tried I heard a hoarse gasp that, fortunately, relieved me — a signal strange and at first formless from the occupant of the high-backed chair.   'Mother wants to speak to you,' Maria then said.

So it appeared from the drop of the old woman's jaw, the expression of her mouth opened as if for the emission of sound. It was difficult to me, somehow, to seem to sympathise without hypocrisy, but, so far as a step nearer could do so, I invited communication.   'Have you heard where Becky's gone ? ' the wonderful witch's white lips then extraordinarily asked.

It drew from Maria, as on my previous visit, an uncontrollable groan, and this, in turn, made me take time to consider. As I considered, however, I had an inspiration.   'To Europe ? '

I must have adorned it with a strange grimace, but my inspiration had been right.   'To Europe,' said Mrs. Rimmle.

PASTE

'I'VE found a lot more things,' her cousin said to her the day after the second funeral; 'they're up in her room — but they're things I wish *you'd* look at.'

The pair of mourners, sufficiently stricken, were in the garden of the vicarage together, before luncheon, waiting to be summoned to that meal, and Arthur Prime had still in his face the intention, she was moved to call it rather than the expression, of feeling something or other. Some such appearance was in itself of course natural within a week of his stepmother's death, within three of his father's; but what was most present to the girl, herself sensitive and shrewd, was that he seemed somehow to brood without sorrow, to suffer without what she in her own case would have called pain. He turned away from her after this last speech — it was a good deal his habit to drop an observation and leave her to pick it up without assistance. If the vicar's widow, now in her turn finally translated, had not really belonged to him it was not for want of her giving herself, so far as he ever would take her; and she had lain for three days all alone at the end of the passage, in the great cold chamber of hospitality, the dampish, greenish room where visitors slept and where several of the ladies of the parish had, without effect, offered, in pairs and successions, piously to watch with her. His personal connection with the parish was now slighter than ever, and he had really not waited for this opportunity to show the ladies what he thought of them. She felt that she herself had, during her doleful month's leave from Bleet, where she was governess, rather taken her place in the same snubbed order; but it was presently, none the less, with a better little hope of coming in for some remembrance, some relic, that she went up to look at the things he had spoken of, the identity of which, as a confused cluster of bright objects on a table in the darkened room, shimmered at her as soon as she had opened the door.

They met her eyes for the first time, but in a moment, before touching them, she knew them as things of the theatre, as very much too fine to have been, with any verisimilitude, things of the vicarage. They were too dreadfully good to be true, for her aunt had had no jewels to speak of, and these were coronets and girdles, diamonds, rubies, and sapphires. Flagrant tinsel and glass, they looked strangely vulgar, but if, after the first queer shock of them, she found herself taking them up, it was for the very proof, never yet so distinct to her, of a far-off faded story. An honest widowed cleric with a small son and a large sense of Shakspeare had, on a brave latitude of habit as well as of taste — since it implied his having in very fact dropped deep into the ' pit ' — conceived for an obscure actress, several years older than himself, an admiration of which the prompt offer of his reverend name and hortatory hand was the sufficiently candid sign. The response had perhaps, in those dim years, in the way of eccentricity, even bettered the proposal, and Charlotte, turning the tale over, had long since drawn from it a measure of the career renounced by the undistinguished *comédienne* — doubtless also tragic, or perhaps pantomimic, at a pinch — of her late uncle's dreams. This career could not have been eminent and must much more probably have been comfortless.

'You see what it is — old stuff of the time she never liked to mention.'

Our young woman gave a start; her companion had, after all, rejoined her and had apparently watched a moment her slightly scared recognition. 'So I said to myself,' she replied. Then, to show intelligence, yet keep clear of twaddle: 'How peculiar they look!'

'They look awful,' said Arthur Prime. 'Cheap gilt, diamonds as big as potatoes. These are trappings of a ruder age than ours. Actors do themselves better now.'

'Oh, now,' said Charlotte, not to be less knowing, 'actresses have real diamonds.'

'Some of them.' Arthur spoke drily.

'I mean the bad ones — the nobodies too.'

'Oh, some of the nobodies have the biggest. But mamma wasn't of that sort.'

'A nobody?' Charlotte risked.

'Not a nobody to whom somebody — well, not a nobody with diamonds. It isn't all worth, this trash, five pounds.'

There was something in the old gewgaws that spoke to her, and she continued to turn them over. 'They're relics. I think they have their melancholy and even their dignity.'

Arthur observed another pause. 'Do you care for them?' he then asked. 'I mean,' he promptly added, 'as a souvenir.'

'Of you?' Charlotte threw off.

'Of me? What have I to do with it? Of your poor dead aunt who was so kind to you,' he said with virtuous sternness.

'Well, I would rather have them than nothing.'

'Then please take them,' he returned in a tone of relief which expressed somehow more of the eager than of the gracious.

'Thank you.' Charlotte lifted two or three objects up and set them down again. Though they were lighter than the materials they imitated they were so much more extravagant that they struck her in truth as rather an awkward heritage, to which she might have preferred even a matchbox or a penwiper. They were indeed shameless pinchbeck. 'Had you any idea she had kept them?'

'I don't at all believe she *had* kept them or knew they were there, and I'm very sure my father didn't. They had quite equally worked off any tenderness for the connection. These odds and ends, which she thought had been given away or destroyed, had simply got thrust into a dark corner and been forgotten.'

Charlotte wondered. 'Where then did you find them?'

'In that old tin box'—and the young man pointed to the receptacle from which he had dislodged them and which stood on a neighbouring chair. 'It's rather a good box still, but I'm afraid I can't give you *that*.'

The girl gave the box no look; she continued only to look at the trinkets. 'What corner had she found?'

'She hadn't "found" it,' her companion sharply insisted; 'she had simply lost it. The whole thing had passed from her mind. The box was on the top shelf of the old schoolroom closet, which, until one put one's head into it from a step-ladder, looked, from below, quite cleared out. The door is narrow and the part of the closet to the left goes well into the wall. The box had stuck there for years.'

Charlotte was conscious of a mind divided and a vision vaguely troubled, and once more she took up two or three of the subjects of this revelation; a big bracelet in the form of a gilt serpent with many twists and beady eyes, a brazen belt studded with emeralds and rubies, a chain, of flamboyant architecture, to which, at the Theatre Royal, Little Peddlington, Hamlet's mother had probably been careful to attach the portrait of the successor to Hamlet's father. 'Are you very sure they're not really worth something? Their mere weight alone——!' she vaguely observed, balancing a moment a royal diadem that might have crowned one of the creations of the famous Mrs. Jarley.

But Arthur Prime, it was clear, had already thought the question over and found the answer easy. 'If they had been worth anything to speak of she would long ago have sold them. My father and she had unfortunately never been in a position to keep any considerable value locked up.' And while his companion took in the obvious force of this he went on with a flourish just marked enough not to escape her: 'If they're worth anything at all — why, you're only the more welcome to them.'

Charlotte had now in her hand a small bag of faded, figured silk — one of those antique conveniences that speak to us, in the terms of evaporated camphor and lavender, of the part they have played in some personal history ; but, though she had for the first time drawn the string, she looked much more at the young man than at the questionable treasure it appeared to contain. 'I shall like them. They're all I have.'

'All you have ——?'

'That belonged to her.'

He swelled a little, then looked about him as if to appeal — as against her avidity — to the whole poor place. 'Well, what else do you want?'

'Nothing. Thank you very much.' With which she bent her eyes on the article wrapped, and now only exposed, in her superannuated satchel — a necklace of large pearls, such as might once have graced the neck of a provincial Ophelia and borne company to a flaxen wig. 'This perhaps *is* worth something. Feel it.' And she passed him the necklace, the weight of which she had gathered for a moment into her hand.

He measured it in the same way with his own, but remained quite detached. 'Worth at most thirty shillings.'

'Not more?'

'Surely not if it's paste?'

'But *is* it paste?'

He gave a small sniff of impatience. 'Pearls nearly as big as filberts?'

'But they're heavy,' Charlotte declared.

'No heavier than anything else.' And he gave them back with an allowance for her simplicity. 'Do you imagine for a moment they're real?'

She studied them a little, feeling them, turning them round. 'Mightn't they possibly be?'

'Of that size — stuck away with that trash?'

'I admit it isn't likely,' Charlotte presently said. 'And pearls are so easily imitated.'

'That's just what — to a person who knows — they're not. These have no lustre, no play.'

'No — they *are* dull. They're opaque.'

'Besides,' he lucidly inquired, 'how could she ever have come by them?'

'Mightn't they have been a present?'

Arthur stared at the question as if it were almost improper. Because actresses are exposed —— ?' He pulled up, however, not saying to what, and before she could supply the deficiency had, with the sharp ejaculation of 'No, they mightn't!' turned his back on her and walked away. His manner made her feel that she had probably been wanting in tact, and before he returned to the subject, the last thing that evening, she had satisfied herself of the ground of his resentment. They had been talking of her departure the next morning, the hour of her train and the fly that would come for her, and it was precisely these things that gave him his effective chance. 'I really can't allow you to leave the house under the impression that my stepmother was at *any* time of her life the sort of person to allow herself to be approached ——'

'With pearl necklaces and that sort of thing?' Arthur had made for her somehow the difficulty that she couldn't show him she understood him without seeming pert.

It at any rate only added to his own gravity. 'That sort of thing, exactly.'

'I didn't think when I spoke this morning — but I see what you mean.'

'I mean that she was beyond reproach,' said Arthur Prime.

'A hundred times yes.'

'Therefore if she couldn't, out of her slender gains, ever have paid for a row of pearls ——'

'She couldn't, in that atmosphere, ever properly have had one? Of course she couldn't. I've seen perfectly since our talk,' Charlotte went on, 'that that string of beads isn't even, as an imitation, very good. The little clasp itself doesn't seem even gold. With false pearls, I suppose,' the girl mused, 'it naturally wouldn't be.'

'The whole thing's rotten paste,' her companion returned as if to have done with it. 'If it were *not*, and she had kept it all these years hidden——'

'Yes?' Charlotte sounded as he paused.

'Why, I shouldn't know what to think!'

'Oh, I see.' She had met him with a certain blankness, but adequately enough, it seemed, for him to regard the subject as dismissed; and there was no reversion to it between them before, on the morrow, when she had with difficulty made a place for them in her trunk, she carried off these florid survivals.

At Bleet she found small occasion to revert to them and, in an air charged with such quite other references, even felt, after she had laid them away, much enshrouded, beneath various piles of clothing, as if they formed a collection not wholly without its note of the ridiculous. Yet she was never, for the joke, tempted to show them to her pupils, though Gwendolen and Blanche, in particular, always wanted, on her return, to know what she had brought back; so that without an accident by which the case was quite changed they might have appeared to enter on a new phase of interment. The essence of the accident was the sudden illness, at the last moment, of Lady Bobby, whose advent had been so much counted on to spice the five days' feast laid out for the coming of age of the eldest son of the house; and its equally marked effect was the despatch of a pressing message, in quite another direction, to Mrs. Guy, who, could she by a miracle be secured — she was always engaged ten parties deep — might be trusted to supply, it was believed, an element of exuberance scarcely less active. Mrs. Guy was already known to several of the visitors already on the scene, but she was not yet known to our young lady, who found her, after many wires and counterwires had at last determined the triumph of her arrival, a strange, charming little red-haired, black-dressed woman, with the face of a baby and the authority of a commodore. She took on the spot the discreet, the exceptional young governess into the confidence of her designs and, still more, of her doubts; intimating that it was a policy she almost always promptly pursued.

'To-morrow and Thursday are all right,' she said frankly to Charlotte on the second day, 'but I'm not half satisfied with Friday.'

'What improvement then do you suggest?'

'Well, my strong point, you know, is *tableaux vivants*.'

'Charming. And what is your favourite character?'

'Boss!' said Mrs. Guy with decision; and it was very markedly under that ensign that she had, within a few hours, completely planned her campaign and recruited her troop. Every word she uttered was to the point, but none more so than, after a general survey of their equipment, her final inquiry of Charlotte. She had been looking about, but half appeased, at the muster of decoration and drapery. 'We shall be dull. We shall want more colour. You've nothing else?'

Charlotte had a thought. 'No — I've *some* things.'

'Then why don't you bring them?'

The girl hesitated. 'Would you come to my room?'

'No,' said Mrs. Guy — 'bring them to-night to mine.'

So Charlotte, at the evening's end, after candlesticks had flickered through brown old passages bedward, arrived at her friend's door with the burden of her aunt's relics. But she promptly expressed a fear. 'Are they too garish?'

When she had poured them out on the sofa Mrs. Guy was but a minute, before the glass, in clapping on the diadem. 'Awfully jolly — we can do Ivanhoe!'

'But they're only glass and tin.'

'Larger than life they are, *rather!* — which is exactly what, for tableaux, is wanted. *Our* jewels, for historic scenes, don't tell — the real thing falls short. Rowena must have rubies

as big as eggs. Leave them with me,' Mrs. Guy continued —
'they'll inspire me. Good-night.'

The next morning she was in fact — yet very strangely —
inspired. 'Yes, *I'll* do Rowena. But I don't, my dear, understand.'

'Understand what?'

Mrs. Guy gave a very lighted stare. 'How you come to
have such things.'

Poor Charlotte smiled. 'By inheritance.'

'Family jewels?'

'They belonged to my aunt, who died some months ago.
She was on the stage a few years in early life, and these are a
part of her trappings.'

'She left them to you?'

'No; my cousin, her stepson, who naturally has no use for
them, gave them to me for remembrance of her. She was a
dear kind thing, always so nice to me, and I was fond of her.'

Mrs. Guy had listened with visible interest. 'But it's *he*
who must be a dear kind thing!'

Charlotte wondered. 'You think so?'

'Is *he*,' her friend went on, 'also "always so nice" to you?'

The girl, at this, face to face there with the brilliant visitor
in the deserted breakfast-room, took a deeper sounding. 'What
is it?'

'Don't you know?'

Something came over her. 'The pearls —— ?' But the
question fainted on her lips.

'Doesn't *he* know?'

Charlotte found herself flushing. 'They're *not* paste?'

'Haven't you looked at them?'

She was conscious of two kinds of embarrassment. '*You*
have?'

'Very carefully.'

'And they're real?'

Mrs. Guy became slightly mystifying and returned for all

answer: 'Come again, when you've done with the children, to my room.'

Our young woman found she had done with the children, that morning, with a promptitude that was a new joy to them, and when she reappeared before Mrs. Guy this lady had already encircled a plump white throat with the only ornament, surely, in all the late Mrs. Prime's — the effaced Miss Bradshaw's — collection, in the least qualified to raise a question. If Charlotte had never yet once, before the glass, tied the string of pearls about her own neck, this was because she had been capable of no such condescension to approved 'imitation'; but she had now only to look at Mrs. Guy to see that, so disposed, the ambiguous objects might have passed for frank originals. 'What in the world have you done to them?'

'Only handled them, understood them, admired them, and put them on. That's what pearls want; they want to be worn — it wakes them up. They're alive, don't you see? How *have* these been treated? They must have been buried, ignored, despised. They were half dead. Don't you *know* about pearls?' Mrs. Guy threw off as she fondly fingered the necklace.

'How *should* I? Do *you?*'

'Everything. These were simply asleep, and from the moment I really touched them — well,' said their wearer lovingly, 'it only took one's eye!'

'It took more than mine — though I did just wonder; and than Arthur's,' Charlotte brooded. She found herself almost panting. 'Then their value ——?'

'Oh, their value's excellent.'

The girl, for a deep moment, took another plunge into the wonder, the beauty and mystery, of them. 'Are you *sure?*'

Her companion wheeled round for impatience. 'Sure? For what kind of an idiot, my dear, do you take me?'

It was beyond Charlotte Prime to say. 'For the same kind as Arthur — and as myself,' she could only suggest. 'But my cousin didn't know. He thinks they're worthless.'

'Because of the rest of the lot? Then your cousin's an ass. But what — if, as I understood you, he gave them to you — has he to do with it?'

'Why, if he gave them to me as worthless and they turn out precious ——'

'You must give them back? I don't see that — if he was such a fool. He took the risk.'

Charlotte fed, in fancy, on the pearls, which, decidedly, were exquisite, but which at the present moment somehow presented themselves much more as Mrs. Guy's than either as Arthur's or as her own. 'Yes — he did take it; even after I had distinctly hinted to him that they looked to me different from the other pieces.'

'Well, then!' said Mrs. Guy with something more than triumph — with a positive odd relief.

But it had the effect of making our young woman think with more intensity. 'Ah, you see he thought they couldn't be different, because — so peculiarly — they shouldn't be.'

'Shouldn't be? I don't understand.'

'Why, how would she have got them?' — so Charlotte candidly put it.

'She? Who?' There was a capacity in Mrs. Guy's tone for a sinking of persons — !

'Why, the person I told you of: his stepmother, my uncle's wife — among whose poor old things, extraordinarily thrust away and out of sight, he happened to find them.'

Mrs. Guy came a step nearer to the effaced Miss Bradshaw. 'Do you mean she may have stolen them?'

'No. But she had been an actress.'

'Oh, well then,' cried Mrs. Guy, 'wouldn't that be just how?'

'Yes, except that she wasn't at all a brilliant one, nor in receipt of large pay.' The girl even threw off a nervous joke. 'I'm afraid she couldn't have been our Rowena.'

Mrs. Guy took it up. 'Was she very ugly?'

'No. She may very well, when young, have looked rather nice.'

'Well, then!' was Mrs. Guy's sharp comment and fresh triumph.

'You mean it was a present? That's just what he so dislikes the idea of her having received — a present from an admirer capable of going such lengths.'

'Because she wouldn't have taken it for nothing? *Speriamo* — that she wasn't a brute. The "length" her admirer went was the length of a whole row. Let us hope she was just a little kind!'

'Well,' Charlotte went on, 'that she was "kind" might seem to be shown by the fact that neither her husband, nor his son, nor I, his niece, knew or dreamed of her possessing anything so precious; by her having kept the gift all the rest of her life beyond discovery — out of sight and protected from suspicion.'

'As if, you mean' — Mrs. Guy was quick — 'she had been wedded to it and yet was ashamed of it? Fancy,' she laughed while she manipulated the rare beads, 'being ashamed of *these!*'

'But you see she had married a clergyman.'

'Yes, she must have been "rum." But at any rate he had married *her*. What did he suppose?'

'Why, that she had never been of the sort by whom such offerings are encouraged.'

'Ah, my dear, the sort by whom they are *not* ——!' But Mrs. Guy caught herself up. 'And her stepson thought the same?'

'Overwhelmingly.'

'Was he, then, if only her stepson ——'

'So fond of her as that comes to? Yes; he had never known, consciously, his real mother, and, without children of her own, she was very patient and nice with him. And *I* liked her so,' the girl pursued, 'that at the end of ten years, in so strange a manner, to "give her away" ——'

'Is impossible to you? Then don't!' said Mrs. Guy with decision.

'Ah, but if they're real I can't keep them!' Charlotte, with her eyes on them, moaned in her impatience. 'It's too difficult.'

'Where's the difficulty, if he has such sentiments that he would rather sacrifice the necklace than admit it, with the presumption it carries with it, to be genuine? You've only to be silent.'

'And keep it? How can *I* ever wear it?'

'You'd have to hide it, like your aunt?' Mrs. Guy was amused. 'You can easily sell it.'

Her companion walked round her for a look at the affair from behind. The clasp was certainly, doubtless intentionally, misleading, but everything else was indeed lovely. 'Well, I must think. Why didn't *she* sell them?' Charlotte broke out in her trouble.

Mrs. Guy had an instant answer. 'Doesn't that prove what they secretly recalled to her? You've only to be silent!' she ardently repeated.

'I must think — I must think!'

Mrs. Guy stood with her hands attached but motionless.

'Then you want them back?'

As if with the dread of touching them Charlotte retreated to the door. 'I'll tell you to-night.'

'But may I wear them?'

'Meanwhile?'

'This evening — at dinner.'

It was the sharp, selfish pressure of this that really, on the spot, determined the girl; but for the moment, before closing the door on the question, she only said: 'As you like!'

They were busy much of the day with preparation and rehearsal, and at dinner, that evening, the concourse of guests was such that a place among them for Miss Prime failed to find itself marked. At the time the company rose she was therefore alone in the schoolroom, where, towards eleven o'clock, she received a visit from Mrs. Guy. This lady's white shoulders heaved, under the pearls, with an emotion that the very red lips which formed, as if for the full effect, the happiest opposition of colour, were not slow to translate. 'My dear, you should have seen the sensation — they've had a success!'

Charlotte, dumb a moment, took it all in. 'It *is* as if they knew it — they're more and more alive. But so much the worse for both of us! I can't,' she brought out with an effort, 'be silent.'

'You mean to return them?'

'If I don't I'm a thief.'

Mrs. Guy gave her a long, hard look: what was decidedly not of the baby in Mrs. Guy's face was a certain air of established habit in the eyes. Then, with a sharp little jerk of her head and a backward reach of her bare beautiful arms, she undid the clasp and, taking off the necklace, laid it on the table. 'If you do, you're a goose.'

'Well, of the two ——!' said our young lady, gathering it up with a sigh. And as if to get it, for the pang it gave, out of sight as soon as possible, she shut it up, clicking the lock, in the drawer of her own little table; after which, when she turned again, her companion, without it, looked naked and plain. 'But what will you say?' it then occurred to her to demand.

'Downstairs — to explain?' Mrs. Guy was, after all, trying at least to keep her temper. 'Oh, I'll put on something else and say that clasp is broken. And you won't of course name *me* to him,' she added.

'As having undeceived me? No — I'll say that, looking at the thing more carefully, it's my own private idea.'

'And does he know how little you really know?'

'As an expert — surely. And he has much, always, the conceit of his own opinion.'

F

'Then he won't believe you — as he so hates to. He'll stick to his judgment and maintain his gift, and we shall have the darlings back!' With which reviving assurance Mrs. Guy kissed for good-night.

She was not, however, to be gratified or justified by any prompt event, for, whether or no paste entered into the composition of the ornament in question, Charlotte shrank from the temerity of despatching it to town by post. Mrs. Guy was thus disappointed of the hope of seeing the business settled — 'by return,' she had seemed to expect — before the end of the revels. The revels, moreover, rising to a frantic pitch, pressed for all her attention, and it was at last only in the general confusion of leave-taking that she made, parenthetically, a dash at her young friend.

'Come, what will you take for them?'

'The pearls? Ah, you'll have to treat with my cousin.'

Mrs. Guy, with quick intensity, lent herself. 'Where then does he live?'

'In chambers in the Temple. You can find him.'

'But what's the use, if *you* do neither one thing nor the other?'

'Oh, I *shall* do the "other,"' Charlotte said; 'I'm only waiting till I go up. You want them so awfully?' She curiously, solemnly again, sounded her.

'I'm dying for them. There's a special charm in them — I don't know what it is: they tell so their history.'

'But what do you know of that?'

'Just what they themselves say. It's all *in* them — and it comes out. They breathe a tenderness — they have the white glow of it. My dear,' hissed Mrs. Guy in supreme confidence and as she buttoned her glove — 'they're things of love!'

'Oh!' our young woman vaguely exclaimed.

'They're things of passion!'

'Mercy!' she gasped, turning short off. But these words

remained, though indeed their help was scarce needed, Charlotte being in private face to face with a new light, as she by
this time felt she must call it, on the dear dead, kind, colourless lady whose career had turned so sharp a corner in the
middle. The pearls had quite taken their place as a revelation. She might have received them for nothing—admit that;
but she couldn't have kept them so long and so unprofitably
hidden, couldn't have enjoyed them only in secret, for nothing; and she had mixed them, in her reliquary, with false
things, in order to put curiosity and detection off the scent.
Over this strange fact poor Charlotte interminably mused: it
became more touching, more attaching for her than she could
now confide to any ear. How bad, or how happy—in the
sophisticated sense of Mrs. Guy and the young man at the
Temple—the effaced Miss Bradshaw must have been to have
had to be so mute! The little governess at Bleet put on the
necklace now in secret sessions; she wore it sometimes under
her dress; she came to feel, verily, a haunting passion for it.
Yet in her penniless state she would have parted with it for
money; she gave herself also to dreams of what in this direction it would do for her. The sophistry of her so often saying
to herself that Arthur had after all definitely pronounced her
welcome to any gain from his gift that might accrue—this
trick remained innocent, as she perfectly knew it for what it
was. Then there was always the possibility of his—as she
could only picture it—rising to the occasion. Mightn't he
have a grand magnanimous moment?—mightn't he just say:
'Oh, of course I couldn't have afforded to let you have it if I
had known; but since you *have* got it, and have made out the
truth by your own wit, I really can't screw myself down to
the shabbiness of taking it back'?

She had, as it proved, to wait a long time—to wait
till, at the end of several months, the great house of
Bleet had, with due deliberation, for the season, transferred
itself to town; after which, however, she fairly snatched at

her first freedom to knock, dressed in her best and armed with her disclosure, at the door of her doubting kinsman. It was still with doubt and not quite with the face she had hoped that he listened to her story. He had turned pale, she thought, as she produced the necklace, and he appeared, above all, disagreeably affected. Well, perhaps there was reason, she more than ever remembered; but what on earth was one, in close touch with the fact, to do? She had laid the pearls on his table, where, without his having at first put so much as a finger to them, they met his hard, cold stare.

'I don't believe in them,' he simply said at last.

'That's exactly, then,' she returned with some spirit, 'what I wanted to hear!'

She fancied that at this his colour changed; it was indeed vivid to her afterwards — for she was to have a long recall of the scene — that she had made him quite angrily flush. 'It's a beastly unpleasant imputation, you know!' — and he walked away from her as he had always walked at the vicarage.

'It's none of *my* making, I'm sure,' said Charlotte Prime. 'If you're afraid to believe they're real ——'

'Well?' — and he turned, across the room, sharp round at her.

'Why, it's not my fault.'

He said nothing more, for a moment, on this; he only came back to the table. 'They're what I originally said they were. They're rotten paste.'

'Then I may keep them?'

'No. I want a better opinion.'

'Than your own?'

'Than *your* own.' He dropped on the pearls another queer stare, then, after a moment, bringing himself to touch them, did exactly what she had herself done in the presence of Mrs. Guy at Bleet — gathered them together, marched off with them to a drawer, put them in and clicked the key. 'You say I'm afraid,' he went on as he again met her; 'but I shan't be afraid to take them to Bond Street.'

'And if the people say they're real ——?'

He hesitated — then had his strangest manner. 'They won't say it! They shan't!'

There was something in the way he brought it out that deprived poor Charlotte, as she was perfectly aware, of any manner at all. 'Oh!' she simply sounded, as she had sounded for her last word to Mrs. Guy; and, within a minute, without more conversation, she had taken her departure.

A fortnight later she received a communication from him, and towards the end of the season one of the entertainments in Eaton Square was graced by the presence of Mrs. Guy. Charlotte was not at dinner, but she came down afterwards, and this guest, on seeing her, abandoned a very beautiful young man on purpose to cross and speak to her. The guest had on a lovely necklace and had apparently not lost her habit of overflowing with the pride of such ornaments.

'Do you see?' She was in high joy.

They were indeed splendid pearls — so far as poor Charlotte could feel that she knew, after what had come and gone, about such mysteries. Charlotte had a sickly smile. 'They're almost as fine as Arthur's.'

'Almost? Where, my dear, are your eyes? They *are* "Arthur's!"' After which, to meet the flood of crimson that accompanied her young friend's start: 'I tracked them — after your folly, and, by miraculous luck, recognised them in the Bond Street window to which he had disposed of them.'

'*Disposed* of them?' the girl gasped. 'He wrote me that I had insulted his mother and that the people had shown him he was right — had pronounced them utter paste.'

Mrs. Guy gave a stare. 'Ah, I told you he wouldn't bear it! No. But I had, I assure you,' she wound up, 'to drive my bargain!'

Charlotte scarce heard or saw; she was full of her private wrong. 'He wrote me,' she panted, 'that he had smashed them.'

Mrs. Guy could only wonder and pity. 'He's really morbid!'
But it was not quite clear which of the pair she pitied; though
Charlotte felt really morbid too after they had separated and
she found herself full of thought. She even went the length
of asking herself what sort of a bargain Mrs. Guy had driven
and whether the marvel of the recognition in Bond Street had
been a veracious account of the matter. Hadn't she perhaps
in truth dealt with Arthur directly? It came back to Charlotte
almost luridly that she had had his address.

THE REAL RIGHT THING

I

WHEN, after the death of Ashton Doyne — but three months after — George Withermore was approached, as the phrase is, on the subject of a 'volume,' the communication came straight from his publishers, who had been, and indeed much more, Doyne's own; but he was not surprised to learn, on the occurrence of the interview they next suggested, that a certain pressure as to the early issue of a Life had been brought to bear upon them by their late client's widow. Doyne's relations with his wife had been, to Withermore's knowledge, a very special chapter — which would present itself, by the way, as a delicate one for the biographer; but a sense of what she had lost, and even of what she had lacked, had betrayed itself, on the poor woman's part, from the first days of her bereavement, sufficiently to prepare an observer at all initiated for some attitude of reparation, some espousal even exaggerated of the interests of a distinguished name. George Withermore was, as he felt, initiated; yet what he had not expected was to hear that she had mentioned him as the person in whose hands she would most promptly place the materials for a book.

These materials — diaries, letters, memoranda, notes, documents of many sorts — were her property, and wholly in her control, no conditions at all attaching to any portion of her heritage; so that she was free at present to do as she liked — free, in particular, to do nothing. What Doyne would have arranged had he had time to arrange could be but supposition and guess. Death had taken him too soon and too suddenly,

and there was all the pity that the only wishes he was known
to have expressed were wishes that put it positively out of
account.   He had broken short off — that was the way of it;
and the end was ragged and needed trimming.   Withermore
was conscious, abundantly, how close he had stood to him, but
he was not less aware of his comparative obscurity.   He was
young, a journalist, a critic, a hand-to-mouth character, with
little, as yet, as was vulgarly said, to show.   His writings were
few and small, his relations scant and vague.   Doyne, on the
other hand, had lived long enough — above all had had talent
enough — to become great, and among his many friends gilded
also with greatness were several to whom his wife would have
struck those who knew her as much more likely to appeal.

The preference she had, at all events, uttered — and uttered
in a roundabout, considerate way that left him a measure of
freedom — made our young man feel that he must at least see
her and that there would be in any case a good deal to talk
about.   He immediately wrote to her, she as promptly named
an hour, and they had it out.   But he came away with his
particular idea immensely strengthened.   She was a strange
woman, and he had never thought her an agreeable one; only
there was something that touched him now in her bustling,
blundering impatience.   She wanted the book to make up,
and the individual whom, of her husband's set, she probably
believed she might most manipulate was in every way to help
it to make up.   She had not taken Doyne seriously enough in
life, but the biography should be a solid reply to every imputation on herself.   She had scantly known how such books
were constructed, but she had been looking and had learned
something.   It alarmed Withermore a little from the first
to see that she would wish to go in for quantity.   She talked
of 'volumes' — but he had his notion of that.

'My thought went straight to *you*, as his own would have
done,' she had said almost as soon as she rose before him there
in her large array of mourning — with her big black eyes, her

big black wig, her big black fan and gloves, her general gaunt, ugly, tragic, but striking and, as might have been thought from a certain point of view, 'elegant' presence. 'You're the one he liked most; oh, *much!*' — and it had been quite enough to turn Withermore's head. It little mattered that he could afterward wonder if she had known Doyne enough, when it came to that, to be sure. He would have said for himself indeed that her testimony on such a point would scarcely have counted. Still, there was no smoke without fire; she knew at least what she meant, and he was not a person she could have an interest in flattering. They went up together, without delay, to the great man's vacant study, which was at the back of the house and looked over the large green garden — a beautiful and inspiring scene, to poor Withermore's view — common to the expensive row.

'You can perfectly work here, you know,' said Mrs. Doyne; 'you shall have the place quite to yourself — I'll give it all up to you; so that in the evenings, in particular, don't you see? for quiet and privacy, it will be perfection.'

Perfection indeed, the young man felt as he looked about — having explained that, as his actual occupation was an evening paper and his earlier hours, for a long time yet, regularly taken up, he would have to come always at night. The place was full of their lost friend; everything in it had belonged to him; everything they touched had been part of his life. It was for the moment too much for Withermore — too great an honour and even too great a care; memories still recent came back to him, and, while his heart beat faster and his eyes filled with tears, the pressure of his loyalty seemed almost more than he could carry. At the sight of his tears Mrs. Doyne's own rose to her lids, and the two, for a minute, only looked at each other. He half expected her to break out: 'Oh, help me to feel as I know you know I want to feel!' And after a little one of them said, with the other's deep assent — it didn't matter which: 'It's here that we're *with*

him.' But it was definitely the young man who put it, before
they left the room, that it was there he was with *them*.

The young man began to come as soon as he could arrange
it, and then it was, on the spot, in the charmed stillness, between the lamp and the fire and with the curtains drawn, that
a certain intenser consciousness crept over him. He turned
in out of the black London November; he passed through the
large, hushed house and up the red-carpeted staircase where
he only found in his path the whisk of a soundless trained
maid, or the reach, out of a doorway, of Mrs. Doyne's queenly
weeds and approving tragic face; and then, by a mere touch
of the well-made door that gave so sharp and pleasant a click,
shut himself in for three or four warm hours with the spirit —
as he had always distinctly declared it — of his master. He
was not a little frightened when, even the first night, it came
over him that he had really been most affected, in the whole
matter, by the prospect, the privilege, and the luxury, of this
sensation. He had not, he could now reflect, definitely considered the question of the book — as to which there was here,
even already, much to consider: he had simply let his affection and admiration — to say nothing of his gratified pride —
meet, to the full, the temptation Mrs. Doyne had offered them.

How did he know, without more thought, he might begin
to ask himself, that the book was, on the whole, to be desired?
What warrant had he ever received from Ashton Doyne himself for so direct and, as it were, so familiar an approach?
Great was the art of biography, but there were lives and lives,
there were subjects and subjects. He confusedly recalled, so
far as that went, old words dropped by Doyne over contemporary compilations, suggestions of how he himself discriminated
as to other heroes and other panoramas. He even remembered
how his friend, at moments, would have seemed to show himself as holding that the 'literary' career might — save in the
case of a Johnson and a Scott, with a Boswell and a Lockhart
to help — best content itself to be represented. The artist was

what he *did* — he was nothing else. Yet how, on the other hand, was not *he*, George Withermore, poor devil, to have jumped at the chance of spending his winter in an intimacy so rich? It had been simply dazzling — that was the fact. It hadn't been the 'terms,' from the publishers — though these were, as they said at the office, all right; it had been Doyne himself, his company and contact and presence — it had been just what it was turning out, the possibility of an intercourse closer than that of life. Strange that death, of the two things, should have the fewer mysteries and secrets! The first night our young man was alone in the room it seemed to him that his master and he were really for the first time together.

II

MRS. DOYNE had for the most part let him expressively alone, but she had on two or three occasions looked in to see if his needs had been met, and he had had the opportunity of thanking her on the spot for the judgment and zeal with which she had smoothed his way. She had to some extent herself been looking things over and had been able already to muster several groups of letters; all the keys of drawers and cabinets she had, moreover, from the first placed in his hands, with helpful information as to the apparent whereabouts of different matters. She had put him, in a word, in the fullest possible possession, and whether or no her husband had trusted her, she at least, it was clear, trusted her husband's friend. There grew upon Withermore, nevertheless, the impression that, in spite of all these offices, she was not yet at peace, and that a certain unappeasable anxiety continued even to keep step with her confidence. Though she was full of consideration, she was at the same time perceptibly *there :* he felt her, through a supersubtle sixth sense that the whole connection had already brought into play, hover, in the still hours, at the top of landings and on the other side of doors, gathered from the soundless brush of her skirts the hint of her watchings and waitings. One evening when, at his friend's table, he had lost himself in the depths of correspondence, he was made to start and turn by the suggestion that some one was behind him. Mrs. Doyne had come in without his hearing the door, and she gave a strained smile as he sprang to his feet. 'I hope,' she said, 'I haven't frightened you.'

'Just a little — I was so absorbed. It was as if, for the instant,' the young man explained, 'it had been himself.'

The oddity of her face increased in her wonder. 'Ashton?'

'He does seem so near,' said Withermore.

'To you too?'

This naturally struck him. 'He does then to you?'

She hesitated, not moving from the spot where she had first stood, but looking round the room as if to penetrate its duskier angles. She had a way of raising to the level of her nose the big black fan which she apparently never laid aside and with which she thus covered the lower half of her face, her rather hard eyes, above it, becoming the more ambiguous. 'Sometimes.'

'Here,' Withermore went on, 'it's as if he might at any moment come in. That's why I jumped just now. The time is so short since he really used to — it only *was* yesterday. I sit in his chair, I turn his books, I use his pens, I stir his fire, exactly as if, learning he would presently be back from a walk, I had come up here contentedly to wait. It's delightful — but it's strange.'

Mrs. Doyne, still with her fan up, listened with interest. 'Does it worry you?'

'No — I like it.'

She hesitated again. 'Do you ever feel as if he were — a — quite — a — personally in the room?'

'Well, as I said just now,' her companion laughed, 'on hearing you behind me I seemed to take it so. What do we want, after all,' he asked, 'but that he shall be with us?'

'Yes, as you said he would be — that first time.' She stared in full assent. 'He *is* with us.'

She was rather portentous, but Withermore took it smiling. 'Then we must keep him. We must do only what he would like.'

'Oh, only that, of course — only. But if he *is* here——?' And her sombre eyes seemed to throw it out, in vague distress, over her fan.

'It shows that he's pleased and wants only to help? Yes, surely; it must show that.'

She gave a light gasp and looked again round the room. 'Well,' she said as she took leave of him, 'remember that I too want only to help.' On which, when she had gone, he felt sufficiently — that she had come in simply to see he was all right.

He was all right more and more, it struck him after this, for as he began to get into his work he moved, as it appeared to him, but the closer to the idea of Doyne's personal presence. When once this fancy had begun to hang about him he welcomed it, persuaded it, encouraged it, quite cherished it, looking forward all day to feeling it renew itself in the evening, and waiting for the evening very much as one of a pair of lovers might wait for the hour of their appointment. The smallest accidents humoured and confirmed it, and by the end of three or four weeks he had come quite to regard it as the consecration of his enterprise. Wasn't it what settled the question of what Doyne would have thought of what they were doing? What they were doing was what he wanted done, and they could go on, from step to step, without scruple or doubt. Withermore rejoiced indeed at moments to feel this certitude: there were times of dipping deep into some of Doyne's secrets when it was particularly pleasant to be able to hold that Doyne desired him, as it were, to know them. He was learning many things that he had not suspected, drawing many curtains, forcing many doors, reading many riddles, going, in general, as they

said, behind almost everything. It was at an occasional sharp
turn of some of the duskier of these wanderings 'behind' that
he really, of a sudden, most felt himself, in the intimate,
sensible way, face to face with his friend; so that he could
scarcely have told, for the instant, if their meeting occurred
in the narrow passage and tight squeeze of the past, or at the
hour and in the place that actually held him. Was it '67, or
was it but the other side of the table?

Happily, at any rate, even in the vulgarest light publicity
could ever shed, there would be the great fact of the way
Doyne was 'coming out.' He was coming out too beautifully
— better yet than such a partisan as Withermore could have
supposed. Yet, all the while, as well, how would this partisan
have represented to any one else the special state of his own
consciousness? It wasn't a thing to talk about — it was only a
thing to feel. There were moments, for instance, when, as he
bent over his papers, the light breath of his dead host was as
distinctly in his hair as his own elbows were on the table before
him. There were moments when, had he been able to look
up, the other side of the table would have shown him this
companion as vividly as the shaded lamplight showed him his
page. That he couldn't at such a juncture look up was his
own affair, for the situation was ruled — that was but natural —
by deep delicacies and fine timidities, the dread of too sudden
or too rude an advance. What was intensely in the air was
that if Doyne *was* there it was not nearly so much for himself
as for the young priest of his altar. He hovered and lingered,
he came and went, he might almost have been, among the
books and the papers, a hushed, discreet librarian, doing the
particular things, rendering the quiet aid, liked by men of
letters.

Withermore himself, meanwhile, came and went, changed
his place, wandered on quests either definite or vague; and
more than once, when, taking a book down from a shelf and
finding in it marks of Doyne's pencil, he got drawn on and lost,

he had heard documents on the table behind him gently shifted and stirred, had literally, on his return, found some letter he had mislaid pushed again into view, some wilderness cleared by the opening of an old journal at the very date he wanted. How should he have gone so, on occasion, to the special box or drawer, out of fifty receptacles, that would help him, had not his mystic assistant happened, in fine prevision, to tilt its lid, or to pull it half open, in just the manner that would catch his eye? — in spite, after all, of the fact of lapses and intervals in which, *could* one have really looked, one would have seen somebody standing before the fire a trifle detached and over-erect — somebody fixing one the least bit harder than in life.

III

THAT this auspicious relation had in fact existed, had continued, for two or three weeks, was sufficiently proved by the dawn of the distress with which our young man found himself aware that he had, for some reason, from a certain evening, begun to miss it. The sign of that was an abrupt, surprised sense — on the occasion of his mislaying a marvellous unpublished page which, hunt where he would, remained stupidly, irrecoverably lost — that his protected state was, after all, exposed to some confusion and even to some depression. If, for the joy of the business, Doyne and he had, from the start, been together, the situation had, within a few days of his first new suspicion of it, suffered the odd change of their ceasing to be so. That was what was the matter, he said to himself, from the moment an impression of mere mass and quantity struck him as taking, in his happy outlook at his material, the place of his pleasant assumption of a clear course and a lively pace. For five nights he struggled; then, never at his table, wandering about the room, taking up his references only to lay them down, looking out of the window, poking the fire, thinking strange thoughts, and listening for signs and sounds not as he suspected or imagined, but as he vainly desired and invoked them, he made up his mind that he was, for the time at least, forsaken.

The extraordinary thing thus became that it made him not only sad not to feel Doyne's presence, but in a high degree uneasy. It was stranger, somehow, that he shouldn't be there than it had ever been that he *was* — so strange, indeed, at last that Withermore's nerves found themselves quite inconsequently affected. They had taken kindly enough to what was of an order impossible to explain, perversely reserving their sharpest state for the return to the normal, the supersession of the false. They were remarkably beyond control when, finally, one night, after resisting an hour or two, he simply edged out of the room. It had only now, for the first time, become impossible to him to remain there. Without design, but panting a little and positively as a man scared, he passed along his usual corridor and reached the top of the staircase. From this point he saw Mrs. Doyne looking up at him from the bottom quite as if she had known he would come ; and the most singular thing of all was that, though he had been conscious of no notion to resort to her, had only been prompted to relieve himself by escape, the sight of her position made him recognise it as just, quickly feel it as a part of some monstrous oppression that was closing over both of them. It was wonderful how, in the mere modern London hall, between the Tottenham Court Road rugs and the electric light, it came up to him from the tall black lady, and went again from him down to her, that he knew what she meant by looking as if he would know. He descended straight, she turned into her own little lower room, and there, the next thing, with the door shut, they were, still in silence and with queer faces, confronted over confessions that had taken sudden life from these two or three movements. Withermore gasped as it came to him why he had lost his friend. 'He has been with *you* ?'

With this it was all out — out so far that neither had to

explain and that, when 'What do you suppose is the matter?' quickly passed between them, one appeared to have said it as much as the other. Withermore looked about at the small, bright room in which, night after night, she had been living her life as he had been living his own upstairs. It was pretty, cosy, rosy; but she had by turns felt in it what he had felt and heard in it what he had heard. Her effect there — fantastic black, plumed and extravagant, upon deep pink — was that of some 'decadent' coloured print, some poster of the newest school. 'You understood he had left me?' he asked.

She markedly wished to make it clear. 'This evening — yes. I've made things out.'

'You knew — before — that he was with me?'

She hesitated again. 'I felt he wasn't with *me*. But on the stairs ——'

'Yes?'

'Well — he passed, more than once. He was in the house. And at your door ——'

'Well?' he went on as she once more faltered.

'If I stopped I could sometimes tell. And from your face,' she added, 'to-night, at any rate, I knew your state.'

'And that was why you came out?'

'I thought you'd come to me.'

He put out to her, on this, his hand, and they thus, for a minute, in silence, held each other clasped. There was no peculiar presence for either, now — nothing more peculiar than that of each for the other. But the place had suddenly become as if consecrated, and Withermore turned over it again his anxiety. 'What *is* then the matter?'

'I only want to do the real right thing,' she replied after a moment.

'And are we not doing it?'

'I wonder. Are *you* not?'

He wondered too. 'To the best of my belief. But we must think.'

G

'We must think,' she echoed. And they did think—thought, with intensity, the rest of that evening together, and thought, independently — Withermore at least could answer for himself — during many days that followed. He intermitted for a little his visits and his work, trying, in meditation, to catch himself in the act of some mistake that might have accounted for their disturbance. Had he taken, on some important point — or looked as if he might take — some wrong line or wrong view? had he somewhere benightedly falsified or inadequately insisted? He went back at last with the idea of having guessed two or three questions he might have been on the way to muddle; after which he had, above stairs, another period of agitation, presently followed by another interview, below, with Mrs. Doyne, who was still troubled and flushed.

'He's there?'

'He's there.'

'I knew it!' she returned in an odd gloom of triumph. Then as to make it clear: 'He has not been again with *me*.'

'Nor with me again to help,' said Withermore.

She considered. 'Not to help?'

'I can't make it out — I'm at sea. Do what I will, I feel I'm wrong.'

She covered him a moment with her pompous pain. 'How do you feel it?'

'Why, by things that happen. The strangest things. I can't describe them — and you wouldn't believe them.'

'Oh yes, I would!' Mrs. Doyne murmured.

'Well, he intervenes.' Withermore tried to explain. 'However I turn, I find him.'

She earnestly followed. '"Find" him?'

'I meet him. He seems to rise there before me.'

Mrs. Doyne, staring, waited a little. 'Do you mean you see him?'

'I feel as if at any moment I may. I'm baffled. I'm checked.' Then he added: 'I'm afraid.'

'Of *him?*' asked Mrs. Doyne.

He thought. 'Well — of what I'm doing.'

'Then what, that's so awful, *are* you doing?'

'What you proposed to me. Going into his life.'

She showed, in her gravity, now, a new alarm. 'And don't you *like* that?'

'Doesn't *he?* That's the question. We lay him bare. We serve him up. What is it called? We give him to the world.'

Poor Mrs. Doyne, as if on a menace to her hard atonement, glared at this for an instant in deeper gloom. 'And why shouldn't we?'

'Because we don't know. There are natures, there are lives, that shrink. He mayn't wish it,' said Withermore. 'We never asked him.'

'How *could* we?'

He was silent a little. 'Well, we ask him now. That's, after all, what our start has, so far, represented. We've put it to him.'

'Then — if he has been with us — we've had his answer.'

Withermore spoke now as if he knew what to believe. 'He hasn't been "with" us — he has been against us.'

'Then why did you think ——'

'What I *did* think, at first — that what he wishes to make us feel is his sympathy? Because, in my original simplicity, I was mistaken. I was — I don't know what to call it — so excited and charmed that I didn't understand. But I understand at last. He only wanted to communicate. He strains forward out of his darkness; he reaches toward us out of his mystery; he makes us dim signs out of his horror.'

'"Horror"?' Mrs. Doyne gasped with her fan up to her mouth.

'At what we're doing.' He could by this time piece it all together. 'I see now that at first ——'

'Well, what?'

'One had simply to feel he was there, and therefore not indifferent. And the beauty of that misled me. But he's there as a protest.'

'Against *my* Life?' Mrs. Doyne wailed.

'Against *any* Life. He's there to *save* his Life. He's there to be let alone.'

'So you give up?' she almost shrieked.

He could only meet her. 'He's there as a warning.'

For a moment, on this, they looked at each other deep. 'You *are* afraid!' she at last brought out.

It affected him, but he insisted. 'He's there as a curse!'

With that they parted, but only for two or three days; her last word to him continuing to sound so in his ears that, between his need really to satisfy her and another need presently to be noted, he felt that he might not yet take up his stake. He finally went back at his usual hour and found her in her usual place. 'Yes, I *am* afraid,' he announced as if he had turned that well over and knew now all it meant. 'But I gather that you're not.'

She faltered, reserving her word. 'What is it you fear?'

'Well, that if I go on I *shall* see him.'

'And then —— ?'

'Oh, then,' said George Withermore, 'I *should* give up!'

She weighed it with her lofty but earnest air. 'I think, you know, we must have a clear sign.'

'You wish me to try again?'

She hesitated. 'You see what it means — for me — to give up.'

'Ah, but *you* needn't,' Withermore said.

She seemed to wonder, but in a moment she went on. 'It would mean that he won't take from me —— ' But she dropped for despair.

'Well, what?'

'Anything,' said poor Mrs. Doyne.

He faced her a moment more. 'I've thought myself of the clear sign. I'll try again.'

As he was leaving her, however, she remembered. 'I'm only afraid that to-night there's nothing ready — no lamp and no fire.'

'Never mind,' he said from the foot of the stairs; 'I'll find things.'

To which she answered that the door of the room would probably, at any rate, be open; and retired again as if to wait for him. She had not long to wait; though, with her own door wide and her attention fixed, she may not have taken the time quite as it appeared to her visitor. She heard him, after an interval, on the stair, and he presently stood at her entrance, where, if he had not been precipitate, but rather, as to step and sound, backward and vague, he showed at least as livid and blank.

'I give up.'

'Then you've seen him?'

'On the threshold — guarding it.'

'Guarding it?' She glowed over her fan. 'Distinct?'

'Immense. But dim. Dark. Dreadful,' said poor George Withermore.

She continued to wonder. 'You didn't go in?'

The young man turned away. 'He forbids!'

'You say *I* needn't,' she went on after a moment. 'Well then, need I?'

'See him?' George Withermore asked.

She waited an instant. 'Give up.'

'You must decide.' For himself he could at last but drop upon the sofa with his bent face in his hands. He was not quite to know afterwards how long he had sat so; it was enough that what he did next know was that he was alone among her favourite objects. Just as he gained his feet, however, with this sense and that of the door standing open to the hall, he found himself afresh confronted, in the light, the warmth, the rosy space, with her big black perfumed presence. He saw at a glance, as she offered him a huger, bleaker stare over the mask of her fan, that she had been above; and so it was that, for the last time, they faced together their strange question. 'You've seen him?' Withermore asked.

He was to infer later on from the extraordinary way she closed her eyes, and, as if to steady herself, held them tight and long, in silence, that beside the unutterable vision of Ashton Doyne's wife his own might rank as an escape. He knew before she spoke that all was over. 'I give up.'

THE GREAT CONDITION

I

'AH there, confound it!' said Bertram Braddle when he had once more frowned, so far as he could frown, over his telegram. 'I *must* catch the train if I'm to have my morning clear in town. And it's a most abominable nuisance!'

'Do you mean on account of — a — *her?*' asked, after a minute's silent sympathy, the friend to whom — in the hall of the hotel, still bestrewn with the appurtenances of the newly disembarked — he had thus querulously addressed himself.

He looked hard for an instant at Henry Chilver, but the hardness was not all produced by Chilver's question. His annoyance at not being able to spend his night at Liverpool was visibly the greatest that such a privation can be conceived as producing, and might have seemed indeed to transcend the limits of its occasion. 'I promised her the second day out that, no matter at what hour we should get in, I would see her up to London and save her having to take a step by herself.'

'And you piled up the assurance' — Chilver somewhat irrelevantly laughed — 'with each successive day!'

'Naturally — for what is there to do between New York and Queenstown but pile up? And now, with this pistol at my head' — crumpling the telegram with an angry fist, he tossed it into the wide public chimney-place — 'I leave her to scramble through to-morrow as she can. She has to go on to Brighton and she doesn't know ——' And Braddle's quickened sense of the perversity of things dropped to a moment's helpless communion with the aggravating face of his watch.

'She doesn't know —— ? ' his friend conscientiously echoed.

'Oh, she doesn't know anything! Should you say it's too late to ask for a word with her?'

Chilver, with his eyes on the big hotel-clock, wondered. 'Lateish — isn't it? — when she must have been gone this quarter of an hour to her room.'

'Yes, I'm bound to say she *has* managed *that* for herself!' and Braddle stuck back his watch. 'So that, as I haven't time to write, there's nothing for me but to wire her — ever so apologetically — the first thing in the morning from town.'

'Surely — as for the steamer special there are now only about five minutes left.'

'Good then — I join you,' said Braddle, with a sigh of submission. 'But where's the brute who took my things? Yours went straight to the station?'

'No — they're still out there on the cab from which I set you down. And there's your chap with your stuff ' — Chilver's eye had just caught the man — 'he's ramming it into the lift. Collar him before it goes up.' Bertram Braddle, on this, sprang forward in time; then while at an office-window that opened into an inner sanctuary he explained his case to a neatly fitted priestess whose cold eyes looked straight through nonsense, putting it before her that he should after all not require the room he had telegraphed for, his companion only turned uneasily about at a distance and made no approach to the arrested four-wheeler that, at the dock, had received both the gentlemen and their effects. 'I join you — I join you,' Braddle repeated as he brought back his larger share of these.

Chilver appeared meanwhile to have found freedom of mind for a decision. 'But, my dear fellow, shall I too then go?'

Braddle stared. 'Why, I thought you so eminently *had* to.'

'Not if I can be of any use to you. I mean by stopping over and offering my — I admit very inferior — aid —— '

'To Mrs. Damerel?' Braddle took in his friend's sudden

and — as it presented itself — singularly obliging change of plan. 'Ah, you want to be of use to *her?*'

'Only if it will take her off your mind till you see her again. I don't mind telling you now,' Chilver courageously continued, 'that I'm not positively in such a hurry. I said I'd catch the train because I thought you wanted to be alone with her.'

The young men stood there now a trifle rigidly, but very expressively, face to face: Bertram Braddle, the younger but much the taller, smooth, handsome, and heavy, with the composition of his dress so elaborately informal, his pleasant monocular scowl so religiously fixed, his hat so despairingly tilted, and his usual air — innocent enough, however — of looking down from some height still greater — as every one knew about the rich, the bloated Braddles — than that of his fine stature; Chilver, slight and comparatively colourless, rather sharp than bright, but with — in spite of a happy brown moustache, scantily professional, but envied by the man whose large, empty, sunny face needed, as some one had said, a little planting — no particular 'looks' save those that dwelt in his intelligent eyes. 'And what then did you think I wanted to do?'

'Exactly what you say. To present yourself in a taking light — to deepen the impression you've been at so much trouble to make. But if you don't care for my stopping——!' And tossing away the end of his cigarette with a gesture of good-humoured renouncement, Chilver moved across the marble slabs to the draughty portal that kept swinging from the street.

There were porters, travellers, other impediments in his way, and this gave Braddle an appreciable time to watch his receding back before it disappeared; the prompt consequence of which was an 'I say, Chilver!' launched after him sharply enough to make him turn round before passing out. The speaker had not otherwise stirred, and the interval of space doubtless took something from the straightness of their further mute communication. This interval, the next minute, as Chilver failed to return, Braddle diminished by gaining the door in company with a porter whose arm he had seized on the way. 'Take this gentleman's things off the cab and put on mine.' Then as he turned to his friend: 'Go and tell the young woman there that you'll have the room I've given up.'

Chilver laid upon him a hand still interrogative enough not to be too grateful. 'Are you very sure it's all right?'

Braddle's face simply followed for a moment, in the outer lamplight, the progress of the operation he had decreed. 'Do you think I'm going to allow you to make out that I'm afraid?'

'Well, my dear chap, why shouldn't you be?' Henry Chilver, with this retort, did nothing; he only, with his hands in his pockets, let the porter and the cabman bestir themselves. 'I simply wanted to be civil.'

'Oh, I'll risk it!' said the younger man with a free enough laugh. 'Be awfully attentive, you know.'

'Of course it won't be anything like the same thing to *her*,' Chilver went on.

'Of course not, but explain. Tell her I'm wiring, writing. Do everything, in short. Good-bye.'

'Good-bye, good-bye, old man.' And Chilver went down with him to the rearranged cab. 'So many thanks.'

'Thanks?' said the other as he got in.

'I mean because I'm — hang it! — just tired enough to be glad to go to bed.'

'Oh!' came rather drily from Braddle out of the window of the cab.

'Shan't I go with you to the station?' his companion asked.

'Dear no — much obliged!'

'Well, you shall have my report!' Chilver continued.

'Ah, I shall have Mrs. Damerel's!' Braddle answered as the cab drove away.

II

THE fatigue of which Chilver had spoken sought relief for the time in a good deal of rather pointless activity, and it was not for an hour after he had taken possession of his room that he lay down to close his eyes. He moved, before this, in his narrow limits, up and down and to and fro; he left his smaller portmanteau gaping but unpacked; he fumbled in his dressing-bag for a book and dropped with it into a chair. But when in this position he let his attention very soon wander and his lids finally droop, it was not at all that sleep had overcome him. Something had overcome him, on the contrary, that, a quarter of an hour later, made him jump up and consult the watch he had transferred from his pocket to his bedside as his only step toward undressing. He quickly restored it to its receptacle and, catching up his hat, left the room and took his course downstairs. Here, for another quarter of an hour, he wandered, waited, looked about. He had been rather positive to his comrade on the question of Mrs. Damerel's possible, impossible reappearance; but his movements, for some time, could have been explained only by an unquenched imagination that, late though the hour, she might 'nip' down — so in fact he mentally phrased it: well, for what? To indulge — it was conceivable — an appetite unappeased by the five and twenty meals (Braddle had seen them all served to her on deck) of the rapid voyage. He kept glancing into the irresponsive coffee-room and peeping through the glass door of a smaller blank, bright apartment in which a lonely, ugly lady, hatted and coated and hugging a bundle of shawls, sat glaring into space with an anxiety of her own. When at last he returned to his room, however, it was quite with the recognition that such a person as Mrs. Damerel wouldn't at all at that hour be knocking about the hotel. On the other hand — his vigil still encouraged the reflection — what appeared less like her than her giving them the slip, on their

all leaving the dock, so unceremoniously; making her independent dash for a good room at the inn the very moment the
Customs people had passed her luggage? It was perhaps the
fatiguing futility of this question that at last sent Henry
Chilver to bed and to sleep.

That restorative proved the next morning to have considerably cleared and settled his consciousness. He found himself
immediately aware of being in no position to say what was or
was not 'like' Mrs. Damerel. He knew as little about her as
Braddle knew, and it was his conviction that Braddle's ignorance had kept regular step with all the rest of the conditions.
These conditions were, to begin with, that, seated next her at
table for the very first repast, Bertram had struck up with her
a friendship of which the leaps and bounds were, in the social,
the sentimental sphere, not less remarkable than those with
which the great hurrying ship took its way through the sea.
They were, further, that, unlike all the other women, so
numerous and, in the fine weather, so 'chatty,' she had succeeded in incurring the acquaintance of nobody in the immense
company but themselves. Three or four men had more or less
made up to her, but with none of the ladies had she found it
inevitable to exchange, to his observation — and oh, his attention, at least, had been deep! — three words. The great fact
above all had been — as it now glimmered back to him — that
he had studied her not so much in her own demonstrations,
which had been few and passive, as in those of his absolutely
alienated companion. He had been reduced to contemplation
resignedly remote, since Braddle now monopolised her, and had
thus seen her largely through his surprise at the constancy
of Braddle's interest. The affinities hitherto — in other cases
— recognised by his friend he had generally made out as of an
order much less fine. There were lots of women on the ship
who might easily have been supposed to be a good deal more
his affair. Not one of them had, however, by any perversity
corresponding with that of the connection under his eyes,

become in any degree Chilver's own.   He had the feeling, on
the huge crowded boat, of making the voyage in singular solitude, a solitude mitigated only by the amusement of finding
Braddle so 'mashed' and of wondering what would come of
it.   Much less, up to that moment, had come of the general
American exposure than each, on their sailing westward for
the more and more prescribed near view, had freely foretold
to the other as the least they were likely to get off with.   The
near view of the big queer country had at last, this summer,
imposed itself: so many other men had got it and were making
it, in talk, not only a convenience but a good deal of a nuisance,
that it appeared to have become, defensively, as necessary as
the electric light in the flat one might wish to let; as to which
the two friends, after their ten bustling weeks, had now in
fact grown to feel that they could press the American button
with the best.

But they had been on the whole — Chilver at least had been
— disappointed in the celebrated (and were they not *all*, in
the United States, celebrated?) native women.   He didn't
quite know what he had expected: something or other, at any
rate, that had not taken place.   He felt as if he had carried
over in his portmanteau a court-suit or a wedding-garment and
were bringing it back untouched, unfolded, in creases unre-
lieved and almost painfully aware of themselves.   They had
taken lots of letters — most of them, some fellow who knew
had told them, awfully good ones; they had been to Wash-
ington and Boston and Newport and Mount Desert, walking
round and round the vociferous whirlpool, but neither tumbling
in nor feeling at any moment, as it appeared, at all dangerously
dizzy; so that here — in relation to Mrs. Damerel — was the
oddity of an impression vertiginous only after everything
might have been supposed to be well over.   This lady was the
first female American they had met, of almost any age, who
was not celebrated; yet she was the one who suggested most
to Chilver something he now imagined himself originally to

have gone forth expecting to feel. She was a person to whom they couldn't possibly have had a letter; she had never in her life been to Newport; she was on her way to England for the first time; she was, in short, most inconsistently, though indeed quite unblushingly, obscure. She was only charming in a new way. It was newer, somehow, than any of the others that were so fresh. Yet what should he call it if he were trying — in a foolish flight of analysis to somebody else — to describe it? When he asked himself this he was verily brought, from one thing to another, to recognising that it was probably in fact as old as the hills. All that was new in it was that he was in love with her; and moreover without in the least knowing her, so completely, so heroically, from the point of honour, had he, for all the six days, left her to poor Braddle. Well, if he should now take her up to town he would be a little less ignorant. He liked, naturally, to think he should be of use to her, but he flattered himself he kept the point of honour well in view. To Braddle — given Braddle's uneasiness — he should be equally of use.

III

THIS last appearance was in a short time abundantly confirmed; not only when, in London, after the discharge of his mission, he submitted to his friend a detailed account of that happy transaction, but ten days later, on Braddle's own return from Brighton, where he had promptly put in a week — a week of which, visibly, the sole and irresistible motive was Mrs. Damerel, established there as a sequel to Chilver's attendance on her from Liverpool to Euston and from Euston, within the hour — so immediately that she got off before her other friend had had time to turn up at either station — to Victoria. This other friend passed in London, while at Brighton, the inside of a day, rapping with a familiar stick — at an hour supposedly not dedicated, in those grey courts, to profane speculation — the door of the dingy Temple chambers in which, after the most extravagant holiday of his life, Henry Chilver had found it salutary to sit and imagine himself 'reading.' But Braddle had always been, portentously, a person of free mornings — his nominal occupation that of looking after his father's 'interests,' and his actual that of spending, though quite without scandal, this personage's money, of which, luckily, there seemed an abundance. What came from him on this occasion connected itself with something that had passed between them on their previous meeting, the one immediately following the incident at Liverpool. Chilver had at that time been rather surprised to hear his friend suddenly bring out: 'You don't then think there's anything "off" about her?'

'Off?' Chilver could at least be perfectly vague. 'Off what?'

'What's the beastly phrase? "Off colour." I mean do you think she's all right?'

'Are you in love with her?' Chilver after a moment demanded.

'Damn it, of course I'm in love with her!' Braddle joylessly articulated.

'Well then, doesn't that give you —— ?'

'Give me what?' he asked with impatience at his companion's pause.

'Well, a sort of searching light ——'

'For reading her clear?' Braddle broke in. 'How can you ask — as a man of the world — anything so idiotic? Where did you ever discover that being in love makes a searching light, makes anything but a most damnable and demoralising darkness? One has been in love with creatures such that one's condition has lighted nothing in the world but one's asininity. *I* have at any rate. And so have you!'

'No, I've never been really in love at all,' said Chilver, good-humouredly.

'The less credit to you then to have — in two or three cases I recall — made such a fool of yourself. I, at all events — I don't mind your knowing,' Braddle went on — 'am harder hit, far and away, than I've ever been. But I don't in the least pretend to place her or to have a free judgment about her. I've already — since we landed — had two letters from her, and I go down to-morrow to see her. That *may* assist me — it ought to — to make her out a little better. But I've a gruesome feeling that it won't!'

'Then how can I help you?' Chilver inquired, with just irritation enough to make him, the next moment — though his interlocutor, interestingly worried but really most inexpert, had no answer for the question — sorry to have shown it. 'If you've heard from her,' he continued, 'did she send me a message?'

'None whatever.'

'Nor say anything about me?'

'Not a word.'

'Ah!' said Henry Chilver, while their eyes again met with some insistence. He somehow liked Mrs. Damerel's silence after the hours he had spent with her; but his state of mind was again predominantly of not wanting Braddle to see in him any emotion. 'A woman may surely be called all right, it seems to me, when she's pretty and clever and good.'

'"Good"?' Braddle echoed. 'How do you know she's good?'

'Why, confound you, she's such a lady.'

'*Isn't* she?' — Braddle took it up with equal promptitude and inconsequence. Then he recovered himself. 'All the same, one has known ladies —— !'

'Yes, one has. But she's quite the best thing that, in the whole time, we've come across.'

'Oh, by a long shot. Think of those women on the ship. It's only that she's so poor,' Braddle added.

Chilver hesitated. 'Is she so awfully?'

'She has evidently to count her shillings.'

'Well, if she had been bad she'd be rich,' Chilver returned after another silence. 'So what more do you want?'

'Nothing. Nothing,' Braddle repeated.

'Good-bye, then.'

'Good-bye.'

On which the elder man had taken leave; so that what was inevitably to follow had to wait for their next meeting. Mrs. Damerel's victim betrayed on this second occasion still more markedly the state of a worried man, and his friend measured his unrest by his obvious need of a patient ear, a need with which Chilver's own nature, this interlocutor felt, would not in the same conditions have been acquainted. Even while he wondered, however, at the freedom his visitor used, Chilver recognised that had it been a case of more or less fatuous happiness Braddle would probably have kept the matter to himself. His host made the reflection that *he*, on the other hand, might have babbled about a confidence, but would never have opened his mouth about a fear. Braddle's fear, like many fears, had a considerable queerness, and Chilver, in presence of it and even before a full glimpse, had begun to describe it to himself as a fixed idea. It was as if according to Braddle, there had been something in Mrs. Damerel's history that she ought really to have told a fellow before letting him in so far.

'But how far?'

'Why, hang it, I'd marry her to-morrow.'

Chilver waited a moment. 'Is what you mean that she'd marry *you?*'

'Yes, blest if I don't believe she certainly would.'

'You mean if you'd let her off —— ?'

'Yes,' Braddle concurred; 'the obligation of letting me know the particular thing that, whatever it is, right or wrong, I've somehow got it so tormentingly into my head that she keeps back.'

H

'When you say "keeps back," do you mean that you've questioned her?'

'Oh, not about *that!*' said Braddle with beautiful simplicity.

'Then do you expect her to volunteer information——'

'That may damage her so awfully with me?' Braddle had taken it up intelligently, but appeared sufficiently at a loss as to what he expected. 'I'm sure she knows well enough I want to know.'

'I don't think I understand what you're talking about,' Chilver replied after a longish stare at the fire.

'Well, about something or other in her life; some awkward passage, some beastly episode or accident; the things that do happen, that often *have* happened, to women you might think perfectly straight — come now! and that they very often quite successfully hide. You know what I'm driving at: some chapter in the book difficult to read aloud — some unlucky page she'd like to tear out. God forgive me, some slip.'

Chilver, quitting the fire, had taken a turn round the room.

'Is it your idea,' he presently inquired, 'that there may have been only *one?* I mean one "slip."'' He pulled up long enough in front of them to give his visitor's eyes time to show a guess at possible derision, then he went on in another manner. 'No, no; I really don't understand. You seem to me to see her as a column of figures each in itself highly satisfactory, but which, when you add them up, make only a total of doubt.'

'That's exactly it!' Braddle spoke almost with admiration of this neat formula. 'She hasn't really *any* references.'

'But, my dear man, it's not as if you were engaging a housemaid.'

Braddle was arrested but a moment. 'It's much worse. For any one else I shouldn't mind——!'

'What I don't grasp,' his companion broke in, 'is your liking her so much as to "mind" so much, without by the same stroke liking her enough not to mind at all.'

Braddle took in without confusion this approach to subtlety. 'But suppose it should be something rather awful?'

It was his confidant, rather, who was a trifle disconcerted. 'Isn't it just as easy — besides being much more comfortable — to suppose there's nothing?'

'No. If it had been, don't you see that I *would* have supposed it? There's something. I don't know what there is; but there's something.'

'Then ask her.'

Braddle wondered. 'Would *you?*'

'Oh dear, no!'

'Then *I* won't!' Braddle returned with an odd air of defiance that made his host break into a laugh. 'Suppose,' he continued, 'she should swear there's nothing.'

'The chance of that is just why it strikes me you might ask her.'

'I "might"? I thought you said one shouldn't.'

'*I* shouldn't. But I haven't your ideas.'

'Ah, but you don't know her.'

Chilver hesitated. 'Precisely. And what you mean is that, even if she should swear there's nothing, you wouldn't believe her?'

Braddle appeared to give a silent and even somewhat diffident assent. 'There's nothing I should hate like that. I should hate it still more than being as I am. If you had seen more of her,' he pursued, 'you would know what I mean by her having no references. Her whole life has been so extraordinarily — so conveniently, as one might say — away from everything.'

'I see — so conveniently for *her.* Beyond verification.'

'Exactly; the record's inaccessible. It's all the "great West." We saw something of the great West, and I thought it rather *too* great. She appears to have put in a lot of California and the Sandwich Islands. I may be too particular, but I don't fancy a Sandwich Islands past. Even for her husband and for her little girl — for their having lived as little as for their having died — she has nothing to show. She hasn't so much as a photograph, a lock of hair, or an announcement in a newspaper.'

Chilver thought. 'But perhaps she wouldn't naturally leave such things about the sitting-room of a Brighton lodging.'

'I dare say not. But it isn't only such things. It's tremendously odd her never having even by mere chance knocked against anything or any one that one has ever heard of or could — if one should want to — get at.'

Again Henry Chilver reflected. 'Well, that's what struck me as especially nice, or rather as very remarkable in her — her being, with all her attraction, one of the obscure seventy millions; a mere little almost nameless tossed-up flower out of the huge mixed lap of the great American people. I mean for the charming person she is. I doubt if, after all, any other huge mixed lap ——'

'Yes, if she were English, on those lines,' Braddle sagaciously interrupted, 'one wouldn't look at her, would one? I say, fancy her English!'

Chilver was silent a little. 'What you don't like is her music.'

His visitor met his eyes. 'Why, it's awfully good.'

'Is it? I mean her having, as you told me on the boat, given lessons.'

'That certainly is not what I most like her to have done — I mean on account of some of the persons she may have given them to; but when her voice broke down she had to do something. She had sung in public — though only in concerts; but that's another thing. She lost her voice after an illness. I don't know what the illness was. It was after her husband's death. She plays quite wonderfully — better, she says, really, than she sang; so she has that resource. She gave the lessons in the Sandwich Islands. She admits that, fighting for her own hand, as she says, she has kept some queer company,

I've asked her for details, but she only says she'll tell me
"some day." Well, *what* day, don't you know? Finally she
inherited a little money — she says from a distant cousin. I
don't call *that* distant — setting her up. It isn't much, but it
made the difference, and there she is. She says she's afraid
of London; but I don't quite see in what sense. She heard
about her place at Brighton from some "Western friends."
But how can I go and ask them?'

'The Western friends?' said Chilver.

'No, the people of the house — about the other people. The
place is rather beastly, but it seems all right. At any rate she
likes it. If there's an awful hole on earth it's Brighton, but
she thinks it "perfectly fascinating." Now isn't that a rum
note? She's the most extraordinary mixture.'

Chilver had listened with an air of strained delicacy to this
broken trickle of anguish, speaking to the point only when it
appeared altogether to have ceased. 'Well, my dear man, what
is it, may I ask in all sympathy, you would like me, in the
circumstances, to do? Do you want me to sound her for you?'

'Don't be *too* excruciatingly funny,' Braddle after a moment
replied.

'Well, then, clear the thing up.'

'But how?'

'By making her let you know the worst.'

'And by what means — if I don't ask her?'

'Simply by proposing.'

'Marriage?'

'Marriage, naturally.'

'You consider,' Braddle inquired, 'that that will infallibly
make her speak?'

'Not infallibly, but probably.'

Braddle looked all round the room. 'But if it shouldn't?'
His friend took another turn about. 'Well — risk it!'

IV

HENRY CHILVER remained for a much longer time than he would have expected in ignorance of the effect of that admonition; two full months elapsed without bringing him news. Something, he meanwhile reasoned, he *should* know — ought to know: it was due to him assuredly that Bertram Braddle shouldn't — quite apart from the distance travelled in the company of Mrs. Damerel — go so far even with *him* without recognising the propriety of going further. But at last, as the weeks passed, he arrived at his own estimate of a situation which had clearly nothing more to give him. It was a situation that had simply ceased to be one. Braddle was afraid and had remained afraid, just as he was ashamed and had remained ashamed. He had bolted, in his embarrassment, to Australia or the Cape; unless indeed he had dashed off once more to America, this time perhaps in quest of his so invidious ' references.' Was he looking for tracks in the great West or listening to twaddle in the Sandwich Islands ? In any case Mrs. Damerel would be alone, and the point of honour, for Chilver himself, would have had its day. The sharpest thing in his life at present was the desire to see her again, and he considered that every hour without information made a difference for the question of avoiding her from delicacy. Finally, one morning, with the first faint winter light, it became vivid to him that the dictate of delicacy was positively the other way — was that, on the basis of Braddle's disappearance, he should make her some sign of recollection. He had not forgotten the address observed on one of her luggage-labels the day he had seen her up from Liverpool. Mightn't he, for instance, run down to her place that very morning ? Braddle couldn't expect ——! What Braddle couldn't expect, however, was lost in the suppressed sound with which, on passing into his sitting-room and taking up his fresh letters, he greeted the superscription of the last of the half-dozen just placed on his table. The envelope bore the postmark of Brighton, and if he had languished for information the very first lines — the note was only of a page — were charged with it. Braddle announced his engagement to Mrs. Damerel, spoke briefly, but with emphasis, of their great happiness and their early nuptials, and hoped very much his correspondent would be able to come down and see them for a day.

Henry Chilver, it may be stated, had, for reasons of feeling — he felt somehow so deeply refuted — to wait a certain time to answer. What had Mrs. Damerel's lover, he wondered, succeeded at last in extracting from her? She had made up her mind as to what she could safely do — she had let him know the worst and he had swallowed it down? What *was* it, the queer suppressed chapter; what was the awkward page they had agreed to tear out together? Chilver found himself envying his friend the romance of having been sustained in the special effort, the extreme sacrifice, involved in such an understanding. But he had for many days, on the whole vision, odd impatiences that were followed by odder recoveries. One of these variations was a sudden drop of the desire to be in presence of the woman for the sight of whom he had all winter consistently been yearning. What was most marked, however, was the shake he had vigorously to give himself on perceiving his thoughts again and again take the direction that poor Braddle had too successfully imparted to them. His curiosity about the concession she might have made to Braddle's was an assumption — without Braddle's excuses — that she had really had something to conceal till she was sure of her man. This was idiotic, because the idea was one that never would have originated with himself.

He did at last fix a day, none the less, and went down; but there, on the spot, his imagination was, to his surprise, freshly excited by the very fact that there were no apparent signs of a drama. It was as if he could see, after all, even face to face with her, what had stirred within the man she had for a time only imperfectly subdued. Why should she have tried to be so simple — too simple? She overdid it, she ignored too much. Clear, soft, sweet, yet not a bit silly, she might well strike a fellow as having had more history than she — what should one call it? — owned up to. There were moments when Chilver thought he got hold of it in saying to himself that she was too clever to be merely what she was. There was something in her that, more than anything ever in any one, gratified his taste and seemed to him to testify to the happiest exercise of her own; and such things brought up the puzzle of how so much taste could have landed her simply where she was. Where she was — well, was doubtless where she would find comfort, for the man she had accepted was now visibly at peace, even though he had not yet, as appeared, introduced her to his people. The fact of which Chilver was at last as at first most conscious was the way she succeeded in withholding from his own penetration every trace of the great question she had had out with her intended, who yet couldn't have failed — one would quite have defied him — to give it to her somehow that he had on two occasions allowed his tongue to betray him to the other person he most trusted. Braddle, whose taste was not his strong point, had probably mentioned this indiscretion to her as a drollery; or else she had simply questioned him, got it out of him. This made their guest a participant, but there was something beautiful and final in the curtain that, on her side, she had dropped. It never gave, all day, the faintest stir. That affected Chilver as the mark of what there might be behind.

Yet when in the evening his friend went with him to the station — for the visitor had declined to sleep and was taking the last train back — he had, after they had walked two or three times up and down the platform, the greatest mystification of all. They were smoking; there were ten minutes to spare, and they moved to and fro in silence. They had been talking all day — mainly in Mrs. Damerel's company, but the circumstance that neither spoke at present was not the less marked. Yet if Chilver was waiting for something on his host's part he could scarcely have said for what. He was aware now that if Mrs. Damerel had, as he privately phrased it, 'spoken,' it was scarcely to be expected that the man with a standpoint altered by a definite engagement would — at the present stage at least — repeat to him her words. He felt, however, as the fruitless moments ebbed, a trifle wronged, at all events disappointed : since he had been dragged into the business, as he always for himself expressed it, it would only have been fair to throw a sop to his conjecture. What, moreover, was Braddle himself so perversely and persistently mum for — without an allusion that should even serve as a penance — unless to draw out some advance which might help him to revert with an approach to grace ?   Chilver nevertheless made no advance, and at last as, ceasing to stroll, they stood at the open door of an empty compartment, the train was almost immediately to start. At this moment they exchanged a long, queer stare.

'Well, good-bye,' said the elder man.

'Good-bye.' Chilver still waited before entering the carriage, but just as he was about to give up his companion added : 'You see I followed your advice.   I took the risk.'

'Oh — about the question we discussed ? ' Chilver broke now, on the instant, into friendly response. 'See then how right I was.'

Braddle looked up and down the train.   'I don't know.'

'You're not satisfied ? '

'Satisfied ? '   Still Braddle looked away.

'With what she has told you.'

Braddle faced him again.   'She has told me nothing.'

'Nothing ? '

'Nothing.   She has accepted me — that's all.   Not a bit else.   So you see you *weren't* so right.'

'Oh — oh!' exclaimed Chilver, protestingly.   The guard at

this moment interposing with a 'Take your seats, please!' and sharply, on his entering the carriage, shutting the door on him, he continued the conversation from the window, on which he rested his elbows. During the movement his protest had changed to something else. 'Ah, but won't she yet —— ?'

'Let me have it? I'm sure I don't know. All I can say is that nothing has come from her.'

'Then it's because there *is* nothing.'

'I hope so,' said Braddle from the platform.

'So you see,' Chilver called out as the train moved, 'I *was* right!' And he leaned forth as the distance grew and Braddle stood motionless and grave, gaily insisting and taking leave with his waving hand. But when he drew in his head and dropped into a seat he rather collapsed, tossing his hat across the compartment and sinking back into a corner and an attitude from which, staring before him and not even lighting another cigarette, he never budged till he reached Victoria.

A fortnight later the footfall of Mrs. Damerel's intended was loud on the old staircase in the Temple and the knob of his stick louder still on the old door. 'It's only that it has rather stuck in my crop,' he presently explained, 'that I let you leave Brighton the other day with the pretension that you had been "right," as you called it, about the risk — attending the particular step — that I took. I can't help it if I want you to know — for it bores me that you're so pleased — that you weren't in the least right. You were most uncommonly wrong.'

'Wrong?'

'Wrong.'

Chilver looked vaguely about as if suddenly in search of something, then moved with an odd general inconsequence to the window. 'As the day's so fine, do you mind our getting out of this beastly stuffy place into the Gardens? We can talk there.' His hat was apparently what he had been looking for, and he took it up, and with it some cigarettes. Braddle,

though seemingly disconcerted by what threatened to be practically a change of subject, replied that he didn't care a hang;
so that, leaving the room, they passed together down to the
court and through other battered courts and crooked ways.
The dim London sunshine in the great surrounded garden had
a kindness, and the hum of the town was as hindered and yet
as present as the faint sense of spring. The two men stopped
together before a bench, but neither for the moment sat down.
'Do you mean she *has* told you?' Chilver at last brought out.

'No — it's just what she hasn't done.'

'Then how the deuce am I wrong?'

'She has admitted that there *is* something.'

Chilver markedly wondered. 'Something? What?'

'That's just what I want to know.'

'Then you *have* asked her?'

Braddle hesitated. 'I couldn't resist my curiosity, my anxiety — call it what you will. I've been too worried. I put
it to her the day after you were down there.'

'And how did you put it?'

'Oh, just simply, brutally, disgustingly. I said: "Isn't
there something about yourself — something or other that has
happened to you — that you're keeping back?"'

Chilver was attentive, but not solemn. 'Well?'

'Oh, she admitted it.'

'And in what terms?'

'"Well, since you really drive me to the wall, there *is*
something."'

Chilver continued to consider. 'And is that all she says?'

'No — she says she *will* tell me.'

'Ah well, then!' And Chilver spoke with a curious — in fact,
a slightly ambiguous — little renewed sound of superiority.

'Yes,' his friend ruefully returned, 'but not, you see, for six
months.'

'Oh, I see! I see!' Chilver thoughtfully repeated. 'So
you've got to wait — which I admit perfectly that you must

find rather a bore. Yet if *she's* willing,' he went on with more
cheer and as if still seeking a justification of his original
judgment — 'if *she's* willing, you see, I wasn't so much out.'

Bertram Braddle demurred. 'But she isn't willing.'

His interlocutor stared. 'I thought you said she proposed
it.'

'Proposed what?'

'Why, the six months' wait — to make sure of you.'

'Ah, but she'll *be* sure of me, after she has married me.
The delay she asks for is not for our marriage,' Braddle
explained, 'but only — from the date of our marriage — for
the information.'

'A-ah!' Chilver murmured, as if only now with a full view.
'She means she'll speak when you *are* married.'

'When we are. And then only on a great condition.'

'How great?'

'Well, that if after the six months I still want it very
much. She argues, you know, that I *shan't* want it.'

'You won't then — you won't!' cried Chilver with a laugh
at the odd word and passing his arm into his friend's to make
him walk again. They talked and they talked; Chilver kept
his companion's arm and they quite had the matter out.

'What's that, you know,' Braddle asked, 'but a way to get
off altogether?'

'You mean for you to get off from knowing?'

'Ah no, for *her* —— '

'To get off from telling? It *is* that, rather, of course,'
Chilver conceded. 'But why shouldn't she get off — if you
should be ready to let her?'

'Oh, but if I shouldn't be?' Braddle broke in.

'Why then, if she promises, she'll tell you.'

'Yes, but by that time the knot will be tight.'

'And what difference will that make if you don't mind?
She argues, as you say, that after that amount of marriage, of
experience of her, you won't care —— !'

'What she does tell me may *be?*' Braddle smoked a moment in silence. 'But suppose it should be one of those things ——' He dropped again.

'Well, what things?'

'That a man can't like in *any* state of satisfaction.'

'I don't know what things you mean.'

'Come, I say — you do! Suppose it should be something really awful.'

'Well, her calculation is that, awful or not,' Chilver said, 'she'll have sufficiently attached you to make you willing either totally to forego her disclosure or else easily to bear it.'

'Oh, I know her calculation — which is very charming as well as very clever and very brave. But my danger ——'

'Oh, you think too much of your danger!'

Braddle stopped short. '*You* don't!'

Chilver, however, who had coloured, spent much of the rest of the time they remained together in assuring him that he allowed this element all its weight. Only he came back at the last to what, practically, he had come back to in their other talks. 'I don't quite see why she doesn't strike you as worth almost *any* risk.'

'Do you mean that that's the way she strikes you?'

'Oh, I've not to tell you at this time of day,' said Chilver, 'how well I think of her.'

His companion was now seated on a bench from which he himself had shortly before risen. 'Ah, but I don't suppose you pretend to know her.'

'No — certainly not, I admit. But I don't see how *you* should either, if you come to that.'

'I don't; but it's exactly what I'm trying for, confound it! Besides,' Braddle pursued, 'she doesn't put you the great condition.'

Chilver took a few steps away; then as he came back, 'No; she doesn't!'

'Wait till some woman does,' Braddle went on. 'Then

you'll see how you feel under it — then you can talk. If I wasn't so infernally fond of her,' he gloomily added, 'I wouldn't mind.'

'Wouldn't mind what?'

'Why, what she has been. What she has done.'

'Oh!' Chilver vaguely ejaculated.

'And I only mind now to the extent of wanting to know.' On which Braddle rose from his seat with a heavy sigh. 'Hang it, I've got to know, you know!' he declared as they walked on together.

V

HENRY CHILVER learned, however, in the course of time that he had won no victory on this, after all, rather reasonable ground — learned it from Mrs. Damerel herself, who came up to town in the spring and established herself, in the neighbourhood of Kensington Square, in modest but decent quarters, where her late suitor's best friend went to pay her his respects. The great condition had, as each party saw it, been fruitlessly maintained, for neither had, under whatever pressure, found a way to give in. The most remarkable thing of all was that Chilver should so rapidly have become aware of owing his acquaintance with these facts directly to Mrs. Damerel. He had, for that matter, on the occasion of his very first call, an impression strangely new to him — the consciousness that they had already touched each other much more than any contact between them explained. They met in the air of a common knowledge, so that when, for instance, almost immediately, without precautions or approaches, she said of Bertram Braddle: 'He has gone off — heaven knows where! — to find out about me,' he was not in the least struck with the length of the jump. He was instantly sensible, on the contrary, of the greatest pleasure in showing by his reply that he needed no explanation. 'And do you think he'll succeed?'

'I don't know. He's so clever.'

This, it seemed to Henry Chilver, was a wonderful speech, and he sat there and candidly admired her for it. There were all sorts of things in it — faint, gentle ironies and humilities, and above all the fact that the description was by no means exact. Poor Braddle was not, for such a measure as hers, clever, or markedly wouldn't be for such an undertaking. The words completely, on the part of the woman who might be supposed to have had a kindness for him, gave him away; but surely that was, in the face of his attitude, a mild revenge. It seemed to Chilver that until in her little makeshift suburban drawing-room he found himself alone with Mrs. Damerel he himself had not effectively judged this position. He saw it now sharply, supremely, as the only one that had been possible to his friend, but finer still was the general state of perception, quickened to a liberal intensity, that made him so see it. He couldn't have expressed the case otherwise than by saying that poor Braddle had had to be right to be so ridiculously wrong. There might well have been, it appeared, in Mrs. Damerel's past a missing link or two; but what was the very office of such a fact — when taken with other facts not a bit less vivid — but to give one a splendid chance to show a confidence? Not the confidence that, as one could only put it to one's self, there had not been anything, but the confidence that, whatever there had been, one wouldn't find that one couldn't — for the sake of the rest — swallow it.

This was at bottom the great result of the first stages of Chilver's now independent, as he felt it to be, acquaintance with Mrs. Damerel — a sudden view of any, of every, dim passage, that was more than a tender acceptance of the particular obscurity, that partook really of the nature of affirmation and insistence. It all made her, with everything that for her advantage happened to help it on, extraordinarily touching to him, clothed her in the beauty of her general admission and her general appeal. Were not this admission and this appeal enough, and could anything be imagined more ponderously clumsy, more tactless and even truculent, than to want to gouge out the bleeding details? The charming woman was, to Chilver's view, about of his own age — not altogether so young, therefore, as Braddle, which was doubtless a note, too, in the latter's embarrassment — and that evidently did give time for a certain quantity of more or less trying, of really complicating experience. There it practically was, this experience, in the character of her delicacy, in her kindly, witty, sensitive face, worn fine, too fine perhaps, but only to its increase of expression. She was neither a young fool nor an old one, assuredly; but if the intenser acquaintance with life had made the object of one's affection neither false nor hard, how could one, on the whole, since the story might be so interesting, wish it away? Mrs. Damerel's admission was so much evidence of her truth and her appeal so much evidence of her softness. She might easily have hated them both for guessing. She was at all events just faded enough to match the small assortment of Chilver's fatigued illusions — those that he had still, for occasions, in somewhat sceptical use, but that had lost their original violence of colour.

The second time he saw her alone he came back to what she had told him of Bertram Braddle. 'If he should succeed — as to what you spoke of, wherever he has gone — would your engagement come on again?'

Mrs. Damerel hesitated, but she smiled. 'Do you mean whether he'll be likely to wish it?'

'No,' said Chilver, with something of a blush; 'I mean whether you'll be.'

She still smiled. 'Dear, no. I consider, you know, that I gave him his chance.'

'That you seem to me certainly to have done. Everything between you, then, as I understand it, is at an end?'

'It's very good of you,' said Mrs. Damerel, 'to desire so much to understand it. But I never give,' she laughed, 'but one chance!'

Chilver met her as he could. 'You evidently can't have given any one very many!'

'Oh, you know,' she replied, 'I don't in the least regard it as a matter of course that, many or few, they should be eagerly seized. Mr. Braddle has only behaved as almost any man in his situation would have done.'

Chilver at first, on this, only lost himself awhile. 'Yes, almost any man. I don't consider that the smallest blame attaches to him.'

'It would be too monstrous.'

Again he was briefly silent, but he had his inspiration. 'Yes, let us speak of him gently.' Then he added: 'You've answered me enough. You're free.'

'Free indeed is what I feel,' she replied with her light irony, 'when I talk to you with this extraordinary frankness.'

'Ah, the frankness is mine! It comes from the fact that from the first, through Braddle, I knew. And you knew I knew. And I knew that too. It has made something between us.'

'It might have made something rather different from this,' said Mrs. Damerel.

He wondered an instant. 'Different from my sitting here so intimately with you?'

'I mightn't have been able to bear that. I might have hated the sight of you.'

'Ah, that would have been only,' said Chilver, 'if you had really liked me!'

She matched quickly enough the spirit of this. 'Oh, but it wasn't so easy to like you little enough!'

'Little enough to endure me? Well, thank heaven, at any rate, we've found a sort of way!' Then he went on with real sincerity: 'I feel as if our friend had tremendously helped me. Oh, how easily I want to let him down! There it is.'

She breathed, after a moment, her assent in a sigh. 'There it is!'

I

There indeed it was for several days during which this sigh frequently came back to him as a note of patience, of dignity in helpless submission, penetrating beyond any that had ever reached him. She had been put completely in his power, her good name handed over to him, by no act of her own, and in all her manner in presence of the awkward fact there was something that blinked it as little as it braved it. He wondered so hard, with this, why, even after the talk I have just reported, they were each not more embarrassed, that it could only take him a tolerably short time to discover the reason. If there was something between them it had been between them, in silence and distance, from the first, from even before the moment when his friend, on the ship, by the favour of better opportunity, had tumbled in deep and temporarily blocked, as it were, the passage. Braddle was good-looking, good-humoured, well-connected, rich; and how could she have known of the impression of the man in the background any more than the man in the background could have known of hers? If she had accepted Braddle hadn't it been just to build out, in her situation, at a stroke, the worry of an alternative that was impossible? Of himself she had seen nothing but that he was out of the question, and she had agreed for conscience, for prudence, as a safeguard and a provision, to throw in her lot with a charming, fortunate fellow who was extremely in love. Chilver had, in his meditations, no sooner read these things clear than he had another flash that completed the vision. Hadn't she then, however, having done so much for reason, stood out, with her intended, on the item of the great condition — made great precisely by the insistence of each — exactly because, after all, that left the door open to her imagination, her dream, her hope? Hadn't her idea been to make for Bertram — troubled herself and wavering for the result — a calculated difficulty, a real test? Oh, if there was a test, how *he* was ready to meet it! Henry Chilver's insistence would take a different line from that of his predecessor.

He stood at the threshold of the door, left open indeed, so that he had only to walk over. By the end of the week he had proposed.

VI

It was at his club, one day of the following year, that he next came upon his old friend, whom he had believed, turning the matter often round, he should — in time, though the time might be long — inevitably meet again on some ground socially workable. That the time might be long had been indicated by a circumstance that came up again as soon as, fairly face to face, they fell, in spite of everything, to talking together. 'Ah, you *will* speak to me then,' said Chilver, 'though you don't answer my letters!'

Braddle showed a strange countenance, partly accounted for by the fact that he was brown, seasoned, a trifle battered, and had almost grown thin. But he had still his good monocular scowl, on the strength of which — it was really so much less a threat than a positive appeal from a supersubtle world — any old friend, recognising it again, would take almost anything from him. Yes indeed, quite anything, Chilver felt after they had been a few minutes together: he had become so quickly conscious of pity, of all sorts of allowances, and this had already operated as such a quickener of his private happiness. He had immediately proposed that they should look for a quiet corner, and they had found one in the smoking-room, always empty in the middle of the afternoon. Here it seemed to him that Braddle showed him what he himself had escaped. He had escaped being as *he* was — that was it: 'as *he* was' was a state that covered now, to Chilver's sense, such vast spaces of exclusion and privation. It wasn't exactly that he was haggard or ill; his case was perhaps even not wholly clear to him, and he had still all the rest of his resources; but he was miserably afloat, and he could only be for Chilver the big, sore, stupid monument of his irretrievable mistake. 'Did you write me more than once?' he finally asked.

'No — but once. But I thought it, I'm bound to say, an awfully good letter, and you took no notice of it, you know, whatever. You never returned me a word.'

'I know,' said Braddle, smoking hard and looking away; 'it reached me at Hawaii. It *was*, I dare say, as good a letter as such a letter could be. I remember — I remember: all right; thanks. But I couldn't answer it. I didn't like it, and yet I couldn't trust myself to tell you so in the right way. So I let it alone.'

'And we've therefore known nothing whatever about you.'

Braddle sat jogging his long foot. 'What is it you've wanted to know?'

The question made Chilver feel a little foolish. What *was* it, after all? 'Well, what had become of you, and that sort of thing. I supposed,' he added, 'that you might be feeling as you say, and there was a lot, in connection with you, of course I myself felt, for me to think about. I even hesitated a good deal to write to you at all, and I waited, you remember, don't you? till after my marriage. I don't know what your state of mind may be to-day, but you'll never, my dear chap, get a "rise" out of me. I bear you no grudge.'

His companion, at this, looked at him again. 'Do you mean for what I said —— ?'

'What you said —— ?'

'About *her*.'

'Oh no — I mean for the way you've treated us.'

'How do you know how I've treated you?' Braddle asked.

'Ah, I only pretend to speak of what I do know! Your not coming near us. You've been in the Sandwich Islands?' Chilver went on after a pause.

'Oh yes.'

'And in California?'

'Yes — all over the place.'

'All the while you've been gone?'

'No, after a time I gave it up. I've been round the world — in extraordinary holes.'

'And have you come back to England,' Chilver asked, 'to stay awhile?'

'I don't know — I don't know!' his friend replied with some impatience.

They kept it up, but with pauses — pauses during which, as they listened, in the big, stale, empty room, always dreary in the absence of talk and the silence of the billiard-balls just beyond — the loud tick of the clock gave their position almost as much an air of awkward penance as if they had had 'lines' to do or were staying after school. Chilver wondered if it would after all practically fail, his desire that they should remain friends. His wife — beautiful creature! — would give every help, so that it would really depend on Braddle himself. It might indeed have been as an issue to the ponderation of some such question on his own part that poor Bertram suddenly exclaimed: 'I see you're happy — I can make *that* out!'

He had said it in a way suggesting that it might make with him a difference for the worse, but Chilver answered none the less good-humouredly. 'I'm afraid I can't pretend that I'm in the least miserable. But is it impossible you should come and see us? — come and judge, as it were, for yourself?'

Braddle looked graver than ever. 'Would it suit your wife?'

'Oh, she's not afraid, I think!' his companion laughed. 'You spoke just now,' he after a moment continued, 'of something that in your absence, in your travels, you "gave up." Let me ask you frankly if you meant that you had undertaken inquiries——'

'Yes; I "nosed round," as they say out there; I looked about and tried to pick something.' Braddle spoke on a drop of his interlocutor, checked evidently by a certain hardness of defiance in his good eyes; but he couldn't know that Chilver wished to draw him out only to be more sorry for him, hesitating simply because of the desire not to put his proceeding to him otherwise than gracefully. 'Awfully low-minded, as well as idiotic, I dare say you'll think it — but I'm not prepared to allow that it was not quite my own affair.'

'Oh, *she* knew!' said Chilver, comfortably enough.

'Knew I shouldn't find out anything? Well, I didn't. So she was right.'

Thus they sat for a moment and seemed to smoke at her infallibility. 'Do you mean anything objectionable?' Chilver presently inquired.

'Anything at all. Not a scrap. Not a trace of her passage — not an echo of her name. That, however — that I wouldn't, that I couldn't,' Braddle added, 'you'll have known for yourself.'

'No, I wasn't sure.'

'Then *she* was.'

'Perhaps,' said Chilver. 'But she didn't tell me.'

His friend hesitated. 'Then what *has* she told you?'

'She has told me nothing.'

'Nothing?'

'Nothing,' said Henry Chilver, smiling as with the enjoyment of his companion's surprise. 'But do come and see us,' he pursued as Braddle abruptly rose and stood — now with a gravity that was almost portentous — looking down at him.

'I'm horribly nervous. Excuse me. You make me so,' the younger man declared after a pause.

Chilver, who with this had got up soothingly and still laughingly, laid a reassuring hand upon him. 'Dear old man — take it easy!'

'Thanks about coming to see you,' Braddle went on. 'I must think of it. Give me time.'

'Time? Haven't you had months?'

Braddle turned it over. 'Yes; but not on seeing you this way. I'm abominably nervous, at all events. There have

been things — my silence among them — which I haven't
known how you'd take.'

'Well, you see how.'

Braddle's stare was after all rather sightless. 'I see — but
I don't understand. I'll tell you what you might do — you
might come to *me.*'

'Oh, delighted. The old place?'

'The old place.' Braddle had taken out his eyeglass to
wipe it, and he cocked it characteristically back. '*Our*
relation's rather rum, you know.'

'Yours and my wife's? Oh, most unconventional; you may
depend on it she feels that herself.'

Braddle kept fixing him. 'Then does *she* want to crow over
me?'

'To crow?' Chilver was vague. 'About what?'

His interlocutor hesitated. 'About having at least got *you.*'

'Oh, she's naturally pleased at that; but her satisfaction's
after all a thing she can keep within bounds; and to see you
again can only, I think, remind her more than anything else
of what she did lose and now misses: your general situation,
your personal advantages, your connections, expectations,
magnificence.'

Braddle, on this, after a lingering frown, turned away, looking at his watch and moving for a minute to the window.
'When will you come? To-night?'

Chilver thought. 'Rather late — yes. With pleasure.'

His friend presently came back with an expression rather
changed. 'What I meant just now was what it all makes of
my relation and yours — the way we go into it.'

'Ah, well, that was extraordinary — the way we went into
it — from the first. It was you, permit me to remark,' Chilver
pleasantly said, 'who originally *began* going into it. Since you
broke the ice I don't in the least mind its remaining broken.'

'Ah, but at that time,' Braddle returned, 'I didn't know in
the least what you were up to.'

'And do I now know any more what *you* are? However,' Chilver went on, 'if you imply that I haven't acted with most scrupulous fairness, we *shall*, my dear fellow, quarrel as much as you please. I pressed you hard for your own interest.'

'Oh, my "interest"!' his companion threw off with another move to some distance; coming back, however, as quickly and before Chilver had time to take this up. 'It's all right — I've nothing to say. Your letter was very clever and very handsome.' Then, 'I'm not "up to" anything,' Braddle added with simplicity.

The simplicity just renewed his interlocutor's mirth. 'In that case why shouldn't we manage?'

'Manage?'

'To make the best, all round, of the situation.'

'I've no difficulty whatever,' said Braddle, 'in doing that. If I'm nervous I'm still much less so than I was before I went away. And as to my having broken off, I feel more and more how impossible it was I should have done anything else.'

'I'm sure of it — so we *will* manage.'

It was as if this prospect, none the less, was still not clear to Braddle. 'Then as you've so much confidence I can ask you why — if what you said just now of me is true — she shouldn't have paid for me a price that she was going, after all, to find herself ready to pay for *you*.'

'A price? What price?'

'Why, the one we've been talking about. That of waiving her great condition.' On which, as Chilver was, a moment — though without embarrassment — silent for this explanation, his interlocutor pursued: 'The condition of your waiting——'

'Ah,' said Chilver, 'it remained. She didn't waive it.'

Oh, how Braddle looked at him! 'You accepted it?'

Chilver gave a laugh at his friend's stare. 'Why are you so surprised when all my urgency to *you* was to accept it and when I thought you were going to?' Bertram had flushed, and he was really astonished. 'Hadn't you then known?'

'Your letter didn't say that.'

'Oh, I didn't go into our terms.'

'No,' said Braddle with some severity, 'you slurred them over. I know what you urged on me and what you thought I was going to do. *I* thought I was going to do it too. But at the scratch I couldn't.'

'So you believed *I* wouldn't?'

Poor Braddle was, after all, candid enough. 'At the scratch, yes; when it came — the question — to yourself, and in spite of your extraordinary preaching. I think I took for granted that she must have done for you what she didn't do for me — that, liking you all for yourself, don't you see? and therefore so much better, she must have come round.'

'For myself, better or worse, I grant you, was the only way she could like me,' Chilver replied. 'But she didn't come round.'

'You married her *with* it?'

This was a question, however — it was in particular an emphasis — as to the interpretation of which he showed a certain reserve. 'With what?'

'Why, damn it, with the condition.'

'Oh, yes — with the condition.' It sounded, on Chilver's lips, positively gay.

'You waited?'

'I waited.'

This answer produced between them for the time — and, as might be said, by its visible effect on the recipient — a hush during which poor Bertram did two or three pointless things: took up an ash-tray that was near them and vaguely examined it, then looked at the clock and at his watch, then again restlessly moved off a few steps and came back. At his watch he gave a second glare. 'I say, after all — *don't* come to-night.'

'You can't stand me?'

'Well, I don't mind telling you you've rather upset me. It's my abject nerves; but they'll settle down in a few days, and then I'll make you a sign. Good-bye.'

'Good-bye.' Chilver held a minute the hand he had put out. 'Don't be too long. My secondary effect on you may perhaps be better.'

'Oh, it isn't really you. I mean it's *her*.'

'Talking about her? Then we'll talk of something else. You'll give me the account——'

'Oh, as I told you, there *was* no account!' Braddle quite artlessly broke in. Chilver laughed out again at this, and his interlocutor went on: 'What's the matter is that, though it's none of my business, I can't resist a brutal curiosity — a kind of suspense.'

'Suspense?' Chilver echoed with good-humoured deprecation.

'Of course I do see you're thoroughly happy.'

'Thoroughly.'

Braddle still waited. 'Then it isn't anything——?'

'Anything?'

'To make a row about. I mean what you know.'

'But I *don't* know.'

'Not yet? She hasn't told you?'

'I haven't asked.'

Braddle wondered. 'But it's six months.'

'It's seven. I've let it pass.'

'Pass?' Braddle repeated with a strange sound.

'So would *you* in my place.'

'Oh, no, I beg your pardon!' Braddle almost exultantly declared. 'But I give you a year.'

'That's what *I've* given,' said Chilver, serenely.

His companion had a gasp. 'Given *her*?'

'I bettered even, in accepting it, the great condition. I allowed her double the time.'

Braddle wondered till he turned almost pale. 'Then it's because you're afraid.'

'To spoil my happiness?'

'Yes — and hers.'

'Well, my dear boy,' said Chilver, cheerfully, 'it may be that.'

'Unless,' his friend went on, 'you're — in the interest of every one, if you'll permit me the expression? — magnificently lying.' Chilver's slow, good-humoured headshake was so clearly, however, the next moment, a sufficient answer to this that the younger man could only add as drily as he might: 'You'll know when you want to.'

'I shall know, doubtless, when I ask. But I feel at present that I shall never ask.'

'Never?'

'Never.'

Braddle waited a moment. 'Then how the devil shall *I* know?'

Something in the tone of it renewed his companion's laughter. 'Have you supposed I'd tell you?'

'Well, you ought to, you know. And — yes — I've believed it.'

'But, my good man, I can't ask for *you*.'

Braddle turned it over. 'Why not, when one thinks of it? You know you owe me something.'

'But — good heavens! — what?'

'Well, some kindness. You know you've all the fun of being awfully sorry for me.'

'My dear chap!' Chilver murmured, patting his shoulder. 'Well, give me time!' he easily added.

'To the end of your year? I'll come back *then*,' said Braddle, going off.

VII

HE came back punctually enough, and one of the results of it was a talk that, a few weeks later, he had one Sunday afternoon with Mrs. Chilver, whom, till this occasion — though it was not his first visit to the house — he had not yet seen alone. It took him then but ten minutes — ten minutes of a marked but subsiding want of ease — to break out with a strong appeal to her on the question of the danger of the possible arrival of somebody else. '*Would* you mind — of course I know it's an immense deal for me to ask — having it just said at the door that you're not at home? I do so want really to get *at* you.'

'Oh, you needn't be afraid of an interruption.' Mrs. Chilver seemed only amused. 'No one comes to us. You see what our life is. Whom have you yet met here?'

He appeared struck with this. 'Yes. Of course your living at Hammersmith——'

'We have to live where we can live for tenpence a year.' He was silent at this touch, with a silence that, like an exclamation, betrayed a kind of helplessness, and she went on explaining as if positively to assist him. 'Besides, we haven't the want. And so few people know us. We're our own company.'

'Yes — that's just it. I never saw such a pair. It's as if you did it on purpose. But it was to show you how I feel at last the luxury of seeing you without Chilver.'

'Ah, but I can't forbid *him* the door!' she laughed.

He kept his eyes for a minute on that of the room. 'Do you mean he *will* come in?'

'Oh, if he does it won't be to hurt you. He's not jealous.'

'Well, *I* am,' said the visitor, frankly, 'and I verily believe it's his not being — and showing it so — that partly has to do with that. If he cared I believe I shouldn't. Besides, what does it matter——?' He threshed about in his place uncomfortably.

She sat there — with all her effaced anxieties — patient and pretty. 'What does what matter?'

'Why, *how* it happens — since it does happen — that he's always here.'

'But you see he isn't!'

He made an eager movement. 'Do you mean then we *can* talk?'

She just visibly hesitated. 'He and I only want to be kind to you.'

'That's just what's awful!' He fell back again. 'It's the way he has kept me on and on. I mean without——' But he had another drop.

'Without what?'

Poor Braddle at last sprang up. 'Do you mind my being in a horrible fidget and floundering about the room?'

She demurred, but without gravity. 'Not if you don't again knock over the lamp. Do you remember the day you did that at Brighton?'

With his ambiguous frown at her he stopped short. 'Yes, and how even that didn't move you.'

'Well, don't presume on it again!' she laughed.

'You mean it might move you this time?' he went on.

'No; I mean that as I've now got better lamps——!'

He roamed there among her decent frugalities and, as regarded other matters as well as lamps, noted once more — as he had done on other occasions — the extreme moderation of the improvement. He had rather imagined on Chilver's part more margin. Then at last suddenly, with an effect of irrelevance: 'Why *don't* people, as you say, come to you?'

'That's the kind of thing,' she smiled, 'you *used* to ask so much.'

'Oh, too much, of course, and it's absurd my still wanting to know. It's none of my business; but, you know, nothing is if you come to that. It's your extraordinary kindness — the way you give me my head — that puts me up to things. Only you're trying the impossible — you can't keep me on. I mean without — well, what I spoke of just now. Do you mind my bringing it bang out like a brute?' he continued, stopping before her again. 'Isn't it a question of either really taking me in or quite leaving me out?' As she had nothing, however, at first, for this inquiry but silence, and as her face made her silence charm-ing, his appeal suddenly changed. 'Do you mind my going on like this?'

'I don't mind anything. You want, I judge, some help. What help can I give you?'

He dropped, at this, straight into his chair again. 'There you are! You pitied me even from the first — regularly beforehand. You're so confoundedly superior' — he almost sufficiently joked. 'Of course I know all our relations are most extraordinary, but I think yours and mine is the strangest — unless it be yours and Chilver's.'

'Let us say it's his and *yours*, and have done with it,' she smiled.

'Do you know what I came back then for? — I mean the second time, *this* time?'

'Why, to see *me*, I've all these days supposed.'

'Well,' said Braddle with a slight hesitation, 'it was, to that extent, to show my confidence.'

But she also hesitated. 'Your confidence in what?'

He had still another impatience, with the force of which he again changed his place. 'Am I giving him away? How much do you know?'

In the air of his deep unrest her soft stillness — lending itself, but only by growing softer — had little by little taken on a beauty. 'I'm trying to follow you — to understand. I know of your meeting with Henry last year at a club.'

'Ah then, if he gave me away ——!'

'I gathered rather, I seem to remember, from what he men-tioned to me, that he must rather have given me too. But I don't in the least mind.'

'Well, what passed between us then,' said Braddle, 'is why I came back. He made me, if I should wait, a sort of promise ——'

'Oh' — she took him up — 'I don't think he was conscious of anything like a promise. He said at least nothing to me of that.' With which, as Braddle's face had exceedingly fallen, 'But I know what you then wanted and what you still want to know,' she added.

On this, for a time, they sat there with a long look. 'I would rather have had it from *him*,' he said at last.

'It would certainly have been more natural,' she intelligently returned. 'But he has given you no chance to press him again?'

'None — and with an evident intention : seeing me only with you.'

'Well, at the present moment he doesn't see you at all. Nor me either!' Mrs. Chilver added, as if to cover something in the accent of her former phrase. 'But if he has avoided close quarters with you, it has been not to disappoint you.'

'He won't, after all, tell me?'

'He can't. He has nothing to tell.'

Poor Bi. ldle showed at this what his disappointment could be. 'He has not even yet asked you?'

'Not even yet — after fifteen months. But don't be hard on him,' she pleaded. ' *You* wouldn't.'

'For all this time?' Braddle spoke almost with indignation at the charge. 'My dear lady — rather!'

'No, no,' she gently insisted, 'not even to tell *him*.'

'He told you then,' Braddle demanded, 'that I thought he ought, if on no other grounds, to ask just *in order* to tell me?'

'Oh dear, no. He only told me he had met you, and where you had been. We don't speak of his "asking,"' she explained.

'Don't you?' Her visitor stared.

'Never.'

'Then how have you known —— ?'

'What you want so much? Why, by having seen it in you before — and just *how* much — and seeing it now. I've been feeling all along,' she said, 'how you must have argued.'

'Oh, we didn't argue!'

'I think *you* did.'

He had slowly got up — now less actively but not less intensely nervous — and stood there heedless of this and rather differently looking at her. 'He never talks with you of his asking?'

'Never,' she repeated.

'And you still stick to it that *I* wouldn't?'

She hesitated. 'Have talked of it?'

'Have asked.'

She was beautiful as she smiled up at him. 'It would have been a little different. *You* would have talked.'

He remained there a little in silence; what he might have done seemed so both to separate them and to hold them together. 'And Chilver, you feel, will now never ask?'

'Never now.'

He seemed to linger for conviction. 'If he was going to, you mean, he would have done it——'

'Yes' — she was prompt — 'the moment his time was up.'

'I see' — and, turning away, he moved slowly about. 'So you're safe?'

'Safe.'

'And I'm just where I was!' he oddly threw off.

'I'm amazed again,' Mrs. Chilver said, 'at your so clinging to it that you would have had the benefit of his information.'

It was a remark that pulled him up as if something like a finer embarrassment had now come to him. 'I've only in mind his information as to the fact that he had made you speak.'

'And what good would *that* have done you?'

'Without the details?' — he was indeed thinking.

'I like your expressions!' said Mrs. Chilver.

'Yes — aren't they hideous?' He had jerked out his glass and, with a returning flush, appeared to affect to smile over it. But the drop of his glass showed something in each of his eyes that, though it might have come from the rage, came evidently — to his companion's vision at least — from the more pardonable pain, of his uncertainty. 'But there we are!'

The manner in which these last words reached her had clearly to do with her finally leaving her place, watching him meanwhile as he wiped his glass. 'Yes — there we are. He did tell me,' she went on, 'that you had told him where you had been and that you could pick up nothing ——'

'Against you?' he broke in. 'Not a beggarly word.'

'And you tried hard?'

'I worked like a nigger. It was no use.'

'But say you had succeeded — what,' she asked, 'was your idea?'

'Why, not to have had the thing any longer between us.'

He brought this out with such simplicity that she stared. 'But if it had been —— ?'

'Yes?' — the way she hung fire made him eager.

'Well — something you would have loathed.'

'*Is* it?' — he almost sprang at her. 'For pity's sake, *what* is it?' he broke out in a key that now filled the room supremely with the strange soreness of his yearning for his justification.

She kept him waiting, after she had taken this in, but another instant. 'You would rather, you say, have had it from *him* ——'

'But I must take it as I can get it? Oh, anyhow!' he fairly panted.

'Then with a condition.'

It threw him back into a wail that was positively droll. 'Another?'

'This one,' she dimly smiled, 'is comparatively easy. You must promise me with the last solemnity ——'

'Yes!'

'On the sacred honour of a gentleman ——'

'Yes!'

'To repeat to no one whatever what you now have from me.'

Thus completely expressed, the condition checked him but a moment. 'Very well!'

K

'You promise?'

'On the sacred honour of a gentleman.'

'Then I invite you to make the inference most directly suggested by the vanity of your researches.'

He looked about him. 'The inference?'

'As to what a fault may have been that it's impossible to find out.'

He got hold as he could. 'It may have been hidden.'

'Then anything hidden, from so much labour, so well——'

'May not have existed?' he stammered after she had given him time to take something from her deep eyes. He glared round and round with it—seemed to have it on his hands before the world. 'Then what did you mean——?'

'Ah, sir, what did *you*? You invented my past.'

'Do you mean you *hadn't* one?' cried Bertram Braddle.

'None I would have mentioned to you. It was *you* who brought it up.'

He appealed, in his stupefaction, to the immensity of the vacancy itself. 'There's *nothing*?'

She made no answer for a moment, only looking, while he dropped hard on her sofa, so far away that her eyes might have been fixed on the blue Pacific. 'There's the upshot of your inquiry.'

He followed her, while she moved before him, from his place. 'What did you then so intensely keep back?'

'What did *you*,' she asked as she paused, 'so intensely put forward? I kept back what you have from me now.'

'*This*,' he gasped from the depths of his collapse, 'is what you would have told me?'

'If, as my loyal husband, you had brought it up again. But you wouldn't!' she once more declared.

'And I should have gone on thinking——'

'Yes,' she interrupted—'that you were, for *not* bringing it up, the most delicate and most generous of men.'

It seemed all to roll over him and sweep him down, but he

gave, in his swift passage, a last clutch. 'You consent to let *him* think you ——?'

'He thinks me what he finds me!' said Mrs. Chilver.

Braddle got up from the sofa, looking about for his hat and stick; but by the time he had reached the door with them he rose again to the surface. 'I, too, then, am to leave him his idea——?'

'Well, of what?' she demanded as he faltered.

'Of your — whatever you called it.'

'I called it nothing. You relieved me of the question of the name.'

He gloomily shook his head. 'You see to what end! Chilver, at any rate,' he said, 'has his view, and to that extent has a name for it.'

'Only to the extent of having the one you gave him.'

'Well, what I gave him he took!' Braddle, with returning spirit, declared. 'What I suggested — God forgive me! — he believed.'

'Yes — that he might make his sacrifice. You speak,' said Mrs. Chilver, 'of his idea. His sacrifice is his idea. And his idea,' she added, 'is his happiness.'

'His sacrifice of your reputation?'

'Well — to whom?'

'To *me*,' said Bertram Braddle. 'Do you expect me now to permit that?'

Mrs. Chilver serenely enough considered. 'I shall protect his happiness, which is above all his vision of his own attitude, and I don't see how you can prevent this save by breaking your oath.'

'Oh, my oath!' And he prolonged the groan of his resentment.

It evidently — what he felt — made her sorry for him, and she spoke in all kindness. 'It's only your punishment!' she sighed after him as he departed.

THE TREE OF KNOWLEDGE

I

It was one of the secret opinions, such as we all have, of
Peter Brench that his main success in life would have consisted in his never having committed himself about the work,
as it was called, of his friend, Morgan Mallow. This was a
subject on which it was, to the best of his belief, impossible,
with veracity, to quote him, and it was nowhere on record
that he had, in the connection, on any occasion and in any
embarrassment, either lied or spoken the truth. Such a triumph
had its honour even for a man of other triumphs — a man who
had reached fifty, who had escaped marriage, who had lived
within his means, who had been in love with Mrs. Mallow for
years without breathing it, and who, last not least, had judged
himself once for all. He had so judged himself in fact that
he felt an extreme and general humility to be his proper portion; yet there was nothing that made him think so well of
his parts as the course he had steered so often through the
shallows just mentioned. It became thus a real wonder that
the friends in whom he had most confidence were just those
with whom he had most reserves. He couldn't tell Mrs. Mallow — or at least he supposed, excellent man, he couldn't —
that she was the one beautiful reason he had never married;
any more than he could tell her husband that the sight of the
multiplied marbles in that gentleman's studio was an affliction
of which even time had never blunted the edge. His victory,
however, as I have intimated, in regard to these productions,
was not simply in his not having let it out that he deplored

them; it was, remarkably, in his not having kept it in by anything else.

The whole situation, among these good people, was verily a marvel, and there was probably not such another for a long way from the spot that engages us — the point at which the soft declivity of Hampstead began at that time to confess in broken accents to St. John's Wood. He despised Mallow's statues and adored Mallow's wife, and yet was distinctly fond of Mallow, to whom, in turn, he was equally dear. Mrs. Mallow rejoiced in the statues — though she preferred, when pressed, the busts; and if she was visibly attached to Peter Brench it was because of his affection for Morgan. Each loved the other, moreover, for the love borne in each case to Lancelot, whom the Mallows respectively cherished as their only child and whom the friend of their fireside identified as the third — but decidedly the handsomest — of his godsons. Already in the old years it had come to that — that no one, for such a relation, could possibly have occurred to any of them, even to the baby itself, but Peter. There was luckily a certain independence, of the pecuniary sort, all round: the Master could never otherwise have spent his solemn *Wanderjahre* in Florence and Rome and continued, by the Thames as well as by the Arno and the Tiber, to add unpurchased group to group and model, for what was too apt to prove in the event mere love, fancy-heads of celebrities either too busy or too buried — too much of the age or too little of it — to sit. Neither could Peter, lounging in almost daily, have found time to keep the whole complicated tradition so alive by his presence. He was massive, but mild, the depositary of these mysteries — large and loose and ruddy and curly, with deep tones, deep eyes, deep pockets, to say nothing of the habit of long pipes, soft hats, and brownish, greyish, weather-faded clothes, apparently always the same.

He had 'written,' it was known, but had never spoken — never spoken, in particular, of that; and he had the air (since, as was believed, he continued to write) of keeping it up in order to have something more — as if he had not, at the worst, enough — to be silent about.   Whatever his air, at any rate, Peter's occasional unmentioned prose and verse were quite truly the result of an impulse to maintain the purity of his taste by establishing still more firmly the right relation of fame to feebleness.   The little green door of his domain was in a garden-wall on which the stucco was cracked and stained, and in the small detached villa behind it everything was old, the furniture, the servants, the books, the prints, the habits, and the new improvements.   The Mallows, at Carrara Lodge, were within ten minutes, and the studio there was on their little land, to which they had added, in their happy faith, to build it.   This was the good fortune, if it was not the ill, of her having brought him, in marriage, a portion that put them in a manner at their ease and enabled them thus, on their side, to keep it up.   And they did keep it up — they always had — the infatuated sculptor and his wife, for whom nature had refined on the impossible by relieving them of the sense of the difficult.   Morgan had, at all events, everything of the sculptor but the spirit of Phidias — the brown velvet, the becoming *beretto*, the 'plastic' presence, the fine fingers, the beautiful accent in Italian, and the old Italian factotum.   He seemed to make up for everything when he addressed Egidio with the 'tu' and waved him to turn one of the rotary pedestals of which the place was full.   They were tremendous Italians at Carrara Lodge, and the secret of the part played by this fact in Peter's life was, in a large degree, that it gave him, sturdy Briton that he was, just the amount of 'going abroad' he could bear.   The Mallows were all his Italy, but it was in a measure for Italy he liked them.   His one worry was that Lance — to which they had shortened his godson — was, in spite of a public school, perhaps a shade too Italian.   Morgan, meanwhile, looked like somebody's flattering idea of somebody's own person as expressed in the great room provided at the Uffizzi museum

for Portraits of Artists by Themselves. The Master's sole
regret that he had not been born rather to the brush than to
the chisel sprang from his wish that he might have contributed to that collection.

It appeared, with time, at any rate, to be to the brush that
Lance had been born; for Mrs. Mallow, one day when the boy
was turning twenty, broke it to their friend, who shared, to
the last delicate morsel, their problems and pains, that it
seemed as if nothing would really do but that he should
embrace the career. It had been impossible longer to remain
blind to the fact that he gained no glory at Cambridge, where
Brench's own college had, for a year, tempered its tone to him
as for Brench's own sake. Therefore why renew the vain
form of preparing him for the impossible? The impossible —
it had become clear — was that he should be anything but an
artist.

'Oh dear, dear!' said poor Peter.

'Don't you believe in it?' asked Mrs. Mallow, who still, at
more than forty, had her violet velvet eyes, her creamy satin
skin, and her silken chestnut hair.

'Believe in what?'

'Why, in Lance's passion.'

'I don't know what you mean by "believing in it." I've
never been unaware, certainly, of his disposition, from his
earliest time, to daub and draw; but I confess I've hoped it
would burn out.'

'But why should it,' she sweetly smiled, 'with his wonderful
heredity? Passion is passion — though of course, indeed, you,
dear Peter, know nothing of that. Has the Master's ever
burned out?'

Peter looked off a little and, in his familiar, formless way,
kept up for a moment a sound between a smothered whistle
and a subdued hum. 'Do you think he's going to be another
Master?'

She seemed scarce prepared to go that length, yet she had,

on the whole, a most marvellous trust. 'I know what you mean by that. Will it be a career to incur the jealousies and provoke the machinations that have been at times almost too much for his father? Well — say it may be, since nothing but clap-trap, in these dreadful days, *can*, it would seem, make its way, and since, with the curse of refinement and distinction, one may easily find one's self begging one's bread. Put it at the worst — say he *has* the misfortune to wing his flight further than the vulgar taste of his stupid countrymen can follow. Think, all the same, of the happiness — the same that the Master has had. He'll *know*.'

Peter looked rueful. 'Ah, but *what* will he know?'

'Quiet joy!' cried Mrs. Mallow, quite impatient and turning away.

II

HE had of course, before long, to meet the boy himself on it and to hear that, practically, everything was settled. Lance was not to go up again, but to go instead to Paris, where, since the die was cast, he would find the best advantages. Peter had always felt that he must be taken as he was, but had never perhaps found him so much as he was as on this occasion. 'You chuck Cambridge then altogether? Doesn't that seem rather a pity?'

Lance would have been like his father, to his friend's sense, had he had less humour, and like his mother had he had more beauty. Yet it was a good middle way, for Peter, that, in the modern manner, he was, to the eye, rather the young stockbroker than the young artist. The youth reasoned that it was a question of time — there was such a mill to go through, such an awful lot to learn. He had talked with fellows and had judged. 'One has got, to-day,' he said, 'don't you see? to know.'

His interlocutor, at this, gave a groan. 'Oh, hang it, *don't* know!'

Lance wondered. '"Don't"? Then what's the use —— ?'
'The use of what?'

'Why, of anything. Don't you think I've talent?'

Peter smoked away, for a little, in silence; then went on:
'It isn't knowledge, it's ignorance that — as we've been beautifully told — is bliss.'

'Don't you think I've talent?' Lance repeated.

Peter, with his trick of queer, kind demonstrations, passed
his arm round his godson and held him a moment. 'How do
I know?'

'Oh,' said the boy, 'if it's your own ignorance you're
defending ——!'

Again, for a pause, on the sofa, his godfather smoked. 'It
isn't. I've the misfortune to be omniscient.'

'Oh, well,' Lance laughed again, 'if you know *too* much ——!'

'That's what I do, and why I'm so wretched.'

Lance's gaiety grew. 'Wretched? Come, I say!'

'But I forgot,' his companion went on — 'you're not to know
about that. It would indeed, for you too, make the too much.
Only I'll tell you what I'll do.' And Peter got up from the
sofa. 'If you'll go up again, I'll pay your way at Cambridge.'

Lance stared, a little rueful in spite of being still more
amused. 'Oh, Peter! You disapprove so of Paris?'

'Well, I'm afraid of it.'

'Ah, I see.'

'No, you don't see — yet. But you will — that is you would.
And you mustn't.'

The young man thought more gravely. 'But one's innocence, already ——'

'Is considerably damaged? Ah, that won't matter,' Peter
persisted — 'we'll patch it up here.'

'Here? Then you want me to stay at home?'

Peter almost confessed to it. 'Well, we're so right — we
four together — just as we are. We're so safe. Come, don't
spoil it.'

The boy, who had turned to gravity, turned from this, on the real pressure in his friend's tone, to consternation. 'Then what's a fellow to be?'

'My particular care. Come, old man'—and Peter now fairly pleaded—'*I'll* look out for you.'

Lance, who had remained on the sofa with his legs out and his hands in his pockets, watched him with eyes that showed suspicion. Then he got up. 'You think there's something the matter with me — that I can't make a success.'

'Well, what do you call a success?'

Lance thought again. 'Why, the best sort, I suppose, is to please one's self. Isn't that the sort that, in spite of cabals and things, is — in his own peculiar line — the Master's?'

There were so much too many things in this question to be answered at once that they practically checked the discussion, which became particularly difficult in the light of such renewed proof that, though the young man's innocence might, in the course of his studies, as he contended, somewhat have shrunken, the finer essence of it still remained. That was indeed exactly what Peter had assumed and what, above all, he desired; yet, perversely enough, it gave him a chill. The boy believed in the cabals and things, believed in the peculiar line, believed, in short, in the Master. What happened a month or two later was not that he went up again at the expense of his godfather, but that a fortnight after he had got settled in Paris this personage sent him fifty pounds.

He had meanwhile, at home, this personage, made up his mind to the worst; and what it might be had never yet grown quite so vivid to him as when, on his presenting himself one Sunday night, as he never failed to do, for supper, the mistress of Carrara Lodge met him with an appeal as to — of all things in the world — the wealth of the Canadians. She was earnest, she was even excited. 'Are many of them *really* rich?'

He had to confess that he knew nothing about them, but he often thought afterwards of that evening. The room in which they sat was adorned with sundry specimens of the Master's genius, which had the merit of being, as Mrs. Mallow herself frequently suggested, of an unusually convenient size. They were indeed of dimensions not customary in the products of the chisel and had the singularity that, if the objects and features intended to be small looked too large, the objects and features intended to be large looked too small. The Master's intention, whether in respect to this matter or to any other, had, in almost any case, even after years, remained undiscoverable to Peter Brench. The creations that so failed to reveal it stood about on pedestals and brackets, on tables and shelves, a little staring white population, heroic, idyllic, allegoric, mythic, symbolic, in which 'scale' had so strayed and lost itself that the public square and the chimney-piece seemed to have changed places, the monumental being all diminutive and the diminutive all monumental; branches, at any rate, markedly, of a family in which stature was rather oddly irrespective of function, age, and sex. They formed, like the Mallows themselves, poor Brench's own family — having at least, to such a degree, a note of familiarity. The occasion was one of those he had long ago learnt to know and to name — short flickers of the faint flame, soft gusts of a kinder air. Twice a year, regularly, the Master believed in his fortune, in addition to believing all the year round in his genius. This time it was to be made by a bereaved couple from Toronto, who had given him the handsomest order for a tomb to three lost children, each of whom they desired to be, in the composition, emblematically and characteristically represented.

Such was naturally the moral of Mrs. Mallow's question: if their wealth was to be assumed, it was clear, from the nature of their admiration, as well as from mysterious hints thrown out (they were a little odd!) as to other possibilities of the same mortuary sort, that their further patronage might be; and not less evident that, should the Master become at all known in those climes, nothing would be more inevitable than a run of Canadian custom. Peter had been present before at runs of custom, colonial and domestic — present at each of those of which the aggregation had left so few gaps in the marble company round him; but it was his habit never, at these junctures, to prick the bubble in advance. The fond illusion, while it lasted, eased the wound of elections never won, the long ache of medals and diplomas carried off, on every chance, by every one but the Master; it lighted the lamp, moreover, that would glimmer through the next eclipse. They lived, however, after all — as it was always beautiful to see — at a height scarce susceptible of ups and downs. They strained a point, at times, charmingly, to admit that the public was, here and there, not too bad to buy; but they would have been nowhere without their attitude that the Master was always too good to sell. They were, at all events, deliciously formed, Peter often said to himself, for their fate; the Master had a vanity, his wife had a loyalty, of which success, depriving these things of innocence, would have diminished the merit and the grace. Any one could be charming under a charm, and, as he looked about him at a world of prosperity more void of proportion even than the Master's museum, he wondered if he knew another pair that so completely escaped vulgarity.

'What a pity Lance isn't with us to rejoice!' Mrs. Mallow on this occasion sighed at supper.

'We'll drink to the health of the absent,' her husband replied, filling his friend's glass and his own and giving a drop to their companion; 'but we must hope that he's preparing himself for a happiness much less like this of ours this evening — excusable as I grant it to be! — than like the comfort we have always — whatever has happened or has not happened — been able to trust ourselves to enjoy. The comfort,' the Master explained, leaning back in the pleasant lamplight and firelight, holding up his glass and looking round at his marble family, quartered more or less, a monstrous brood, in every room — 'the comfort of art in itself!'

Peter looked a little shily at his wine. 'Well—I don't care what you may call it when a fellow doesn't—but Lance must learn to *sell*, you know. I drink to his acquisition of the secret of a base popularity!'

'Oh yes, *he* must sell,' the boy's mother, who was still more, however, this seemed to give out, the Master's wife, rather artlessly conceded.

'Oh,' the sculptor, after a moment, confidently pronounced, 'Lance *will*. Don't be afraid. He will have learnt.'

'Which is exactly what Peter,' Mrs. Mallow gaily returned —'why in the world were you so perverse, Peter?—wouldn't, when he told him, hear of.'

Peter, when this lady looked at him with accusatory affection—a grace, on her part, not infrequent—could never find a word; but the Master, who was always all amenity and tact, helped him out now as he had often helped him before. 'That's his old idea, you know—on which we've so often differed: his theory that the artist should be all impulse and instinct. *I* go in, of course, for a certain amount of school. Not too much—but a due proportion. There's where his protest came in,' he continued to explain to his wife, 'as against what *might*, don't you see? be in question for Lance.'

'Ah, well,'—and Mrs. Mallow turned the violet eyes across the table at the subject of this discourse,—'he's sure to have meant, of course, nothing but good; but that wouldn't have prevented him, if Lance *had* taken his advice, from being, in effect, horribly cruel.'

They had a sociable way of talking of him to his face as if he had been in the clay or—at most—in the plaster, and the Master was unfailingly generous. He might have been waving Egidio to make him revolve. 'Ah, but poor Peter was not so wrong as to what it may, after all, come to that he *will* learn.'

'Oh, but nothing artistically bad,' she urged—still, for poor Peter, arch and dewy.

'Why, just the little French tricks,' said the Master: on which their friend had to pretend to admit, when pressed by Mrs. Mallow, that these æsthetic vices had been the objects of his dread.

III

'I KNOW now,' Lance said to him the next year, 'why you were so much against it.' He had come back, supposedly for a mere interval, and was looking about him at Carrara Lodge, where indeed he had already, on two or three occasions, since his expatriation, briefly appeared. This had the air of a longer holiday. 'Something rather awful has happened to me. It *isn't* so very good to know.'

'I'm bound to say high spirits don't show in your face,' Peter was rather ruefully forced to confess. 'Still, are you very sure you do know?'

'Well, I at least know about as much as I can bear.' These remarks were exchanged in Peter's den, and the young man, smoking cigarettes, stood before the fire with his back against the mantel. Something of his bloom seemed really to have left him.

Poor Peter wondered. 'You're clear then as to what in particular I wanted you not to go for?'

'In particular?' Lance thought. 'It seems to me that, in particular, there can have been but one thing.'

They stood for a little sounding each other. 'Are you quite sure?'

'Quite sure I'm a beastly duffer? Quite — by this time.'

'Oh!' — and Peter turned away as if almost with relief.

'It's *that* that isn't pleasant to find out.'

'Oh, I don't care for "that,"' said Peter, presently coming round again. 'I mean I personally don't.'

'Yet I hope you can understand a little that I myself should!'

'Well, what do you mean by it?' Peter sceptically asked.

And on this Lance had to explain — how the upshot of his studies in Paris had inexorably proved a mere deep doubt of his means. These studies had waked him up, and a new light was in his eyes; but what the new light did was really to show him too much. 'Do you know what's the matter with me? I'm too horribly intelligent. Paris was really the last place for me. I've learnt what I can't do.'

Poor Peter stared — it was a staggerer; but even after they had had, on the subject, a longish talk in which the boy brought out to the full the hard truth of his lesson, his friend betrayed less pleasure than usually breaks into a face to the happy tune of 'I told you so!' Poor Peter himself made now indeed so little a point of having told him so that Lance broke ground in a different place a day or two after. 'What was it then that — before I went — you were afraid I should find out?' This, however, Peter refused to tell him — on the ground that if he hadn't yet guessed perhaps he never would, and that nothing at all, for either of them, in any case, was to be gained by giving the thing a name. Lance eyed him, on this, an instant, with the bold curiosity of youth — with the air indeed of having in his mind two or three names, of which one or other would be right. Peter, nevertheless, turning his back again, offered no encouragement, and when they parted afresh it was with some show of impatience on the side of the boy. Accordingly, at their next encounter, Peter saw at a glance that he had now, in the interval, divined and that, to sound his note, he was only waiting till they should find themselves alone. This he had soon arranged, and he then broke straight out. 'Do you know your conundrum has been keeping me awake? But in the watches of the night the answer came over me — so that, upon my honour, I quite laughed out. Had you been supposing I had to go to Paris to learn *that*?' Even now, to see him still so sublimely on his guard, Peter's young friend had to laugh afresh. 'You won't give a sign till you're sure? Beautiful old Peter!' But Lance at last produced it. 'Why, hang it, the truth about the Master.'

It made between them, for some minutes, a lively passage, full of wonder, for each, at the wonder of the other. 'Then how long have you understood——'

'The true value of his work? I understood it,' Lance recalled, 'as soon as I began to understand anything. But I didn't begin fully to do that, I admit, till I got là-bas.'

'Dear, dear!'—Peter gasped with retrospective dread.

'But for what have you taken me? I'm a hopeless muff— that I *had* to have rubbed in. But I'm not such a muff as the Master!' Lance declared.

'Then why did you never tell me——?'

'That I hadn't, after all'—the boy took him up— 'remained such an idiot? Just because I never dreamed *you* knew. But I beg your pardon. I only wanted to spare you. And what I don't now understand is how the deuce then, for so long, you've managed to keep bottled.'

Peter produced his explanation, but only after some delay and with a gravity not void of embarrassment. 'It was for your mother.'

'Oh!' said Lance.

'And that's the great thing now—since the murder *is* out. I want a promise from you. I mean'—and Peter almost feverishly followed it up—'a vow from you, solemn and such as you owe me, here on the spot, that you'll sacrifice anything rather than let her ever guess——'

'That *I've* guessed?'—Lance took it in. 'I see.' He evidently, after a moment, had taken in much. 'But what is it you have in mind that I may have a chance to sacrifice?'

'Oh, one has always something.'

Lance looked at him hard. 'Do you mean that *you've* had——?' The look he received back, however, so put the question by that he found soon enough another. 'Are you really sure my mother doesn't know?'

Peter, after renewed reflection, was really sure. 'If she does, she's too wonderful.'

'But aren't we all too wonderful?'

'Yes,' Peter granted — 'but in different ways. The thing's so desperately important because your father's little public consists only, as you know then,' Peter developed — 'well, of how many?'

'First of all,' the Master's son risked, 'of himself. And last of all too. I don't quite see of whom else.'

Peter had an approach to impatience. 'Of your mother, I say — *always*.'

Lance cast it all up. 'You absolutely feel that?'

'Absolutely.'

'Well then, with yourself, that makes three.'

'Oh, *me!*' — and Peter, with a wag of his kind old head, modestly excused himself. 'The number is, at any rate, small enough for any individual dropping out to be too dreadfully missed. Therefore, to put it in a nutshell, take care, my boy — that's all — that *you're* not!'

'I've got to keep on humbugging?' Lance sighed.

'It's just to warn you of the danger of your failing of that that I've seized this opportunity.'

'And what do you regard in particular,' the young man asked, 'as the danger?'

'Why, this certainty: that the moment your mother, who feels so strongly, should suspect your secret — well,' said Peter desperately, 'the fat would be on the fire.'

Lance, for a moment, seemed to stare at the blaze. 'She'd throw me over?'

'She'd throw *him* over.'

'And come round to us?'

Peter, before he answered, turned away. 'Come round to *you*.' But he had said enough to indicate — and, as he evidently trusted, to avert — the horrid contingency.

L

IV

WITHIN six months again, however, his fear was, on more occasions than one, all before him. Lance had returned to Paris, to another trial; then had reappeared at home and had had, with his father, for the first time in his life, one of the scenes that strike sparks. He described it with much expression to Peter, as to whom — since they had never done so before — it was a sign of a new reserve on the part of the pair at Carrara Lodge that they at present failed, on a matter of intimate interest, to open themselves — if not in joy, then in sorrow — to their good friend. This produced perhaps, practically, between the parties, a shade of alienation and a slight intermission of commerce — marked mainly indeed by the fact that, to talk at his ease with his old playmate, Lance had, in general, to come to see him. The closest, if not quite the gayest, relation they had yet known together was thus ushered in. The difficulty for poor Lance was a tension at home, begotten by the fact that his father wished him to be, at least, the sort of success he himself had been. He hadn't 'chucked' Paris — though nothing appeared more vivid to him than that Paris had chucked him; he would go back again because of the fascination in trying, in seeing, in sounding the depths — in learning one's lesson, in fine, even if the lesson were simply that of one's impotence in the presence of one's larger vision. But what did the Master, all aloft in his senseless fluency, know of impotence, and what vision — to be called such — had he, in all his blind life, ever had? Lance, heated and indignant, frankly appealed to his godparent on this score.

His father, it appeared, had come down on him for having, after so long, nothing to show, and hoped that, on his next return, this deficiency would be repaired. *The* thing, the Master complacently set forth, was — for any artist, however inferior to himself — at least to 'do' something. 'What can you do? That's all I ask!' *He* had certainly done enough, and there was no mistake about what he had to show. Lance had tears in his eyes when it came thus to letting his old friend know how great the strain might be on the 'sacrifice' asked of him. It wasn't so easy to continue humbugging — as from son to parent — after feeling one's self despised for not grovelling in mediocrity. Yet a noble duplicity was what, as they intimately faced the situation, Peter went on requiring; and it was still, for a time, what his young friend, bitter and sore, managed loyally to comfort him with. Fifty pounds, more than once again, it was true, rewarded, both in London and in Paris, the young friend's loyalty; none the less sensibly, doubtless, at the moment, that the money was a direct advance on a decent sum for which Peter had long since privately prearranged an ultimate function. Whether by these arts or others, at all events, Lance's just resentment was kept for a season — but only for a season — at bay. The day arrived when he warned his companion that he could hold out — or hold in — no longer. Carrara Lodge had had to listen to another lecture delivered from a great height — an infliction really heavier, at last, than, without striking back or in some way letting the Master have the truth, flesh and blood could bear.

'And what I don't see is,' Lance observed with a certain irritated eye for what was, after all, if it came to that, due to himself too — 'What I don't see is, upon my honour, how *you*, as things are going, can keep the game up.'

'Oh, the game for me is only to hold my tongue,' said placid Peter. 'And I have my reason.'

'Still my mother?'

Peter showed, as he had often shown before — that is by turning it straight away — a queer face. 'What will you have? I haven't ceased to like her.'

'She's beautiful — she's a dear, of course,' Lance granted;

'but what is she to you, after all, and what is it to you that, as to anything whatever, she should or she shouldn't?'

Peter, who had turned red, hung fire a little. 'Well — it's all, simply, what I make of it.'

There was now, however, in his young friend, a strange, an adopted, insistence. 'What are you, after all, to *her?*'

'Oh, nothing. But that's another matter.'

'She cares only for my father,' said Lance the Parisian.

'Naturally — and that's just why.'

'Why you've wished to spare her?'

'Because she cares so tremendously much.'

Lance took a turn about the room, but with his eyes still on his host. 'How awfully — always — you must have liked her!'

'Awfully. Always,' said Peter Brench.

The young man continued for a moment to muse — then stopped again in front of him. 'Do you know how much she cares?' Their eyes met on it, but Peter, as if his own found something new in Lance's, appeared to hesitate, for the first time for so long, to say he did know. '*I've* only just found out,' said Lance. 'She came to my room last night, after being present, in silence and only with her eyes on me, at what I had had to take from him; she came — and she was with me an extraordinary hour.'

He had paused again, and they had again for a while sounded each other. Then something — and it made him suddenly turn pale — came to Peter. 'She *does* know?'

'She does know. She let it all out to me — so as to demand of me no more than that, as she said, of which she herself had been capable. She has always, always known,' said Lance without pity.

Peter was silent a long time; during which his companion might have heard him gently breathe and, on touching him, might have felt within him the vibration of a long, low sound suppressed. By the time he spoke, at last, he had taken everything in. 'Then I do see how tremendously much.'

'Isn't it wonderful?' Lance asked.

'Wonderful,' Peter mused.

'So that if your original effort to keep me from Paris was to keep me from knowledge ——!' Lance exclaimed as if with a sufficient indication of this futility.

It might have been at the futility that Peter appeared for a little to gaze. 'I think it must have been — without my quite at the time knowing it — to keep *me!*' he replied at last as he turned away.

THE ABASEMENT OF THE NORTHMORES

I

WHEN Lord Northmore died public reference to the event took for the most part rather a ponderous and embarrassed form. A great political figure had passed away. A great light of our time had been quenched in mid-career. A great usefulness had somewhat anticipated its term, though a great part, none the less, had been signally played. The note of greatness, all along the line, kept sounding, in short, by a force of its own, and the image of the departed evidently lent itself with ease to figures and flourishes, the poetry of the daily press. The newspapers and their purchasers equally did their duty by it — arranged it neatly and impressively, though perhaps with a hand a little violently expeditious, upon the funeral car, saw the conveyance properly down the avenue, and then, finding the subject suddenly quite exhausted, proceeded to the next item on their list. His lordship had been a person, in fact, in connection with whom there was almost nothing but the fine monotony of his success to mention. This success had been his profession, his means as well as his end; so that his career admitted of no other description and demanded, indeed suffered, no further analysis. He had made politics, he had made literature, he had made land, he had made a bad manner and a great many mistakes, he had made a gaunt, foolish wife, two extravagant sons, and four awkward daughters — he had made everything, as he *could* have made almost anything, thoroughly pay. There had been something deep down in him that did it, and his old friend Warren Hope, the person knowing him earliest and probably, on the whole, best, had never, even to the last, for curiosity, quite made out what it was. The secret was one that this distinctly distanced competitor had in fact mastered as little for intellectual relief as for emulous use; and there was quite a kind of tribute to it in the way that, the night before the obsequies and addressing himself to his wife, he said after some silent thought: 'Hang it, you know, I must see the old boy through. I must go to the grave.'

Mrs. Hope looked at her husband at first in anxious silence. 'I've no patience with you. You're much more ill than *he* ever was.'

'Ah, but if that qualifies me but for the funerals of others——!'

'It qualifies you to break my heart by your exaggerated chivalry, your renewed refusal to consider your interests. You sacrifice them to him, for thirty years, again and again, and from this supreme sacrifice—possibly that of your life—you might, in your condition, I think, be absolved.' She indeed lost patience. 'To the grave—in this weather—after his treatment of you!'

'My dear girl,' Hope replied, 'his treatment of me is a figment of your ingenious mind—your too-passionate, your beautiful loyalty. Loyalty, I mean, to *me*.'

'I certainly leave it to you,' she declared, 'to have any to *him!*'

'Well, he was, after all, one's oldest, one's earliest friend. I'm not in such bad case—I do go out; and I want to do the decent thing. The fact remains that we never broke—we always kept together.'

'Yes indeed,' she laughed in her bitterness, 'he always took care of that! He never recognised you, but he never let you go. You kept him up, and he kept you down. He used you, to the last drop he could squeeze, and left you the only one to wonder, in your incredible idealism and your incorrigible modesty, how on earth such an idiot made his way. He

made his way on your back. You put it candidly to others —
" What in the world was his gift ? " And others are such
gaping idiots that they too haven't the least idea. *You* were
his gift ! '

'And you're mine, my dear ! ' her husband, pressing her to
him, more resignedly laughed. He went down the next day
by 'special' to the interment, which took place on the great
man's own property, in the great man's own church. But he
went alone — that is, in a numerous and distinguished party,
the flower of the unanimous, gregarious demonstration; his
wife had no wish to accompany him, though she was anxious
while he was absent. She passed the time uneasily, watching
the weather and fearing the cold; she roamed from room to
room, pausing vaguely at dull windows, and before he came
back she had thought of many things. It was as if, while he
saw the great man buried, she also, by herself, in the con-
tracted home of their later years, stood before an open grave.
She lowered into it, with her weak hands, the heavy past and
all their common dead dreams and accumulated ashes. The
pomp surrounding Lord Northmore's extinction made her feel
more than ever that it was not Warren who had made anything pay. He had been always what he was still, the clev-
erest man and the hardest worker she knew; but what was
there, at fifty-seven, as the vulgar said, to 'show' for it all
but his wasted genius, his ruined health, and his paltry pension? It was the term of comparison conveniently given her
by his happy rival's now foreshortened splendour that fixed
these things in her eye. It was as happy rivals to their own
flat union that she always had thought of the Northmore pair;
the two men, at least, having started together, after the
University, shoulder to shoulder and with — superficially
speaking — much the same outfit of preparation, ambition, and
opportunity. They had begun at the same point and wanting
the same things — only wanting them in such different ways.
Well, the dead man had wanted them in the way that got

them; had got too, in his peerage, for instance, those Warren
had never wanted: there was nothing else to be said. There
was nothing else, and yet, in her sombre, her strangely appre-
hensive solitude at this hour, she said much more than I can
tell. It all came to this — that there had been, somewhere
and somehow, a wrong. Warren was the one who should have
succeeded. But she was the one person who knew it now, the
single other person having descended, with *his* knowledge, to
the tomb.

She sat there, she roamed there, in the waiting greyness of
her small London house, with a deepened sense of the several
odd knowledges that had flourished in their company of three.
Warren had always known everything and, with his easy
power — in nothing so high as for indifference — had never
cared. John Northmore had known, for he had, years and
years before, told her so; and thus had had a reason the more
— in addition to not believing her stupid — for guessing at her
view. She lived back; she lived it over; she had it all there
in her hand. John Northmore had known her first, and how
he had wanted to marry her the fat little bundle of his love-
letters still survived to tell. He had introduced Warren Hope
to her — quite by accident and because, at the time they had
chambers together, he couldn't help it: that was the one thing
he *had* done for them. Thinking of it now, she perhaps saw
how much he might conscientiously have considered that it
disburdened him of more. Six months later she had accepted
Warren, and for just the reason the absence of which had
determined her treatment of his friend. She had believed in
his future. She held that John Northmore had never afterwards remitted the effort to ascertain the degree in which she
felt herself 'sold.' But, thank God, she had never shown him.

Her husband came home with a chill, and she put him
straight to bed. For a week, as she hovered near him, they
only looked deep things at each other; the point was too
quickly passed at which she could bearably have said 'I told

you so!' That his late patron should never have had difficulty in making *him* pay was certainly no marvel. But it was indeed a little too much, after all, that he should have made him pay with his life. This was what it had come to — she was sure, now, from the first. Congestion of the lungs, that night, declared itself, and on the morrow, sickeningly, she was face to face with pneumonia. It was more than — with all that had gone before — they could meet. Warren Hope ten days later succumbed. Tenderly, divinely, as he loved her, she felt his surrender, through all the anguish, as an unspeakable part of the sublimity of indifference into which his hapless history had finally flowered. 'His easy power, his easy power!' — her passion had never yet found such relief in that simple, secret phrase for him. He was so proud, so fine, and so flexible, that to fail a little had been as bad for him as to fail much; therefore he had opened the flood-gates wide — had thrown, as the saying was, the helve after the hatchet. He had amused himself with seeing what the devouring world would take. Well, it had taken all.

II

But it was after he had gone that his name showed as written in water. What had he left? He had only left *her* and her grey desolation, her lonely piety and her sore, unresting rebellion. Sometimes, when a man died, it did something for him that life had not done; people, after a little, on one side or the other, discovered and named him, annexing him to their flag. But the sense of having lost Warren Hope appeared not in the least to have quickened the world's wit; the sharper pang for his widow indeed sprang just from the commonplace way in which he was spoken of as known. She received letters enough, when it came to that, for of course, personally, he had been liked; the newspapers were fairly copious and perfectly stupid; the three or four societies, 'learned' and other, to which he had belonged, passed resolutions of regret and condolence, and the three or four colleagues about whom he himself used to be most amusing stammered eulogies; but almost anything, really, would have been better for her than the general understanding that the occasion had been met. Two or three solemn noodles in 'administrative circles' wrote her that she must have been gratified at the unanimity of regret, the implication being clearly that she was ridiculous if she were not. Meanwhile what she felt was that she could have borne well enough his not being noticed at all; what she couldn't bear was this treatment of him as a minor celebrity. He was, in economics, in the higher politics, in philosophic history, a splendid unestimated genius, or he was nothing. He wasn't, at any rate — heaven forbid! — a 'notable figure.' The waters, none the less, closed over him as over Lord Northmore; which was precisely, as time went on, the fact she found it hardest to accept. That personage, the week after his death, without an hour of reprieve, the place swept as clean of him as a hall, lent for a charity, of the tables and booths of a three-days' bazaar — that personage had gone straight to the bottom, dropped like a crumpled circular into the waste-basket. Where, then, was the difference? — if the end *was* the end for each alike? For Warren it should have been properly the beginning.

During the first six months she wondered what she could herself do, and had much of the time the sense of walking by some swift stream on which an object dear to her was floating out to sea. All her instinct was to keep up with it, not to lose sight of it, to hurry along the bank and reach in advance some point from which she could stretch forth and catch and save it. Alas, it only floated and floated; she held it in sight, for the stream was long, but no convenient projection offered itself to the rescue. She ran, she watched, she lived with her great fear; and all the while, as the distance to the sea diminished, the current visibly increased. At the last, to do anything, she must hurry. She went into his papers, she ransacked his drawers; something of that sort, at least, she might do. But there were difficulties, the case was special; she lost herself in the labyrinth, and her competence was questioned; two or three friends to whose judgment she appealed struck her as tepid, even as cold, and publishers, when sounded — most of all in fact the house through which his three or four important volumes had been given to the world — showed an absence of eagerness for a collection of literary remains. It was only now that she fully understood how remarkably little the three or four important volumes had 'done.' He had successfully kept that from her, as he had kept other things she might have ached at: to handle his notes and memoranda was to come at every turn, in the wilderness, the wide desert, upon the footsteps of his scrupulous soul. But she had at last to accept the truth that it was only for herself, her own relief, she must follow him. His work, unencouraged and interrupted, failed of a final form: there would have been nothing to offer but fragments of fragments. She felt, all the same, in recognising this, that she abandoned him; he died for her at that hour over again.

The hour, moreover, happened to coincide with another hour, so that the two mingled their bitterness. She received a note from Lady Northmore, announcing a desire to gather in and publish his late lordship's letters, so numerous and so interesting, and inviting Mrs. Hope, as a more than probable depositary, to be so good as to contribute to the project those addressed to her husband. This gave her a start of more kinds than one. The long comedy of his late lordship's greatness was *not* then over? The monument was to be built to him that she had but now schooled herself to regard as impossible for his defeated friend? Everything was to break out afresh, the comparisons, the contrasts, the conclusions so invidiously in his favour? — the business all cleverly managed to place him in the light and keep every one else in the shade? Letters? — had John North-

more indited three lines that could, at that time of day, be of
the smallest consequence ? Whose idea was such a publication,
and what infatuated editorial patronage could the family have
secured ? She, of course, didn't know, but she should be surprised if there were material. Then it came to her, on reflection, that editors and publishers must of course have flocked —
his star would still rule. Why shouldn't he make his letters
pay in death as he had made them pay in life ? Such as they
were they *had* paid. They would be a tremendous success.
She thought again of her husband's rich, confused relics —
thought of the loose blocks of marble that could only lie now
where they had fallen; after which, with one of her deep and
frequent sighs, she took up anew Lady Northmore's communication.

His letters to Warren, kept or not kept, had never so much
as occurred to her. Those to herself were buried and safe —
she knew where her hand would find them; but those to herself her correspondent had carefully not asked for and was
probably unaware of the existence of. They belonged, moreover, to that phase of the great man's career that was distinctly
— as it could only be called — previous : previous to the greatness, to the proper subject of the volume, and, in especial, to
Lady Northmore. The faded fat packet lurked still where it
had lurked for years; but she could no more to-day have said
why she had kept it than why — though he knew of the early
episode — she had never mentioned her preservation of it to
Warren. This last circumstance certainly absolved her from
mentioning it to Lady Northmore, who, no doubt, knew of the
episode too. The odd part of the matter was, at any rate, that
her retention of these documents had not been an accident.
She had obeyed a dim instinct or a vague calculation. A calculation of what ? She couldn't have told : it had operated, at
the back of her head, simply as a sense that, not destroyed, the
complete little collection made for safety. But for whose, just
heaven ? Perhaps she should still see; though nothing, she

trusted, would occur requiring her to touch the things or to read them over. She wouldn't have touched them or read them over for the world.

She had not as yet, at all events, overhauled those receptacles in which the letters Warren kept would have accumulated; and she had her doubts of their containing any of Lord Northmore's. Why should he have kept any? Even she herself had had more reasons. Was his lordship's later epistolary manner supposed to be good, or of the kind that, on any grounds, prohibited the waste-basket or the fire? Warren had lived in a deluge of documents, but these perhaps he might have regarded as contributions to contemporary history. None the less, surely, he wouldn't have stored up many. She began to look, in cupboards, boxes, drawers yet unvisited, and she had her surprises both as to what he had kept and as to what he hadn't. Every word of her own was there — every note that, in occasional absence, he had ever had from her. Well, that matched happily enough her knowing just where to put her finger on every note that, on such occasions, she herself had received. *Their* correspondence at least was complete. But so, in fine, on one side, it gradually appeared, was Lord Northmore's. The superabundance of these missives had not been sacrificed by her husband, evidently, to any passing convenience; she judged more and more that he had preserved every scrap; and she was unable to conceal from herself that she was — she scarce knew why — a trifle disappointed. She had not quite unhopefully, even though vaguely, seen herself writing to Lady Northmore that, to her great regret and after an exhausting search, she could find nothing at all.

She found, alas, in fact, everything. She was conscientious and she hunted to the end, by which time one of the tables quite groaned with the fruits of her quest. The letters appeared moreover to have been cared for and roughly classified — she should be able to consign them to the family in excellent order. She made sure, at the last, that she had overlooked nothing, and then, fatigued and distinctly irritated, she prepared to answer in a sense so different from the answer she had, as might have been said, planned. Face to face with her note, however, she found she couldn't write it; and, not to be alone longer with the pile on the table, she presently went out of the room. Late in the evening — just before going to bed — she came back, almost as if she hoped there might have been since the afternoon some pleasant intervention in the interest of her distaste. Mightn't it have magically happened that her discovery was a mistake? — that the letters were either not there or were, after all, somebody's else? Ah, they *were* there, and as she raised her lighted candle in the dusk the pile on the table squared itself with insolence. On this, poor lady, she had for an hour her temptation.

It was obscure, it was absurd; all that could be said of it was that it was, for the moment, extreme. She saw herself, as she circled round the table, writing with perfect impunity: 'Dear Lady Northmore, I have hunted high and low and have found nothing whatever. My husband evidently, before his death, destroyed everything. I'm *so* sorry — I should have liked so much to help you. Yours most truly.' She should have only, on the morrow, privately and resolutely to annihilate the heap, and those words would remain an account of the matter that nobody was in a position to challenge. What good it would do her? — was *that* the question? It would do her the good that it would make poor Warren seem to have been just a little less used and duped. This, in her mood, would ease her off. Well, the temptation was real; but so, she after a while felt, were other things. She sat down at midnight to her note. 'Dear Lady Northmore, I am happy to say I have found a great deal — my husband appears to have been so careful to keep everything. I have a mass at your disposition if you can conveniently send. So glad to be able to help your work. Yours most truly.' She stepped out as she was and dropped the letter into the nearest pillar-box.

By noon the next day the table had, to her relief, been cleared. Her ladyship sent a responsible servant — her butler, in a four-wheeler, with a large japanned box.

III

AFTER this, for a twelvemonth, there were frequent announcements and allusions. They came to her from every side, and there were hours at which the air, to her imagination, contained almost nothing else. There had been, at an early stage, immediately after Lady Northmore's communication to her, an official appeal, a circular *urbi et orbi*, reproduced, applauded, commented in every newspaper, desiring all possessors of letters to remit them without delay to the family. The family, to do it justice, rewarded the sacrifice freely — so far as it was a reward to keep the world informed of the rapid progress of the work. Material had shown itself more copious than was to have been conceived. Interesting as the imminent volumes had naturally been expected to prove, those who had been favoured with a glimpse of their contents already felt warranted in promising the public an unprecedented treat. They would throw upon certain sides of the writer's mind and career lights hitherto unsuspected. Lady Northmore, deeply indebted for favours received, begged to renew her solicitation ; gratifying as the response had been, it was believed that, particularly in connection with several dates, which were given, a residuum of buried treasure might still be looked for.

Mrs. Hope saw, she felt, as time went on, fewer and fewer people ; yet her circle was even now not too narrow for her to hear it blown about that Thompson and Johnson had 'been asked.' Conversation in the London world struck her for a time as almost confined to such questions and such answers. 'Have *you* been asked ? ' 'Oh yes — rather. Months ago. And you ? ' The whole place was under contribution, and the striking thing was that being asked had been clearly accom-

panied, in every case, with the ability to respond. The spring
had but to be touched — millions of letters flew out. Ten volumes, at such a rate, Mrs. Hope mused, would not exhaust the
supply. She mused a great deal — did nothing but muse; and,
strange as this may at first appear, it was inevitable that one
of the final results of her musing should be a principle of
doubt. It could only seem possible, in view of such unanimity,
that she should, after all, have been mistaken. It *was*, then, to
the general sense, the great departed's, a reputation sound and
safe. It wasn't he who had been at fault — it was her silly
self, still burdened with the fallibility of Being. He had been
a giant, then, and the letters would triumphantly show it. She
had looked only at the envelopes of those she had surrendered,
but she was prepared for anything. There was the fact, not
to be blinked, of Warren's own marked testimony. The attitude of others was but *his* attitude; and she sighed as she perceived him in this case, for the only time in his life, on the side
of the chattering crowd.

She was perfectly aware that her obsession had run away
with her, but as Lady Northmore's publication really loomed
into view — it was now definitely announced for March, and
they were in January — her pulses quickened so that she found
herself, in the long nights, mostly lying awake. It was in one
of these vigils that, suddenly, in the cold darkness, she felt the
brush of almost the only thought that, for many a month, had
not made her wince; the effect of which was that she bounded
out of bed with a new felicity. Her impatience flashed, on
the spot, up to its maximum — she could scarce wait for day
to give herself to action. Her idea was neither more nor less
than immediately to collect and put forth the letters of *her*
hero. She would publish her husband's own — glory be to
God! — and she even wasted none of her time in wondering
why she had waited. She *had* waited — all too long; yet it
was perhaps no more than natural that, for eyes sealed with
tears and a heart heavy with injustice, there should not have

M

been an instant vision of where her remedy lay. She thought of it already as her remedy — though she would probably have found an awkwardness in giving a name, publicly, to her wrong. It was a wrong to feel, but not, doubtless, to talk about. And lo, straightway, the balm had begun to drop: the balance would so soon be even. She spent all that day in reading over her own old letters, too intimate and too sacred — oh, unluckily! — to figure in her project, but pouring wind, nevertheless, into its sails and adding magnificence to her presumption. She had of course, with separation, all their years, never frequent and never prolonged, known her husband as a correspondent much less than others; still, these relics constituted a property — she was surprised at their number — and testified hugely to his inimitable gift.

He was a letter-writer if you liked — natural, witty, various, vivid, playing, with the idlest, lightest hand, up and down the whole scale. His easy power — his easy power: everything that brought him back brought back that. The most numerous were of course the earlier, and the series of those during their engagement, witnesses of their long probation, which were rich and unbroken; so full indeed and so wonderful that she fairly groaned at having to defer to the common measure of married modesty. There was discretion, there was usage, there was taste; but she would fain have flown in their face. If there were pages too intimate to publish, there were too many others too rare to suppress. Perhaps after her death —— ! It not only pulled her up, the happy thought of that liberation alike for herself and for her treasure, making her promise herself straightway to arrange: it quickened extremely her impatience for the term of her mortality, which would leave a free field to the justice she invoked. Her great resource, however, clearly, would be the friends, the colleagues, the private admirers to whom he had written for years, to whom she had known him to write, and many of whose own letters, by no means remarkable, she had come upon in her recent sortings and siftings. She drew up a list of these persons and immediately wrote to them or, in cases in which they had passed away, to their widows, children, representatives; reminding herself in the process not disagreeably, in fact quite inspiringly, of Lady Northmore. It had struck her that Lady Northmore took, somehow, a good deal for granted; but this idea failed, oddly enough, to occur to her in regard to Mrs. Hope. It was indeed with her ladyship she began, addressing her exactly in the terms of this personage's own appeal, every word of which she remembered.

Then she waited, but she had not, in connection with that quarter, to wait long. 'Dear Mrs. Hope, I have hunted high and low and have found nothing whatever. My husband evidently, before his death, destroyed everything. I'm so sorry — I should have liked so much to help you. Yours most truly.' This was all Lady Northmore wrote, without the grace of an allusion to the assistance she herself had received; though even in the first flush of amazement and resentment our friend recognised the odd identity of form between her note and another that had never been written. She was answered as she had, in the like case, in her one evil hour, dreamed of answering. But the answer was not over with this — it had still to flow in, day after day, from every other source reached by her question. And day after day, while amazement and resentment deepened, it consisted simply of three lines of regret. Everybody had looked, and everybody had looked in vain. Everybody would have been so glad, but everybody was reduced to being, like Lady Northmore, so sorry. Nobody could find anything, and nothing, it was therefore to be gathered, had been kept. Some of these informants were more prompt than others, but all replied in time, and the business went on for a month, at the end of which the poor woman, stricken, chilled to the heart, accepted perforce her situation and turned her face to the wall. In this position, as it were, she remained for days, taking heed of nothing and only feeling and nursing her wound. It was a wound the more cruel for having found her so unguarded. From the moment her remedy had been whispered to her, she had not had an hour of doubt, and the beautiful side of it had seemed that it was, above all, so easy. The strangeness of the issue was even greater than the pain. Truly it was a world *pour rire*, the world in which John Northmore's letters were classed and labelled for posterity and Warren Hope's kindled fires. All sense, all measure of anything, could only leave one — leave one indifferent and dumb. There was nothing to be done — the show was upside-down. John Northmore was immortal and Warren Hope was damned. And for herself, she was finished. She was beaten. She leaned thus, motionless, muffled, for a time of which, as I say, she took no account; then at last she was reached by a great sound that made her turn her veiled head. It was the report of the appearance of Lady Northmore's volumes.

IV

THIS was a great noise indeed, and all the papers, that day, were particularly loud with it. It met the reader on the threshold, and the work was everywhere the subject of a 'leader' as well as of a review. The reviews moreover, she saw at a glance, overflowed with quotation; it was enough to look at two or three sheets to judge of the enthusiasm. Mrs. Hope looked at the two or three that, for confirmation of the single one she habitually received, she caused, while at breakfast, to be purchased; but her attention failed to penetrate further; she couldn't, she found, face the contrast between the pride of the Northmores on such a morning and her own humiliation. The papers brought it too sharply home; she pushed them away and, to get rid of them, not to feel their presence, left the house early. She found pretexts for remaining out; it was as if there had been a cup prescribed for her to drain, yet she could put off the hour of the ordeal. She filled the time as she might; bought things, in shops, for which she had no use, and called on friends for whom she had no taste. Most of her friends, at present, were reduced to that category, and she had to choose, for visits, the houses guiltless, as she might have said, of her husband's blood. She couldn't speak to the people who had answered in such dreadful terms her late circular; on the other hand, the people out of its range were such as would also be stolidly unconscious of Lady Northmore's publication and from whom the sop of sympathy could be but circuitously extracted. As she had lunched at a pastrycook's, so she stopped out to tea, and the March dusk had fallen when she got home. The first thing she then saw in her lighted hall was a large neat package on the table; whereupon she knew before approaching it that Lady Northmore had sent her the book. It had arrived, she learned, just after her going out; so that, had she not done this, she might have spent the day with it. She now quite understood her prompt instinct of flight. Well, flight had helped her, and the touch of the great indifferent general life. She would at last face the music.

She faced it, after dinner, in her little closed drawing-room, unwrapping the two volumes — *The Public and Private Correspondence of the Right Honourable, &c., &c.* — and looking well, first, at the great escutcheon on the purple cover and at the various portraits within, so numerous that wherever she opened she came on one. It had not been present to her before that he was so perpetually 'sitting,' but he figured in every phase and in every style, and the gallery was enriched with views of his successive residences, each one a little grander than the last. She had ever, in general, found that, in portraits, whether of the known or the unknown, the eyes seemed to seek and to meet her own; but John Northmore everywhere looked straight away from her, quite as if he had been in the room and were unconscious of acquaintance. The effect of this was, oddly

enough, so sharp that at the end of ten minutes she found herself sinking into his text as if she had been a stranger and
beholden, vulgarly and accidentally, to one of the libraries.
She had been afraid to plunge, but from the moment she got
in she was — to do every one, all round, justice — thoroughly
held.   She sat there late, and she made so many reflections
and discoveries that — as the only way to put it — she passed
from mystification to stupefaction.   Her own contribution had
been almost exhaustively used; she had counted Warren's letters before sending them and perceived now that scarce a
dozen were not all there — a circumstance explaining to her
Lady Northmore's present.   It was to these pages she had
turned first, and it was as she hung over them that her stupefaction dawned.   It took, in truth, at the outset, a particular
form — the form of a sharpened wonder at Warren's unnatural
piety.   Her original surprise had been keen — when she had
tried to take reasons for granted; but her original surprise
was as nothing to her actual bewilderment.   The letters to
Warren had been practically, she judged, for the family, the
great card; yet if the great card made only that figure, what
on earth was one to think of the rest of the pack?

She pressed on, at random, with a sense of rising fever; she
trembled, almost panting, not to be sure too soon; but wherever she turned she found the prodigy spread.   The letters to
Warren were an abyss of inanity; the others followed suit as
they could; the book was surely then a sandy desert, the publication a theme for mirth.   She so lost herself, as her perception of the scale of the mistake deepened, in uplifting visions,
that when her parlour-maid, at eleven o'clock, opened the door
she almost gave the start of guilt surprised.   The girl, with-
drawing for the night, had come but to say so, and her mistress supremely wide-awake, and with remembrance kindled,
appealed to her, after a blank stare, with intensity.   ' What
have you done with the papers?'

' The papers, ma'am?'

'All those of this morning — don't tell me you've destroyed them! Quick, quick — bring them back.' The young woman, by a rare chance, had not destroyed them; she presently re-appeared with them, neatly folded; and Mrs. Hope, dismissing her with benedictions, had at last, in a few minutes, taken the time of day. She saw her impression portentously reflected in the public prints. It was not then the illusion of her jealousy — it was the triumph, unhoped for, of her justice. The reviewers observed a decorum, but, frankly, when one came to look, their stupefaction matched her own. What she had taken in the morning for enthusiasm proved mere perfunctory attention, unwarned in advance and seeking an issue for its mystification. The question was, if one liked, asked civilly, but it was asked, none the less, all round: 'What *could* have made Lord Northmore's family take him for a letter-writer?' Pompous and ponderous, yet loose and obscure, he managed, by a trick of his own, to be both slipshod and stiff. Who, in such a case, had been primarily responsible, and under what strangely belated advice had a group of persons destitute of wit themselves been thus deplorably led thus astray? With fewer accomplices in the preparation, it might almost have been assumed that they had been dealt with by practical jokers.

They had at all events committed an error of which the most merciful thing to say was that, as founded on loyalty, it was touching. These things, in the welcome offered, lay perhaps not quite on the face, but they peeped between the lines and would force their way through on the morrow. The long quotations given were quotations marked Why? — 'Why,' in other words, as interpreted by Mrs. Hope, 'drag to light such helplessness of expression? why give the text of his dulness and the proof of his fatuity?' The victim of the error had certainly been, in his way and day, a useful and remarkable person, but almost any other evidence of the fact might more happily have been adduced. It rolled over her, as she paced her room in the small hours, that the wheel had come full circle. There was after all a rough justice. The monument that had over-darkened her was reared, but it would be within a week the opportunity of every humourist, the derision of intelligent London. Her husband's strange share in it continued, that night, between dreams and vigils, to puzzle her, but light broke with her final waking, which was comfortably late. She opened her eyes to it, and, as it stared straight into them, she greeted it with the first laugh that had for a long time passed her lips. How could she, idiotically, not have guessed? Warren, playing insidiously the part of a guardian, had done what he had done on purpose! He had acted to an end long foretasted, and the end — the full taste — had come.

V

It was after this, none the less — after the other organs of criticism, including the smoking-rooms of the clubs, the lobbies of the House, and the dinner-tables of everywhere, had duly embodied their reserves and vented their irreverence, and the unfortunate two volumes had ranged themselves, beyond appeal, as a novelty insufficiently curious and prematurely stale — it was when this had come to pass that Mrs. Hope really felt how beautiful her own chance would now have been and how sweet her revenge. The success of *her* volumes, for the inevitability of which nobody had had an instinct, would have been as great as the failure of Lady Northmore's, for the inevitability of which everybody had had one. She read over and over her letters and asked herself afresh if the confidence that had preserved *them* might not, at such a crisis, in spite of everything, justify itself. Did not the discredit to English wit, as it were, proceeding from the uncorrected attribution to an established public character of such mediocrity of thought and form, really demand, for that matter, some such redemptive stroke as the appearance of a collection of masterpieces gathered from a similar walk? To have such a collection under one's hand and yet sit and see one's self not use it was a torment through which she might well have feared to break down.

But there was another thing she might do, not redemptive indeed, but perhaps, after all, as matters were going, apposite. She fished out of their nook, after long years, the packet of John Northmore's epistles to herself, and, reading them over in the light of his later style, judged them to contain to the full the promise of that inimitability; felt that they would deepen the impression and that, in the way of the *inédit*, they constituted her supreme treasure. There was accordingly a terrible week for her in which she itched to put them forth. She composed mentally the preface, brief, sweet, ironic, representing her as prompted by an anxious sense of duty to a great reputation and acting upon the sight of laurels so lately gathered. There would naturally be difficulties; the documents were her own, but the family, bewildered, scared, suspicious, figured to her fancy as a dog with a dust-pan tied to its tail and ready for any dash to cover at the sound of the clatter of tin. They would have, she surmised, to be consulted, or, if not consulted, would put in an injunction; yet of the two courses, that of scandal braved for the man she had rejected drew her on, while the charm of this vision worked, still further than that of delicacy over-ridden for the man she had married.

The vision closed round her and she lingered on the idea — fed, as she handled again her faded fat packet, by re-perusals more richly convinced. She even took opinions as to the interference open to her old friend's relatives; took, in fact, from this time on, many opinions; went out anew, picked up old threads, repaired old ruptures, resumed, as it was called, her place in society. She had not been for years so seen of men as during the few weeks that followed the abasement of the Northmores. She called, in particular, on every one she had cast out after the failure of her appeal. Many of these

persons figured as Lady Northmore's contributors, the unwit-
ting agents of the unprecedented exposure; they having, it
was sufficiently clear, acted in dense good faith. Warren, fore-
seeing and calculating, might have the benefit of such subtlety,
but it was not for any one else. With every one else — for
they did, on facing her, as she said to herself, look like fools
— she made inordinately free; putting right and left the
question of what, in the past years, they, or their progenitors,
could have been thinking of. 'What on earth had you in
mind, and where, among you, were the rudiments of intelligence, when you burnt up my husband's priceless letters and
clung as if for salvation to Lord Northmore's? You see how
you have been saved!' The weak explanations, the imbecility, as she judged it, of the reasons given, were so much balm
to her wound. The great balm, however, she kept to the last:
she would go to see Lady Northmore only when she had exhausted all other comfort. That resource would be as supreme
as the treasure of the fat packet. She finally went and, by a
happy chance, if chance could ever be happy in such a house,
was received. She remained half an hour — there were other
persons present, and, on rising to go, felt that she was satisfied. She had taken in what she desired, had sounded what
she saw; only, unexpectedly, something had overtaken her
more absolute than the hard need she had obeyed or the vin-
dictive advantage she had cherished. She had counted on
herself for almost anything but for pity of these people, yet
it was in pity that, at the end of ten minutes, she felt everything else dissolve.

They were suddenly, on the spot, transformed for her by
the depth of their misfortune, and she saw them, the great
Northmores, as — of all things — consciously weak and flat.
She neither made nor encountered an allusion to volumes
published or frustrated; and so let her arranged inquiry die
away that when, on separation, she kissed her wan sister in
widowhood, it was not with the kiss of Judas. She had

meant to ask lightly if she mightn't have *her* turn at editing; but the renunciation with which she re-entered her house had formed itself before she left the room. When she got home indeed she at first only wept — wept for the commonness of failure and the strangeness of life. Her tears perhaps brought her a sense of philosophy ; it was all as broad as it was long. When they were spent, at all events, she took out for the last time the faded fat packet. Sitting down by a receptacle daily emptied for the benefit of the dustman, she destroyed, one by one, the gems of the collection in which each piece had been a gem. She tore up, to the last scrap, Lord Northmore's letters. It would never be known now, as regards this series, either that they had been hoarded or that they had been sacrificed. And she was content so to let it rest. On the following day she began another task. She took out her husband's and attacked the business of transcription. She copied them piously, tenderly, and, for the purpose to which she now found herself settled, judged almost no omissions imperative. By the time they should be published ——! She shook her head, both knowingly and resignedly, as to criticism so remote. When her transcript was finished she sent it to a printer to set up, and then, after receiving and correcting proof, and with every precaution for secrecy, had a single copy struck off and the type, under her eyes, dispersed. Her last act but one — or rather perhaps but two — was to put these sheets, which, she was pleased to find, would form a volume of three hundred pages, carefully away. Her next was to add to her testamentary instrument a definite provision for the issue, after her death, of such a volume. Her last was to hope that death would come in time.

THE GIVEN CASE

I

BARTON REEVE waited, with outward rigour and inward rage, till every one had gone: there was in particular an objectionable, travelled, superior young man — a young man with a long neck and bad shoes, especially great on Roumania — whom he was determined to outstay. He could only wonder the while whether he most hated designed or unconscious unpleasantness. It was a Sunday afternoon, the time in the week when, for some subtle reason, 'such people' — Reeve freely generalised them — most take liberties. But even when the young man had disappeared there still remained Mrs. Gorton, Margaret Hamer's sister, and actual hostess — it was with this lady that Miss Hamer was at present staying. He was sustained, however, as he had been for half an hour previous, by the sense that the charming girl knew perfectly he had something to say to her and was trying covertly to help him. 'Only hang on: leave the rest to me' — something of that sort she had already conveyed to him. He left it to her now to get rid of her sister, and was struck by the wholly natural air with which she soon achieved this feat. It was not absolutely hidden from him that if he had not been so insanely in love he might like her for herself. As it was, he could only like her for Mrs. Despard. Mrs. Gorton was dining out, but Miss Hamer was not; that promptly turned up, with the effect of bringing on, for the former lady, the question of time to dress. She still remained long enough to say over and over that it *was* time. Meanwhile, a little awkwardly, they hung about by the fire. Mrs. Gorton looked at her pretty shoe on the

172

fender, but Barton Reeve and Miss Hamer were on their feet as if to declare that they were fixed.

'You're dining all alone?' he said to the girl.

'Women never dine alone,' she laughed. 'When they're alone they don't dine.'

Mrs. Gorton looked at her with an expression of which Reeve became aware: she was so handsome that, but for its marked gravity, it might have represented the pleasure and pride of sisterhood. But just when he most felt such complacency to be natural his hostess rather sharply mystified him. 'She won't *be* alone — more's the pity!' Mrs. Gorton spoke with more intention than he could seize, and the next moment he was opening the door for her.

'I shall have a cup of coffee and a biscuit — and also, propped up before me, Gardiner's *Civil War*. Don't you always read when you dine alone?' Miss Hamer asked as he came back.

Women were strange — he was not to be drawn in that direction. She had been showing him for an hour that she knew what he wanted; yet now that he had got his chance — which she moreover had given him — she looked as innocent as the pink face in the oval frame above the chimney. It took him, however, but a moment to see more: her innocence was her answer to the charge with which her sister had retreated, a charge into which, the next minute, her conscious blankness itself helped him to read a sense. Margaret Hamer was never alone, because Phil Mackern was always — But it was none of *his* business! She lingered there on the rug, and it somehow passed between them before anything else was done that he quite recognised that. After the point was thus settled he took his own affair straight up. 'You know why I'm here. It's because I believe you can help me.'

'Men always think that. They think every one can "help" them but themselves.'

'And what do women think?' Barton Reeve asked with some asperity. 'It might be a little of a light for me if you were able to tell me *that*.　What do they think a man is made of?　What does *she* think —— ?'

A little embarrassed, Margaret looked round her, wishing to show she could be kind and patient, yet making no movement to sit down.　Mrs. Gorton's allusion was still in the air — it had just affected their common comfort.　'I know what you mean.　You assume she tells me everything.'

'I assume that you're her most intimate friend.　I don't know to whom else to turn.'

The face the girl now took in was smooth-shaven and fine, a face expressing penetration up to the limit of decorum.　It was full of the man's profession — passionately legal.　Barton Reeve was certainly concerned with advice, but not with taking it.　'What particular thing,' she asked, 'do you want me to do?'

'Well, to make her see what she's doing to me.　From you she'll take it.　She won't take it from me.　She doesn't believe me — she thinks I'm "prejudiced."　But she'll believe you.'

Miss Hamer smiled, but not with cruelty.　'And whom shall *I* believe?'

'Ah, that's not kind of you!'　Barton Reeve returned; after which, for a moment, as he stood there sombre and sensitive, something visibly came to him that completed his thought, but that he hesitated to produce.　Presently, as if to keep it back, he turned away with a jerk.　He knew all about the girl herself — the woman of whom they talked had, out of the fulness of her own knowledge, told him; he knew what would have given him a right to say: 'Oh, come; don't pretend I've to reveal to *you* what the dire thing makes of us!'　He moved across the room and came back — felt himself even at this very moment, in the grip of his passion, shaken as a rat by a terrier.　But just that was what he showed by his silence.　As he rejoined her by the chimney-piece he was extravagantly nervous.　'Oh Lord, Lord!' he at last simply exclaimed.

'I believe you — I believe you,' she replied. 'But *she* really does too.'

'Then why does she treat me so? — it's a refinement of perversity and cruelty. She never gives me an inch but she takes back the next day ten yards; never shows me a gleam of sincerity without making up for it as soon as possible by something that leaves me in no doubt of her absolute heartless coquetry. Of whom the deuce is she afraid?'

His companion hesitated. 'You perhaps might remember once in a while that she has a husband.'

'Do I ever forget it for an instant? Isn't my life one long appeal to her to get rid of him?'

'Ah,' said his friend as if she knew all about it, 'getting rid of husbands isn't so easy!'

'I beg your pardon ' — Reeve spoke with much more gravity and a still greater competence — 'there's every facility for it when the man's a proved brute and the woman an angel whom, for three years, he has not troubled himself so much as to look at.'

'Do you think,' Miss Hamer inquired, 'that, even for an angel, extreme intimacy with another angel — such another as you: angels of a feather flock together! — positively adds to the facility?'

Barton could perfectly meet her. 'It adds to the reason — that's what it adds to; and the reason *is* the facility. I only know one way,' he went on, 'of showing her I want to marry her. I can't show it by never going near her.'

'But need you also show Colonel Despard?'

'Colonel Despard doesn't care a rap!'

'He cares enough to have given her all this time nothing whatever — for divorcing him, if you mean that — to take hold of.'

'I do mean that,' Barton Reeve declared; 'and I must ask you to believe that I know what I'm talking about. He hates her enough for any perversity, but he has given her exactly what is necessary. Enough's as good as a feast!'

Miss Hamer looked away — looked now at the clock; but it was none the less apparent that she understood. 'Well — she of course has a horror of that. I mean of doing anything herself.'

'Then why does she go so far?'

Margaret still looked at the clock. 'So far —— ?'

'With me, month after month, in every sort of way!'

Moving away from the fire, she gave him an irrelevant smile. 'Though I *am* to be alone, my time's up.'

He kept his eyes on her. 'Women don't feed for themselves, but they do dress, eh?'

'I must go to my room.'

'But that isn't an answer to my question.'

She thought a moment. 'About poor Kate's going so far? I thought your complaint was of her not going far enough.'

'It all depends,' said Reeve, impatiently, 'upon her having some truth in her. She shouldn't do what she does if she doesn't care for me.'

'She does care for you,' said the girl.

'Well then, damn it, she should do much more!'

Miss Hamer put out her hand. 'Good-bye. I'll speak to her.'

Reeve held her fast. 'She does care for me?'

She hesitated but an instant. 'Far too much. It's excessively awkward.'

He still detained her, pressing her with his sincerity, almost with his crudity. 'That's exactly why I've come to you.' Then he risked: '*You* know —— !' But he faltered.

'I know what?'

'Why, what it is.'

She threw back her head, releasing herself. 'To be impertinent? Never!' She fairly left him — the man was in the hall to let him out; and he walked away with a sense not diminished, on the whole, of how viciously fate had seasoned his draught. Yet he believed Margaret Hamer *would* speak for him. She had a kind of nobleness.

II

At Pickenham, on the Saturday night, it came round some-how to Philip Mackern that Barton Reeve was to have been of the party, and that Mrs. Despard's turning up without him — so it was expressed — had somewhat disconcerted their hostess. This, in the smoking-room, made him silent more to think than to listen — he knew whom *he* had 'turned up' without. The next morning, among so many, there were some who went to church; Mackern always went now because Miss Hamer had told him she wished it. He liked it, moreover, for the time: it was an agreeable symbol to him of the way his situation made him 'good.' Besides, he had a plan; he knew what Mrs. Despard would do; *her* situation made her good too. The morning, late in May, was bright, and the walk, though short, charming; they all straggled, in vivid twos and threes, across the few fields — passing stiles and gates, drawing out, scattering their colour over the green, as if they had the 'tip' for some new sport. Mrs. Despard, with two companions, was one of the first; Mackern himself, as it happened, quitted the house by the side of Lady Orville, who, before they had gone many steps, completed the information given him the night before.

'That's just the sort of thing Kate Despard's always up to. I'm too tired of her!'

Phil Mackern wondered. 'But do you mean she prevented him —— ?'

'I asked her only to make him come — it was *him* I wanted. But she's a goose: she hasn't the courage ——'

'Of her reckless passion?' Mackern asked, as his companion's candour rather comically dropped.

'Of her ridiculous flirtation. She doesn't know what she wants — she's in and out of her hole like a frightened mouse. On knowing she's invited he immediately accepts, and she encourages him in the fond thought of the charming time

N

they'll have. Then at the eleventh hour she finds it will never do. It will be too "marked"! Marked it would certainly have been,' Lady Orville pursued. 'But there would have been a remedy!'

'For *her* to have stayed away?'

Her ladyship waited. 'What horrors you make me say!'

'Well,' Mackern replied, 'I'm glad she came. I particularly want her.'

'You? — what have *you* to do with her? You're as bad as she!' his hostess added, quitting him, however, for some other attention, before he had need to answer.

He sought no second companion — he had matter for thought as he went on; but he reached the door of the church before Mrs. Despard had gone in, and he observed that when, glancing back, she saw him pass the gate, she immediately waited for him. She had turned off a little into the churchyard, and as he came up he was struck with the prettiness that, beneath the old grey tower and among the crooked headstones, she presented to the summer morning.

'It's just to say, before any one else gets hold of you, that I want you, when we come out, to walk home with me. I want most particularly to speak to you.'

'*Comme cela se trouve!*' Mackern laughed. 'That's exactly what I want to do to you!'

'Oh, I warn you that you won't like it; but you will have, all the same, to take it!' Mrs. Despard declared. 'In fact, it's why I came,' she added.

'To speak to *me?*'

'Yes, and you needn't attempt to look innocent and interesting. You know perfectly what it's about!' With which she passed into church.

It scarce prepared the young man for his devotions; he thought more of what it might be about — whether he knew or not — than he thought of what, ostensibly, he had come for. He was not seated near Mrs. Despard, but he appropriated

her, after service, before they had left the place; and then,
on the walk back, took care they should be quite by themselves. She opened fire with a promptitude clearly intended
to deprive him of every advantage.

'Don't you think it's about time, you know, to let Margaret
Hamer alone?'

He found his laugh again a resource. 'Is that what you
came down to say to me?'

'I suppose what you mean is that in that case I might as
well have stayed at home. But I can assure you,' Mrs. Despard continued, 'that if you don't care for her, I at least do.
I'd do anything for her!'

'Would you?' Philip Mackern asked. 'Then, for God's
sake, try to induce her to show me some frankness and reason.
Knowing that you know all about it and that I should find
you here, that's what determined me. And I find you talking
to me,' he went on, ' about giving her up. How *can* I give her
up? What do you mean by my not caring for her? Don't I
quite sufficiently show — and to the point absolutely of making
a public fool of myself — that I don't care for anything else
in life?'

Mrs. Despard, slightly to his surprise and pacing beside him
a moment in silence, seemed arrested by this challenge. But
she presently found her answer. 'That's not the way, you
know, to get on at the Treasury.'

'I don't pretend it is; and it's just one of the things that I
thought of asking you to bring home to her better than any
one else can. She plays the very devil with my work. She
makes me hope just enough to be all upset, and yet never, for
an hour, enough to be — well, what you may call made strong;
enough to know where I am.'

'You're where you've no business to be — that's where you
are,' said Mrs. Despard. 'You've no right whatever to perse-
cute a girl who, to listen to you, will have to do something that
she doesn't want, and that would be most improper if she did.'

'You mean break off —— ? '

'I mean break off — with Mr. Grove-Stewart.'

'And why shouldn't she? '

'Because they've been engaged three years.'

'And could there be a better reason? ' Philip Mackern asked with heat. 'A man who's engaged to a girl three years without marrying her — what sort of a man is that, and what tie to him is she, or is any one else, bound to recognise? '

'He's an extremely nice person,' Mrs. Despard somewhat sententiously replied, 'and he's to return from India — and not to go back, you know — this autumn at latest.'

'Then that's all the more reason for my acting successfully before he comes — for my insisting on an understanding without the loss of another week.'

The young man, who was tall and straight, had squared his shoulders and, throwing back his massive, fair head, appeared to proclaim to earth and air the justice of his cause. Mrs. Despard, for an instant, answered nothing, but, as if to take account of his manner, she presently stopped short. 'I think I ought to express to you my frank belief that for you, Mr. Mackern, there can be nothing but loss. I'm sorry for you, to a certain point; but you happen to have got hold of a girl who's incapable of anything dishonourable.' And with this — as if *that* were settled — she resumed her walk.

Mackern, however, stood quite still — only too glad of the opportunity for emphasis given him by their pause; so that after a few steps she turned round. 'Do you know that that's exactly on what I wanted to appeal to you? *Is* she the woman to chuck me now? '

Mrs. Despard, all face and figure in the mild brightness, looked at him across the grass and appeared to give some extension to the question of what, in general at least, a woman might be the woman to do. 'Now? '

'Now. After all she has done.'

Mrs. Despard, however, wouldn't hear of what Margaret

Hamer had done; she only walked straight off again, shaking everything away as Mackern overtook her. 'Leave her alone — leave her alone!'

He held his tongue for some minutes, but he swished the air with his stick in a way that made her presently look at him. She found him positively pale, and he looked away from her. 'You should have given me that advice,' he remarked with dry derision, 'a good many weeks ago!'

'Well, it's never too late to mend!' she retorted with some vivacity.

'I beg your pardon. It's often too late — altogether too late. And as for "mending,"' Mackern went on almost sternly, 'you know as well as I that if I *had* — in time, or anything of that sort — tried to back out or pull up, you would have been the first to make her out an injured innocent and declare I had shamefully used her.'

This proposition took, as appeared, an instant or two to penetrate Mrs. Despard's consciousness; but when it had fairly done so it produced, like a train of gunpowder, an audible report. 'Why, you strange, rude man!' — she fairly laughed for indignation. 'Permit me not to answer you: I can't discuss any subject with you in that key.'

They had reached a neat white gate and paused for Mackern to open it; but, with his hand on the top, he only held it a little, fixing his companion with insistence and seemingly in full indifference to her protest. 'Upon my soul, the way women treat men —— !'

'Well?' she demanded, while he gasped as if it were more than he could express.

'It's too execrable! There's only one thing for her to do.' He clearly wished to show he was not to be humbugged.

'And what wonderful thing is that?'

'There's only one thing for *any* woman to do,' he pursued with an air of conscious distinctness, 'when she has drawn a man on to believe there's nothing she's not ready for.'

Mrs. Despard waited; she watched, over the gate, the gambols, in the next field, of a small white lamb. 'Will you kindly let me pass?' she then asked.

But he went on as if he had not heard her. 'It's to make up to him for what she has cost him. It's simply to do everything.'

Mrs. Despard hesitated. 'Everything?' she then vaguely asked.

'Everything,' Mackern said as he opened the gate. '*Won't* you help me?' he added more appealingly as they got into the next field.

'No.' She was as distinct as himself. She followed with her eyes the little white lamb. She dismissed the subject. 'You're simply wicked.'

III

BARTON REEVE, of a Sunday, sometimes went for luncheon to his sister, who lived in Great Cumberland Place, and this particular Sunday was so fine that, from the Buckingham Palace Road, he walked across the Park. There, in the eastern quarter, he encountered many persons who appeared, on the return from church, to have assembled to meet each other and who had either disposed themselves on penny chairs or were passing to and fro near the Park Lane palings. The sitters looked at the walkers, the walkers at the sitters, and Barton Reeve, with his sharp eyes, at every one. Thus it was that he presently perceived, under a spreading tree, Miss Hamer and her sister, who, however, though in possession of chairs, were not otherwise engaged. He went straight up to them, and, while he stood talking, they were approached by another friend, an elderly intimate, as it seemed, of Mrs. Gorton's, whom he recognised as one of the persons so trying to his patience the day of his long wait in her drawing-room. Barton Reeve looked very hard at the younger lady, and was perfectly conscious of the effect he produced of always reminding her that there was a subject between them. He was, on the other hand, probably not aware of the publicity that his manner struck his alert young friend as conferring on this circumstance, nor of the degree in which, as an illustration of his intensity about his own interests, his candour appeared to her comic. What *was* comic, on his part, was the excessive frankness — clever man though he was — of his assumption that he finely, quite disinterestedly, extended their subject by this very looking of volumes. She and her affairs figured in them all, and there was a set of several in a row by the time that, laughing in spite of herself, she now said to him: 'Will you take me a little walk?' He left her in no doubt of his alacrity, and in a moment Mrs. Gorton's visitor was in her chair and our couple away from the company and out in the open.

'I want you to know,' the girl immediately began, 'that I've said what I could for you — that I say it whenever I can. But I've asked you to speak to me now just because you mustn't be under any illusion or flatter yourself that I'm doing——' she hesitated, for his attention had made her stop short — 'well, what I'm not. I may as well tell you, at any rate,' she added, 'that I do maturely consider she cares for you. But what will you have? She's a woman of duty.'

'Duty? What do you mean by duty?'

Barton Reeve's irritation at this name had pierced the air with such a sound that Margaret Hamer looked about for a caution. But they were in an empty circle — a wide circle of smutty sheep. She showed a slight prevision of embarrassment — even of weariness: she had hoped for an absence of that. 'You know what I mean. What else is there to mean? I mean Colonel Despard.'

'Was it her duty to Colonel Despard to be as consciously charming to me as if there had been no such person alive? Has she explained to you that?' he demanded.

'She hasn't explained to me anything — I don't need it,' said the girl, with some spirit. 'I've only explained to *her*.'

'Well?' — he was almost peremptory.

She didn't mind it. 'Well, her excuse — for her false position, I mean — is really a perfectly good one.' Miss Hamer had been standing, but with this she walked on. 'She found she — what do you call it? — liked you.'

'Then what's the matter?'

'Why, that she didn't know how much you'd like her, how far you'd — what do you call it? — "go." It's odious to be talking of such things, I think,' she pursued; 'and I assure you I wouldn't do it for other people — for any one but you and her. It makes it all sound so vulgar. She didn't think you cared — on the contrary. Then when she began to see, she had got in too deep.'

'She had made my life impossible to me without her? She certainly has "got in" to that extent,' said Barton Reeve, 'and it's precisely my contention. Can you pretend for her that to have found out that she has done this leaves open to her, in common decency, any but the one course?'

'I don't pretend anything!' his companion replied with some confusion and still more impatience. 'I'm bound to say I don't see what responsibility you're trying to fix on me.'

He just cast about him, making little wild jerks with his stick. 'I'm not trying anything and you're awfully good to me. I dare say my predicament makes me a shocking bore — makes me, in fact, ridiculous. But I don't speak to you only because you're her friend — her friend, and therefore not indifferent to the benefit for her of what, take it altogether, I have to offer. It's because I feel so sure of how, in her place, you would generously, admirably take your own line.'

'Heaven forbid I should ever be in her place!' Margaret exclaimed with a laugh in which it pleased Reeve, at the moment, to discover a world of dissimulation.

'You're already there — I say, come!' the young man had

it on his tongue's end to reply. But he stopped himself in time, and felt extraordinarily delicate and discreet. 'I don't say it's the easiest one in the world; but here I stand, after all — and I'm not supposed to be such an ass — ready to give her every conceivable assistance.' His friend, at this, replied nothing; but he presently spoke again. 'What has she invented, at Pickenham, to-day, but to keep me from coming?'

'Is Kate to-day at Pickenham?' Miss Hamer inquired.

Barton Reeve, in his acuteness, caught something in the question — an energy of profession of ignorance — in which he again saw depths. It presented Pickenham and whomsoever might be there as such a blank that he felt quite forced to say:

'I rather imagined — till I spied you just now — that you would have gone.'

'Well, you see I haven't.' With which our young lady paused again, turning on him more frankly. It struck him that, as from a conscious effort, she had a heightened colour. 'You must know far better than I what she feels, but I repeat it to you, once for all, as, the last time I saw her, she gave it me. I said just now she hadn't explained, but she did explain that.' The girl just faltered, but she brought it out. 'She can't divorce. And if she can't, you know, she can't!'

'I never heard such twaddle,' Barton Reeve declared. 'As if a woman with a husband who hates her so he would like to kill her couldn't obtain any freedom —— !' And he gave such a passionate whirl of his stick that it flew straight away from him.

His companion waited till he had picked it up. 'Ah, but there's freedom and freedom.'

'She can do anything on all the wide earth she likes.' He had gone on as if not hearing her, and, lost in the vastness of his meaning, he absolutely glared awhile at the distance. 'But she's afraid!'

Miss Hamer, in her turn, stared at the way he sounded it; then she gave a vague laugh. 'How you say that!'

Barton Reeve said it again — said it with rage and scorn. 'She's afraid, she's afraid!'

Margaret continued to look at him; then she turned away. 'Yes — she is.'

'Well, who wouldn't be?' came to her, as a reply, across the grass. Mrs. Gorton, with two gentlemen, now rejoined them.

IV

ON hearing from Mrs. Despard that she must see him, Philip Mackern's action was immediate: she had named the morrow for his call, but he knocked at her door, on the chance, an hour after reading her note. The footman demurred, but at the same moment Barton Reeve, taking his departure, appeared in the hall, and Mackern instantly appealed to him.

'She *is* at home, I judge — isn't she?' The young man was so impatient that it was only afterwards he took into account a queerness of look on Reeve's part — a queerness that seemed to speak of a different crisis and that indeed something in his own face might, to his friend's eyes, remarkably have matched. Like two uneasy Englishmen, at any rate, they somehow passed each other, and when, a minute later, in the drawing-room, Mrs. Despard, who, with her back presented, was at the window, turned about at the sound of his name, she showed him an expression in which nothing corresponded to that of her other visitor. It may promptly be mentioned that, even through what followed, this visitor's presence was, to Mackern's sense, still in the air; only it was also just one of the things ministering, for our friend, to the interest of retrospect that such a fact — the fact that Mrs. Despard could be so 'wonderful' — conveyed a reminder of the superior organisation of women. 'I know you said to-morrow,' he quickly began; 'but I'll come to-morrow too. Is it bad or good?' he went on — 'I mean what you have to tell me. Even if I just know it's bad, I believe I can wait — if you haven't time now.'

'I haven't time, at all, now,' Mrs. Despard replied very sweetly. 'I can only give you two minutes — my dressmaker's waiting. But it isn't bad,' she added.

'Then it's good?' he eagerly asked.

'Oh, I haven't the least idea you'll think it so! But it's because it's exactly what I myself have been wanting and hoping that I wrote to you. It strikes me that the sooner you know the better. I've just heard from Bombay — from Amy Warden.'

'Amy Warden?' Philip Mackern wondered.

'John Grove-Stewart's sister — the nice one. He comes home immediately — doesn't wait till the autumn. So there you are!' said Mrs. Despard.

Philip Mackern looked straight at the news, with which she now presented herself as brilliantly illuminated. 'I don't see that I'm anywhere but where I've always been. I haven't expected anything of his absence that I shan't expect of his presence.'

Mrs. Despard thought a moment, but with perfect serenity. 'Have you expected quite fatally to compromise her?'

He gave her question an equal consideration. 'To compromise her?'

'That's what you are doing, you know — as deliberately as ever you can.'

Again the young man thought. They were in the middle of the room — she had not asked him to sit down. 'Quite fatally, you say?'

'Well, she has just one chance to save herself.'

Mackern, whom Mrs. Despard had already, more than once, seen turn pale under the emotion of which she could touch the spring, gave her again — and with it a smile that struck her as strange — this sign of sensibility. 'Yes — she may have only one chance. But it's such a good one!' he laughed. 'What is Mr. Grove-Stewart coming home for?'

'Because it has reached him that the whole place is filled

with the wonder of her conduct. Amy Warden thinks that, as so intimate a friend, I should hear what he has decided to do. She takes for granted, I suppose — though she doesn't say it — that I'll let Margaret know.'

Philip Mackern looked at the ceiling. 'She doesn't know yet?'

Mrs. Despard hesitated. 'I suppose he means it as a surprise.'

'So you won't tell her?'

'On the contrary — I shall tell her immediately. But I thought it best to tell you first.'

'I'm extremely obliged to you,' said Philip Mackern.

'Of course you hate me — but I don't care!' Mrs. Despard declared. 'You've made her talked about in India — you may be proud!'

Once more Philip Mackern considered. 'I'm not at all proud — but I think I'm very glad.'

'I think you're very horrible then. But I've said what I wanted. Good-bye.' Mrs. Despard had nodded at the footman, who, returning, had announced her carriage. He had left, on retiring, the door open, and as she followed him to go to her room her visitor went out with her. She gave Mackern, on the landing, a last word. 'Her one chance is to marry him as soon as he arrives.'

Mackern's strange smile, in his white face, was now fixed. 'Her one chance, dear lady, is to marry *me*.'

His hostess, suddenly flushing on this, showed a passion that startled him. 'Stuff!' she crudely cried, and turned away with such impatience that, quitting her, he passed half downstairs. But she more quickly turned back to him; calling his name, she came to the top, while, checked, he looked up at her. Then she spoke with a particular solemnity. 'To marry you, Mr. Mackern,' — it was quite portentous, — 'will be the very worst thing for her good name.'

The young man stood staring, then frankly emulated his friend. 'Rubbish!' he rang out as he swiftly descended.

V

'MRS. GORTON has come in?'

'No, miss; but Mrs. Despard is here. She said she'd wait for you.'

'Then I'm not at home to any one.' Margaret Hamer went straight upstairs and found her visitor in the smaller drawing-room, not seated, erect before the fireplace and with the air of having for some time restlessly paced and turned. Mrs. Despard hailed her with an instant cry.

'It has come at last!'

'Do you mean you've seen your husband?'

'He dropped on me to-day — out of the blue. He came in just before luncheon. If the house is his own —— !' And Mrs. Despard, who, as with the first relief to her impatience, had flung herself, to emphasise her announcement on the sofa, gave a long, sombre sigh.

'If the house is his own he can come when he likes?' Standing before her and looking grave and tired, Margaret Hamer showed interest, but kept expression down. 'And yet you were so splendidly sure,' she continued, 'that he wouldn't come!'

'I wasn't sure — I see now I wasn't; I only tried to convince myself. I knew — at the back of my head — that he probably *was* in England; I felt in all my bones — six weeks ago, you know — that he would really have returned and, in his own infamous, underhand way, would be somewhere looking out. He told me to-day about ninety distinct lies. I don't know how he has kept so dark, but he has been at one of the kind of places he likes — some fourth-rate watering-place.'

Margaret waited a moment. 'With any one?'

'I don't know. I don't care.' This time, for emphasis, Mrs. Despard jumped up and, wandering, like a caged creature, to a distance, stopped before a glass and gave a touch or two to the position of her hat. 'It makes no difference. Nothing makes any.'

Her friend, across the room, looked at her with a certain blankness. 'Of what does he accuse you?'

'Of nothing whatever,' said Mrs. Despard, turning round. 'Not of the least little thing!' she sighed, coming back.

'Then he made no scene?'

'No — it was too awful.'

Again the girl faltered. 'Do you mean he was —— ?'

'I mean he was dreadful. I mean I can't bear it.'

'Does he want to come back?'

'Immediately and forever. "Beginning afresh," he calls it. Fancy,' the poor woman cried, rueful and wide-eyed as with a vision of more things than she could name — 'fancy beginning afresh!' Once more, in her fidget, appalled, she sank into the nearest seat.

This image of a recommencement had just then, for both ladies, in all the circumstances, a force that filled the room — that seemed for a little fairly to make a hush. 'But if he can't oblige you?' Margaret presently returned.

Mrs. Despard sat sombre. 'He *can* oblige me.'

'Do you mean by law?'

'Oh,' she wailed, 'I mean by everything! By my having been the fool —— !' She dropped to her intolerable sense of it.

Margaret watched her an instant. 'Oh, if you say it of yourself!'

Mrs. Despard gave one of her springs. 'And don't *you* say it?'

Margaret met her eyes, but changed colour. 'Say it of you?'

'Say it of *your*self.'

They fixed each other awhile; it was deep — it was even hard. 'Yes,' said the girl at last. But she turned away.

Her companion's eyes followed her as she moved; then Mrs.

Despard broke out. 'Do you mean you're not going to keep faith?'

'What faith do you *call* faith?'

'You know perfectly what I call faith for *you*, and in how little doubt, from the first, I've left you about it!'

This reply had been sharp enough to jerk the speaker for a moment, as by the toss of her head, out of her woe, but Margaret met it at first only by showing her again a face that enjoined patience and pity. They continued to look indeed, each out of her peculiar distress, more things than they found words for. 'I don't know,' Margaret Hamer finally said. 'I have time — I've a little; I've more than you — that's what makes me so sorry for you. I've been very possibly the direst idiot — I'll admit anything you like; though I won't pretend I see now how it could have been different. It couldn't — it couldn't. I don't know, I don't know,' she wearily, mechanically repeated. There was something in her that had surrendered by this time all the importance of her personal question; she wished to keep it back or to get rid of it. 'Don't, at any rate, think one is selfish and all taken up. I'm perfectly quiet — it's only about you I'm nervous. You're worse than I, dear,' she added with a dim smile.

But Mrs. Despard took it more than gravely. 'Worse?'

'I mean you've more to think of. And perhaps even *he's* worse.'

Mrs. Despard thought again. 'He's terrible.'

Her companion hesitated — she had perhaps mistaken the allusion. 'I don't mean your husband.'

Mrs. Despard *had* mistaken the allusion, but she carried it off. 'Barton Reeve is terrible. It's more than I deserve.'

'Well, he really cares. There it is.'

'Yes, there it is!' Mrs. Despard echoed. 'And much *that* helps me!'

They hovered about, but shifting their relation now and

each keeping something back. 'When are you to see him
again?' Margaret asked.

This time Mrs. Despard knew whom she meant. 'Never —
never again. What I may feel for him — what I may feel
for myself — has nothing to do with it. Never as long as I
live!' Margaret's visitor declared. 'You don't believe it?'
she, however, the next moment demanded.

'I don't believe it. You know how I've always liked him.
But what has *that* to do with it either?' the girl almost inco-
herently continued. 'I don't believe it — no,' she repeated.
'I don't want to make anything harder for you, but you won't
find it so easy.'

'I shan't find anything easy, and I must row my own boat.
But not seeing him will be the least impossibility.'

Margaret looked away. 'Well!' — she spoke at last vaguely
and conclusively.

Something in her tone so arrested her friend that she found
herself suddenly clutched by the arm. 'Do you mean to say
you'll see Mr. Mackern?'

'I don't know.'

'Then *I* do!' Mrs. Despard pronounced with energy.
'You're lost.'

'Ah!' wailed Margaret with the same wan detachment.

'Yes, simply lost!' It rang out — would have rung out
indeed too loud had it not caught itself just in time. Mrs.
Gorton at that moment opened the door.

VI

MRS. DESPARD at last came down — he had been sure it
would be but a question of time. Barton Reeve had, to this
end, presented himself, on the Sunday morning, early: he had
allowed a margin for difficulty. He was armed with a note
of three lines, which, on the butler's saying to him that she
was not at home, he simply, in a tone before which even a

butler prompted and primed must quail, requested him to carry straight up. Then unannounced and unaccompanied, not knowing in the least whom he should find, he had taken, for the hundredth time in four months, his quick course to the drawing-room, where emptiness, as it proved, reigned, but where, notwithstanding, he felt, at the end of an hour, rather more than less in possession. To express it, to put it to her, to put it to any one, would perhaps have been vain and vulgar; but the whole assurance on which he had proceeded was his sense that, on the spot, he had, to a certain point, an effect. He was enough on the spot from the moment she knew he was, and she would know it — know it by divination, as she had often before shown how extraordinarily she knew things — even if that pompous ass had not sent up his note. To what point his effect would prevail in the face of the biggest obstacle he had yet had to deal with was exactly what he had come to find out. It was enough, to begin with, that he did, after a weary wait, draw her — draw her in spite of everything: he felt that as he at last heard her hand on the door-knob. He heard it indeed pause as well as move — pause while he himself kept perfectly still. During this minute, it must be added, he looked straight at the ugliest of the whole mixed row of possibilities. Something had yielded — yes; but what had yielded was quite most probably not her softness. It might well be her hardness. Her hardness was her love of the sight of her own effect.

Dressed for church, though it was now much too late, she was more breathless than he had ever seen her; in spite of which, beginning immediately, he gave her not a moment. 'I make a scandal, your letter tells me — I make it, you say, even before the servants, whom you appear to have taken in the most extraordinary way into your confidence. You greatly exaggerate — but even suppose I do: let me assure you frankly that I care not one rap. What you've done you've done, and I'm here in spite of your letter — and in spite of

9

anything, of everything, any one else may say — on the perfectly solid ground of your having irretrievably done it. Don't
talk to me,' Reeve went on, 'about your husband and new
complications: to do that now is horribly unworthy of you
and quite the sort of thing that adds — well, you know what
— to injury. There isn't a single complication that there
hasn't always been and that we haven't, on the whole, completely mastered and put in its place. There was nothing in
your husband that prevented, from the first hour we met, your
showing yourself, and every one else you chose, what you
could do with me. What you could do you did systematically
and without a scruple — without a pang of real compunction
or a movement of real retreat.'

Mrs. Despard had not come down unprepared, and her impenetrable face now announced it. She was even strong
enough to speak softly — not to meet anger with anger. Yet
she was also clearly on her defence. 'If I was kind to you —
if I had the frankness and confidence to let it be seen I liked
you — it's because I thought I was safe.'

'Safe?' Barton Reeve echoed. 'Yes, I've no doubt you did!
And how safe did you think *I* was? Can't you give me some
account of the attention you gave to *that?*' She looked at
him without reply to his challenge, but the full beauty of her
silent face had only, as in two or three still throbs, to come
out, to affect him suddenly with all the force of a check. The
plea of her deep, pathetic eyes took the place of the admission
that his passion vainly desired to impose upon her. They
broke his resentment down; all his tenderness welled up with
the change; it came out in supplication. 'I can't look at you
and believe any ill of you. I feel for you everything I ever
felt, and that we're committed to each other by a power that
not even death can break. How can you look at *me* and not
know to what depths I'm yours? You've the finest, sweetest
chance that ever a woman had!'

She waited a little, and the firmness in her face, the intensity of her effort to possess herself, settled into exaltation, at the same time that she might have struck a spectator as staring at some object of fear. 'I see my chance — I see it; but I don't see it as you see it. You must forgive me. My chance is not *that* chance. It has come to me — God knows why! — but in the hardest way of all. I made a great mistake — I recognise it.'

'So *I* must pay for it?' Barton Reeve asked.

She continued to look at him with her protected dread. 'We both did — so we must both pay.'

'Both? I beg your pardon,' said the young man: 'I utterly deny it — I made no mistake whatever. I'm just where I was — and everything else is. Everything but you!'

She looked away from him, but going on as if she had not heard him. 'We must do our duty — when once we see it. I didn't know — I didn't understand. But now I do. It's when one's eyes are opened — that the wrong is wrong.' Not as a lesson got by heart, not as a trick rehearsed in her room, but delicately, beautifully, step by step, she made it out for herself — and for him so far as he would take it. 'I can only follow the highest line.' Then, after faltering a moment, 'We must thank God,' she said, 'it isn't worse. My husband's here,' she added with a sufficient strangeness of effect.

But Barton Reeve accepted the mere fact as relevant. 'Do you mean he's in the house?'

'Not at this moment. He's on the river — for the day. But he comes back to-morrow.'

'And he has been here since Friday?' She was silent, on this, so long that her visitor continued: 'It's none of my business?'

Again she hesitated, but at last she replied. 'Since Friday.'

'And you hate him as much as ever?'

This time she spoke out. 'More.'

Reeve made, with a sound irrepressible and scarce articulate, a motion that was a sort of dash at her. 'Ah, my *own* own!'

But she retreated straight before him, checking him with a gesture of horror, her first outbreak of emotion. 'Don't touch me!' He turned, after a minute, away; then, like a man dazed, looked, without sight, about for something. It proved to be his hat, which he presently went and took up. 'Don't talk, don't talk — you're not *in* it!' she continued. 'You speak of "paying," but it's I who pay.' He reached the door and, having opened it, stood with his hand on the knob and his eyes on her face. She was far away, at the most distant of the windows. 'I shall never care for any one again,' she kept on.

Reeve had dropped to something deeper than resentment; more abysmal, even, it seemed to him, than renouncement or despair. But all he did was slowly to shake his helpless head at her. 'I've no words for you.'

'It doesn't matter. Don't think of me.'

He was closing the door behind him, but, still hearing her voice, kept it an instant. 'I'm all right!' — that was the last that came to him as he drew the door to.

VII

'I ONLY speak of the given case,' Philip Mackern said; 'that's the only thing I have to do with, and on what I've expressed to you of the situation it has made for me I don't yield an inch.'

Mrs. Gorton, to whom, in her own house, he had thus, in defence, addressed himself, was in a flood of tears which rolled, however, in their current not a few hard grains of asperity. 'You're *always* speaking of it, and it acts on my nerves, and I don't know what you mean by it, and I don't care, and I think you're horrible. The case is like any other case that can be mended if people will behave decently.'

Philip Mackern moved slowly about the room; impatience and suspense were in every step he took, but he evidently had

himself well in hand and he met his hostess with studied indulgence. She had made her appearance, in advance, to prepare
him for her sister, who had agreed by letter to see him, but
who, through a detention on the line, which she had wired from
Bath to explain, had been made late for the appointment she
was on her way back to town to keep. Margaret Hamer had
gone home precipitately — to Devonshire — five days before, the
day after her last interview with Mrs. Despard; on which had
ensued, with the young man, whom she had left London without seeing, a correspondence resulting in her present return.
She had forbidden him, in spite of his insistence, either to come
down to her at her mother's or to be at Paddington to meet her,
and had finally, arriving from these places, but just alighted
in Manchester Square, where, while he awaited her, Mackern's
restless measurement of the empty drawing-room had much in
common with the agitation to which, in a similar place, his
friend Barton Reeve had already been condemned. Mrs. Gorton, emerging from a deeper retreat, had at last, though not out
of compassion, conferred on him her company; she left him
from the first instant in no doubt of the spirit in which she
approached him. Margaret was at last almost indecently
there, Margaret was upstairs, Margaret was coming down; but
he would render the whole family an inestimable service by
quietly taking up his hat and departing without further parley.
Philip Mackern, whose interest in this young lady was in no
degree whatever an interest in other persons connected with
her, only transferred his hat from the piano to the window-seat
and put it kindly to Mrs. Gorton that such a departure would
be, if the girl had come to take leave of him, a brutality, and
if she had come to do anything else an imbecility. His inward
attitude was that his interlocutress was an insufferable busy-
body : he took his stand, he considered, upon admirable facts ;
Margaret Hamer's age and his own — twenty-six and thirty-
two — her independence, her intelligence, his career, his prospects, his general and his particular situation, his income, his

extraordinary merit, and perhaps even his personal appearance. He left his sentiments, in his private estimate, out of account — he was almost too proud to mention them even to himself. Yet he found, after the first moment, that he had to mention them to Mrs. Gorton.

'I don't know what you mean,' he said, 'by my "always" speaking of anything whatever that's between your sister and me; for I must remind you that this is the third time, at most, that we've had any talk of the matter. If I did, however, touch, to you, last month, on what I hold that a woman is, in certain circumstances — circumstances that, mind you, would never have existed without her encouragement, her surrender — bound in honour to do, it was because you yourself, though I dare say you didn't know with what realities you were dealing, called my attention precisely to the fact of the "given case." It isn't always, it isn't often, given, perhaps — but when it is one knows it. And it's given now if it ever was in the world,' Mackern still, with his suppression of violence, but with an emphasis the more distinct for its peculiar amenity, asserted as he resumed his pacing.

Mrs. Gorton watched him a moment through such traces of tears as still resisted the extreme freedom of her pocket-handkerchief. 'Admit then as much as you like that you've been a pair of fools and criminals' — the poor woman went far: 'what business in the world have you to put the whole responsibility on her?'

Mackern pulled up short; nothing could exceed the benevolence of his surprise. 'On "her"? Why, don't I absolutely take an equal share of it?'

'Equal? Not a bit! You're not engaged to any one else.'

'Oh, thank heaven, no!' said Philip Mackern with a laugh of questionable discretion and instant effect.

His companion's cheek assumed a deeper hue and her eyes a drier light. 'You cause her to be outrageously talked about, and then have the assurance to come and prate to us of " honour " ! '

Mackern turned away again — again he measured his cage. 'What is there I'm not ready to make good ? ' — and he gave, as he passed, a hard, anxious smile.

Mrs. Gorton said nothing for a moment; then she spoke with an accumulation of dignity. 'I think you both — if you want to know — absolutely improper persons, and if I had had my wits about me I would have declined, in time, to lend my house again to any traffic that might take place between you. But you're hatefully here, to my shame, and the wretched creature, whom I myself got off, has come up, and the fat's cn the fire, and it's too late to prevent it. It's not too late, however, just to say this: that if you've come, an1 if you intend, to bully and browbeat her——'

'Well ? ' Philip Mackern asked.

She had faltered and paused, and the next moment he saw why. The door had opened without his hearing it — Margaret Hamer stood and looked at them. He made no movement; he only, after a minute, held her eyes long enough to fortify him, as it were, in his attempted intensity of stillness. He felt already as if some process, something complex and exquisite, were going on that a sound, that a gesture, might spoil. But his challenge to Mrs. Gorton was still in the air, and she apparently, on her vision of her sister, had seen something pass. She fixed the girl and she fixed Mackern; then, highly flushed and moving to the door, she answered him. 'Why, you're a brute and a coward ! ' With which she banged the door behind her.

The way the others met without speech or touch was extraordinary, and still more singular perhaps the things that, in their silence, Philip Mackern thought. There was no freedom of appeal for him — he instantly felt that; there was neither burden nor need. He wondered Margaret didn't notice in some way what Mrs. Gorton had said; there was a strangeness in her not, on one side or the other, taking that up. There was a strangeness as well, he was perfectly aware, in his finding himself surprised and even, for ten seconds, as it happened, mercilessly disappointed, at her not looking quite so 'badly' as her encounter with a grave crisis might have been entitled to present her. She looked beautiful, perversely beautiful: he couldn't indeed have said just how directly his presumption of visible ravage was to have treated her handsome head. Meanwhile, as she carried this handsome head — in a manner he had never quite seen her carry it before — to the window and stood looking blindly out, there deepened in him almost to quick anguish the fear even of breathing upon the hour they had reached. That she had come back to him, to whatever end, was somehow in itself so divine a thing that lips and hands were gross to deal with it. What, moreover, in the extremity of a man's want, had he not already said? They were simply shut up there with their moment, and he, at least, felt it throb and throb in the hush.

At last she turned round. 'He will never, never understand that I can have been so base.'

Mackern awkwardly demurred. 'Base?'

'Letting you, from the first, make, to me, such a difference.'

'I don't think you could help it.' He was still awkward.

'How can he believe that? How can he admit it?'

She asked it too wofully to expect a reply, but the young man thought a moment. 'You can't look to me to speak for him' — he said it as feeling his way and without a smile. 'He should have looked out for himself.'

'He trusted me. He trusted me,' she repeated.

'So did I — so did I.'

'Yes. Yes.' She looked straight at him, as if tasting all her bitterness. 'But I pity him so that it kills me!'

'And only him?' — and Philip Mackern came nearer. 'It's perfectly simple,' he went on. 'I'll abide by that measure. It shall be the one you pity most.'

She kept her eyes on him till she burst into tears. 'Pity *me* — pity *me !* '

He drew her to him and held her close and long, and even at that high moment it was perhaps the deepest thing in his gratitude that he did pity her.

JOHN DELAVOY

I

The friend who kindly took me to the first night of poor Windon's first — which was also poor Windon's last : it was removed as fast as, at an unlucky dinner, a dish of too perceptible a presence — also obligingly pointed out to me the notabilities in the house. So it was that we came round, just opposite, to a young lady in the front row of the balcony — a young lady in mourning so marked that I rather wondered to see her at a place of pleasure. I dare say my surprise was partly produced by my thinking her face, as I made it out at the distance, refined enough to aid a little the contradiction. I remember at all events dropping a word about the manners and morals of London — a word to the effect that, for the most part, elsewhere, people so bereaved as to be so becraped were bereaved enough to stay at home. We recognised of course, however, during the wait, that nobody ever did stay at home ; and, as my companion proved vague about my young lady, who was yet somehow more interesting than any other as directly in range, we took refuge in the several theories that might explain her behaviour. One of these was that she had a sentiment for Windon which could override superstitions ; another was that her scruples had been mastered by an influence discernible on the spot. This was nothing less than the spell of a gentleman beside her, whom I had at first mentally disconnected from her on account of some visibility of difference. He was not, as it were, quite good enough to have come with her ; and yet he was strikingly handsome, whereas she, on the contrary, would in all likelihood have been pronounced almost occultly so. That

202

was what, doubtless, had led me to put a question about her; the fact of her having the kind of distinction that is quite independent of beauty. Her friend, on the other hand, whose clustering curls were fair, whose moustache and whose fixed monocular glass particularly, if indescribably, matched them, and whose expanse of white shirt and waistcoat had the air of carrying out and balancing the scheme of his large white forehead — her friend had the kind of beauty that is quite independent of distinction. That he was her friend — and very much — was clear from his easy imagination of all her curiosities. He began to show her the company, and to do much better in this line than my own companion did for me, inasmuch as he appeared even to know who we ourselves were. That gave a propriety to my finding, on the return from a dip into the lobby in the first entr'acte, that the lady beside me was at last prepared to identify him. I, for my part, knew too few people to have picked up anything. She mentioned a friend who had edged in to speak to her and who had named the gentleman opposite as Lord Yarracome.

Somehow I questioned the news.   'It sounds like the sort of thing that's too good to be true.'

'Too good?'

'I mean he's too much like it.'

'Like what?   Like a lord?'

'Well, like the name, which is expressive, and — yes — even like the dignity.   Isn't that just what lords are usually not?' I didn't, however, pause for a reply, but inquired further if his lordship's companion might be regarded as his wife.

'Dear, no.   She's Miss Delavoy.'

I forget how my friend had gathered this — not from the informant who had just been with her; but on the spot I accepted it, and the young lady became vividly interesting. 'The daughter of the great man?'

'What great man?'

'Why, the wonderful writer, the immense novelist: the one

who died last year.' My friend gave me a look that led me to add: 'Did you never hear of him?' and, though she professed inadvertence, I could see her to be really so vague that — perhaps a trifle too sharply — I afterwards had the matter out with her. Her immediate refuge was in the question of Miss Delavoy's mourning. It was for *him*, then, her illustrious father; though that only deepened the oddity of her coming so soon to the theatre, and coming with a lord. My companion spoke as if the lord made it worse, and, after watching the pair a moment with her glass, observed that it was easy to see he could do anything he liked with his young lady. I permitted her, I confess, but little benefit from this diversion, insisting on giving it to her plainly that I didn't know what we were coming to and that there was in the air a gross indifference to which perhaps more almost than anything else the general density on the subject of Delavoy's genius testified. I even let her know, I am afraid, how scant, for a supposedly clever woman, I thought the grace of these *lacunæ;* and I may as well immediately mention that, as I have had time to see, we were not again to be just the same allies as before my explosion. This was a brief, thin flare, but it expressed a feeling, and the feeling led me to concern myself for the rest of the evening, perhaps a trifle too markedly, with Lord Yarracome's victim. She was the image of a nearer approach, of a personal view : I mean in respect to my great artist, on whose consistent aloofness from the crowd I needn't touch, any more than on his patience in going his way and attending to his work, the most unadvertised, unreported, uninterviewed, unphotographed, uncriticised of all originals. Was he not the man of the time about whose private life we delightfully knew least? The young lady in the balcony, with the stamp of her close relation to him in her very dress, was a sudden opening into that region. I borrowed my companion's glass; I treated myself, in this direction, — yes, I was momentarily gross, — to an excursion of some minutes. I came back from it with the sense of something gained; I felt as if I had been studying Delavoy's own face, no portrait of which I had ever met. The result of it all, I easily recognised, would be to add greatly to my impatience for the finished book he had left behind, which had not yet seen the light, which was announced for a near date, and as to which rumour — I mean, of course, only in the particular warm air in which it lived at all — had already been sharp. I went out after the second act to make room for another visitor — they buzzed all over the place — and when I rejoined my friend she was primed with rectifications.

'He isn't Lord Yarracome at all. He's only Mr. Beston.'

I fairly jumped; I see, as I now think, that it was as if I had read the future in a flash of lightning. 'Only ——? The mighty editor?'

'Yes, of the celebrated *Cynosure*.' My interlocutress was determined this time not to be at fault. 'He's always at first nights.'

'What a chance for me, then,' I replied, 'to judge of my particular fate!'

'Does that depend on Mr. Beston?' she inquired; on which I again borrowed her glass and went deeper into the subject.

'Well, my literary fortune does. I sent him a fortnight ago the best thing I've ever done. I've not as yet had a sign from him, but I can perhaps make out in his face, in the light of his type and expression, some little portent or promise.' I did my best, but when after a minute my companion asked what I discovered I was obliged to answer 'Nothing!' The next moment I added: 'He won't take it.'

'Oh, I hope so!'

'That's just what I've been doing.' I gave back the glass. 'Such a face is an abyss.'

'Don't you think it handsome?'

'Glorious. Gorgeous. Immense. Oh, I'm lost! What does Miss Delavoy think of it?' I then articulated.

'Can't you see?' My companion used her glass. 'She's

under the charm — she has succumbed. How else can he have dragged her here in her state?' I wondered much, and indeed her state seemed happy enough, though somehow, at the same time, the pair struck me as not in the least matching. It was only for half a minute that my friend made them do so by going on: 'It's perfectly evident. She's not a daughter, I should have told you, by the way — she's only a sister. They've struck up an intimacy in the glow of his having engaged to publish from month to month the wonderful book that, as I understand you, her brother has left behind.'

That was plausible, but it didn't bear another look. 'Never!' I at last returned. 'Daughter or sister, that fellow won't touch him.'

'Why in the world —— ?'

'Well, for the same reason that, as you'll see, he won't touch *me*. It's wretched, but we're too good for him.' My explanation did as well as another, though it had the drawback of leaving me to find another for Miss Delavoy's enslavement. I was not to find it that evening, for as poor Windon's play went on we had other problems to meet, and at the end our objects of interest were lost to sight in the general blinding blizzard. The affair was a bitter 'frost,' and if we were all in our places to the last everything else had disappeared. When I got home it was to be met by a note from Mr. Beston accepting my article almost with enthusiasm, and it is a proof of the rapidity of my fond revulsion that before I went to sleep, which was not till ever so late, I had excitedly embraced the prospect of letting him have, on the occasion of Delavoy's new thing, my peculiar view of the great man. I must add that I was not a little ashamed to feel I had made a fortune the very night Windon had lost one.

II

MR. BESTON really proved, in the event, most kind, though his appeal, which promised to become frequent, was for two or three quite different things before it came round to my peculiar view of Delavoy. It in fact never addressed itself at all to that altar, and we met on the question only when, the posthumous volume having come out, I had found myself wound up enough to risk indiscretions. By this time I had twice been with him and had had three or four of his notes. They were the barest bones, but they phrased, in a manner, a connection. This was not a triumph, however, to bring me so near to him as to judge of the origin and nature of his relations with Miss Delavoy. That his magazine would, after all, publish no specimens was proved by the final appearance of the new book at a single splendid bound. The impression it made was of the deepest — it remains the author's highest mark; but I heard, in spite of this, of no emptying of table-drawers for Mr. Beston's benefit. What the book is we know still better to-day, and perhaps even Mr. Beston does; but there was no approach at the time to a general rush, and I therefore of course saw that if he was thick with the great man's literary legatee — as I, at least, supposed her — it was on some basis independent of his bringing anything out. Nevertheless he quite rose to the idea of my study, as I called it, which I put before him in a brief interview.

'You ought to have something. That thing has brought him to the front with a leap——!'

'The front? What do you call the front?'

He had laughed so good-humouredly that I could do the same. 'Well, the front is where you and I **are**.' I told him my paper was already finished.

'Ah then, you must write it again.'

'Oh, but look at it first——!'

'You must write it again,' Mr. Beston only repeated. Before I left him, however, he had explained a little. 'You must see his sister.'

'I shall be delighted to do that.'

'She's a great friend of mine, and my having something

may please her — which, though my first, my only duty is to please my subscribers and shareholders, is a thing I should rather like to do. I'll take from you something of the kind you mention, but only if she's favourably impressed by it.'

I just hesitated, and it was not without a grain of hypocrisy that I artfully replied : 'I would much rather *you* were!'

'Well, I shall be if she is.'   Mr. Beston spoke with gravity. 'She can give you a good deal, don't you know ? — all sorts of leads and glimpses. She naturally knows more about him than any one.   Besides, she's charming herself.'

To dip so deep could only be an enticement; yet I already felt so saturated, felt my cup so full, that I almost wondered what was left to me to learn, almost feared to lose, in greater waters, my feet and my courage.   At the same time I welcomed without reserve the opportunity my patron offered, making as my one condition that if Miss Delavoy assented he would print my article as it stood.   It was arranged that he should tell her that I would, with her leave, call upon her, and I begged him to let her know in advance that I was prostrate before her brother.   He had all the air of thinking that he should have put us in a relation by which *The Cynosure* would largely profit, and I left him with the peaceful consciousness that if I had baited my biggest hook he had opened his widest mouth.   I wondered a little, in truth, how he could care enough for Delavoy without caring more than enough, but I may at once say that I was, in respect to Mr. Beston, now virtually in possession of my point of view.   This had revealed to me an intellectual economy of the rarest kind.   There was not a thing in the world — with a single exception, on which I shall presently touch — that he valued for itself, and not a scrap he knew about anything save whether or no it would do.   To 'do' with Mr. Beston, was to do for *The Cynosure*.   The wonder was that he could know that of things of which he knew nothing else whatever.

There are a hundred reasons, even in this most private

record, which, from a turn of mind so unlike Mr. Beston's, I keep exactly for a love of the fact in itself : there are a hundred confused delicacies, operating however late, that hold my hand from any motion to treat the question of the effect produced on me by first meeting with Miss Delavoy. I say there are a hundred, but it would better express my sense perhaps to speak of them all in the singular. Certain it is that one of them embraces and displaces the others. It was not the first time, and I dare say it was not even the second, that I grew sure of a shyness on the part of this young lady greater than any exhibition in such a line that my kindred constitution had ever allowed me to be clear about. My own diffidence, I may say, kept me in the dark so long that my perception of hers had to be retroactive — to go back and put together and, with an element of relief, interpret and fill out. It failed, inevitably, to operate in respect to a person in whom the infirmity of which I speak had none of the awkwardness, the tell-tale anguish, that makes it as a rule either ridiculous or tragic. It was too deep, too still, too general — it was perhaps even too proud. I must content myself, however, with saying that I have in all my life known nothing more beautiful than the faint, cool morning-mist of confidence less and less embarrassed in which it slowly evaporated. We have made the thing all out since, and we understand it all now. It took her longer than I measured to believe that a man without her particular knowledge could make such an approach to her particular love. The approach was made in my paper, which I left with her on my first visit and in which, on my second, she told me she had not an alteration to suggest. She said of it what I had occasionally, to an artist, heard said, or said myself, of a likeness happily caught : that to touch it again would spoil it, that it had ' come ' and must only be left. It may be imagined that after such a speech I was willing to wait for anything; unless indeed it be suggested that there could be then nothing more to wait for. A great deal more,

P

at any rate, seemed to arrive, and it was all in conversation about Delavoy that we ceased to be hindered and hushed. The place was still full of him, and in everything there that spoke to me I heard the sound of his voice. I read his style into everything — I read it into his sister. She was surrounded by his relics, his possessions, his books; all of which were not many, for he had worked without material reward: this only, however, made each more charged, somehow, and more personal. He had been her only devotion, and there were moments when she might have been taken for the guardian of a temple or a tomb. That was what brought me nearer than I had got even in my paper; the sense that it was he, in a manner, who had made her, and that to be with her was still to be with himself. It was not only that I could talk to him so; it was that he listened and that he also talked. Little by little and touch by touch she built him up to me; and then it was, I confess, that I felt, in comparison, the shrinkage of what I had written. It grew faint and small — though indeed only for myself; it had from the first, for the witness who counted so much more, a merit that I have ever since reckoned the great good fortune of my life, and even, I will go so far as to say, a fine case of inspiration. I hasten to add that this case had been preceded by a still finer. Miss Delavoy had made of her brother the year before his death a portrait in pencil that was precious for two rare reasons. It was the only representation of the sort in existence, and it was a work of curious distinction. Conventional but sincere, highly finished and smaller than life, it had a quality that, in any collection, would have caused it to be scanned for some signature known to the initiated. It was a thing of real vision, yet it was a thing of taste, and as soon as I learned that our hero, sole of his species, had succeeded in never, save on this occasion, sitting, least of all to a photographer, I took the full measure of what the studied strokes of a pious hand would some day represent for generations more aware of John Delavoy than, on the whole, his own had been. My feeling for them was not diminished, moreover, by learning from my young lady that Mr. Beston, who had given them some attention, had signified that, in the event of his publishing an article, he would like a reproduction of the drawing to accompany it. The 'pictures' in *The Cynosure* were in general a marked chill to my sympathy: I had always held that, like good wine, honest prose needed, as it were, no bush. I took them as a sign that if good wine, as we know, is more and more hard to meet, the other commodity was becoming as scarce. The bushes, at all events, in *The Cynosure*, quite planted out the text; but my objection fell in the presence of Miss Delavoy's sketch, which already, in the forefront of my study, I saw as a flower in the coat of a bridegroom.

I was obliged just after my visit to leave town for three weeks and was, in the country, surprised at their elapsing without bringing me a proof from Mr. Beston. I finally wrote to ask of him an explanation of the delay; for which in turn I had again to wait so long that before I heard from him I received a letter from Miss Delavoy, who, thanking me as for a good office, let me know that our friend had asked her for the portrait. She appeared to suppose that I must have put in with him some word for it that availed more expertly than what had passed on the subject between themselves. This gave me occasion, on my return to town, to call on her for the purpose of explaining how little as yet, unfortunately, she owed me. I am not indeed sure that it didn't quicken my return. I knocked at her door with rather a vivid sense that if Mr. Beston had her drawing I was yet still without my proof. My privation was the next moment to feel a sharper pinch, for on entering her apartment I found Mr. Beston in possession. Then it was that I was fairly confronted with the problem given me from this time to solve. I began at that hour to look it straight in the face. What I in the first place saw was that Mr. Beston was 'making up' to our hostess; what I saw in the second — what at any rate I believed I saw — was that she had come a certain distance to meet him; all of which would have been simple and usual enough had not the very things that gave it such a character been exactly the things I should least have expected. Even this first time, as my patron sat there, I made out somehow that in that position at least he was sincere and sound. Why should this have surprised me? Why should I immediately have asked myself how he would make it pay? He was there because he liked to be, and where was the wonder of his liking? There was no wonder in my own, I felt, so that my state of mind must have been already a sign of how little I supposed we could like the same things. This even strikes me, on looking back, as an implication sufficiently ungraceful of the absence on Miss Delavoy's part of direct and designed attraction. I dare say indeed that Mr. Beston's subjection would have seemed to me a clearer thing if I had not had by the same stroke to account for his friend's. She liked him, and I grudged her that, though with the actual limits of my knowledge of both parties I had literally to invent reasons for its being a perversity, I could only in private treat it as one, and this in spite of Mr. Beston's notorious power to please. He was the handsomest man in 'literary' London, and, controlling the biggest circulation — a body of subscribers as vast as a conscript army — he represented in a manner the modern poetry of numbers. He was in love, moreover, or he thought he was; that flushed with a general glow the large surface he presented. This surface, from my quiet corner, struck me as a huge tract, a sort of particoloured map, a great spotted social chart. He abounded in the names of things, and his mind was like a great staircase at a party — you heard them bawled at the top. He ought to have liked Miss Delavoy because *her* name, so announced, sounded well, and I grudged him, as I grudged the young lady, the higher motive of an intelligence of her charm. It was a charm so fine and so veiled that if she had been a piece of prose or of verse I was sure he would never have discovered it. The oddity was that, as the case stood, he had seen she would 'do.' I, too, had seen it, but then I was a critic: these remarks will sadly have miscarried if they fail to show the reader how much of one.

III

I MENTIONED my paper and my disappointment, but I think it was only in the light of subsequent events that I could fix an impression of his having, at the moment, looked a trifle embarrassed. He smote his brow and took out his tablets; he deplored the accident of which I complained, and promised to look straight into it. An accident it could only have been, the result of a particular pressure, a congestion of work. Of course he had had my letter and had fully supposed it had been answered and acted on. My spirits revived at this, and I almost thought the incident happy when I heard Miss Delavoy herself put a clear question.

'It won't be for April, then, which was what I had hoped?'

It was what *I* had hoped, goodness knew, but if I had had no anxiety I should not have caught the low, sweet ring of her own. It made Mr. Beston's eyes fix her a moment, and, though the thing has as I write it a fatuous air, I remember thinking that he must at this instant have seen in her face almost all his contributor saw. If he did he couldn't wholly have enjoyed it; yet he replied genially enough: 'I'll put it into June.'

'Oh, June!' our companion murmured in a manner that I took as plaintive — even as exquisite.

Mr. Beston had got up. I had not promised myself to sit him out, much less to drive him away; and at this sign of his retirement I had a sense still dim, but much deeper, of being literally lifted by my check. Even before it was set up my article was somehow operative, so that I could look from one of my companions to the other and quite magnanimously smile. 'June will do very well.'

'Oh, if *you* say so——!' Miss Delavoy sighed and turned away.

'We must have time for the portrait; it will require great care,' Mr. Beston said.

'Oh, please be sure it has the greatest!' I eagerly returned.

But Miss Delavoy took this up, speaking straight to Mr. Beston. 'I attach no importance to the portrait. My impatience is all for the article.'

'The article's very neat. It's very neat,' Mr. Beston repeated. 'But your drawing's our great prize.'

'Your great prize,' our young lady replied, 'can only be the thing that tells most about my brother.'

'Well, that's the case with your picture,' Mr. Beston protested.

'How can you say that? My picture tells nothing in the world but that he never sat for another.'

'Which is precisely the enormous and final fact!' I laughingly exclaimed.

Mr. Beston looked at me as if in uncertainty and just the least bit in disapproval; then he found his tone. 'It's the big fact for *The Cynosure*. I shall leave you in no doubt of *that!*' he added, to Miss Delavoy, as he went away.

I was surprised at his going, but I inferred that, from the pressure at the office, he had no choice; and I was at least not too much surprised to guess the meaning of his last remark to have been that our hostess must expect a handsome draft. This allusion had so odd a grace on a lover's lips that, even after the door had closed, it seemed still to hang there between Miss Delavoy and her second visitor. Naturally, however, we let it gradually drop; she only said with a kind of conscious quickness: 'I'm really very sorry for the delay.' I thought her beautiful as she spoke, and I felt that I had taken with her a longer step than the visible facts explained. 'Yes, it's a great bore. But to an editor — one doesn't show it.'

She seemed amused. 'Are they such queer fish?'

I considered. 'You know the great type.'

'Oh, I don't know Mr. Beston as an editor.'

'As what, then?'

'Well, as what you call, I suppose, a man of the world. A very kind, clever one.'

'Of course *I* see him mainly in the saddle and in the charge — at the head of his hundreds of thousands. But I mustn't undermine him,' I added, smiling, 'when he's doing so much for me.'

She appeared to wonder about it. 'Is it really a great deal?'

'To publish a thing like that? Yes — as editors go. They're all tarred with the same brush.'

'Ah, but he has immense ideas. He goes in for the best in all departments. That's his own phrase. He has often assured me that he'll never stoop.'

'He wants none but "first-class stuff." That's the way he has expressed it to *me;* but it comes to the same thing. It's our great comfort. He's charming.'

'He's charming,' my friend replied; and I thought for the moment we had done with Mr. Beston. A rich reference to him, none the less, struck me as flashing from her very next words — words that she uttered without appearing to have noticed any I had pronounced in the interval. 'Does no one, then, really care for my brother?'

I was startled by the length of her flight. 'Really care?'

'No one but you? Every month your study doesn't appear is at this time a kind of slight.'

'I see what you mean. But of course *we*'re serious.'

'Whom do you mean by "we"?'

'Well, you and me.'

She seemed to look us all over and not to be struck with our mass. 'And no one else? No one else is serious?'

'What I should say is that no one *feels* the whole thing, don't you know? as much.'

Miss Delavoy hesitated. 'Not even so much as Mr. Beston?'

And her eyes, as she named him, waited, to my surprise, for my answer.

I couldn't quite see why she returned to him, so that my answer was rather lame. 'Don't ask me too many things; else there are some *I* shall have to ask.'

She continued to look at me; after which she turned away. 'Then I won't — for I don't understand him.' She turned away, I say, but the next moment had faced about with a fresh, inconsequent question. 'Then why in the world has he cooled off?'

'About my paper? *Has* he cooled? Has he shown you that otherwise?' I asked.

'Than by his delay?   Yes, by silence — and by worse.'

'What do you call worse?'

'Well, to say of it — and twice over — what he said just now.'

'That it's very "neat"? You don't think it *is* ?' I laughed.

'I don't say it;' and with that she smiled. 'My brother might hear!'

Her tone was such that, while it lingered in the air, it deepened, prolonging the interval, whatever point there was in this; unspoken things therefore had passed between us by the time I at last brought out: 'He hasn't read me! It doesn't matter,' I quickly went on; 'his relation to what I may do or not do is, for his own purposes, quite complete enough without that.'

She seemed struck with this. 'Yes, his relation to almost anything is extraordinary.'

'His relation to everything!' It rose visibly before us and, as we felt, filled the room with its innumerable, indistinguishable objects. 'Oh, it's the making of him!'

She evidently recognised all this, but after a minute she again broke out: 'You say he hasn't read you and that it doesn't matter. But has he read my brother? Doesn't *that* matter?'

I waved away the thought. 'For what do you take him, and why in the world should it? He knows perfectly what he wants to do, and his postponement is quite in your interest. The reproduction of the drawing ——'

She took me up. 'I hate the drawing!'

'So do I,' I laughed, 'and I rejoice in there being something on which we can feel so together!'

IV

WHAT may further have passed between us on this occasion loses, as I try to recall it, all colour in the light of a communication that I had from her four days later. It consisted of a note in which she announced to me that she had heard from Mr. Beston in terms that troubled her: a letter from Paris — he had dashed over on business — abruptly proposing that she herself should, as she quoted, give him something; something that her intimate knowledge of the subject — which was of course John Delavoy — her rare opportunities for observation and study would make precious, would make as unique as the work of her pencil. He appealed to her to gratify him in this particular, exhorted her to sit right down to her task, reminded her that to tell a loving sister's tale was her obvious, her highest duty. She confessed to mystification and invited me to explain. Was this sudden perception of her duty a result on Mr. Beston's part of any difference with myself? Did he want two papers? Did he want an alternative to mine? Did he want hers as a supplement or as a substitute? She begged instantly to be informed if anything had happened to mine. To meet her request I had first to make sure, and I repaired on the morrow to Mr. Beston's office in the eager hope that he was back from Paris. This hope was crowned; he had crossed in the night and was in his room; so that on sending up my card I was introduced to his presence, where I promptly

broke ground by letting him know that I had had even yet
no proof.

'Oh, yes! about Delavoy. Well, I've rather expected you,
but you must excuse me if I'm brief. My absence has put me
back; I've returned to arrears. Then from Paris I meant to
write to you, but even there I was up to my neck. I think,
too, I've instinctively held off a little. You won't like what I
have to say — you *can't!*' He spoke almost as if I might wish
to prove I could. 'The fact is, you see, your thing won't do.
No — not even a little.'

Even after Miss Delavoy's note it was a blow, and I felt
myself turn pale. 'Not even a little? Why, I thought you
wanted it so!'

Mr. Beston just perceptibly braced himself. 'My dear man,
we didn't want *that!* We couldn't do it. I've every desire to
be agreeable to you, but we really couldn't.'

I sat staring. 'What in the world's the matter with it?'

'Well, it's impossible. That's what's the matter with it.'

'Impossible?' There rolled over me the ardent hours and
a great wave of the feeling that I had put into it.

He hung back but an instant — he faced the music. 'It's
indecent.'

I could only wildly echo him. 'Indecent? Why, it's absolutely, it's almost to the point of a regular chill, expository.
What in the world is it but critical?'

Mr. Beston's retort was prompt. 'Too critical by half!
That's just where it is. It says too much.'

'But what it says is all about its subject.'

'I dare say, but I don't think we want quite so much about
its subject.'

I seemed to swing in the void and I clutched, fallaciously,
at the nearest thing. 'What you do want, then — what is *that*
to be about?'

'That's for you to find out — it's not my business to tell
you.'

It was dreadful, this snub to my happy sense that I *had* found out. 'I thought you wanted John Delavoy. I've simply stuck to him.'

Mr. Beston gave a dry laugh. 'I should think you had!' Then after an instant he turned oracular. 'Perhaps we wanted him — perhaps we didn't. We didn't at any rate want indelicacy.'

'Indelicacy?' I almost shrieked. 'Why, it's pure portraiture.'

'"Pure," my dear fellow, just begs the question. It's most objectionable — that's what it is. For portraiture of *such* things, at all events, there's no place in our scheme.'

I speculated. 'Your scheme for an account of Delavoy?'

Mr. Beston looked as if I trifled. 'Our scheme for a successful magazine.'

'No place, do I understand you, for criticism? No place for the great figures ——? If you don't want too much detail,' I went on, 'I recall perfectly that I was careful not to go into it. What I tried for was a general vivid picture — which I really supposed I arrived at. I boiled the man down — I gave the three or four leading notes. *Them* I did try to give with some intensity.'

Mr. Beston, while I spoke, had turned about and, with a movement that confessed to impatience and even not a little, I thought, to irritation, fumbled on his table among a mass of papers and other objects; after which he had pulled out a couple of drawers. Finally he fronted me anew with my copy in his hand, and I had meanwhile added a word about the disadvantage at which he placed me. To have made me wait was unkind; but to have made me wait for such news ——! I ought at least to have been told it earlier. He replied to this that he had not at first had time to read me, and, on the evidence of my other things, had taken me pleasantly for granted: he had only been enlightened by the revelation of the proof. What he had fished out of his drawer was, in effect, not my

manuscript, but the 'galleys' that had never been sent me.
The thing was all set up there, and my companion, with eyeglass and thumb, dashed back the sheets and looked up and
down for places. The proof-reader, he mentioned, had so
waked him up with the blue pencil that he had no difficulty
in finding them. They were all in his face when he again
looked at me. 'Did you candidly think that we were going
to print this?'

All my silly young pride in my performance quivered as if
under the lash. 'Why the devil else should I have taken the
trouble to write it? If you're not going to print it, why the
devil did you ask me for it?'

'I didn't ask you. You proposed it yourself.'

'You jumped at it; you quite agreed you ought to have it:
it comes to the same thing. So indeed you ought to have it.
It's too ignoble, your not taking up such a man.'

He looked at me hard. 'I *have* taken him up. I do want
something about him, and I've got his portrait there — coming
out beautifully.'

'Do you mean you've taken him up,' I inquired, 'by asking
for something of his sister? Why, in that case, do you speak
as if I had forced on you the question of a paper? If you
want one you want one.'

Mr. Beston continued to sound me. 'How do you know
what I've asked of his sister?'

'I know what Miss Delavoy tells me. She let me know it
as soon as she had heard from you.'

'Do you mean that you've just seen her?'

'I've not seen her since the time I met you at her house;
but I had a note from her yesterday. She couldn't understand your appeal — in the face of knowing what I've done
myself.'

Something seemed to tell me at this instant that she had not
yet communicated with Mr. Beston, but that he wished me not
to know she hadn't. It came out still more in the temper with

which he presently said: 'I want what Miss Delavoy can do, but I don't want this kind of thing!' And he shook my proof at me as if for a preliminary to hurling it.

I took it from him, to show I anticipated his violence, and, profoundly bewildered, I turned over the challenged pages. They grinned up at me with the proof-reader's shocks, but the shocks, as my eye caught them, bloomed on the spot like flowers. I didn't feel abased — so many of my good things came back to me. 'What on earth do you seriously mean? This thing isn't bad. It's awfully good — it's beautiful.'

With an odd movement he plucked it back again, though not indeed as if from any new conviction. He had had after all a kind of contact with it that had made it a part of his stock. 'I dare say it's clever. For the kind of thing it is, it's as beautiful as you like. It's simply not *our* kind.' He seemed to break out afresh. 'Didn't you know more —— ? '

I waited. 'More what?'

He in turn did the same. 'More everything. More about Delavoy. The whole point was that I thought you did.'

I fell back in my chair. 'You think my article shows ignorance? I sat down to it with the sense that I knew more than any one.'

Mr. Beston restored it again to my hands. 'You've kept that pretty well out of sight then. Didn't you get anything out of *her?* It was simply for that I addressed you to her.'

I took from him with this, as well, a silent statement of what it had not been for. 'I got everything in the wide world I could. We almost worked together, but what appeared was that all her own knowledge, all her own view, quite fell in with what I had already said. There appeared nothing to subtract or to add.'

He looked hard again, not this time at me, but at the document in my hands. 'You mean she has gone into all that — seen it just as it stands there?'

'If I've still,' I replied, 'any surprise left, it's for the surprise your question implies. You put our heads together, and you've surely known all along that they've remained so. She told me a month ago that she had immediately let you know the good she thought of what I had done.'

Mr. Beston very candidly remembered, and I could make out that if he flushed as he did so it was because what most came back to him was his own simplicity. 'I see. That must have been why I trusted you—sent you, without control, straight off to be set up. But now that I see you——!' he went on.

'You're surprised at her indulgence?'

Once more he snatched at the record of my rashness — once more he turned it over. Then he read out two or three paragraphs. 'Do you mean she has gone into all that?'

'My dear sir, what do you take her for? There wasn't a line we didn't thresh out, and our talk wouldn't for either of us have been a bit interesting if it hadn't been really frank. Have you to learn at this time of day,' I continued, 'what her feeling is about her brother's work? She's not a bit stupid. She has a kind of worship for it.'

Mr. Beston kept his eyes on one of my pages. 'She passed her life with him and was extremely fond of him.'

'Yes, and she has the point of view and no end of ideas. She's tremendously intelligent.'

Our friend at last looked up at me, but I scarce knew what to make of his expression. 'Then she'll do me exactly what I want.'

'Another article, you mean, to replace mine?'

'Of a totally different sort. Something the public *will* stand.' His attention reverted to my proof, and he suddenly reached out for a pencil. He made a great dash against a block of my prose and placed the page before me. Do you pretend to me they'll stand *that?*'

'That' proved, as I looked at it, a summary of the subject, deeply interesting, and treated, as I thought, with extraordinary art, of the work to which I gave the highest place in my author's

array. I took it in, sounding it hard for some hidden vice, but with a frank relish, in effect, of its lucidity; than I answered: 'If they won't stand it, what will they stand?'

Mr. Beston looked about and put a few objects on his table to rights. 'They won't stand anything.' He spoke with such pregnant brevity as to make his climax stronger. 'And quite right too! *I*'m right, at any rate; I can't plead ignorance. I know where I am, and I want to stay there. That single page would have cost me five thousand subscribers.'

'Why, that single page is a statement of the very essence —— !'

He turned sharp round at me. 'Very essence of what?'

'Of my very topic, damn it.'

'Your very topic is John Delavoy.'

'And what's *his* very topic? Am I not to attempt to utter it? What under the sun else am I writing about?'

'You're not writing in *The Cynosure* about the relations of the sexes. With those relations, with the question of sex in any degree, I should suppose you would already have seen that we have nothing whatever to do. If you want to know what our public won't stand, there you have it.'

I seem to recall that I smiled sweetly as I took it. 'I don't know, I think, what you mean by those phrases, which strike me as too empty and too silly, and of a nature therefore to be more deplored than any, I'm positive, that I use in my analysis. I don't use a single one that even remotely resembles them. I simply try to express my author, and if your public won't stand his being expressed, mention to me kindly the source of its interest in him.'

Mr. Beston was perfectly ready. 'He's all the rage with the clever people — that's the source. The interest of the public is whatever a clever article may make it.'

'I don't understand you. How can an article be clever, to begin with, and how can it make anything of anything, if it doesn't avail itself of material?'

'There *is* material, which I'd hoped you'd use. Miss Delavoy has lots of material. I don't know what she has told you, but I know what she has told *me*.' He hung fire but an instant. 'Quite lovely things.'

'And have you told *her*——?'

'Told her what?' he asked as I paused.

'The lovely things you've just told me.'

Mr. Beston got up; folding the rest of my proof together, he made the final surrender with more dignity than I had looked for. 'You can do with this what you like.' Then as he reached the door with me: 'Do you suppose that I talk with Miss Delavoy on such subjects?' I answered that he could leave that to me — I shouldn't mind so doing; and I recall that before I quitted him something again passed between us on the question of her drawing. 'What we want,' he said, 'is just the really nice thing, the pleasant, right thing to go with it. That drawing's going to take!'

V

A FEW minutes later I had wired to our young lady that, should I hear nothing from her to the contrary, I would come to her that evening. I had other affairs that kept me out; and on going home I found a word to the effect that though she should not be free after dinner she hoped for my presence at five o'clock: a notification betraying to me that the evening would, by arrangement, be Mr. Beston's hour and that she wished to see me first. At five o'clock I was there, and as soon as I entered the room I perceived two things. One of these was that she had been highly impatient; the other was that she had not heard, since my call on him, from Mr. Beston, and that her arrangement with him therefore dated from earlier. The tea-service was by the fire — she herself was at the window; and I am at a loss to name the particular revelation that I drew from this fact of her being restless on general grounds. My telegram had fallen in with complications at which I could only guess; it had not found her quiet; she was living in a troubled air. But her wonder leaped from her lips. 'He does want two?'

I had brought in my proof with me, putting it in my hat and my hat on a chair. 'Oh, no — he wants only one, only yours.'

Her wonder deepened. 'He won't print ——?'

'My poor old stuff! He returns it with thanks.'

'Returns it? When he had accepted it!'

'Oh, that doesn't prevent — when he doesn't like it.'

'But he does; he did. He liked it to *me*. He called it "sympathetic."'

'He only meant that *you* are — perhaps even that I myself am. He hadn't read it then. He read it but a day or two ago, and horror seized him.'

Miss Delavoy dropped into a chair. 'Horror?'

'I don't know how to express to you the fault he finds with it.' I had gone to the fire, and I looked to where it peeped out of my hat; my companion did the same, and her face showed the pain she might have felt, in the street, at sight of the victim of an accident. 'It appears it's indecent.'

She sprang from her chair. 'To describe my brother?'

'As *I*'ve described him. That, at any rate, is how my account sins. What I've said is unprintable.' I leaned against the chimney-piece with a serenity of which, I admit, I was conscious; I rubbed it in and felt a private joy in watching my influence.

'Then what *have* you said?'

'You know perfectly. You heard my thing from beginning to end. You said it was beautiful.'

She remembered as I looked at her; she showed all the things she called back. 'It *was* beautiful.' I went over and picked it up; I came back with it to the fire. 'It was the best thing ever said about him,' she went on. 'It was the finest and truest.'

Q

'Well, then——!' I exclaimed.

'But what have you done to it since?'

'I haven't touched it since.'

'You've put nothing else in?'

'Not a line — not a syllable. Don't you remember how you warned me against spoiling it? It's of the thing we read together, liked together, went over and over together; it's of this dear little serious thing of good sense and good faith' — and I held up my roll of proof, shaking it even as Mr. Beston had shaken it — 'that he expresses that opinion.'

She frowned at me with an intensity that, though bringing me no pain, gave me a sense of her own. 'Then that's why he has asked *me*——?'

'To do something instead. But something pure. You, he hopes, won't be indecent.'

She sprang up, more mystified than enlightened; she had pieced things together, but they left the question gaping. 'Is he mad? What is he talking about?'

'Oh, *I* know — now. Has he specified what he wants of you?'

She thought a moment, all before me. 'Yes — to be very "personal."'

'Precisely. You mustn't speak of the work.'

She almost glared. 'Not speak of it?'

'That's indecent.'

'My brother's work?'

'To speak of it.'

She took this from me as she had not taken anything. 'Then how can I speak of him at all? — how can I articulate? He *was* his work.'

'Certainly he was. But that's not the kind of truth that will stand in Mr. Beston's way. Don't you know what he means by wanting you to be personal?'

In the way she looked at me there was still for a moment a dim desire to spare him — even perhaps a little to save him. None the less, after an instant, she let herself go. 'Something horrible?'

'Horrible; so long, that is, as it takes the place of something more honest and really so much more clean. He wants — what do they call the stuff ? — anecdotes, glimpses, gossip, chat; a picture of his " home life," domestic habits, diet, dress, arrangements — all his little ways and little secrets, and even, to better it still, all your own, your relations with him, your feelings about him, his feelings about *you:* both his and yours, in short, about anything else you can think of. Don't you see what I mean ? ' She saw so well that, in the dismay of it, she grasped my arm an instant, half as if to steady herself, half as if to stop me. But she couldn't stop me. ' He wants you just to write round and round that portrait.'

She was lost in the reflections I had stirred, in apprehensions and indignations that slowly surged and spread; and for a moment she was unconscious of everything else. 'What portrait ? '

' Why, the beautiful one you did. The beautiful one you gave him.'

' Did I give it to him ? Oh, yes ! ' It came back to her, but this time she blushed red, and I saw what had occurred to her. It occurred, in fact, at the same instant to myself. ' Ah, *par exemple,*' she cried, ' he shan't have it ! '

I couldn't help laughing. ' My dear young lady, unfortunately he *has* got it ! '

' He shall send it back. He shan't use it.'

' I'm afraid he *is* using it,' I replied. ' I'm afraid he *has* used it. They've begun to work on it.'

She looked at me almost as if I were Mr. Beston. ' Then they must stop working on it.' Something in her decision somehow thrilled me. ' Mr. Beston must send it straight back. Indeed, I'll wire to him to bring it to-night.'

' Is he coming to-night ? ' I ventured to inquire.

She held her head very high. ' Yes, he's coming to-night. It's most happy ! ' she bravely added, as if to forestall any suggestion that it could be anything else.

I thought a moment; first about that, then about something that presently made me say: 'Oh, well, if he brings it
back —— !'

She continued to look at me. 'Do you mean you doubt his
doing so?'

I thought again. 'You'll probably have a stiff time with
him.'

She made, for a little, no answer to this but to sound me
again with her eyes; our silence, however, was carried off by
her then abruptly turning to her tea-tray and pouring me out
a cup. 'Will you do me a favour?' she asked as I took it.

'Any favour in life.'

'Will you be present?'

'Present?' — I failed at first to imagine.

'When Mr. Beston comes.'

It was so much more than I had expected that I of course
looked stupid in my surprise. 'This evening — here?'

'This evening — here. Do you think my request very
strange?'

I pulled myself together. 'How can I tell when I'm so
awfully in the dark?'

'In the dark —— ?' She smiled at me as if I were a person
who carried such lights!

'About the nature, I mean, of your friendship.'

'With Mr. Beston?' she broke in. Then in the wonderful
way that women say such things: 'It has always been so
pleasant.'

'Do you think it will be pleasant for *me*?' I laughed.

'Our friendship? I don't care whether it is or not!'

'I mean what you'll have out with him — for of course you
will have it out. Do you think it will be pleasant for *him*?'

'To find you here — or to see you come in? I don't feel
obliged to think. This is a matter in which I now care for no
one but my brother — for nothing but his honour. I stand
only on that.'

I can't say how high, with these words, she struck me as
standing, nor how the look that she gave me with them
seemed to make me spring up beside her. We were at this
elevation together a moment. ' I'll do anything in the world
you say.'

'Then please come about nine.'

That struck me as so tantamount to saying ' And please
therefore go this minute' that I immediately turned to the
door. Before I passed it, however, I gave her time to ring
out clear : 'I know what I'm about !' She proved it the next
moment by following me into the hall with the request that
I would leave her my proof. I placed it in her hands, and
if she knew what she was about I wondered, outside, what *I*
was.

VI

I DARE say it was the desire to make this out that, in the
evening, brought me back a little before my time. Mr. Beston
had not arrived, and it's worth mentioning — for it was rather
odd — that while we waited for him I sat with my hostess in
silence. She spoke of my paper, which she had read over —
but simply to tell me she had done so; and that was practically all that passed between us for a time at once so full and
so quiet that it struck me neither as short nor as long. We
felt, in the matter, so indivisible that we might have been
united in some observance or some sanctity — to go through
something decorously appointed. Without an observation we
listened to the door-bell, and, still without one, a minute later,
saw the person we expected stand there and show his surprise.
It was at me he looked as he spoke to her.

'I'm not to see you alone ? '

'Not just yet, please,' Miss Delavoy answered. 'Of what
has suddenly come between us this gentleman is essentially a
part, and I really think he'll be less present if we speak before
him than if we attempt to deal with the question without him.'

Mr. Beston was amused, but not enough amused to sit down, and we stood there while, for the third time, my proof-sheets were shaken for emphasis. 'I've been reading these over,' she said as she held them up.

Mr. Beston, on what he had said to me of them, could only look grave; but he tried also to look pleasant, and I foresaw that, on the whole, he would really behave well. 'They're remarkably clever.'

'And yet you wish to publish instead of them something from so different a hand?'

He smiled now very kindly. 'If you'll only let me have it! *Won't* you let me have it? I'm sure you know exactly the thing I want.'

'Oh, perfectly!'

'I've tried to give her an idea of it,' I threw in.

Mr. Beston promptly saw his way to make this a reproach to me. 'Then, after all, you had one yourself?'

'I think I couldn't have kept so clear of it if I hadn't had!' I laughed.

'I'll write you something,' Miss Delavoy went on, 'if you'll print this as it stands.' My proof was still in her keeping.

Mr. Beston raised his eyebrows. 'Print two? Whatever do I want with two? What do I want with the wrong one if I can get the beautiful right?'

She met this, to my surprise, with a certain gaiety. 'It's a big subject — a subject to be seen from different sides. Don't you want a full, a various treatment? Our papers will have nothing in common.'

'I should hope not!' Mr. Beston said good-humouredly. 'You have command, dear lady, of a point of view too good to spoil. It so happens that your brother has been really less handled than any one, so that there's a kind of obscurity about him, and in consequence a kind of curiosity, that it seems to me quite a crime not to work. There's just the perfection, don't you know? of a little sort of mystery — a tantalising *demi-jour.*' He continued to smile at her as if he thoroughly hoped to kindle her, and it was interesting at that moment to get this vivid glimpse of his conception.

I could see it quickly enough break out in Miss Delavoy, who sounded for an instant almost assenting. 'And you want the obscurity and the mystery, the tantalising *demi-jour*, cleared up?'

'I want a little lovely, living thing! Don't be perverse,' he pursued, 'don't stand in your own light and in your brother's and in this young man's — in the long run, and in mine too and in every one's: just let us have him out as no one but you can bring him and as, by the most charming of chances and a particular providence, he has been kept all this time just on purpose for you to bring. Really, you know' — his vexation *would* crop up — 'one could howl to see such good stuff wasted!'

'Well,' our young lady returned, 'that holds good of one thing as well as of another. I can never hope to describe or express my brother as these pages describe and express him; but, as I tell you, approaching him from a different direction, I promise to do my very best. Only, my condition remains.'

Mr. Beston transferred his eyes from her face to the little bundle in her hand, where they rested with an intensity that made me privately wonder if it represented some vain vision of a snatch defeated in advance by the stupidity of his having suffered my copy to be multiplied. 'My printing that?'

'Your printing this.'

Mr. Beston wavered there between us: I could make out in him a vexed inability to keep us as distinct as he would have liked. But he was triumphantly light. 'It's impossible. Don't be a pair of fools!'

'Very well, then,' said Miss Delavoy; 'please send me back my drawing.'

'Oh dear, no!' Mr. Beston laughed. 'Your drawing we must have at any rate.'

'Ah, but I forbid you to use it! This gentleman is my witness that my prohibition is absolute.'

'Was it to be your witness that you sent for the gentleman?
You take immense precautions!' Mr. Beston exclaimed. Be-
fore she could retort, however, he came back to his strong point.
'Do you coolly ask of me to sacrifice ten thousand subscribers?'

The number, I noticed, had grown since the morning, but
Miss Delavoy faced it boldly. 'If you do, you'll be well rid of
them. They must be ignoble, your ten thousand subscribers.'

He took this perfectly. 'You dispose of them easy! Ignoble
or not, what I have to do is to keep them and if possible add
to their number; not to get rid of them.'

'You'd rather get rid of my poor brother instead?'

'I don't get rid of him. I pay him a signal attention. Reduc-
ing it to the least, I publish his portrait.'

'His portrait — the only one worth speaking of? Why, you
turn it out with horror.'

'Do you call the only one worth speaking of that misguided
effort?' And, obeying a restless impulse, he appeared to reach
for my tribute; not, I think, with any conscious plan, but with
a vague desire in some way again to point his moral with it.

I liked immensely the motion with which, in reply to this,
she put it behind her: her gesture expressed so distinctly her
vision of her own lesson. From that moment, somehow, they
struck me as forgetting me, and I seemed to see them as they
might have been alone together; even to see a little what, for
each, had held and what had divided them. I remember how,
at this, I almost held my breath, effacing myself to let them
go, make them show me whatever they might. 'It's the only
one,' she insisted, 'that tells, about its subject, anything that's
any one's business. If you really want John Delavoy, there he
is. If you don't want him, don't insult him with an evasion
and a pretence. Have at least the courage to say that you're
afraid of him!'

I figured Mr. Beston here as much incommoded; but all too

simply, doubtless, for he clearly held on, smiling through flushed discomfort and on the whole bearing up. 'Do you think I'm afraid of *you* ?' He might forget me, but he would have to forget me a little more to yield completely to his visible impulse to take her hand. It was visible enough to herself to make her show that she declined to meet it, and even that his effect on her was at last distinctly exasperating. Oh, how I saw at that moment that in the really touching good faith of his personal sympathy he didn't measure his effect! If he had done so he wouldn't have tried to rush it, to carry it off with tenderness. He dropped to that now so rashly that I was in truth sorry for him. 'You *could* do so gracefully, so naturally, what we want. What we want, don't you see? is perfect taste. I know better than you do yourself how perfect yours would be. I always know better than people do themselves.' He jested and pleaded, getting in, benightedly, deeper. Perhaps I didn't literally hear him ask in the same accents if she didn't care for him at all, but I distinctly saw him look as if he were on the point of it, and something, at any rate, in a lower tone, dropped from him that he followed up with the statement that if she did even just a little she would help him.

VII

SHE made him wait a deep minute for her answer to this, and that gave me time to read into it what he accused her of failing to do. I recollect that I was startled at their having come so far, though I was reassured, after a little, by seeing that he had come much the furthest. I had now I scarce know what amused sense of knowing our hostess so much better than he. 'I think you strangely inconsequent,' she said at last. 'If you associate with — what you speak of — the idea of help, does it strike you as helping *me* to treat in that base fashion the memory I most honour and cherish?' As I was quite sure of what he spoke of, I could measure the force of this challenge. 'Have you never discovered, all this time, that my brother's work is my pride and my joy?'

'Oh, my dear thing!'—and Mr. Beston broke into a cry that combined in the drollest way the attempt to lighten his guilt with the attempt to deprecate hers. He let it just flash upon us that, should he be pushed, he would show as—well, scandalised.

The tone in which Miss Delavoy again addressed him offered a reflection of this gleam. 'Do you know what my brother would think of you?'

He was quite ready with his answer, and there was no moment in the whole business at which I thought so well of him. 'I don't care a hang what your brother would think!'

'Then why do you wish to commemorate him?'

'How can you ask so innocent a question? It isn't for *him.*'

'You mean it's for the public?'

'It's for the magazine,' he said with a noble simplicity.

'The magazine *is* the public,' it made me so far forget myself as to suggest.

'You've discovered it late in the day! Yes,' he went on to our companion, 'I don't in the least mind saying I don't care. I don't—I don't!' he repeated with a sturdiness in which I somehow recognised that he was, after all, a great editor. He looked at me a moment as if he even guessed what I saw, and, not unkindly, desired to force it home. 'I don't care for anybody. It's not my business to care. That's not the way to run a magazine. Except of course as a mere man!'—and he added a smile for Miss Delavoy. He covered the whole ground again. 'Your reminiscences would make a talk!'

She came back from the greatest distance she had yet reached. 'My reminiscences?'

'To accompany the head.' He must have been as tender as if I had been away. 'Don't I see how you'd do them?'

She turned off, standing before the fire and looking into it;

after which she faced him again.   'If you'll publish our friend here, I'll do them.'

'Why are you so awfully wound up about our friend here?'

'Read his article over — with a little intelligence — and your question will be answered.'

Mr. Beston glanced at me and smiled as if with a loyal warning; then, with a good conscience, he let me have it. 'Oh, damn his article!'

I was struck with her replying exactly what I should have replied if I had not been so detached.   'Damn it as much as you like, but publish it.'   Mr. Beston, on this, turned to me as if to ask me if I had not heard enough to satisfy me : there was a visible offer in his face to give me more if I insisted. This amounted to an appeal to me to leave the room at least for a minute ; and it was perhaps from the fear of what might pass between us that Miss Delavoy once more took him up. 'If my brother's as vile as you say —— !'

'Oh, I don't say *he*'s vile!' he broke in.

'You only say *I* am!' I commented.

'You've entered so into him,' she replied to me, 'that it comes to the same thing.   And Mr. Beston says further that out of this unmentionableness he wants somehow to make something — some money or some sensation.'

'My dear lady,' said Mr. Beston, 'it's a very great literary figure!'

'Precisely.   You advertise yourself with it because it's a very great literary figure, and it's a very great literary figure because it wrote very great literary things that you wouldn't for the world allow to be intelligibly or critically named.   So you bid for the still more striking tribute of an intimate picture — an unveiling of God knows what! — without even having the pluck or the logic to say on what ground it is that you go in for naming him at all.   Do you know, dear Mr. Beston,' she asked, 'that you make me very sick?   I count on

receiving the portrait,' she concluded, 'by to-morrow evening
at latest.'

I felt, before this speech was over, so sorry for her interlocutor that I was on the point of asking her if she mightn't
finish him without my help. But I had lighted a flame that
was to consume me too, and I was aware of the scorch of it
while I watched Mr. Beston plead frankly, if tacitly, that,
though there was something in him not to be finished, she
must yet give him a moment and let him take his time to look
about him at pictures and books. He took it with more cool-
ness than I; then he produced his answer. 'You shall receive
it to-morrow morning if you'll do what I asked the last time.'
I could see more than he how the last time had been overlaid
by what had since come up; so that, as she opposed a momen-
tary blank, I felt almost a coarseness in his recall of it with
an 'Oh, you know — you know!'

Yes, after a little she knew, and I need scarcely add that I
did. I felt, in the oddest way, by this time, that she was
conscious of my penetration and wished to make me, for the
loss now so clearly beyond repair, the only compensation in
her power. This compensation consisted of her showing me
that she was indifferent to my having guessed the full extent
of the privilege that, on the occasion to which he alluded, she
had permitted Mr. Beston to put before her. The balm for
my wound was therefore to see what she resisted. She resisted Mr. Beston in more ways than one. 'And if I don't do
it?' she demanded.

'I'll simply keep your picture!'

To what purpose if you don't use it?'

'To keep it *is* to use it,' Mr. Beston said.

'He has only to keep it long enough,' I added, and with the
intention that may be imagined, 'to bring you round, by the
mere sense of privation, to meet him on the other ground.'

Miss Delavoy took no more notice of this speech than if she
had not heard it, and Mr. Beston showed that he had heard it

only enough to show, more markedly, that he followed her example. 'I'll do anything, I'll do everything for you in life,' he declared to her, 'but publish such a thing as that.'

She gave in all decorum to this statement the minute of concentration that belonged to it; but her analysis of the matter had for sole effect to make her at last bring out, not with harshness, but with a kind of wondering pity: 'I think you're really very dreadful!'

'In what esteem then, Mr. Beston,' I asked, 'do you hold John Delavoy's work?'

He rang out clear. 'As the sort of thing that's out of our purview!' If for a second he had hesitated it was partly, I judge, with just resentment at my so directly addressing him, and partly, though he wished to show our friend that he fairly faced the question, because experience had not left him in such a case without two or three alternatives. He had already made plain indeed that he mostly preferred the simplest.

'Wonderful, wonderful purview!' I quite sincerely, or at all events very musingly, exclaimed.

'Then, if you could ever have got one of his novels——?' Miss Delavoy inquired.

He smiled at the way she put it; it made such an image of the attitude of *The Cynosure*. But he was kind and explicit. 'There isn't one that wouldn't have been beyond us. We could never have run him. We could never have handled him. We could never, in fact, have touched him. We should have dropped to—oh, Lord!' He saw the ghastly figure he couldn't name—he brushed it away with a shudder.

I turned, on this, to our companion. 'I wish awfully you'd do what he asks!' She stared an instant, mystified; then I quickly explained to which of his requests I referred. 'I mean I wish you'd do the nice familiar chat about the sweet home-life. You might make it inimitable, and, upon my word, I'd give you for it the assistance of my general lights. The thing is—don't you see?—that it would put Mr. Beston in a grand position. Your position would be grand,' I hastened to add as I looked at him, 'because it would be so admirably false.' Then, more seriously, I felt the impulse even to warn him. 'I don't think you're quite aware of what you'd make it. Are you really quite conscious?' I went on with a benevolence that struck him, I was presently to learn, as a depth of fatuity.

He was to show once more that he was a rock. 'Conscious? Why should I be? Nobody's conscious.'

He was splendid; yet before I could control it I had risked the challenge of a 'Nobody?'

'Who's anybody? The public isn't!'

'Then why are you afraid of it?' Miss Delavoy demanded.

'Don't ask him that,' I answered; 'you expose yourself to his telling you that, if the public isn't anybody, that's still more the case with your brother.'

Mr. Beston appeared to accept as a convenience this somewhat inadequate protection; he at any rate under cover of it again addressed us lucidly. 'There's only one false position — the one you seem so to wish to put me in.'

I instantly met him. 'That of losing —— ?'

'That of losing —— !'

'Oh, fifty thousand — yes. And they wouldn't see anything the matter —— ?'

'With the position,' said Mr. Beston, 'that you qualify, I neither know nor care why, as false.' Suddenly, in a different tone, almost genially, he continued: 'For what do you take them?'

For what indeed? — but it didn't signify. 'It's enough that I take *you* — for one of the masters.' It's literal that as he stood there in his florid beauty and complete command I felt his infinite force, and, with a gush of admiration, wondered how, for our young lady, there could be at such a moment another man. 'We represent different sides,' I rather lamely said. However, I picked up. 'It isn't a question of where we are, but of what. You're not on a side — you *are* a side.

You're the right one. What a misery,' I pursued, 'for us not to be "on" you!'

His eyes showed me for a second that he yet saw how our not being on him did just have for it that it could facilitate such a speech; then they rested afresh on Miss Delavoy, and that brought him back to firm ground. 'I don't think you can imagine how it will come out.'

He was astride of the portrait again, and presently again she had focussed him. 'If it does come out——!' she began, poor girl; but it was not to take her far.

'Well, if it does——?'

'He means what will you do then?' I observed, as she had nothing to say.

'Mr. Beston will see,' she at last replied with a perceptible lack of point.

He took this up in a flash. 'My dear young lady, it's *you* who'll see; and when you've seen you'll forgive me. Only wait till you do!' He was already at the door, as if he quite believed in what he should gain by the gain, from this moment, of time. He stood there but an instant — he looked from one of us to the other. 'It will be a ripping little thing!' he remarked; and with that he left us gaping.

VIII

THE first use I made of our rebound was to say with intensity: 'What *will* you do if he does?'

'Does publish the picture?' There was an instant charm to me in the privacy of her full collapse and the sudden high tide of our common defeat. 'What *can* I? It's all very well; but there's nothing to be done. I want never to see him again. There's only something,' she went on, 'that *you* can do.'

'Prevent him? — get it back? I'll do, be sure, my utmost; but it will be difficult without a row.'

'What do you mean by a row?' she asked.

'I mean it will be difficult without publicity. I don't think we want publicity.'

She turned this over. 'Because it will advertise him?'

'His magnificent energy. Remember what I just now told him. He's the right side.'

'And we're the wrong!' she laughed. 'We mustn't make that known — I see. But, all the same, save my sketch!'

I held her hands. 'And if I do?'

'Ah, get it back first!' she answered, ever so gently and with a smile, but quite taking them away.

I got it back, alas! neither first nor last; though indeed at the end this was to matter, as I thought and as I found, little enough. Mr. Beston rose to his full height and was not to abate an inch even on my offer of another article on a subject notoriously unobjectionable. The only portrait of John Delavoy was going, as he had said, to take, and nothing was to stand in its way. I besieged his office, I waylaid his myrmidons, I haunted his path, I poisoned, I tried to flatter myself, his life; I wrote him at any rate letters by the dozen and showed him up to his friends and his enemies. The only thing I didn't do was to urge Miss Delavoy to write to her solicitors or to the newspapers. The final result, of course, of what I did and what I didn't was to create, on the subject of the sole copy of so rare an original, a curiosity that, by the time *The Cynosure* appeared with the reproduction, made the month's sale, as I was destined to learn, take a tremendous jump. The portrait of John Delavoy, prodigiously 'paragraphed' in advance and with its authorship flushing through, was accompanied by a page or two, from an anonymous hand, of the pleasantest, liveliest comment. The press was genial, the success immense, current criticism had never flowed so full, and it was universally felt that the handsome thing had been done. The process employed by Mr. Beston had left, as he had promised, nothing to be desired; and the sketch itself, the next week, arrived in safety, and with only a smutch or two, by the post. I placed my article, naturally, in another magazine, but was disappointed, I confess, as to what it discoverably did in literary circles for its subject. This ache, however, was muffled. There was a worse victim than I, and there was consolation of a sort in our having out together the question of literary circles. The great orb of *The Cynosure*, wasn't that a literary circle? By the time we had fairly to face this question we had achieved the union that — at least for resistance or endurance — is supposed to be strength.

THE THIRD PERSON

I

WHEN, a few years since, two good ladies, previously not intimate nor indeed more than slightly acquainted, found themselves domiciled together in the small but ancient town of Marr, it was as a result, naturally, of special considerations. They bore the same name and were second cousins; but their paths had not hitherto crossed; there had not been coincidence of age to draw them together; and Miss Frush, the more mature, had spent much of her life abroad. She was a bland, shy, sketching person, whom fate had condemned to a monotony — triumphing over variety — of Swiss and Italian *pensions;* in any one of which, with her well-fastened hat, her gauntlets and her stout boots, her camp-stool, her sketch-book, her Tauchnitz novel, she would have served with peculiar propriety as a frontispiece to the natural history of the English old maid. She would have struck you indeed, poor Miss Frush, as so happy an instance of the type that you would perhaps scarce have been able to equip her with the dignity of the individual. This was what she enjoyed, however, for those brought nearer — a very insistent identity, once even of prettiness, but which now, blanched and bony, timid and inordinately queer, with its utterance all vague interjection and its aspect all eyeglass and teeth, might be acknowledged without inconvenience and deplored without reserve. Miss Amy, her kinswoman, who, ten years her junior, showed a different figure — such as, oddly enough, though formed almost wholly in English air, might have appeared much more to betray a foreign influence — Miss Amy was brown, brisk,

and expressive: when really young she had even been pronounced showy. She had an innocent vanity on the subject
of her foot, a member which she somehow regarded as a guarantee of her wit, or at least of her good taste. Even had it
not been pretty she flattered herself it would have been shod:
she would never — no, never, like Susan — have given it up.
Her bright brown eye was comparatively bold, and she had
accepted Susan once for all as a frump. She even thought
her, and silently deplored her as, a goose. But she was none
the less herself a lamb.

They had benefited, this innocuous pair, under the will of
an old aunt, a prodigiously ancient gentlewoman, of whom, in
her later time, it had been given them, mainly by the office
of others, to see almost nothing; so that the little property
they came in for had the happy effect of a windfall. Each, at
least, pretended to the other that she had never dreamed — as
in truth there had been small encouragement for dreams in
the sad character of what they now spoke of as the late lady's
'dreadful *entourage.*' Terrorised and deceived, as they considered, by her own people, Mrs. Frush was scantily enough
to have been counted on for an act of almost inspired justice.
The good luck of her husband's nieces was that she had really
outlived, for the most part, their ill-wishers and so, at the
very last, had died without the blame of diverting fine Frush
property from fine Frush use. Property quite of her own she
had done as she liked with; but she had pitied poor expa-
triated Susan and had remembered poor unhusbanded Amy,
though lumping them together perhaps a little roughly in her
final provision. Her will directed that, should no other
arrangement be more convenient to her executors, the old
house at Marr might be sold for their joint advantage. What
befell, however, in the event, was that the two legatees,
advised in due course, took an early occasion — and quite
without concert — to judge their prospects on the spot. They
arrived at Marr, each on her own side, and they were so

pleased with Marr that they remained. So it was that they met: Miss Amy, accompanied by the office-boy of the local solicitor, presented herself at the door of the house to ask admittance of the caretaker. But when the door opened it offered to sight not the caretaker, but an unexpected, unexpecting lady in a very old waterproof, who held a long-handled eyeglass very much as a child holds a rattle. Miss Susan, already in the field, roaming, prying, meditating in the absence on an errand of the woman in charge, offered herself in this manner as in settled possession; and it was on that idea that, through the eyeglass, the cousins viewed each other with some penetration even before Amy came in. Then at last when Amy did come in it was not, any more than Susan, to go out again.

It would take us too far to imagine what might have happened had Mrs. Frush made it a condition of her benevolence that the subjects of it should inhabit, should live at peace together, under the roof she left them; but certain it is that as they stood there they had at the same moment the same unprompted thought. Each became aware on the spot that the dear old house itself was exactly what she, and exactly what the other, wanted; it met in perfection their longing for a quiet harbour and an assured future; each, in short, was willing to take the other in order to get the house. It was therefore not sold; it was made, instead, their own, as it stood, with the dead lady's extremely 'good' old appurtenances not only undisturbed and undivided, but piously reconstructed and infinitely admired, the agents of her testamentary purpose rejoicing meanwhile to see the business so simplified. They might have had their private doubts — or their wives might have; might cynically have predicted the sharpest of quarrels, before three months were out, between the deluded yoke-fellows, and the dissolution of the partnership with every circumstance of recrimination. All that need be said is that such prophets would have prophesied vulgarly.

The Misses Frush were not vulgar; they had drunk deep of the cup of singleness and found it prevailingly bitter; they were not unacquainted with solitude and sadness, and they recognised with due humility the supreme opportunity of their lives. By the end of three months, moreover, each knew the worst about the other. Miss Amy took her evening nap before dinner, an hour at which Miss Susan could never sleep — it was so odd; whereby Miss Susan took hers after that meal, just at the hour when Miss Amy was keenest for talk. Miss Susan, erect and unsupported, had feelings as to the way in which, in almost any posture that could pass for a seated one, Miss Amy managed to find a place in the small of her back for two out of the three sofa-cushions — a smaller place, obviously, than they had ever been intended to fit.

But when this was said all was said; they continued to have, on either side, the pleasant consciousness of a personal soil, not devoid of fragmentary ruins, to dig in. They had a theory that their lives had been immensely different, and each appeared now to the other to have conducted her career so perversely only that she should have an unfamiliar range of anecdote for her companion's ear. Miss Susan, at foreign *pensions*, had met the Russian, the Polish, the Danish, and even an occasional flower of the English, nobility, as well as many of the most extraordinary Americans, who, as she said, had made everything of her and with whom she had remained, often, in correspondence; while Miss Amy, after all less conventional, at the end of long years of London, abounded in reminiscences of literary, artistic, and even — Miss Susan heard it with bated breath — theatrical society, under the influence of which she had written — there, it came out! — a novel that had been anonymously published and a play that had been strikingly type-copied. Not the least charm, clearly, of this picturesque outlook at Marr would be the support that might be drawn from it for getting back, as she hinted, with 'general society' bravely sacrificed, to 'real work.' She had in her head hundreds of plots — with which the future, accordingly, seemed to bristle for Miss Susan. The latter, on her side, was only waiting for the wind to go down to take up again her sketching. The wind at Marr was often high, as was natural in a little old huddled, red-roofed, historic south-coast town which had once been in a manner mistress, as the cousins reminded each other, of the 'Channel,' and from which, high and dry on its hilltop though it might be, the sea had not so far receded as not to give, constantly, a taste of temper. Miss Susan came back to English scenery with a small sigh of fondness to which the consciousness of Alps and Apennines only gave more of a quaver; she had picked out her subjects and, with her head on one side and a sense that they were easier abroad, sat sucking her water-colour brush and nervously — perhaps even a little inconsistently — waiting and hesitating. What had happened was that they had, each for herself, re-discovered the country; only Miss Amy, emergent from Bloomsbury lodgings, spoke of it as primroses and sunsets, and Miss Susan, rebounding from the Arno and the Reuss, called it, with a shy, synthetic pride, simply England.

The country was at any rate in the house with them as well as in the little green girdle and in the big blue belt. It was in the objects and relics that they handled together and wondered over, finding in them a ground for much inferred importance and invoked romance, stuffing large stories into very small openings and pulling every faded bell-rope that might jingle rustily into the past. They were still here in the presence, at all events, of their common ancestors, as to whom, more than ever before, they took only the best for granted. Was not the best, for that matter, — the best, that is, of little melancholy, middling, disinherited Marr, — seated in every stiff chair of the decent old house and stitched into the patchwork of every quaint old counterpane? Two hundred years of it squared themselves in the brown, panelled parlour, creaked patiently on the wide staircase, and bloomed herba-

ceously in the red-walled garden.   There was nothing any one
had ever done or been at Marr that a Frush hadn't done it or
been it.   Yet they wanted more of a picture and talked themselves into the fancy of it; there were portraits — half a
dozen, comparatively recent (they called 1800 comparatively
recent), and something of a trial to a descendant who had
copied Titian at the Pitti; but they were curious of detail and
would have liked to people a little more thickly their backward space, to set it up behind their chairs as a screen
embossed with figures.   They threw off theories and small
imaginations, and almost conceived themselves engaged in
researches; all of which made for pomp and circumstance.
Their desire was to discover something, and, emboldened by
the broader sweep of wing of her companion, Miss Susan herself was not afraid of discovering something bad.   Miss Amy
it was who had first remarked, as a warning, that this was
what it might all lead to.   It was she, moreover, to whom
they owed the formula that, had anything *very* bad ever happened at Marr, they should be sorry if a Frush hadn't been in
it.   This was the moment at which Miss Susan's spirit had
reached its highest point: she had declared, with her odd,
breathless laugh, a prolonged, an alarmed or alarming gasp,
that she should really be quite ashamed.   And so they rested
awhile; not saying quite how far they were prepared to go in
crime — not giving the matter a name.   But there would have
been little doubt for an observer that each supposed the other
to mean that she not only didn't draw the line at murder, but
stretched it so as to take in — well, gay deception.   If Miss
Susan could conceivably have asked whether Don Juan had
ever touched at that port, Miss Amy would, to a certainty,
have wanted to know by way of answer at what port he had
not touched.   It was only unfortunately true that no one of
the portraits of gentlemen looked at all like him and no one of
those of ladies suggested one of his victims.

At last, none the less, the cousins had a find, came upon a

box of old odds and ends, mainly documentary; partly printed matter, newspapers and pamphlets yellow and grey with time, and, for the rest, epistolary — several packets of letters, faded, scarce decipherable, but clearly sorted for preservation and tied, with sprigged ribbon of a far-away fashion, into little groups. Marr, below ground, is solidly founded — underlaid with great straddling cellars, sound and dry, that are like the groined crypts of churches and that present themselves to the meagre modern conception as the treasure-chambers of stout merchants and bankers in the old bustling days. A recess in the thickness of one of the walls had yielded up, on resolute investigation — that of the local youth employed for odd jobs and who had happened to explore in this direction on his own account — a collection of rusty superfluities among which the small chest in question had been dragged to light. It produced of course an instant impression and figured as a discovery; though indeed as rather a deceptive one on its having, when forced open, nothing better to show, at the best, than a quantity of rather illegible correspondence. The good ladies had naturally had for the moment a fluttered hope of old golden guineas — a miser's hoard; perhaps even of a hatful of those foreign coins of old-fashioned romance, ducats, doubloons, pieces of eight, as are sometimes found to have come to hiding, from over seas, in ancient ports. But they had to accept their disappointment — which they sought to do by making the best of the papers, by agreeing, in other words, to regard them as wonderful. Well, they *were*, doubtless, wonderful; which didn't prevent them, however, from appearing to be, on superficial inspection, also rather a weary labyrinth. Baffling, at any rate, to Miss Susan's unpractised eyes, the little pale-ribboned packets were, for several evenings, round the fire, while she luxuriously dozed, taken in hand by Miss Amy; with the result that on a certain occasion when, toward nine o'clock, Miss Susan woke up, she found her fellow-labourer fast asleep. A slightly irritated confes-

sion of ignorance of the Gothic character was the further consequence, and the upshot of this, in turn, was the idea of
appeal to Mr. Patten. Mr. Patten was the vicar and was
known to interest himself, as such, in the ancient annals of
Marr; in addition to which — and to its being even held a
little that his sense of the affairs of the hour was sometimes
sacrificed to such inquiries — he was a gentleman with a humour
of his own, a flushed face, a bushy eyebrow, and a black wide-
awake worn sociably askew. 'He will tell us,' said Amy
Frush, 'if there's anything in them.'

'Yet if it should be,' Susan suggested, 'anything we mayn't
like?'

'Well, that's just what I'm thinking of,' returned Miss
Amy in her offhand way. 'If it's anything we shouldn't
know ——'

'We've only to tell him not to tell us? Oh, certainly,' said
mild Miss Susan. She took upon herself even to give him
that warning when, on the invitation of our friends, Mr.
Patten came to tea and to talk things over; Miss Amy sitting
by and raising no protest, but distinctly promising herself
that, whatever there might be to be known, and however objectionable, she would privately get it out of their initiator.
She found herself already hoping that it *would* be something
too bad for her cousin — too bad for any one else at all — to
know, and that it most properly might remain between them.
Mr. Patten, at sight of the papers, exclaimed, perhaps a trifle
ambiguously, and by no means clerically, 'My eye, what a
lark!' and retired, after three cups of tea, in an overcoat
bulging with his spoil.

II

AT ten o'clock that evening the pair separated, as usual,
on the upper landing, outside their respective doors, for the
night; but Miss Amy had hardly set down her candle on her

dressing-table before she was startled by an extraordinary sound, which appeared to proceed not only from her companion's room, but from her companion's throat. It was something she would have described, had she ever described it, as between a gurgle and a shriek, and it brought Amy Frush, after an interval of stricken stillness that gave her just time to say to herself 'Some one under her bed!' breathlessly and bravely back to the landing. She had not reached it, however, before her neighbour, bursting in, met her and stayed her.

'There's some one in my room!'

They held each other. 'But who?'

'A man.'

'Under the bed?'

'No — just standing there.'

They continued to hold each other, but they rocked. 'Standing? Where? How?'

'Why, right in the middle — before my dressing-glass.'

Amy's blanched face by this time matched her mate's, but its terror was enhanced by speculation. 'To look at himself?'

'No — with his back to it. To look at *me*,' poor Susan just audibly breathed. 'To keep me off,' she quavered. 'In strange clothes — of another age; with his head on one side.'

Amy wondered. 'On one side?'

'Awfully!' the refugee declared while, clinging together, they sounded each other.

This, somehow, for Miss Amy, was the convincing touch; and on it, after a moment, she was capable of the effort of darting back to close her own door. 'You'll remain then with me.'

'Oh!' Miss Susan wailed with deep assent; quite, as if, had she been a slangy person, she would have ejaculated 'Rather!' So they spent the night together; with the assumption thus marked, from the first, both that it would have been vain to confront their visitor as they didn't even pretend to each other that they would have confronted a housebreaker; and that by leaving the place at his mercy nothing worse could happen than had already happened. It was Miss Amy's approaching the door again as with intent ear and after a hush that had represented between them a deep and extraordinary interchange — it was this that put them promptly face to face with the real character of the occurrence. 'Ah,' Miss Susan, still under her breath, portentously exclaimed, 'it isn't any one —— !'

'No' — her partner was already able magnificently to take her up. 'It isn't any one ——'

'Who can really hurt us' — Miss Susan completed her thought. And Miss Amy, as it proved, had been so indescribably prepared that this thought, before morning, had, in the strangest, finest way, made for itself an admirable place with them. The person the elder of our pair had seen in her room was not — well, just simply was not any one in from outside. He was a different thing altogether. Miss Amy had felt it as soon as she heard her friend's cry and become aware of her commotion; as soon, at all events, as she saw Miss Susan's face. That was all — and there it was. There had been something hitherto wanting, they felt, to their small state and importance; it was present now, and they were as handsomely conscious of it as if they had previously missed it. The element in question, then, was a third person in their association, a hovering presence for the dark hours, a figure that with its head very much — too much — on one side, could be trusted to look at them out of unnatural places; yet only, it doubtless might be assumed, to look at them. They had it at last — had what was to be had in an old house where many, too many, things had happened, where the very walls they touched and floors they trod could have told secrets and named names, where every surface was a blurred mirror of life and death, of the endured, the remembered, the forgotten. Yes; the place was h——, but they stopped at sounding the word.

And by morning, wonderful to say, they were used to it — had quite lived into it.

Not only this indeed, but they had their prompt theory. There was a connection between the finding of the box in the vault and the appearance in Miss Susan's room. The heavy air of the past had been stirred by the bringing to light of what had so long been hidden. The communication of the papers to Mr. Patten had had its effect. They faced each other in the morning at breakfast over the certainty that their queer roused inmate was the sign of the violated secret of these relics. No matter; for the sake of the secret they would put up with his attention; and — this, in them, was most beautiful of all — they must, though he was such an addition to their grandeur, keep him quite to themselves. Other people might hear of what was in the letters, but they should never hear of *him*. They were not afraid that either of the maids should see him — he was not a matter for maids. The question indeed was whether — should he keep it up long — they themselves would find that they could really live with him. Yet perhaps his keeping it up would be just what would make them indifferent. They turned these things over, but spent the next nights together; and on the third day, in the course of their afternoon walk, descried at a distance the vicar, who, as soon as he saw them, waved his arms violently — either as a warning or as a joke — and came more than halfway to meet them. It was in the middle — or what passed for such — of the big, bleak, blank, melancholy square of Marr; a public place, as it were, of such an absurd capacity for a crowd; with the great ivy-mantled choir and stopped transept of the nobly planned church, telling of how many centuries ago it had, for its part, given up growing.

'Why, my dear ladies,' cried Mr. Patten as he approached, 'do you know what, of all things in the world, I seem to make out for you from your funny old letters?' Then as they waited, extremely on their guard now: 'Neither more nor less, if you please, than that one of your ancestors in the last century — Mr. Cuthbert Frush, it would seem, by name — was hanged.'

They never knew afterwards which of the two had first found composure — found even dignity — to respond. 'And pray, Mr. Patten, for what?'

'Ah, that's just what I don't yet get hold of. But if you don't mind my digging away' — and the vicar's bushy, jolly brows turned from one of the ladies to the other — 'I think I can run it to earth. They hanged, in those days, you know,' he added as if he had seen something in their faces, 'for almost any trifle!'

'Oh, I hope it wasn't for a trifle!' Miss Susan strangely tittered.

'Yes, of course one would like that, while he was about it — well, it had been, as they say,' Mr. Patten laughed, 'rather for a sheep than for a lamb!'

'Did they hang at that time for a sheep?' Miss Amy wonderingly asked.

It made their friend laugh again. 'The question's whether *he* did! But we'll find out. Upon my word, you know, I quite want to myself. I'm awfully busy, but I think I can promise you that you shall hear. You *don't* mind?' he insisted.

'I think we could bear *anything*,' said Miss Amy.

Miss Susan gazed at her, on this, as for reference and appeal. 'And what is he, after all, at this time of day, *to* us?'

Her kinswoman, meeting the eyeglass fixedly, spoke with gravity. 'Oh, an ancestor's always an ancestor.'

'Well said and well felt, dear lady!' the vicar declared. 'Whatever they may have done——'

'It isn't every one,' Miss Amy replied, 'that has them to be ashamed of.'

'And we're not ashamed *yet!*' Miss Frush jerked out.

'Let me promise you then that you shan't be. Only, for I am busy,' said Mr. Patten, 'give me time.'

'Ah, but we want the truth!' they cried with high emphasis as he quitted them. They were much excited now.

He answered by pulling up and turning round as short as if his professional character had been challenged. 'Isn't it just in the truth — and the truth only — that I deal?'

This they recognised as much as his love of a joke, and so they were left there together in the pleasant, if slightly over-done, void of the square, which wore at moments the air of a conscious demonstration, intended as an appeal, of the shrink-age of the population of Marr to a solitary cat. They walked on after a little, but they waited till the vicar was ever so far away before they spoke again; all the more that their doing so must bring them once more to a pause. Then they had a long look. 'Hanged!' said Miss Amy — yet almost exultantly.

This was, however, because it was not she who had seen. 'That's why his head——' but Miss Susan faltered.

Her companion took it in. 'Oh, has such a dreadful twist?'

'It *is* dreadful!' Miss Susan at last dropped, speaking as if she had been present at twenty executions.

There would have been no saying, at any rate, what it didn't evoke from Miss Amy. 'It breaks their neck,' she contributed after a moment.

Miss Susan looked away. 'That's why, I suppose, the head turns so fearfully awry. It's a most peculiar effect.'

So peculiar, it might have seemed, that it made them silent afresh. 'Well, then, I hope he killed some one!' Miss Amy broke out at last.

Her companion thought. 'Wouldn't it depend on whom —— ?'

'No!' she returned with her characteristic briskness — a briskness that set them again into motion.

That Mr. Patten was tremendously busy was evident indeed, as even by the end of the week he had nothing more to impart. The whole thing meanwhile came up again — on the Sunday afternoon; as the younger Miss Frush had been quite confident that, from one day to the other, it must. They went inveterately to evening church, to the close of which supper was postponed; and Miss Susan, on this occasion, ready the first, patiently awaited her mate at the foot of the stairs. Miss Amy at last came down, buttoning a glove, rustling the tail of a frock, and looking, as her kinswoman always thought, conspicuously young and smart. There was no one at Marr, she held, who dressed like her; and Miss Amy, it must be owned, had also settled to this view of Miss Susan, though taking it in a different spirit. Dusk had gathered, but our frugal pair were always tardy lighters, and the grey close of day, in which the elder lady, on a high-backed hall chair, sat with hands patiently folded, had for all cheer the subdued glow — always subdued — of the small fire in the drawing-room, visible through a door that stood open. Into the drawing-room Miss Amy passed in search of the prayer-book she had laid down there after morning church, and from it, after a minute, without this volume, she returned to her companion. There was something in her movement that spoke — spoke for a moment so largely that nothing more was said till, with a quick unanimity, they had got themselves straight out of the house. There, before the door, in the cold, still twilight of the winter's end, while the church bells rang and the windows of the great choir showed across the empty square faintly red, they had it out again. But it was Miss Susan herself, this time, who had to bring it.

'He's there?'

'Before the fire — with his back to it.'

'Well, now you see!' Miss Susan exclaimed with elation and as if her friend had hitherto doubted her.

'Yes, I see — and what you mean.' Miss Amy was deeply thoughtful.

'About his head?'

'It *is* on one side,' Miss Amy went on. 'It makes him ——'
she considered. But she faltered as if still in his presence.

'It makes him awful!' Miss Susan murmured. 'The way,' she softly moaned, 'he looks at you!'

Miss Amy, with a glance, met this recognition. 'Yes — doesn't he?' Then her eyes attached themselves to the red windows of the church. 'But it means something.'

'The Lord knows what it means!' her associate gloomily sighed. Then, after an instant, 'Did he move?' Miss Susan asked.

'No — and *I* didn't.'

'Oh, I did!' Miss Susan declared, recalling her more precipitous retreat.

'I mean I took my time. I waited.'

'To see him fade?'

Miss Amy for a moment said nothing. 'He doesn't fade. That's *it*.'

'Oh, then you did move!' her relative rejoined.

Again for a little she was silent. 'One *has* to. But I don't know what really happened. Of course I came back to you. What I mean is that I took him thoroughly in. He's young,' she added.

'But he's *bad!*' said Miss Susan.

'He's handsome!' Miss Amy brought out after a moment. And she showed herself even prepared to continue: 'Splendidly.'

'"Splendidly"! — with his neck broken and with that terrible look?'

'It's just the look that makes him so. It's the wonderful eyes. They mean something,' Amy Frush brooded.

She spoke with a decision of which Susan presently betrayed the effect. 'And what do they mean?'

Her friend had stared again at the glimmering windows of St. Thomas of Canterbury. 'That it's time we should get to church.'

III

THE curate that evening did duty alone; but on the morrow the vicar called and, as soon as he got into the room, let them again have it. 'He was hanged for smuggling!'

They stood there before him almost cold in their surprise and diffusing an air in which, somehow, this misdemeanour sounded out as the coarsest of all. '*Smuggling?*' Miss Susan disappointedly echoed — as if it presented itself to the first chill of their apprehension that he had, then, only been vulgar.

'Ah, but they hanged for it freely, you know, and I was an idiot for not having taken it, in his case, for granted. If a man swung, hereabouts, it *was* mostly for that. Don't you know it's on that we stand here to-day, such as we are — on the fact of what our bold, bad forefathers were not afraid of? It's in the floors we walk on and under the roofs that cover us. They smuggled so hard that they never had time to do anything else; and if they broke a head not their own it was only in the awkwardness of landing their brandy-kegs. I mean, dear ladies,' good Mr. Patten wound up, 'no disrespect to *your* forefathers when I tell you that — as I've rather been supposing that, like all the rest of us, you were aware — they conveniently lived by it.'

Miss Susan wondered — visibly almost doubted. 'Gentle-folks?'

'It was the gentlefolks who were the worst.'

'They must have been the bravest!' Miss Amy interjected. She had listened to their visitor's free explanation with a rapid return of colour. 'And since if they lived by it they also died for it ——'

'There's nothing at all to be said against them? I quite agree with you,' the vicar laughed, 'for all my cloth; and I even go so far as to say, shocking as you may think me, that we owe them, in our shabby little shrunken present, the sense of a bustling background, a sort of undertone of romance.

s

They give us '— he humorously kept it up, verging perilously near, for his cloth, upon positive paradox —'our little handful of legend and our small possibility of ghosts.' He paused an instant, with his lighter pulpit manner, but the ladies exchanged no look. They were, in fact, already, with an immense revulsion, carried quite as far away. 'Every penny in the place, really, that hasn't been earned by subtler — not nobler — arts in our own virtuous time, and though it's a pity there are not more of 'em: every penny in the place was picked up, somehow, by a clever trick, and at the risk of your neck, when the backs of the king's officers were turned. It's shocking, you know, what I'm saying to you, and I wouldn't say it to every one, but I think of some of the shabby old things about us, that represent such pickings, with a sort of sneaking kindness — as of relics of our heroic age. What are we now? We were at any rate devils of fellows then!'

Susan Frush considered it all solemnly, struggling with the spell of this evocation. 'But must we forget that they were wicked?'

'Never!' Mr. Patten laughed. 'Thank you, dear friend, for reminding me. Only I'm worse than they!'

'But would you do it?'

'Murder a coastguard —— ?' The vicar scratched his head.

'I hope,' said Miss Amy rather surprisingly, 'you'd defend yourself.' And she gave Miss Susan a superior glance. '*I* would!' she distinctly added.

Her companion anxiously took it up. 'Would you defraud the revenue?'

Miss Amy hesitated but a moment; then with a strange laugh, which she covered, however, by turning instantly away, 'Yes!' she remarkably declared.

Their visitor, at this, amused and amusing, eagerly seized her arm. 'Then may I count on you on the stroke of midnight to help me —— ?'

'To help you——?'

'To land the last new Tauchnitz.'

She met the proposal as one whose fancy had kindled, while her cousin watched them as if they had suddenly improvised a drawing-room charade. 'A service of danger?'

'Under the cliff — when you see the lugger stand in!'

'Armed to the teeth?'

'Yes — but invisibly. Your old waterproof——!'

'Mine is new. I'll take Susan's!'

This good lady, however, had her reserves. 'Mayn't one of them, all the same — here and there — have been sorry?'

Mr. Patten wondered. 'For the jobs he muffed?'

'For the wrong — as it *was* wrong — he did.'

'"One" of them?' She had gone too far, for the vicar suddenly looked as if he divined in the question a reference.

They became, however, as promptly unanimous in meeting this danger, as to which Miss Susan in particular showed an inspired presence of mind. 'Two of them!' she sweetly smiled. 'May not Amy and I——?'

'Vicariously repent?' said Mr. Patten. 'That depends — for the true honour of Marr — on how you show it.'

'Oh, we *shan't* show it!' Miss Amy cried.

'Ah, then,' Mr. Patten returned, 'though atonements, to be efficient, are supposed to be public, you may do penance in secret as much as you please!'

'Well, *I* shall do it,' said Susan Frush.

Again, by something in her tone, the vicar's attention appeared to be caught. 'Have you then in view a particular form——?'

'Of atonement?' She coloured now, glaring rather helplessly, in spite of herself, at her companion. 'Oh, if you're sincere you'll always find one.'

Amy came to her assistance. 'The way she often treats me has made her — though there's after all no harm in her — familiar with remorse. Mayn't we, at any rate,' the younger lady continued, 'now have our letters back?' And the vicar left them with the assurance that they should receive the bundle on the morrow.

They were indeed so at one as to shrouding their mystery that no explicit agreement, no exchange of vows, needed to pass between them; they only settled down, from this moment, to an unshared possession of their secret, an economy in the use and, as may even be said, the enjoyment of it, that was part of their general instinct and habit of thrift. It had been the disposition, the practice, the necessity of each to keep, fairly indeed to clutch, everything that, as they often phrased it, came their way; and this was not the first time such an influence had determined for them an affirmation of property in objects to which ridicule, suspicion, or some other inconvenience might attach. It was their simple philosophy that one never knew of what service an odd object might *not* be; and there were days now on which they felt themselves to have made a better bargain with their aunt's executors than was witnessed in those law-papers which they had at first timorously regarded as the record of advantages taken of them in matters of detail. They had got, in short, more than was vulgarly, more than was even shrewdly supposed — such an indescribable unearned increment as might scarce more be divulged as a dread than as a delight. They drew together, old-maidishly, in a suspicious, invidious grasp of the idea that a dread of their very own — and blissfully not, of course, that of a failure of any essential supply — might, on nearer acquaintance, positively turn to a delight.

Upon some such attempted consideration of it, at all events, they found themselves embarking after their last interview with Mr. Patten, an understanding conveyed between them in no redundancy of discussion, no flippant repetitions nor profane recurrences, yet resting on a sense of added margin, of appropriated history, of liberties taken with time and space, that would leave them prepared both for the worst and for the best. The best would be that something that would turn out to their advantage might prove to be hidden about the place; the worst would be that they might find themselves growing to depend only too much on excitement. They found themselves amazingly reconciled, on Mr. Patten's information, to the particular character thus fixed on their visitor; they knew by tradition and fiction that even the highwaymen of the same picturesque age were often gallant gentlemen; therefore a smuggler, by such a measure, fairly belonged to the aristocracy of crime. When their packet of documents came back from the vicarage Miss Amy, to whom her associate continued to leave them, took them once more in hand; but with an effect, afresh, of discouragement and languor — a headachy sense of faded ink, of strange spelling and crabbed characters, of allusions she couldn't follow and parts she couldn't match. She placed the tattered papers piously together, wrapping them tenderly in a piece of old figured silken stuff; then, as solemnly as if they had been archives or statutes or title-deeds, laid them away in one of the several small cupboards lodged in the thickness of the wainscoted walls. What really most sustained our friends in all ways was their consciousness of having, after all — and so contrariwise to what appeared — a man in the house. It removed them from that category of the manless into which no lady really lapses till every issue is closed. Their visitor was an issue — at least to the imagination, and they arrived finally, under provocation, at intensities of flutter in which they felt themselves so compromised by his hoverings that they could only consider with relief the fact of nobody's knowing.

The real complication indeed at first was that for some weeks after their talks with Mr. Patten the hoverings quite ceased; a circumstance that brought home to them in some degree a sense of indiscretion and indelicacy. They hadn't mentioned him, no; but they had come perilously near it, and they had doubtless, at any rate, too recklessly let in the light on old buried and sheltered things, old sorrows and shames. They roamed about the house themselves at times, fitfully and singly, when each supposed the other out or engaged; they paused and lingered, like soundless apparitions, in corners, doorways, passages, and sometimes suddenly met, in these experiments, with a suppressed start and a mute confession. They talked of him practically never; but each knew how the other thought — all the more that it was (oh yes, unmistakably!) in a manner different from her own. They were together, none the less, in feeling, while, week after week, he failed again to show, as if they had been guilty of blowing, with an effect of sacrilege, on old-gathered silvery ashes. It frankly came out for them that, possessed as they so strangely, yet so ridiculously were, they should be able to settle to nothing till their consciousness was yet again confirmed. Whatever the subject of it might have for them of fear or favour, profit or loss, he had taken the taste from everything else. He had converted *them* into wandering ghosts. At last, one day, with nothing they could afterwards perceive to have determined it, the change came — came, as the previous splash in their stillness had come, by the pale testimony of Miss Susan.

She waited till after breakfast to speak of it — or Miss Amy, rather, waited to hear her; for she showed during the meal the face of controlled commotion that her comrade already knew and that must, with the game loyally played, serve as preface to a disclosure. The younger of the friends really watched the elder, over their tea and toast, as if seeing her for the first time as possibly tortuous, suspecting in her some intention of keeping back what had happened. What had happened was that the image of the hanged man had reappeared in the night; yet only after they had moved together to the drawing-room did Miss Amy learn the facts.

'I was beside the bed — in that low chair; about' — since Miss Amy must know — 'to take off my right shoe. I had

noticed nothing before, and had had time partly to undress —
had got into my wrapper. So, suddenly — as I happened to look
— there he was. And there,' said Susan Frush, 'he stayed.'

'But where do you mean?'

'In the high-backed chair, the old flowered chintz "ear-
chair" beside the chimney.'

'All night? — and you in your wrapper?' Then as if this
image almost challenged her credulity, 'Why didn't you go to
bed?' Miss Amy inquired.

'With a — a person in the room?' her friend wonderfully
asked; adding after an instant as with positive pride: 'I never
broke the spell!'

'And didn't freeze to death?'

'Yes, almost. To say nothing of not having slept, I can
assure you, one wink. I shut my eyes for long stretches, but
whenever I opened them he was still there, and I never for
a moment lost consciousness.'

Miss Amy gave a groan of conscientious sympathy. 'So
that you're feeling now, of course, half dead.'

Her companion turned to the chimney-glass a wan, glazed
eye. 'I dare say I *am* looking impossible.'

Miss Amy, after an instant, found herself still conscientious.
'You are.' Her own eyes strayed to the glass, lingering there
while she lost herself in thought. 'Really,' she reflected with
a certain dryness, 'if that's the kind of thing it's to be ——!'
there would seem, in a word, to be no withstanding it for
either. Why, she afterwards asked herself in secret, should
the restless spirit of a dead adventurer have addressed itself,
in its trouble, to such a person as her queer, quaint, inefficient
housemate? It was in *her*, she dumbly and somewhat sorely
argued, that an unappeased soul of the old race should show
a confidence. To this conviction she was the more directed
by the sense that Susan had, in relation to the preference
shown, vain and foolish complacencies. She had her idea of
what, in their prodigious predicament, should be, as she called

it, 'done,' and that was a question that Amy from this time began to nurse the small aggression of not so much as discussing with her. She had certainly, poor Miss Frush, a new, an obscure reticence, and since she wouldn't speak first she should have silence to her fill. Miss Amy, however, peopled the silence with conjectural visions of her kinswoman's secret communion. Miss Susan, it was true, showed nothing, on any particular occasion, more than usual; but this was just a part of the very felicity that had begun to harden and uplift her. Days and nights hereupon elapsed without bringing felicity of any order to Amy Frush. If she had no emotions it was, she suspected, because Susan had them all; and — it would have been preposterous had it not been pathetic — she proceeded rapidly to hug the opinion that Susan was selfish and even something of a sneak. Politeness, between them, still reigned, but confidence had flown, and its place was taken by open ceremonies and confessed precautions. Miss Susan looked blank but resigned; which maintained again, unfortunately, her superior air and the presumption of her duplicity. Her manner was of not knowing where her friend's shoe pinched; but it might have been taken by a jaundiced eye for surprise at the challenge of her monopoly. The unexpected resistance of her nerves was indeed a wonder: was that, then, the result, even for a shaky old woman, of shocks sufficiently repeated? Miss Amy brooded on the rich inference that, if the first of them didn't prostrate and the rest didn't undermine, one might keep them up as easily as — well, say an unavowed acquaintance or a private commerce of letters. She was startled at the comparison into which she fell — but what was this but an intrigue like another? And fancy Susan carrying one on! That history of the long night hours of the pair in the two chairs kept before her — for it was always present — the extraordinary measure. Was the situation it involved only grotesque — or was it quite grimly grand? It struck her as both; but that was the case with all their situations. Would it be in herself, at any rate, to show such a front? She put herself such questions till she was tired of them. A few good moments of her own would have cleared the air. Luckily they were to come.

IV

IT was on a Sunday morning in April, a day brimming over with the turn of the season. She had gone into the garden before church; they cherished alike, with pottering intimacies and opposed theories and a wonderful apparatus of old gloves and trowels and spuds and little botanical cards on sticks, this feature of their establishment, where they could still differ without fear and agree without diplomacy, and which now, with its vernal promise, threw beauty and gloom and light and space, a great good-natured ease, into their wavering scales. She was dressed for church; but when Susan, who had, from a window, seen her wandering, stooping, examining, touching, appeared in the doorway to signify a like readiness, she suddenly felt her intention checked. 'Thank you,' she said, drawing near; 'I think that, though I've dressed, I won't, after all, go. Please, therefore, proceed without me.'

Miss Susan fixed her. 'You're not well?'

'Not particularly. I shall be better — the morning's so perfect — here.'

'Are you really ill?'

'Indisposed; but not enough so, thank you, for you to stay with me.'

'Then it has come on but just now?'

'No — I felt not quite fit when I dressed. But it won't do.'

'Yet you'll stay out here?'

Miss Amy looked about. 'It will depend!'

Her friend paused long enough to have asked what it would depend on, but abruptly, after this contemplation, turned instead and, merely throwing over her shoulder an 'At least take care of yourself!' went rustling, in her stiffest Sunday fashion, about her business. Miss Amy, left alone, as she clearly desired to be, lingered awhile in the garden, where the sense of things was somehow made still more delicious by the sweet, vain sounds from the church tower; but by the end of ten minutes she had returned to the house. The sense of things was not delicious there, for what it had at last come to was that, as they thought of each other what they couldn't say, all their contacts were hard and false. The real wrong was in what Susan thought — as to which she was much too proud and too sore to undeceive her. Miss Amy went vaguely to the drawing-room.

They sat as usual, after church, at their early Sunday dinner, face to face; but little passed between them save that Miss Amy felt better, that the curate had preached, that nobody else had stayed away, and that everybody had asked why Amy had. Amy, hereupon, satisfied everybody by feeling well enough to go in the afternoon; on which occasion, on the other hand — and for reasons even less luminous than those that had operated with her mate in the morning — Miss Susan remained within. Her comrade came back late, having, after church, paid visits; and found her, as daylight faded, seated in the drawing-room, placid and dressed, but without so much as a Sunday book — the place contained whole shelves of such reading — in her hand. She looked so as if a visitor had just left her that Amy put the question: 'Has any one called?'

'Dear, no; I've been quite alone.'

This again was indirect, and it instantly determined for Miss Amy a conviction — a conviction that, on her also sitting down just as she was and in a silence that prolonged itself, promoted in its turn another determination. The April dusk gathered, and still, without further speech, the companions sat there. But at last Miss Amy said in a tone not quite her commonest: 'This morning he came — while you were at church. I suppose it must have been really — though of course I couldn't know it — what I was moved to stay at home for.' She spoke now — out of her contentment — as if to oblige with explanations.

But it was strange how Miss Susan met her. 'You stay at home for him? *I* don't!' She fairly laughed at the triviality of the idea.

Miss Amy was naturally struck by it and after an instant even nettled. 'Then why did you do so this afternoon?'

'Oh, it wasn't for *that!*' Miss Susan lightly quavered. She made her distinction. 'I *really* wasn't well.'

At this her cousin brought it out. 'But he has been with you?'

'My dear child,' said Susan, launched unexpectedly even to herself, 'he's with me so often that if I put myself out for him ——!' But as if at sight of something that showed, through the twilight, in her friend's face, she pulled herself up.

Amy, however, spoke with studied stillness. 'You've ceased then to put yourself out? You gave me, you remember, an instance of how you once did!' And she tried, on her side, a laugh.

'Oh yes — that was at first. But I've seen such a lot of him since. Do you mean *you* hadn't?' Susan asked. Then as her companion only sat looking at her: 'Has this been really the first time for you — since we last talked?'

Miss Amy for a minute said nothing. 'You've actually believed me ——'

'To be enjoying on your own account what *I* enjoy? How couldn't I, at the very least,' Miss Susan cried — 'so grand and strange as you must allow me to say you've struck me?'

Amy hesitated. 'I hope I've sometimes struck you as decent!'

But it was a touch that, in her friend's almost amused preoccupation with the simple fact, happily fell short. 'You've only been waiting for what didn't come?'

Miss Amy coloured in the dusk. 'It came, as I tell you, to-day.'

'Better late than never!' And Miss Susan got up.

Amy Frush sat looking. 'It's because you thought you had ground for jealousy that *you*'ve been extraordinary?'

Poor Susan, at this, quite bounced about. 'Jealousy?'

It was a tone — never heard from her before — that brought Amy Frush to her feet; so that for a minute, in the unlighted room where, in honour of the spring, there had been no fire and the evening chill had gathered, they stood as enemies. It lasted, fortunately, even long enough to give one of them time suddenly to find it horrible. 'But why should we quarrel *now*?' Amy broke out in a different voice.

Susan was not too alienated quickly enough to meet it. 'It *is* rather wretched.'

'Now when we're equal,' Amy went on.

'Yes — I suppose we are.' Then, however, as if just to attenuate the admission, Susan had her last lapse from grace. 'They say, you know, that when women do quarrel it's usually about a man.'

Amy recognised it, but also with a reserve. 'Well, then, let there first *be* one!'

'And don't you call *him* —— ?'

'No!' Amy declared and turned away, while her companion showed her a vain wonder for what she could in that case have expected. Their identity of privilege was thus established, but it is not certain that the air with which she indicated that the subject had better drop didn't press down for an instant her side of the balance. She knew that she knew most about men.

The subject did drop for the time, it being agreed between them that neither should from that hour expect from the other any confession or report. They would treat all occurrences now as not worth mentioning — a course easy to pursue from the moment the suspicion of jealousy had, on each side, been so completely laid to rest. They led their life a month or two on the smooth ground of taking everything for granted; by the end of which time, however, try as they would, they had set up no question that — while they met as a pair of gentlewomen living together only must meet — could successfully pretend to take the place of that of Cuthbert Frush. The spring softened and deepened, reached out its tender arms and scattered its shy graces; the earth broke, the air stirred, with emanations that were as touches and voices of the past; our friends bent their backs in their garden and their noses over its symptoms; they opened their windows to the mildness and tracked it in the lanes and by the hedges; yet the plant of conversation between them markedly failed to renew itself with the rest. It was not indeed that the mildness was not within them as well as without; all asperity, at least, had melted away; they were more than ever pleased with their general acquisition, which, at the winter's end, seemed to give out more of its old secrets, to hum, however faintly, with more of its old echoes, to creak, here and there, with the expiring throb of old aches. The deepest sweetness of the spring at Marr was just in its being in this way an attestation of age and rest. The place never seemed to have lived and lingered so long as when kind nature, like a maiden blessing a crone, laid rosy hands on its grizzled head. Then the new season was a light held up to show all the dignity of the years, but also all the wrinkles and scars. The good ladies in whom we are interested changed, at any rate, with the happy days, and it finally came out not only that the invidious note had dropped, but that it had positively turned to music. The whole tone of the time made so for tenderness that it really seemed as if at moments they were sad for each other. They had their grounds at last: each found them in her own consciousness; but it was as if each waited, on the other hand, to be sure she could speak without offence. Fortunately, at last, the tense cord snapped.

The old churchyard at Marr is still liberal; it does its immemorial utmost to people, with names and dates and memories and eulogies, with generations fore-shortened and confounded, the high empty table at which the grand old cripple of the church looks down over the low wall. It serves as an easy thoroughfare, and the stranger finds himself pausing in it with a sense of respect and compassion for the great maimed, ivied shoulders — as the image strikes him — of stone. Miss Susan and Miss Amy were strangers enough still to have sunk down one May morning on the sun-warmed tablet of an ancient tomb and to have remained looking about them in a sort of anxious peace. Their walks were all pointless now, as if they always stopped and turned, for an unconfessed want of interest, before reaching their object. That object presented itself at every start as the same to each, but they had come back too often without having got near it. This morning, strangely, on the return and almost in sight of their door, they were more in presence of it than they had ever been, and they seemed fairly to touch it when Susan said at last, quite in the air and with no traceable reference: 'I hope you don't mind, dearest, if I'm awfully sorry for you.'

'Oh, I know it,' Amy returned — 'I've felt it. But what does it do for us?' she asked.

Then Susan saw, with wonder and pity, how little resentment for penetration or patronage she had had to fear and out of what a depth of sentiment similar to her own her companion helplessly spoke. 'You're sorry for *me* ?'

Amy at first only looked at her with tired eyes, putting out a hand that remained awhile on her arm. 'Dear old girl! You might have told me before,' she went on as she took everything in; 'though, after all, haven't we each really known it?'

'Well,' said Susan, 'we've waited. We could only wait.'

'Then if we've waited together,' her friend returned, 'that *has* helped us.'

'Yes — to keep him in his place. Who would ever believe in him?' Miss Susan wearily wondered. 'If it wasn't for you and for me ——'

'Not doubting of each other?' — her companion took her up: 'yes, there wouldn't be a creature. It's lucky for us,' said Miss Amy, 'that we *don't* doubt.'

'Oh, if we did we shouldn't be sorry.'

'No — except, selfishly, for ourselves. I am, I assure you, for *my*self — it has made me older. But, luckily, at any rate, we trust each other.'

'We do,' said Miss Susan.

'We do,' Miss Amy repeated — they lingered a little on that. 'But except making one feel older, what has it done for one?'

'There it is!'

'And though we've kept him in his place,' Miss Amy continued, 'he has also kept us in ours. We've lived with it,' she declared in melancholy justice. 'And we wondered at first if we could!' she ironically added. 'Well, isn't just what we feel now that we can't any longer?'

'No — it must stop. And I've my idea,' said Susan Frush.

'Oh, I assure you I've mine!' her cousin responded.

'Then if you want to act, don't mind me.'

'Because you certainly won't *me*? No, I suppose not. Well!' Amy sighed, as if, merely from this, relief had at last come. Her comrade echoed it; they remained side by side; and nothing could have had more oddity than what was assumed alike in what they had said and in what they still kept back. There would have been this at least in their favour for a questioner of their case, that each, charged dejectedly with her own experience, took, on the part of the other, the extraordinary — the ineffable, in fact — all for granted. They never named it again — as indeed it was not easy to name; the whole matter shrouded itself in personal discriminations and privacies; the comparison of notes had become a thing

impossible. What was definite was that they had lived into
their queer story, passed through it as through an observed, a
studied, eclipse of the usual, a period of reclusion, a financial,
social, or moral crisis, and only desired now to live out of it
again. The questioner we have been supposing might even
have fancied that each, on her side, had hoped for something
from it that she finally perceived it was never to give, which
would have been exactly, moreover, the core of her secret and
the explanation of her reserve. They, at least, as the business
stood, put each other to no test, and, if they were in fact dis-
illusioned and disappointed, came together, after their long
blight, solidly on that. It fully appeared between them that
they felt a great deal older. When they got up from their sun-
warmed slab, however, reminding each other of luncheon, it
was with a visible increase of ease and with Miss Susan's hand
drawn, for the walk home, into Miss Amy's arm. Thus the
'idea' of each had continued unspoken and ungrudged. It
was as if each wished the other to try her own first; from
which it might have been gathered that they alike presented
difficulty and even entailed expense. The great questions
remained. What then did he mean? what then did he want?
Absolution, peace, rest, his final reprieve — merely to say *that*
saw them no further on the way than they had already come.
What were they at last to do for him? What could they
give him that he would take? The ideas they respectively
nursed still bore no fruit, and at the end of another month
Miss Susan was frankly anxious about Miss Amy. Miss Amy
as freely admitted that people *must* have begun to notice strange
marks in them and to look for reasons. They were changed —
they must change back.

V

YET it was not till one morning at midsummer, on their
meeting for breakfast, that the elder lady fairly attacked the

younger's last entrenchment. 'Poor, poor Susan!' Miss Amy had said to herself as her cousin came into the room; and a moment later she brought out, for very pity, her appeal. 'What then *is* yours?'

'My idea?' It was clearly, at last, a vague comfort to Miss Susan to be asked. Yet her answer was desolate. 'Oh, it's no use!'

'But how do you know?'

'Why, I tried it — ten days ago, and I thought at first it had answered. But it hasn't.'

'He's back again?'

Wan, tired, Miss Susan gave it up. 'Back again.'

Miss Amy, after one of the long, odd looks that had now become their most frequent form of intercourse, thought it over. 'And just the same?'

'Worse.'

'Dear!' said Miss Amy, clearly knowing what that meant. 'Then what did you do?'

Her friend brought it roundly out. 'I made my sacrifice.'

Miss Amy, though still more deeply interrogative, hesitated. 'But of what?'

'Why, of my little all — or almost.'

The 'almost' seemed to puzzle Miss Amy, who, moreover, had plainly no clue to the property or attribute so described. 'Your "little all"?'

'Twenty pounds.'

'Money?' Miss Amy gasped.

Her tone produced on her companion's part a wonder as great as her own. 'What then is it yours to give?'

'My idea? It's not to *give!*' cried Amy Frush.

At the finer pride that broke out in this poor Susan's blankness flushed. 'What then is it to do?'

But Miss Amy's bewilderment outlasted her reproach. 'Do you mean he takes money?'

'The Chancellor of the Exchequer does — for "conscience."'

T

Her friend's exploit shone larger. 'Conscience-money? You sent it to Government?' Then while, as the effect of her surprise, her mate looked too much a fool, Amy melted to kindness. 'Why, you secretive old thing!'

Miss Susan presently pulled herself more together. 'When your ancestor has robbed the revenue and his spirit walks for remorse ——'

'You pay to get rid of him? I see — and it becomes what the vicar called his atonement by deputy. But what if it isn't remorse?' Miss Amy shrewdly asked.

'But it *is* — or it seemed to me so.'

'Never to me,' said Miss Amy.

Again they searched each other. 'Then, evidently, with you he's different.'

Miss Amy looked away. 'I dare say!'

'So what *is* your idea?'

Miss Amy thought. 'I'll tell you only if it works.'

'Then, for God's sake, try it!'

Miss Amy, still with averted eyes and now looking easily wise, continued to think. 'To try it I shall have to leave you. That's why I've waited so long.' Then she fully turned, and with expression: 'Can you face three days alone?'

'Oh — "alone"! I wish I ever were!'

At this her friend, as for very compassion, kissed her; for it seemed really to have come out at last — and welcome! — that poor Susan was the worse beset. 'I'll do it! But I must go up to town. Ask me no questions. All I can tell you now is ——'

'Well?' Susan appealed while Amy impressively fixed her.

'It's no more remorse than *I'm* a smuggler.'

'What is it then?'

'It's bravado.'

An 'Oh!' more shocked and scared than any that, in the whole business, had yet dropped from her, wound up poor Susan's share in this agreement, appearing as it did to represent for her a somewhat lurid inference. Amy, clearly, had lights of her own. It was by their aid, accordingly, that she immediately prepared for the first separation they had had yet to suffer; of which the consequence, two days later, was that Miss Susan, bowed and anxious, crept singly, on the return from their parting, up the steep hill that leads from the station of Marr and passed ruefully under the ruined town-gate, one of the old defences, that arches over it.

But the full sequel was not for a month — one hot August night when, under the dim stars, they sat together in their little walled garden. Though they had by this time, in general, found again — as women only can find — the secret of easy speech, nothing, for the half-hour, had passed between them: Susan had only sat waiting for her comrade to wake up. Miss Amy had taken of late to interminable dozing — as if with forfeits and arrears to recover; she might have been a convalescent from fever repairing tissue and getting through time. Susan Frush watched her in the warm dimness, and the question between them was fortunately at last so simple that she had freedom to think her pretty in slumber and to fear that she herself, so unguarded, presented an appearance less graceful. She was impatient, for her need had at last come, but she waited, and while she waited she thought. She had already often done so, but the mystery deepened to-night in the story told, as it seemed to her by her companion's frequent relapses. What had been, three weeks before, the effort intense enough to leave behind such a trail of fatigue? The marks, sure enough, had shown in the poor girl that morning of the termination of the arranged absence for which not three days, but ten, without word or sign, were to prove no more than sufficient. It was at an unnatural hour that Amy had turned up, dusty, dishevelled, inscrutable, confessing for the time to nothing more than a long night-journey. Miss Susan prided herself on having played the game and respected, however tormenting, the conditions. She had her conviction that her friend had been out of the country, and she marvelled, thinking of her own old wanderings and her present settled fears, at the spirit with which a person who, whatever she had previously done, had not travelled, could carry off such a flight. The hour had come at last for this person to name her remedy. What determined it was that as Susan Frush sat there, she took home the fact that the remedy was by this time not to be questioned. It had acted as her own had not, and Amy, to all appearance, had only waited for her to admit it. Well, she was ready when Amy woke — woke immediately to meet her eyes and to show, after a moment, in doing so, a vision of what was in her mind. 'What *was* it now?' Susan finally said.

'My idea? Is it possible you've not guessed?'

'Oh, you're deeper, much deeper,' Susan sighed, 'than I.'

Amy didn't contradict that — seemed indeed, placidly enough, to take it for truth; but she presently spoke as if the difference, after all, didn't matter now. 'Happily for us to-day — isn't it so? — our case is the same. I can speak, at any rate, for myself. He has left me.'

'Thank God, then!' Miss Susan devoutly murmured. 'For he has left *me*.'

'Are you sure?'

'Oh, I think so.'

'But how?'

'Well,' said Miss Susan after an hesitation, 'how are *you?*'

Amy, for a little, matched her pause. 'Ah, that's what I can't tell you. I can only answer for it that he's gone.'

'Then allow me also to prefer not to explain. The sense of relief has for some reason grown strong in me during the last half-hour. That's such a comfort that it's enough, isn't it?'

'Oh, plenty!' The garden-side of their old house, a window or two dimly lighted, massed itself darkly in the summer night, and, with a common impulse, they gave it, across the little lawn, a long, fond look. Yes, they could be sure. 'Plenty!' Amy repeated. 'He's gone.'

Susan's elder eyes hovered, in the same way, through her elegant glass, at his purified haunt. 'He's gone. And how,' she insisted, ' *did* you do it ? '

' Why, you dear goose,' — Miss Amy spoke a little strangely, — 'I went to Paris.'

'To Paris ? '

'To see what I could bring back — that I mightn't, that I shouldn't. To do a stroke with !' Miss Amy brought out.

But it left her friend still vague. 'A stroke —— ? '

' To get through the Customs — under their nose.'

It was only with this that, for Miss Susan, a pale light dawned. ' You wanted to smuggle ? *That* was your idea ? '

' It was *his*,' said Miss Amy. 'He wanted no "conscience-money" spent for him,' she now more bravely laughed ; ' it was quite the other way about — he wanted some bold deed done, of the old wild kind ; he wanted some big risk taken. And I took it.' She sprang up, rebounding, in her triumph.

Her companion, gasping, gazed at her. 'Might they have hanged you too ? '

Miss Amy looked up at the dim stars. 'If I had defended myself. But luckily it didn't come to that. What I brought in I brought' — she rang out, more and more lucid, now, as she talked — 'triumphantly. To appease him — I braved them. I chanced it, at Dover, and they never knew.'

' Then you hid it —— ? '

' About my person.'

With the shiver of this Miss Susan got up, and they stood there duskily together. ' It was so small ? ' the elder lady wonderingly murmured.

' It was big enough to have satisfied him,' her mate replied with just a shade of sharpness. 'I chose it, with much thought, from the forbidden list.'

The forbidden list hung a moment in Miss Susan's eyes, suggesting to her, however, but a pale conjecture. 'A Tauch-nitz ? '

Miss Amy communed again with the August stars. 'It was the *spirit* of the deed that told.'

'A Tauchnitz?' her friend insisted.

Then at last her eyes again dropped, and the Misses Frush moved together to the house. 'Well, he's satisfied.'

'Yes, and'— Miss Susan mused a little ruefully as they went— 'you got at last your week in Paris!'

MAUD–EVELYN

On some allusion to a lady who, though unknown to myself, was known to two or three of the company, it was asked by one of these if we had heard the odd circumstance of what she had just 'come in for' — the piece of luck suddenly over-taking, in the grey afternoon of her career, so obscure and lonely a personage. We were at first, in our ignorance, mainly reduced to crude envy; but old Lady Emma, who for a while had said nothing, scarcely even appearing to listen, and letting the chatter, which was indeed plainly beside the mark, subside of itself, came back from a mental absence to observe that if what had happened to Lavinia was wonderful, certainly what had for years gone before it, led up to it, had likewise not been without some singular features. From this we perceived that Lady Emma had a story — a story, moreover, out of the ken even of those of her listeners acquainted with the quiet person who was the subject of it. Almost the oddest thing — as came out afterwards — was that such a situation should for the world have remained so in the background of this person's life. By 'afterwards' I mean simply before we separated; for what came out came on the spot, under encour-agement and pressure, our common, eager solicitation. Lady Emma, who always reminded me of a fine old instrument that has first to be tuned, agreed, after a few of our scrapings and fingerings, that, having said so much, she couldn't, without wantonly tormenting us, forbear to say all. She had known Lavinia, whom she mentioned throughout only by that name, from far away, and she had also known —— But what she had known I must give as nearly as possible as she herself

279

gave it. She talked to us from her corner of the sofa, and the flicker of the firelight in her face was like the glow of memory, the play of fancy from within.

I

'THEN why on earth don't you take him?' I asked. I think that was the way that, one day when she was about twenty — before some of you perhaps were born — the affair, for me, must have begun. I put the question because I knew she had had a chance, though I didn't know how great a mistake her failure to embrace it was to prove. I took an interest because I liked them both — you see how I like young people still — and because, as they had originally met at my house, I had in a manner to answer to each for the other. I'm afraid I'm thrown baldly back on the fact that if the girl was the daughter of my earliest, almost my only governess, to whom I had remained much attached and who, after leaving me, had married — for a governess — 'well,' Marmaduke (it isn't *his* real name!) was the son of one of the clever men who had — I was charming then, I assure you I was — wanted, years before, and this one as a widower, to marry me. I hadn't cared, somehow, for widowers, but even after I had taken somebody else I was conscious of a pleasant link with the boy whose step-mother it had been open to me to become and to whom it was perhaps a little a matter of vanity with me to show that I should have been for him one of the kindest. This was what the woman his father eventually did marry was not, and that threw him upon me the more.

Lavinia was one of nine, and her brothers and sisters, who had never done anything for her, help, actually, in different countries and on something, I believe of that same scale, to people the globe. There were mixed in her then, in a puzzling way, two qualities that mostly exclude each other, — an extreme timidity and, as the smallest fault that could qualify a harmıess creature for a world of wickedness, a self-complacency hard in tiny, unexpected spots, for which I used sometimes to take her up, but which, I subsequently saw, would have done something for the flatness of her life had they not evaporated with everything else. She was at any rate one of those persons as to whom you don't know whether they might have been attractive if they had been happy, or might have been happy if they had been attractive. If I was a trifle vexed at her not jumping at Marmaduke, it was probably rather less because I expected wonders of him than because I thought she took her own prospect too much for granted. She had made a mistake and, before long, admitted it; yet I remember that when she expressed to me a conviction that he would ask her again, I also thought this highly probable, for in the meantime I had spoken to him. 'She does care for you,' I declared; and I can see at this moment, long ago though it be, his handsome empty young face look, on the words, as if, in spite of itself for a little, it really thought. I didn't press the matter, for he had, after all, no great things to offer; yet my conscience was easier, later on, for having not said less. He had three hundred and fifty a year from his mother, and one of his uncles had promised him something — I don't mean an allowance, but a place, if I recollect, in a business. He assured me that he loved as a man loves — a man of twenty-two! — but once. He said it, at all events, as a man says it but once.

'Well, then,' I replied, 'your course is clear.'

'To speak to her again, you mean?'

'Yes — try it.'

He seemed to try it a moment in imagination; after which, a little to my surprise, he asked: 'Would it be very awful if she should speak to *me*?'

I stared. 'Do you mean pursue you — overtake you? Ah, if you're running away ——'

'I'm not running away!' — he was positive as to that. 'But when a fellow has gone so far ——'

'He can't go any further? Perhaps,' I replied drily. 'But in that case he shouldn't talk of "caring."'

'Oh, but I do, I do.'

I shook my head. 'Not if you're too proud!' On which I turned away, looking round at him again, however, after he had surprised me by a silence that seemed to accept my judgment. Then I saw he had not accepted it; I perceived it indeed to be essentially absurd. He expressed more, on this, than I had yet seen him do — had the queerest, frankest, and, for a young man of his conditions, saddest smile.

'I'm *not* proud. It isn't *in* me. If you're not, you're not, you know. I don't think I'm proud enough.'

It came over me that this was, after all, probable; yet somehow I didn't at the moment like him the less for it, though I spoke with some sharpness. 'Then what's the matter with you?'

He took a turn or two about the room, as if what he had just said had made him a little happier. 'Well, how can a man say more?' Then, just as I was on the point of assuring him that I didn't know what he had said, he went on: 'I swore to her that I would never marry. Oughtn't that to be enough?'

'To make her come after you?'

'No — I suppose scarcely that; but to make her feel sure of me — to make her wait.'

'Wait for what?'

'Well, till I come back.'

'Back from where?'

'From Switzerland — haven't I told you? I go there next month with my aunt and my cousin.'

He was quite right about not being proud — this was an alternative distinctly humble.

II

AND yet see what it brought forth — the beginning of which was something that, early in the autumn, I learned from poor

Lavinia. He had written to her, they were still such friends; and thus it was that she knew his aunt and his cousin to have come back without him. He had stayed on — stayed much longer and travelled much further: he had been to the Italian lakes and to Venice; he was now in Paris. At this I vaguely wondered, knowing that he was always short of funds and that he must, by his uncle's beneficence, have started on the journey on a basis of expenses paid. 'Then whom has he picked up?' I asked; but feeling sorry, as soon as I had spoken, to have made Lavinia blush. It was almost as if he had picked up some improper lady, though in this case he wouldn't have told her, and it wouldn't have saved him money.

'Oh, he makes acquaintance so quickly, knows people in two minutes,' the girl said. 'And every one always wants to be nice to him.'

This was perfectly true, and I saw what she saw in it. 'Ah, my dear, he will have an immense circle ready for you!'

'Well,' she replied, 'if they do run after us I'm not likely to suppose it will ever be for me. It will be for *him*, and they may do to me what they like. My pleasure will be — but you'll see.' I already saw — saw at least what she supposed she herself saw: her drawing-room crowded with female fashion and her attitude angelic. 'Do you know what he said to me again before he went?' she continued.

I wondered; he *had* then spoken to her. 'That he will never, never marry ——'

'Any one but *me!*' She ingenuously took me up. 'Then you knew?'

It might be. 'I guessed.'

'And don't you believe it?'

Again I hesitated. 'Yes.' Yet all this didn't tell me why she had changed colour. 'Is it a secret — whom he's with?'

'Oh no, they seem so nice. I was only struck with the way you know him — your seeing immediately that it must be a new friendship that has kept him over. It's the devotion of the Dedricks,' Lavinia said. 'He's travelling with them.'

Once more I wondered. 'Do you mean they're taking him about?'

'Yes — they've invited him.'

No, indeed, I reflected — he wasn't proud. But what I said was: 'Who in the world are the Dedricks?'

'Kind, good people whom last month he accidentally met. He was walking some Swiss pass — a long, rather stupid one, I believe, without his aunt and his cousin, who had gone round some other way and were to meet him somewhere. It came on to rain in torrents, and while he was huddling under a shelter he was overtaken by some people in a carriage who kindly made him get in. They drove him, I gather, for several hours; it began an intimacy, and they've continued to be charming to him.'

I thought a moment. 'Are they ladies?'

Her own imagination meanwhile had also strayed a little. 'I think about forty.'

'Forty ladies?'

She quickly came back. 'Oh no; I mean Mrs. Dedrick is.'

'About forty? Then Miss Dedrick ——'

'There isn't any Miss Dedrick.'

'No daughter?'

'Not with them, at any rate. No one but the husband.'

I thought again. 'And how old is *he*?'

Lavinia followed my example. 'Well, about forty, too.'

'About forty-two?' We laughed, but 'That's all right!' I said; and so, for the time, it seemed.

He continued absent, none the less, and I saw Lavinia repeatedly, and we always talked of him, though this represented a greater concern with his affairs than I had really supposed myself committed to. I had never sought the acquaintance of his father's people, nor seen either his aunt or his cousin, so that the account given by these relatives of

the circumstances of their separation reached me at last only
through the girl, to whom, also, — for she knew them as little,
— it had circuitously come.   They considered, it appeared,
the poor ladies he had started with, that he had treated them
ill and thrown them over, sacrificing them selfishly to company picked up on the road — a reproach deeply resented by
Lavinia, though about the company too I could see she was
not much more at her ease. 'How can he help it if he's so
taking?' she asked; and to be properly indignant in one
quarter she had to pretend to be delighted in the other.
Marmaduke *was* 'taking'; yet it also came out between us at
last that the Dedricks must certainly be extraordinary. We
had scant added evidence, for his letters stopped, and that
naturally was one of our signs. I had meanwhile leisure to
reflect — it was a sort of study of the human scene I always
liked — on what to be taking consisted of. The upshot of my
meditations, which experience has only confirmed, was that
it consisted simply of itself. It was a quality implying no
others. Marmaduke *had* no others. What indeed was his
need of any?

III

He at last, however, turned up; but then it happened that
if, on his coming to see me, his immediate picture of his
charming new friends quickened even more than I had expected my sense of the variety of the human species, my
curiosity about them failed to make me respond when he
suggested I should go to see them. It's a difficult thing to
explain, and I don't pretend to put it successfully, but doesn't
it often happen that one may think well enough of a person
without being inflamed with the desire to meet — on the ground
of any such sentiment — other persons who think still better?
Somehow — little harm as there was in Marmaduke — it was
but half a recommendation of the Dedricks that they were

crazy about him. I didn't say this — I was careful to say little; which didn't prevent his presently asking if he mightn't then bring them to *me*. 'If not, why not?' he laughed. He laughed about everything.

'Why not? Because it strikes me that your surrender doesn't require any backing. Since you've done it you must take care of yourself.'

'Oh, but they're as safe,' he returned, 'as the Bank of England. They're wonderful — for respectability and goodness.'

'Those are precisely qualities to which my poor intercourse can contribute nothing.' He hadn't, I observed, gone so far as to tell me they would be 'fun,' and he *had*, on the other hand, promptly mentioned that they lived in Westbourne Terrace. They were not forty — they were forty-five; but Mr. Dedrick had already, on considerable gains, retired from some primitive profession. They were the simplest, kindest, yet most original and unusual people, and nothing could exceed, frankly, the fancy they had taken to him. Marmaduke spoke of it with a placidity of resignation that was almost irritating. I suppose I should have despised him if, after benefits accepted, he had said they bored him; yet their not boring him vexed me even more than it puzzled. 'Whom do they know?'

'No one but me. There are people in London like that.'

'Who know no one but you?'

'No — I mean no one at all. There are extraordinary people in London, and awfully nice. You haven't an idea. You people don't know every one. They lead their lives — they go their way. One finds — what do you call it? — refinement, books, cleverness, don't you know, and music, and pictures, and religion, and an excellent table — all sorts of pleasant things. You only come across them by chance; but it's all perpetually going on.'

I assented to this: the world was very wonderful, and one must certainly see what one could. In my own quarter too I found wonders enough. 'But are you,' I asked, 'as fond of them ——— '

'As they are of *me?*' He took me up promptly, and his eyes were quite unclouded. 'I'm quite sure I shall become so.'

'Then are you taking Lavinia —— ? '

'Not to see them — no.' I saw, myself, the next minute, of course, that I had made a mistake. 'On what footing *can* I ? '

I bethought myself. 'I keep forgetting you're not engaged.'

'Well,' he said after a moment, 'I shall never marry another.'

It somehow, repeated again, gave on my nerves. 'Ah, but what good will that do her, or me either, if you don't marry *her?*'

He made no answer to this — only turned away to look at something in the room; after which, when he next faced me, he had a heightened colour. 'She ought to have taken me that day,' he said gravely and gently, fixing me also as if he wished to say more.

I remember that his very mildness irritated me; some show of resentment would have been a promise that the case might still be righted. But I dropped it, the silly case, without letting him say more, and, coming back to Mr. and Mrs. Dedrick, asked him how in the world, without either occupation or society, they passed so much of their time. My question appeared for a moment to leave him at a loss, but he presently found light; which, at the same time, I saw on my side, really suited him better than further talk about Lavinia. 'Oh, they live for Maud-Evelyn.'

'And who's Maud-Evelyn ? '

'Why, their daughter.'

'Their daughter ? ' I had supposed them childless.

He partly explained. 'Unfortunately they've lost her.'

'Lost her ? ' I required more.

He hesitated again. 'I mean that a great many people would take it that way. But *they* don't — they won't.'

I speculated. 'Do you mean other people would have given her up ? '

'Yes — perhaps even tried to forget her. But the Dedricks can't.'

I wondered what she had done: had it been anything very bad? However, it was none of my business, and I only said: 'They communicate with her?'

'Oh, all the while.'

'Then why isn't she with them?'

Marmaduke thought. 'She *is* — now.'

'"Now"? Since when?'

'Well, this last year.'

'Then why do you say they've lost her?'

'Ah,' he said, smiling sadly, '*I* should call it that. I, at any rate,' he went on, 'don't see her.'

Still more I wondered. 'They keep her apart?'

He thought again. 'No, it's not that. As I say, they live for her.'

'But they don't want *you* to — is that it?'

At this he looked at me for the first time, as I thought, a little strangely. 'How *can* I?'

He put it to me as if it were bad of him, somehow, that he shouldn't; but I made, to the best of my ability, a quick end of that. 'You can't. Why in the world *should* you? Live for *my* girl. Live for Lavinia.'

IV

I HAD unfortunately run the risk of boring him again with that idea, and, though he had not repudiated it at the time, I felt in my having returned to it the reason why he never re-appeared for weeks. I saw 'my girl,' as I had called her, in the interval, but we avoided with much intensity the subject of Marmaduke. It was just this that gave me my perspective for finding her constantly full of him. It determined me, in all the circumstances, not to rectify her mistake about the child-lessness of the Dedricks. But whatever I left unsaid, her naming the young man was only a question of time, for at the end of a month she told me he had been twice to her mother's and that she had seen him on each of these occasions.

'Well then?'

'Well then, he's very happy.'

'And still taken up——'

'As much as ever, yes, with those people. He didn't tell me so, but I could see it.'

I could too, and her own view of it. 'What, in that case, did he tell you?'

'Nothing — but I think there's something he wants to. Only not what *you* think,' she added.

I wondered then if it were what I had had from him the last time. 'Well, what prevents him?' I asked.

'From bringing it out? I don't know.'

It was in the tone of this that she struck, to my ear, the first note of an acceptance so deep and a patience so strange that they gave me, at the end, even more food for wonderment than the rest of the business. 'If he can't speak, why does he come?'

She almost smiled. 'Well, I think I *shall* know.'

I looked at her; I remember that I kissed her. 'You're admirable; but it's very ugly.'

'Ah,' she replied, 'he only wants to be kind!'

'To *them?* Then he should let others alone. But what I call ugly is his being content to be so "beholden"——'

'To Mr. and Mrs. Dedrick?' She considered as if there might be many sides to it. 'But mayn't he do them some good?'

The idea failed to appeal to me. 'What good can Marmaduke do? There's one thing,' I went on, 'in case he should want you to know them. Will you promise me to refuse?'

She only looked helpless and blank. 'Making their acquaintance?'

'Seeing them, going near them — ever, ever.'

U

Again she brooded. 'Do you mean *you* won't?'

'Never, never.'

'Well, then, I don't think I want to.'

'Ah, but that's not a promise.' I kept her up to it. 'I want your word.'

She demurred a little. 'But why?'

'So that at least he shan't make use of you,' I said with energy.

My energy overbore her, though I saw how she would really have given herself. 'I promise, but it's only because it's something I know he will never ask.'

I differed from her at the time, believing the proposal in question to have been exactly the subject she had supposed him to be wishing to broach; but on our very next meeting I heard from her of quite another matter, upon which, as soon as she came in, I saw her to be much excited.

'You know then about the daughter without having told me? He called again yesterday,' she explained as she met my stare at her unconnected plunge, 'and now I know that he *has* wanted to speak to me. He at last brought it out.'

I continued to stare. 'Brought what?'

'Why, everything.' She looked surprised at my face. 'Didn't he tell you about Maud-Evelyn?'

I perfectly recollected, but I momentarily wondered. 'He spoke of there being a daughter, but only to say that there's something the matter with her. What is it?'

The girl echoed my words. 'What "is" it? — you dear, strange thing! The matter with her is simply that she's dead.'

'Dead?' I was naturally mystified. 'When, then, did she die?'

'Why, years and years ago — fifteen, I believe. As a little girl. Didn't you understand it so?'

'How *should* I? — when he spoke of her as "with" them and said that they lived for her!'

'Well,' my young friend explained, 'that's just what he meant — they live for her memory. She *is* with them in the sense that they think of nothing else.'

I found matter for surprise in this correction, but also, at first, matter for relief. At the same time it left, as I turned it over, a fresh ambiguity. 'If they think of nothing else, how can they think so much of Marmaduke?'

The difficulty struck her, though she gave me even then a dim impression of being already, as it were, rather on Marmaduke's side, or, at any rate — almost as against herself — in sympathy with the Dedricks. But her answer was prompt: 'Why, that's just their reason — that they can talk to him so much about her.'

'I see.' Yet still I wondered. 'But what's *his* interest——?'

'In being drawn into it?' Again Lavinia met her difficulty. 'Well, that she was so interesting! It appears she was lovely.'

I doubtless fairly gaped. 'A little girl in a pinafore?'

'She was out of pinafores; she was, I believe, when she died, about fourteen. Unless it was sixteen! She was at all events wonderful for beauty.'

'That's the rule. But what good does it do him if he has never seen her?'

She thought a moment, but this time she had no answer. 'Well, you must ask him!'

I determined without delay to do so; but I had before me meanwhile other contradictions. 'Hadn't I better ask him on the same occasion what he means by their "communicating"?'

Oh, this was simple. 'They go in for "mediums," don't you know, and raps, and sittings. They began a year or two ago.'

'Ah, the idiots!' I remember, at this, narrow-mindedly exclaiming. 'Do they want to drag *him* in——?'

'Not in the least; they don't desire it, and he has nothing to do with it.'

'Then where does his fun come in?'

Lavinia turned away; again she seemed at a loss. At last she brought out: 'Make him show you her little photograph.'

But I remained unenlightened. 'Is her little photograph his fun?'

Once more she coloured for him. 'Well, it represents a young loveliness!'

'That he goes about showing?'

She hesitated. 'I think he has only shown it to *me*.'

'Ah, you're just the last one!' I permitted myself to observe.

'Why so, if I'm also struck?'

There was something about her that began to escape me, and I must have looked at her hard. 'It's very good of you to be struck!'

'I don't only mean by the beauty of the face,' she went on; 'I mean by the whole thing — by that also of the attitude of the parents, their extraordinary fidelity, and the way that, as he says, they have made of her memory a real religion. That was what, above all, he came to tell me about.'

I turned away from her now, and she soon afterwards left me; but I couldn't help its dropping from me before we parted that I had never supposed him to be *that* sort of fool.

V

If I were really the perfect cynic you probably think me, I should frankly say that the main interest of the rest of this matter lay for me in fixing the sort of fool I *did* suppose him. But I'm afraid, after all, that my anecdote amounts mainly to a presentation of my own folly. I shouldn't be so in possession of the whole spectacle had I not ended by accepting it, and I shouldn't have accepted it had it not, for my imagination, been saved somehow from grotesqueness. Let me say at once, however, that grotesqueness, and even indeed something worse, did at first appear to me strongly to season it. After that talk with Lavinia I immediately addressed to our friend a request that he would come to see me; when I took the liberty of challenging him outright on everything she had told me. There was one point in particular that I desired to clear up and that seemed to me much more important even than the colour of Maud-Evelyn's hair or the length of her pinafores: the question, I of course mean, of my young man's good faith. Was he altogether silly or was he only altogether mercenary? I felt my choice restricted for the moment to these alternatives.

After he had said to me 'It's as ridiculous as you please, but they've simply adopted me,' I had it out with him, on the spot, on the issue of common honesty, the question of what he was conscious, so that his self-respect should be saved, of being able to give such benefactors in return for such bounty. I'm obliged to say that to a person so inclined at the start to quarrel with him his amiability could yet prove persuasive. His contention was that the equivalent he represented was something for his friends alone to measure. He didn't for a moment pretend to sound deeper than the fancy they had taken to him. He had not, from the first, made up to them in any way: it was all their own doing, their own insistence, their own eccentricity, no doubt, and even, if I liked, their own insanity. Wasn't it enough that he was ready to declare to me, looking me straight in the eye, that he was 'really and truly' fond of them and that they didn't bore him a mite? I had evidently — didn't I see? — an ideal for him that he wasn't at all, if I didn't mind, the fellow to live up to. It was he himself who put it so, and it drew from me the pronouncement that there *was* something irresistible in the refinement of his impudence. 'I don't go near Mrs. Jex,' he said— Mrs. Jex was their favourite medium: 'I do find *her* ugly and vulgar and tiresome, and I hate that part of the business. Besides,' he added in words that I afterwards remembered, 'I don't require it: I do beautifully without it. But my friends themselves,' he pursued, 'though they're of a type you've never come within miles of, are not ugly, are not vulgar, are not in any degree whatever any sort of a " dose." They're, on the contrary, in their own unconventional way, the very best company. They're endlessly amusing. They're delightfully queer and quaint and kind — they're like people in some old story or of some old time. It's at any rate our own affair — mine and theirs — and I beg you to believe that I should make short work of a remonstrance on the subject from any one but you.'

I remember saying to him three months later: 'You've never yet told me what they really want of you;' but I'm afraid this was a form of criticism that occurred to me precisely because I had already begun to guess. By that time indeed I had had great initiations, and poor Lavinia had had them as well — hers in fact throughout went further than mine — and we had shared them together, and I had settled down to a tolerably exact sense of what I was to see. It was what Lavinia added to it that really made the picture. The portrait of the little dead girl had evoked something attractive, though one had not lived so long in the world without hearing of plenty of little dead girls; and the day came when I felt as if I had actually sat with Marmaduke in each of the rooms converted by her parents — with the aid not only of the few small, cherished relics, but that of the fondest figments and fictions, ingenious imaginary mementos and tokens, the unexposed make-believes of the sorrow that broods and the passion that clings — into a temple of grief and worship. The child, incontestably beautiful, had evidently been passionately loved, and in the absence from their lives — I suppose originally a mere accident — of such other elements, either new pleasures or new pains, as abound for most people, their feeling had drawn to itself their whole consciousness: it had become mildly maniacal. The idea was fixed, and it kept others out.

The world, for the most part, allows no leisure for such a ritual, but the world had consistently neglected this plain, shy couple, who were sensitive to the wrong things and whose sincerity and fidelity, as well as their tameness and twaddle, were of a rigid, antique pattern.

I must not represent that either of these objects of interest, or my care for their concerns, took up all my leisure; for I had many claims to meet and many complications to handle, a hundred preoccupations and much deeper anxieties. My young woman, on her side, had other contacts and contingencies — other troubles, too, poor girl; and there were stretches of time in which I neither saw Marmaduke nor heard a word of the Dedricks. Once, only once, abroad, in Germany at a railway station, I met him in their company. They were colourless, commonplace, elderly Britons, of the kind you identify by the livery of their footman, of the labels of their luggage, and the mere sight of them justified me to my conscience in having avoided, from the first, the stiff problem of conversation with them. Marmaduke saw me on the spot and came over to me. There was no doubt whatever of *his* vivid bloom. He had grown fat — or almost, but not with grossness — and might perfectly have passed for the handsome, happy, full-blown son of doting parents who couldn't let him out of view and to whom he was a model of respect and solicitude. They followed him with placid, pleased eyes when he joined me, but asking nothing at all for themselves and quite fitting into his own manner of saying nothing about them. It has its charm, I confess, the way he could be natural and easy, and yet intensely conscious, too, on such a basis. What he was conscious of was that there were things I by this time knew; just as, while we stood there and good-humouredly sounded each other's faces — for, having accepted everything at last, I was only a little curious — I knew that he measured my insight. When he returned again to his doting parents I had to admit that, doting as they were, I felt him not to have been spoiled.

It was incongruous in such a career, but he was rather more of a man. There came back to me with a shade of regret after I had got on this occasion into my train, which was not theirs, a memory of some words that, a couple of years before, I had uttered to poor Lavinia. She had said to me, speaking in reference to what was then our frequent topic and on some fresh evidence that I have forgotten: 'He feels now, you know, about Maud-Evelyn quite as the old people themselves do.'

'Well,' I had replied, 'it's only a pity he's paid for it!'

'Paid?' She had looked very blank.

'By all the luxuries and conveniences,' I had explained, 'that he comes in for through living with them. For that's what he practically does.'

At present I saw how wrong I had been. He was paid, but paid differently, and the mastered wonder of that was really what had been between us in the waiting-room of the station. Step by step, after this, I followed.

VI

I can see Lavinia, for instance, in her ugly new mourning immediately after her mother's death. There had been long anxieties connected with this event, and she was already faded, already almost old. But Marmaduke, on her bereavement, had been to her, and she came straightway to me.

'Do you know what he thinks now?' she soon began. 'He thinks he knew her.'

'Knew the child?' It came to me as if I had half expected it.

'He speaks of her now as if she hadn't been a child.' My visitor gave me the strangest fixed smile. 'It appears that she wasn't so young — it appears she had grown up.'

I stared. 'How can it "appear"? They know, at least! There were the facts.'

'Yes,' said Lavinia, 'but they seem to have come to take a different view of them. He talked to me a long time, and all about *her*. He told me things.'

'What kind of things? Not trumpery stuff, I hope, about "communicating"—about his seeing or hearing her?'

'Oh no, he doesn't go in for that; he leaves it to the old couple, who, I believe, cling to their mediums, keep up their sittings and their rappings, and find in it all a comfort, an amusement, that he doesn't grudge them and that he regards as harmless. I mean anecdotes—memories of his own. I mean things she said to him and that they did together—places they went to. His mind is full of them.'

I turned it over. 'Do you think he's decidedly mad?'

She shook her head with her bleached patience. 'Oh no, it's too beautiful!'

'Then are *you* taking it up? I mean the preposterous theory——'

'It *is* a theory,' she broke in, 'but it isn't necessarily preposterous. Any theory has to suppose something,' she sagely pursued, 'and it depends at any rate on what it's a theory *of*. It's wonderful to see this one work.'

'Wonderful always to see the growth of a legend!' I laughed. 'This is a rare chance to watch one in formation. They're all three in good faith building it up. Isn't that what you made out from him?'

Her tired face fairly lighted. 'Yes—you understand it; and you put it better than I. It's the gradual effect of brooding over the past; the past, that way, grows and grows. They make it and make it. They've persuaded each other—the parents—of so many things that they've at last also persuaded *him*. It has been contagious.'

'It's you who put it well,' I returned. 'It's the oddest thing I ever heard of, but it is, in its way, a reality. Only we mustn't speak of it to others.'

She quite accepted that precaution. 'No — to nobody. *He* doesn't. He keeps it only for me.'

'Conferring on you thus,' I again laughed, 'such a precious privilege!'

She was silent a moment, looking away from me. 'Well, he has kept his vow.'

'You mean of not marrying? Are you very sure?' I asked. 'Didn't he perhaps —— ?' But I faltered at the boldness of my joke.

The next moment I saw I needn't. 'He *was* in love with her,' Lavinia brought out.

I broke now into a peal which, however provoked, struck even my own ear at the moment as rude almost to profanity. 'He literally tells you outright that he's making believe?'

She met me effectively enough. 'I don't think he *knows* he is. He's just completely in the current.'

'The current of the old people's twaddle?'

Again my companion hesitated; but she knew what she thought. 'Well, whatever we call it, I like it. It isn't so common, as the world goes, for any one — let alone for two or three — to feel and to care for the dead as much as that. It's self-deception, no doubt, but it comes from something that — well,' she faltered again, 'is beautiful when one does hear of it. They make her out older, so as to imagine they had her longer; and they make out that certain things really happened to her, so that she shall have had more life. They've invented a whole experience for her, and Marmaduke has become a part of it. There's one thing, above all, they want her to have had.' My young friend's face, as she analysed the mystery, fairly grew bright with her vision. It came to me with a faint dawn of awe that the attitude of the Dedricks *was* contagious. 'And she did have it!' Lavinia declared.

I positively admired her, and if I could yet perfectly be rational without being ridiculous, it was really, more than anything else, to draw from her the whole image. 'She had the bliss of knowing Marmaduke? Let us agree to it, then, since she's not here to contradict us. But what I don't get over is the scant material for *him!*' It may easily be conceived how little, for the moment, I could get over it. It was the last time my impatience was to be too much for me, but I remember how it broke out. 'A man who might have had *you!*'

For an instant I feared I had upset her — thought I saw in her face the tremor of a wild wail. But poor Lavinia was magnificent. 'It wasn't that he might have had "me" — that's nothing: it was, at the most, that I might have had *him*. Well, isn't that just what has happened? He's mine from the moment no one else has him. I give up the past, but don't you see what it does for the rest of life? I'm surer than ever that he won't marry.'

'Of course, he won't — to quarrel, with those people!'

For a minute she answered nothing; then, 'Well, for whatever reason!' she simply said. Now, however, I had gouged out of her a couple of still tears, and I pushed away the whole obscure comedy.

VII

I MIGHT push it away, but I couldn't really get rid of it; nor, on the whole, doubtless, did I want to, for to have in one's life, year after year, a particular question or two that one couldn't comfortably and imposingly make up one's mind about was just the sort of thing to keep one from turning stupid. There had been little need of my enjoining reserve upon Lavinia: she obeyed, in respect to impenetrable silence save with myself, an instinct, an interest of her own. We never therefore gave poor Marmaduke, as you call it, 'away'; we were much too tender, let alone that she was also too proud; and, for himself, evidently, there was not, to the end, in London, another person in his confidence. No echo of the queer part he played ever came back to us; and I can't tell you how this fact, just by itself, brought home to me, little by little, a sense of the charm he was under. I met him 'out' at long intervals — met him usually at dinner. He had grown like a person with a position and a history. Rosy and rich-looking, fat, moreover, distinctly fat at last, there was almost in him something of the bland — yet not too bland — young head of an hereditary business. If the Dedricks had been bankers, he might have constituted the future of the house. There was none the less a long middle stretch during which, though we were all so much in London, he dropped out of my talks with Lavinia. We were conscious, she and I, of his absence from them; but we clearly felt in each quarter that there are things after all unspeakable, and the fact, in any case, had nothing to do with her seeing or not seeing our friend. I was sure, as it happened, that she did see him. But there were moments that for myself still stand out.

One of these was a certain Sunday afternoon when it was so dismally wet that, taking for granted I should have no visitors, I had drawn up to the fire with a book — a successful novel of the day — that I promised myself comfortably to finish. Suddenly, in my absorption, I heard a firm rat-tat-tat; on which I remember giving a groan of inhospitality. But my visitor proved in due course Marmaduke, and Marmaduke proved — in a manner even less, at the point we had reached, to have been counted on — still more attaching than my novel. I think it was only an accident that he became so; it would have been the turn of a hair either way. He hadn't come to speak — he had only come to talk, to show once more that we could continue good old friends without his speaking. But somehow there were the circumstances: the insidious fireside, the things in the room, with their reminders of his younger time; perhaps even too the open face of my book, looking at him from where I had laid it down for him and giving him a chance to feel that he could supersede Wilkie Collins. There was at all events a promise of intimacy, of opportunity for him in the cold lash of the windows by the storm. We should be alone; it was cosy; it was safe.

The action of these impressions was the more marked that what was touched by them, I afterwards saw, was not at all a desire for an effect — was just simply a spirit of happiness that needed to overflow. It had finally become too much for him. His past, rolling up year after year, had grown too interesting. But he was, all the same, directly stupefying. I forget what turn of our preliminary gossip brought it out, but it came, in explanation of something or other, as it had not yet come: 'When a man has had for a few months what *I* had, you know!' The moral appeared to be that nothing in the way of human experience of the exquisite could again particularly matter. He saw, however, that I failed immediately to fit his reflection to a definite case, and he went on with the frankest smile: 'You look as bewildered as if you suspected me of alluding to some sort of thing that isn't usually spoken of; but I assure you I mean nothing more reprehensible than our blessed engagement itself.'

'Your blessed engagement?' I couldn't help the tone in which I took him up; but the way he disposed of that was something of which I feel to this hour the influence. It was only a look, but it put an end to my tone forever. It made me, on my side, after an instant, look at the fire — look hard and even turn a little red. During this moment I saw my alternatives and I chose; so that when I met his eyes again I was fairly ready. 'You still feel,' I asked with sympathy, 'how much it did for you?'

I had no sooner spoken than I saw that that would be from that moment the right way. It instantly made all the difference. The main question would be whether I could keep it up. I remember that only a few minutes later, for instance, this question gave a flare. His reply had been abundant and imperturbable — had included some glance at the way death brings into relief even the faintest things that have preceded it; on which I felt myself suddenly as restless as if I had grown afraid of him. I got up to ring for tea; he went on talking — talking about Maud-Evelyn and what she had been for him; and when the servant had come up I prolonged, nervously, on purpose, the order I had wished to give. It made time, and I could speak to the footman sufficiently without thinking: what I thought of really was the risk of turning right round with a little outbreak. The temptation was strong; the same influences that had worked for my companion just worked, in their way, during that minute or two, for me. *Should* I, taking him unaware, flash at him a plain 'I say, just settle it for me once for all. *Are* you the boldest and basest of fortune-hunters, or have you only, more innocently and perhaps more pleasantly, suffered your brain slightly to soften?' But I missed the chance — which I didn't in fact afterwards regret. My servant went out, and I faced again to my visitor, who continued to converse. I met his eyes once more, and their effect was repeated. If anything had happened to his brain this effect was perhaps the domination of the madman's stare. Well, he was the easiest and gentlest of madmen. By the time the footman came back with tea I was in for it; I was in for everything. By 'everything' I mean my whole subsequent treatment of the case. It *was* — the case was — really beautiful. So, like all the rest, the hour comes back to me: the sound of the wind and the rain; the look of the empty, ugly, cabless square and of the stormy spring light; the way that, uninterrupted and absorbed, we had tea together by my fire. So it was that he found me receptive and that I found myself able to look merely grave and kind when he said, for example: 'Her father and mother, you know, really, that first day — the day they picked me up on the Splügen — recognised me as the proper one.'

'The proper one?'

'To make their son-in-law. They wanted her so,' he went on, 'to have had, don't you know, just everything.'

'Well, if she did have it'—I tried to be cheerful—'isn't the whole thing then all right?'

'Oh, it's all right *now*,' he replied—'now that we've got it all there before us. You see, they couldn't like me so much'—he wished me thoroughly to understand—'without wanting me to have been the man.'

'I see—that was natural.'

'Well,' said Marmaduke, 'it prevented the possibility of any one else'

'Ah, that would never have done!' I laughed.

His own pleasure at it was impenetrable, splendid. 'You see, they couldn't do much, the old people—and they can do still less now—with the future; so they had to do what they could with the past.'

'And they seem to have done,' I concurred, 'remarkably much.'

'Everything, simply. Everything,' he repeated. Then he had an idea, though without insistence or importunity—I noticed it just flicker in his face. 'If you *were* to come to Westbourne Terrace——'

'Oh, don't speak of that!' I broke in. 'It wouldn't be decent now. I should have come, if at all, ten years ago.'

But he saw, with his good humour, further than this. 'I see what you mean. But there's much more in the place now than then.'

'I dare say. People get new things. All the same——!' I was at bottom but resisting my curiosity.

Marmaduke didn't press me, but he wanted me to know. 'There are our rooms—the whole set; and I don't believe you ever saw anything more charming, for *her* taste was extraordinary. I'm afraid, too, that I myself have had much to say to them.' Then as he made out that I was again a little at sea, 'I'm talking,' he went on, 'of the suite prepared for her marriage.' He 'talked' like a crown prince. 'They were ready, to the last touch—there was nothing more to be done. And they're just as they were — not an object moved, not an arrangement altered, not a person but ourselves coming in: they're only exquisitely kept. All our presents are there — I should have liked you to see them.'

It had become a torment by this time — I saw that I had made a mistake. But I carried it off. 'Oh, I couldn't have borne it!'

'They're not sad,' he smiled — 'they're too lovely to be sad. They're happy. And the things——!' He seemed, in the excitement of our talk, to have them before him.

'They're so very wonderful?'

'Oh, selected with a patience that makes them almost priceless. It's really a museum. There was nothing they thought too good for her.'

I had lost the museum, but I reflected that it could contain no object so rare as my visitor. 'Well, you've helped them — you could do *that*.'

He quite eagerly assented. 'I could do that, thank God — I could do that! I felt it from the first, and it's what I *have* done.' Then as if the connection were direct: 'All *my* things are there.'

I thought a moment. 'Your presents?'

'Those I made her. She loved each one, and I remember about each the particular thing she said. Though I do say it,' he continued, 'none of the others, as a matter of fact, come near mine. I look at them every day, and I assure you I'm not ashamed.' Evidently, in short, he had spared nothing, and he talked on and on. He really quite swaggered.

VIII

In relation to times and intervals I can only recall that if this visit of his to me had been in the early spring it was one day in the late autumn — a day, which couldn't have been in the same year, with the difference of hazy, drowsy sunshine and brown and yellow leaves — that, taking a short cut across Kensington Gardens, I came, among the untrodden ways, upon a couple occupying chairs under a tree, who immediately rose at the sight of me. I had been behind them at recognition, the fact that Marmaduke was in deep mourning having perhaps, so far as I had observed it, misled me. In my desire both not to look flustered at meeting them and to spare their own confusion I bade them again be seated and asked leave, as a third chair was at hand, to share a little their rest. Thus it befell that after a minute Lavinia and I had sat down, while our friend, who had looked at his watch, stood before us among the fallen foliage and remarked that he was sorry to have to leave us. Lavinia said nothing, but I expressed regret; I couldn't, however, as it struck me, without a false or a vulgar note speak as if I had interrupted a tender passage or separated a pair of lovers. But I could look him up and down, take in his deep mourning. He had not made, for going off, any other pretext than that his time was up and that he was due at home. 'Home,' with him now, had but one meaning: I knew him to be completely quartered in Westbourne Terrace. 'I hope nothing has happened,' I said — 'that you've lost no one whom *I* know.'

Marmaduke looked at my companion, and she looked at Marmaduke. 'He has lost his wife,' she then observed.

Oh, this time, I fear, I had a small quaver of brutality; but it was at him I directed it. 'Your wife? I didn't know you had *had* a wife!'

'Well,' he replied, positively gay in his black suit, his black gloves, his high hatband, 'the more we live in the past, the more things we find in it. That's a literal fact. You would see the truth of it if your life had taken such a turn.'

'*I* live in the past,' Lavinia put in gently and as if to help us both.

'But with the result, my dear,' I returned, 'of not making,

x

I hope, such extraordinary discoveries!' It seemed absurd to be afraid to be light.

'May none of her discoveries be more fatal than mine!' Marmaduke wasn't uproarious, but his treatment of the matter had the good taste of simplicity. 'They've wanted it so for her,' he continued to me wonderfully, 'that we've at last seen our way to it — I mean to what Lavinia has mentioned.' He hesitated but three seconds — he brought it brightly out. 'Maud-Evelyn had *all* her young happiness.'

I stared, but Lavinia was, in her peculiar manner, as brilliant. 'The marriage *did* take place,' she quietly, stupendously explained to me.

Well, I was determined not to be left. 'So you're a widower,' I gravely asked, 'and these are the signs?'

'Yes; I shall wear them always now.'

'But isn't it late to have begun?'

My question had been stupid, I felt the next instant; but it didn't matter — he was quite equal to the occasion. 'Oh, I had to wait, you know, till all the facts about my marriage had given me the right.' And he looked at his watch again. 'Excuse me — I *am* due. Good-bye, good-bye.' He shook hands with each of us, and as we sat there together watching him walk away I was struck with his admirable manner of looking the character. I felt indeed as our eyes followed him that we were at one on this, and I said nothing till he was out of sight. Then by the same impulse we turned to each other.

'I thought he was never to marry!' I exclaimed to my friend.

Her fine wasted face met me gravely. 'He isn't — ever. He'll be still more faithful.'

'Faithful this time to whom?'

'Why, to Maud-Evelyn.' I said nothing — I only checked an ejaculation; but I put out a hand and took one of hers, and for a minute we kept silence. 'Of course it's only an idea,' she began again at last, 'but it seems to me a beautiful one.' Then she continued resignedly and remarkably: 'And now *they* can die.'

'Mr. and Mrs. Dedrick?' I pricked up my ears. 'Are they dying?'

'Not quite, but the old lady, it appears, is failing, steadily weakening; less, as I understand it, from any definite ailment than because she just feels her work done and her little sum of passion, as Marmaduke calls it, spent. Fancy, with her convictions, all her reasons for wanting to die! And if she goes, he says, Mr. Dedrick won't long linger. It will be quite "John Anderson my jo."'

'Keeping her company down the hill, to lie beside her at the foot?'

'Yes, having settled all things.'

I turned these things over as we walked away, and how they had settled them — for Maud-Evelyn's dignity and Marmaduke's high advantage; and before we parted that afternoon — we had taken a cab in the Bayswater Road and she had come home with me — I remember saying to her: 'Well, then, when they die won't he be free?'

She seemed scarce to understand. 'Free?'

'To do what he likes.'

She wondered. 'But he does what he likes now.'

'Well, then, what *you* like!'

'Oh, you know what *I* like ——!'

Ah, I closed her mouth! 'You like to tell horrid fibs — yes, I know it!'

What she had then put before me, however, came in time to pass: I heard in the course of the next year of Mrs. Dedrick's extinction, and some months later, without, during the interval, having seen a sign of Marmaduke, wholly taken up with his bereaved patron, learned that her husband had touchingly followed her. I was out of England at the time; we had had to put into practice great economies and let our little place; so that, spending three winters successively in Italy, I devoted the periods between, at home, altogether to visits among people, mainly relatives, to whom these friends of mine were not known.   Lavinia of course wrote to me — wrote, among many things, that Marmaduke was ill and had not seemed at all himself since the loss of his 'family,' and this in spite of the circumstance, which she had already promptly communicated, that they had left him, by will, 'almost everything.'   I knew before I came back to remain that she now saw him often and, to the extent of the change that had overtaken his strength and his spirits, greatly ministered to him. As soon as we at last met I asked for news of him; to which she replied: 'He's gradually going.'   Then on my surprise: 'He has had his life.'

'You mean that, as he said of Mrs. Dedrick, his sum of passion is spent?'

At this she turned away.   'You've never understood.'

I *had*, I conceived; and when I went subsequently to see him I was moreover sure.   But I only said to Lavinia on this first occasion that I would immediately go; which was precisely what brought out the climax, as I feel it to be, of my story.   'He's not now, you know,' she turned round to admonish me, 'in Westbourne Terrace.   He has taken a little old house in Kensington.'

'Then he hasn't kept the things?'

'He has kept everything.'   She looked at me still more as if I had never understood.

'You mean he has moved them?'

She was patient with me.   'He has moved nothing.   Everything is as it was, and kept with the same perfection.'

I wondered.   'But if he doesn't live there?'

'It's just what he does.'

'Then how can he be in Kensington?'

She hesitated, but she had still more than her old grasp of it.   'He's in Kensington — without living.'

'You mean that at the other place —— ?'

'Yes, he spends most of his time. He's driven over there every day — he remains there for hours. He keeps it for that.'

'I see — it's still the museum.'

'It's still the temple!' Lavinia replied, with positive austerity.

'Then why did he move?'

'Because, you see, there' — she faltered again — 'I could come to him. And he wants me,' she said, with admirable simplicity.

Little by little I took it in. 'After the death of the parents, even, you never went?'

'Never.'

'So you haven't seen anything?'

'Anything of hers? Nothing.'

I understood, oh perfectly; but I won't deny that I was disappointed: I had hoped for an account of his wonders, and I immediately felt that it wouldn't be for me to take a step that she had declined. When, a short time later, I saw them together in Kensington Square — there were certain hours of the day that she regularly spent with him — I observed that everything about him was new, handsome, and simple. They were, in their strange, final union — if union it could be called — very natural and very touching; but he was visibly stricken — he had his ailment in his eyes. She moved about him like a sister of charity — at all events like a sister. He was neither robust nor rosy now, nor was his attention visibly very present, and I privately and fancifully asked myself where it wandered and waited. But poor Marmaduke was a gentleman to the end — he wasted away with an excellent manner. He died twelve days ago; the will was opened; and last week, having meanwhile heard from her of its contents, I saw Lavinia. He leaves her everything that he himself had inherited. But she spoke of it all in a way that caused me to say in surprise: 'You haven't yet been to the house?'

'Not yet. I've only seen the solicitors, who tell me there will be no complications.'

There was something in her tone that made me ask more. 'Then you're not curious to see what's there?'

She looked at me with a troubled — almost a pleading — sense, which I understood; and presently she said: 'Will you go with me?'

'Some day, with pleasure — but not the first time. You must go alone then. The "relics" that you'll find there,' I added — for I had read her look — 'you must think of now not as hers ——'

'But as his?'

'Isn't that what his death — with his so close relation to them — has made them for you?'

Her face lighted — I saw it was a view she could thank me for putting into words. 'I see — I see. They *are* his. I'll go.'

She went, and three days ago she came to me. They're really marvels, it appears, treasures extraordinary, and she has them all. Next week I go with her — I shall see them at last. Tell *you* about them, you say? My dear man, everything.

MISS GUNTON OF POUGHKEEPSIE

'It's astonishing what you take for granted!' Lady
Champer had exclaimed to her young friend at an early
stage; and this might have served as a sign that even then
the little plot had begun to thicken. The reflection was
uttered at the time the outlook of the charming American
girl in whom she found herself so interested was still much in
the rough. They had often met, with pleasure to each, during
a winter spent in Rome; and Lily had come to her in London
towards the end of May with further news of a situation the
dawn of which, in March and April, by the Tiber, the Arno,
and the Seine, had considerably engaged her attention. The
Prince had followed Miss Gunton to Florence and then with
almost equal promptitude to Paris, where it was both clear and
comical for Lady Champer that the rigour of his uncertainty
as to parental commands and remittances now detained him.
This shrewd woman promised herself not a little amusement
from her view of the possibilities of the case. Lily was on
the whole showing a wonder; therefore the drama would lose
nothing from her character, her temper, her tone. She was
waiting — this was the truth she had imparted to her clever
protectress — to see if her Roman captive would find himself
drawn to London. Should he really turn up there she would
the next thing start for America, putting him to the test of
that wider range and declining to place her confidence till he
should have arrived in New York at her heels. If he remained
in Paris or returned to Rome she would stay in London and,
as she phrased it, have a good time by herself. Did he expect
her to go back to Paris for him? Why not in that case just

as well go back to Rome at once? The first thing for her,
Lily intimated to her London adviser, was to show what, in
her position, *she* expected.

Her position meanwhile was one that Lady Champer, try as
she would, had as yet succeeded neither in understanding nor
in resigning herself not to understand. It was that of being
extraordinarily pretty, amazingly free, and perplexingly good,
and of presenting these advantages in a positively golden light.
How was one to estimate a girl whose nearest approach to a
drawback — that is to an encumbrance — appeared to be a
grandfather carrying on a business in an American city her
ladyship had never otherwise heard of, with whom communication was all by cable and on the subject of 'drawing'?
Expression was on the old man's part moreover as concise as
it was expensive, consisting as it inveterately did of but the
single word 'Draw.' Lily drew, on every occasion in life, and
it at least could not be said of the pair — when the 'family
idea,' as embodied in America, was exposed to criticism —
that they were not in touch. Mr. Gunton had given her
further Mrs. Brine, to come out with her, and with this provision and the perpetual pecuniary he plainly figured — to
Lily's own mind — as solicitous to the point of anxiety. Mrs.
Brine's scheme of relations seemed in truth to be simpler still.
There was a transatlantic 'Mr. Brine,' of whom she often
spoke — and never in any other way; but she wrote for newspapers; she prowled in catacombs, visiting more than once
even those of Paris; she haunted hotels; she picked up com-
patriots; she spoke above all a language that often baffled
comprehension. She mattered, however, but little; she was
mainly so occupied in having what Lily had likewise independently glanced at — a good time by herself. It was difficult enough indeed to Lady Champer to see the wonderful
girl reduced to that, yet she was a little person who kept one
somehow in presence of the incalculable. Old measures and
familiar rules were of no use at all with her — she had so

broken the moulds and so mixed the marks. What was confounding was her disparities — the juxtaposition in her of beautiful sun-flushed heights and deep dark holes. She had none of the things that the other things implied. She dangled in the air in a manner that made one dizzy; though one took comfort, at the worst, in feeling that one was there to catch her if she fell. Falling, at the same time, appeared scarce one of her properties, and it was positive for Lady Champer at moments that if one held out one's arms one might be, after all, much more likely to be pulled up. That was really a part of the excitement of the acquaintance.

'Well,' said this friend and critic on one of the first of the London days, 'say he does, on your return to your own country, go after you: how do you read, on that occurrence, the course of events?'

'Why, if he comes after me I'll have him.'

'And do you think it so easy to "have" him?'

Lily appeared, lovely and candid, — and it was an air and a way she often had, — to wonder what she thought. 'I don't know that I think it any easier than he seems to think it to have *me*. I know moreover that, though he wants awfully to see the country, he wouldn't just now come to America unless to marry me; and if I take him at all,' she pursued, 'I want first to be able to show him to the girls.'

'Why "first"?' Lady Champer asked. 'Wouldn't it do as well last?'

'Oh, I should want them to see me in Rome, too,' said Lily. 'But, dear me, I'm afraid I want a good many things! What I most want of course is that he should show me unmistakably what *he* wants. Unless he wants me more than anything else in the world, I don't want him. Besides, I hope he doesn't think I'm going to be married anywhere but in my own place.'

'I see,' said Lady Champer. 'It's for your wedding you want the girls. And it's for the girls you want the Prince.'

'Well, we're all bound by that promise. And of course *you*'ll come!'

'Ah, my dear child —— !' Lady Champer gasped.

'You can come with the old Princess. You'll be just the right company for her.'

The elder friend considered afresh, with depth, the younger's beauty and serenity. 'You *are*, love, beyond everything!'

The beauty and serenity took on for a moment a graver cast. 'Why do you so often say that to me?'

'Because you so often make it the only thing to say. But you'll some day find out why,' Lady Champer added with an intention of encouragement.

Lily Gunton, however, was a young person to whom encouragement looked queer; she had grown up without need of it, and it seemed indeed scarce required in her situation. 'Do you mean you believe his mother won't come?'

'Over mountains and seas to see you married? — and to be seen also of the girls? If she does, *I* will. But we had perhaps better,' Lady Champer wound up, 'not count our chickens before they're hatched.' To which, with one of the easy returns of gaiety that were irresistible in her, Lily made answer that neither of the ladies in question struck her quite as chickens.

The Prince at all events presented himself in London with a promptitude that contributed to make the warning gratuitous. Nothing could have exceeded, by this time, Lady Champer's appreciation of her young friend, whose merits 'town' at the beginning of June threw into renewed relief; but she had the imagination of greatness and, though she believed she tactfully kept it to herself, she thought what the young man had thus done a great deal for a Roman prince to do. Take him as he was, with the circumstances — and they were certainly peculiar, and he was charming — it was a far cry for him from Piazza Colonna to Clarges Street. If Lady Champer had the imagination of greatness, which the Prince in all sorts of ways gratified, Miss Gunton of Poughkeepsie — it was vain to pretend the contrary — was not great in any particular save one. She was great when she 'drew.' It was true that at the beginning of June she did draw with unprecedented energy and in a manner that, though Mrs. Brine's remarkable nerve apparently could stand it, fairly made a poor baronet's widow, little as it was her business, hold her breath. It was none of her business at all, yet she talked of it even with the Prince himself — to whom it was indeed a favourite subject and whose greatness, oddly enough, never appeared to shrink in the effect it produced upon him. The line they took together was that of wondering if the scale of Lily's drafts made really most for the presumption that the capital at her disposal was rapidly dwindling, or for that of its being practically infinite. 'Many a fellow,' the young man smiled, 'would marry her to pull her up.' He was in any case of the opinion that it was an occasion for deciding — one way or the other — quickly. Well, he did decide — so quickly that, within the week, Lily communicated to her friend that he had offered her his hand, his heart, his fortune, and all his titles, grandeurs, and appurtenances. She had given him his answer, and he was in bliss; though nothing, as yet, was settled but that.

Tall, fair, active, educated, amiable, simple, carrying so naturally his great name and pronouncing so kindly Lily's small one, the happy youth, if he was one of the most ancient of princes, was one of the most modern of Romans. This second character it was his special aim and pride to cultivate. He would have been pained at feeling himself an hour behind his age; and he had a way — both touching and amusing to some observers — of constantly comparing his watch with the dial of the day's news. It was in fact easy to see that in deciding to ally himself with a young alien of vague origin, whose striking beauty was reinforced only by her presumptive money, he had even put forward a little the fine hands of his timepiece. No one else, however, — not even Lady Champer, and least of all Lily herself, — had quite taken the measure, in this connection, of his merit. The quick decision he had spoken of was really a flying leap. He desired incontestably to rescue Miss Gunton's remainder; but to rescue it he had to take it for granted, and taking it for granted was nothing less than — at whatever angle considered — a risk. He never, naturally, used the word to her, but he distinctly faced a peril. The sense of what he had staked on a vague return gave him, at the height of the London season, bad nights, or rather bad mornings — for he danced with his intended, as a usual thing, conspicuously, till dawn — besides obliging him to take, in the form of long explanatory, argumentative, and persuasive letters to his mother and sisters, his uncles, aunts, cousins, and preferred confidants, large measures of justification at home. The family sense was strong in his huge old house, just as the family array was numerous; he was dutifully conscious of the trust reposed in him, and moved from morning till night, he perfectly knew, as the observed of a phalanx of observers; whereby he the more admired himself for his passion, precipitation, and courage. He had only a probability to go upon, but he was — and by the romantic tradition of his race — so in love that he should surely not be taken in.

His private agitation of course deepened when, to do honour to her engagement and as if she would have been ashamed to do less, Lily 'drew' again most gloriously; but he managed to smile beautifully on her asking him if he didn't want her to be splendid, and at his worst hours he went no further than to wish that he might be married on the morrow. Unless it were the next day, or at most the next month, it really at moments seemed best that it should never be at all. On the most favourable view — with the solidity of the residuum fully assumed — there were still minor questions and dangers. A vast America, arching over his nuptials, bristling with expectant bridesmaids and underlaying their feet with expensive flowers, stared him in the face and prompted him to the reflection that if she dipped so deep into the mere remote overflow her dive into the fount itself would verily be a header. If she drew at such a rate in London how wouldn't she draw at Poughkeepsie? he asked himself, and practically asked Lady Champer; yet bore the strain of the question, without an answer, so nobly that when, with small delay, Poughkeepsie seemed simply to heave with reassurances, he regarded the ground as firm and his tact as rewarded. 'And now at last, dearest,' he said, 'since everything's so satisfactory, you *will* write?' He put it appealingly, endearingly, yet as if he could scarce doubt.

'Write, love? Why,' she replied, 'I've done nothing *but* write! I've written ninety letters.'

'But not to mamma,' he smiled.

'Mamma?' — she stared. 'My dear boy, I've not at this time of day to remind you that I've the misfortune to have no mother. I lost mamma, you know, as you lost your father, in childhood. You may be sure,' said Lily Gunton, 'that I wouldn't otherwise have waited for you to prompt me.'

There came into his face a kind of amiable convulsion. 'Of course, darling, I remember — your beautiful mother (she *must* have been beautiful!) whom I should have been so glad to know. I was thinking of *my* mamma — who'll be so delighted to hear from you.' The Prince spoke English in perfection — had lived in it from the cradle and appeared, particularly when alluding to his home and family, to matters familiar and of fact, or to those of dress and sport, of general recreation, to draw such a comfort from it as made the girl think of him as scarce more a foreigner than a pleasant, auburn, slightly awkward, slightly slangy, and extremely well-tailored young Briton would have been. He sounded 'mamma' like a rosy English schoolboy; yet just then, for the first time, the things with which he was connected struck her as in a manner strange and far-off. Everything in him, none the less — face and voice and tact, above all his deep desire — laboured to bring them near and make them natural. This was intensely the case as he went on: 'Such a little letter as you *might* send would really be awfully jolly.'

'My dear child,' Lily replied on quick reflection, 'I'll write to her with joy the minute I hear from her. Won't she write to *me?*'

The Prince just visibly flushed. 'In a moment if you'll only ——'

'Write to her first?'

'Just pay her a little — no matter how little — your respects.'

His attenuation of the degree showed perhaps a sense of a weakness of position; yet it was no perception of this that made the girl immediately say: 'Oh, *caro*, I don't think I can begin. If you feel that *she* won't — as you evidently do — is it because you've asked her and she has refused?' The next moment, 'I see you *have!*' she exclaimed. His rejoinder to this was to catch her in his arms, to press his cheek to hers, to murmur a flood of tender words in which contradiction, confession, supplication, and remonstrance were oddly confounded; but after he had sufficiently disengaged her to allow her to speak again, his effusion was checked by what came. 'Do you really mean you can't induce her?' It renewed itself on the first return of ease; or it, more correctly perhaps, in order to renew itself, took this return — a trifle too soon — for granted. Singular, for the hour, was the quickness with which ease could leave them — so blissfully at one as they were; and, to be brief, it had not come back even when Lily spoke of the matter to Lady Champer. It is true that she waited but little to do so. She then went straight to the point. 'What would you do if his mother doesn't write?'

'The old Princess — to *you?*' Her ladyship had not had time to mount guard in advance over the tone of this, which was doubtless (as she instantly, for that matter, herself became aware) a little too much that of 'Have you really expected she would?' What Lily had expected found itself therefore not unassisted to come out — and came out indeed to such a tune that with all kindness, but with a melancholy deeper than any she had ever yet in the general connection used, Lady Champer was moved to remark that the situation might have been found more possible had a little more historic sense been brought to it.   'You're the dearest thing in the world, and I can't imagine a girl's carrying herself in any way, in a difficult position, better than you do; only I'm bound to say I think you ought to remember that you're entering a very great house, of tremendous antiquity, fairly groaning under the weight of ancient honours, the heads of which — through the tradition of the great part they've played in the world — are accustomed to a great deal of deference. The old Princess, my dear, you see' — her ladyship gathered confidence a little as she went — 'is a most prodigious personage.'

'Why, Lady Champer, of course she is, and that's just what I like her for!' said Lily Gunton.

'She has never in her whole life made an advance, any more than any one has ever dreamed of expecting it of her. It's a pity that while you were there you didn't see her, for I think it would have helped you to understand.   However, as you did see his sisters, the two Duchesses and dear little Donna Claudia, you know how charming they all *can* be.   They only want to be nice, I know, and I dare say that on the smallest opportunity you'll hear from the Duchesses.'

The plural had a sound of splendour, but Lily quite kept her head.   'What do you call an opportunity?   Am I not giving them, by accepting their son and brother, the best — and in fact the only — opportunity they could desire?'

'I like the way, darling,' Lady Champer smiled, 'you talk about "accepting"!'

Lily thought of this — she thought of everything.   'Well, say it would have been a better one still for them if I had refused him.'

Her friend caught her up. 'But you haven't.'

'Then they must make the most of the occasion as it is.' Lily was very sweet, but very lucid. 'The Duchesses may write or not, as they like; but I'm afraid the Princess simply *must*.' She hesitated, but after a moment went on: 'He oughtn't to be willing moreover that I shouldn't expect to be welcomed.'

'He isn't!' Lady Champer blurted out.

Lily jumped at it. 'Then he has told you? It's her attitude?'

She had spoken without passion, but her friend was scarce the less frightened. 'My poor child, what can he do?'

Lily saw perfectly. 'He can make her.'

Lady Champer turned it over, but her fears were what was clearest. 'And if he doesn't?'

'If he "doesn't"?' The girl ambiguously echoed it.

'I mean if he can't.'

Well, Lily, more cheerfully, declined, for the hour, to consider this. He would certainly do for her what was right; so that after all, though she had herself put the question, she disclaimed the idea that an answer was urgent. There was time, she conveyed — which Lady Champer only desired to believe; a faith moreover somewhat shaken in the latter when the Prince entered her room the next day with the information that there was none — none at least to leave everything in the air. Lady Champer had not yet made up her mind as to which of these young persons she liked most to draw into confidence, nor as to whether she most inclined to take the Roman side with the American or the American side with the Roman. But now in truth she was settled; she gave proof of it in the increased lucidity with which she spoke for Lily.

'Wouldn't the Princess depart — a — from her usual attitude for such a great occasion?'

The difficulty was a little that the young man so well understood his mother. 'The devil of it is, you see, that it's for Lily herself, so much more, she thinks the occasion great.'

Lady Champer mused. 'If you hadn't her consent I could understand it. But from the moment she thinks the girl good enough for you to marry —— '

'Ah, she doesn't!' the Prince gloomily interposed. 'However,' he explained, 'she accepts her because there are reasons — my own feeling, now so my very life, don't you see? But it isn't quite open arms. All the same, as I tell Lily, the arms *would* open.'

'If she'd make the first step? Hum!' said Lady Champer, not without the note of grimness. 'She'll be obstinate.'

The young man, with a melancholy eye, quite coincided. 'She'll be obstinate.'

'So that I strongly recommend you to manage it,' his friend went on after a pause. 'It strikes me that if the Princess can't do it for Lily she might at least do it for you. Any girl you marry becomes thereby somebody.'

'Of course — doesn't she? She certainly ought to do it for *me*. I'm after all the head of the house.'

'Well, then, make her!' said Lady Champer a little impatiently.

'I will. Mamma adores me, and I adore *her*.'

'And you adore Lily, and Lily adores you — therefore everybody adores everybody, especially as I adore you both. With so much adoration all round, therefore, things ought to march.'

'They shall!' the young man declared with spirit. 'I adore you, too — you don't mention that; for you help me immensely. But what do you suppose she'll do if she doesn't?'

The agitation already visible in him ministered a little to vagueness; but his friend after an instant disembroiled it. 'What do I suppose Lily will do if your mother remains stiff?' Lady Champer faltered, but she let him have it, 'She'll break.'

Y

His wondering eyes became strange.   'Just for that?'

'You may certainly say it isn't much — when people love as you do.'

'Ah, I'm afraid then Lily doesn't!' — and he turned away in his trouble.

She watched him while he moved, not speaking for a minute.   'My dear young man, are you afraid of your mamma?'

He faced short about again.   'I'm afraid of this — that if she does do it she won't forgive her. She *will* do it — yes. But Lily will be for her, in consequence, ever after, the person who has made her submit herself. She'll hate her for that — and then she'll hate me for being concerned in it.' The Prince presented it all with clearness — almost with charm.   'What do you say to that?'

His friend had to think.   'Well, only, I fear, that we belong, Lily and I, to a race unaccustomed to counting with such passions. Let her hate!' she, however, a trifle inconsistently wound up.

'But I love her so!'

'Which?'   Lady Champer asked it almost ungraciously; in such a tone at any rate that, seated on the sofa with his elbows on his knees, his much-ringed hands nervously locked together and his eyes of distress wide open, he met her with visible surprise.   What she met *him* with is perhaps best noted by the fact that after a minute of it his hands covered his bent face and she became aware she had drawn tears. This produced such regret in her that before they parted she did what she could to attenuate and explain — making a great point, at all events, of her rule, with Lily, of putting only his own side of the case.   'I insist awfully, you know, on your greatness!'

He jumped up, wincing.   'Oh, that's horrid.'

'I don't know. Whose fault is it, then, at any rate, if trying to help you may have that side?'   This was a question that, with the tangle he had already to unwind, only added a twist; yet she went on as if positively to add another. 'Why on earth don't you, all of you, leave them alone?'

'Leave them —— ? '

'All your Americans.'

'Don't you like them then — the women?'

She hesitated. 'No. Yes. They're an interest. But they're a nuisance. It's a question, very certainly, if they're worth the trouble they give.'

This at least it seemed he could take in. 'You mean that one should be quite sure first what they *are* worth?'

He made her laugh now. 'It would appear that you never *can* be. But also really that you can't keep your hands off.'

He fixed the social scene an instant with his heavy eye. 'Yes. Doesn't it?'

'However,' she pursued as if he again a little irritated her, 'Lily's position is quite simple.'

'Quite. She just loves me.'

'I mean simple for herself. She really makes no differences. It's only we — you and I — who make them all.'

The Prince wondered. 'But she tells me she delights in us; has, that is, such a sense of what we are supposed to "represent."'

'Oh, she *thinks* she has. Americans think they have all sorts of things; but they haven't. That's just *it*' — Lady Champer was philosophic. 'Nothing but their Americanism. If you marry anything, you marry that; and if your mother accepts anything that's what she accepts.' Then, though the young man followed the demonstration with an apprehension almost pathetic, she gave him without mercy the whole of it. 'Lily's rigidly logical. A girl — as *she* knows girls — is "welcomed," on her engagement, before anything else can happen, by the family of her young man; and the motherless girl, alone in the world, more punctually than any other. His mother — if she's a "lady" — takes it upon herself. Then the girl goes and stays with them. But she does nothing before. *Tirez-vous de là.*'

The young man sought on the spot to obey this last injunction, and his effort presently produced a flash. 'Oh, if she'll come and *stay* with us ' — all would, easily, be well! The flash went out, however, when Lady Champer returned: 'Then let the Princess invite her.'

Lily a fortnight later simply said to her, from one hour to the other, 'I'm going home,' and took her breath away by sailing on the morrow with the Bransbys. The tense cord had somehow snapped; the proof was in the fact that the Prince, dashing off to his good friend at this crisis an obscure, an ambiguous note, started the same night for Rome. Lady Champer, for the time, sat in darkness, but during the summer many things occurred; and one day in the autumn, quite unheralded and with the signs of some of them in his face, the Prince appeared again before her. He was not long in telling her his story, which was simply that he had come to her, all the way from Rome, for news of Lily and to talk of Lily. She was prepared, as it happened, to meet his impatience; yet her preparation was but little older than his arrival and was deficient moreover in an important particular. She was not prepared to knock him down, and she made him talk to gain time. She had however, to understand, put a primary question: 'She never wrote, then?'

'Mamma? Oh yes — when she at last got frightened at Miss Gunton's having become so silent. She wrote in August; but Lily's own decisive letter — letter to me, I mean — crossed with it. It was too late — that put an end.'

'A *real* end?'

Everything in the young man showed how real. 'On the ground of her being willing no longer to keep up, by the stand she had taken, such a relation between mamma and *me*. But her rupture,' he wailed, 'keeps it up more than anything else.'

'And is it very bad?'

'Awful, I assure you. I've become for my mother a person who has made her make, all for nothing, an unprecedented advance, a humble submission; and she's so disgusted, all round, that it's no longer the same old charming thing for us to be together. It makes it worse for her that I'm still madly in love.'

'Well,' said Lady Champer after a moment, 'if you're still madly in love I can only be sorry for you.'

'You can *do* nothing for me? — don't advise me to go over?'

She had to take a longer pause. 'You don't at all know then what has happened? — that old Mr. Gunton has died and left her everything?'

All his vacancy and curiosity came out in a wild echo. '"Everything"?'

'She writes me that it's a great deal of money.'

'You've just heard from her, then?'

'This morning. I seem to make out,' said Lady Champer, 'an extraordinary number of dollars.'

'Oh, I was sure it was!' the young man moaned.

'And she's engaged,' his friend went on, 'to Mr. Bransby.'

He bounded, rising before her. 'Mr. Bransby?'

'"Adam P."'— the gentleman with whose mother and sisters she went home. *They*, she writes, have beautifully welcomed her.'

'*Dio mio!*' The Prince stared; he had flushed with the blow, and the tears had come into his eyes. 'And I believed she loved me!'

'*I* didn't!' said Lady Champer with some curtness.

He gazed about; he almost rocked; and, unconscious of her words, he appealed, inarticulate and stricken. At last, however, he found his voice. 'What on earth then shall I do? I can less than ever go back to mamma!'

She got up for him, she thought for him, pushing a better chair into her circle. 'Stay here with me, and I'll ring for tea, Sit there nearer the fire — you're cold.'

'Awfully!' he confessed as he sank. 'And I believed she loved me!' he repeated as he stared at the fire.

'*I* didn't!' Lady Champer once more declared. This time, visibly, he heard her, and she immediately met his wonder. 'No — it was all the rest; your great historic position, the glamour of your name, and your past. Otherwise what she stood out for wouldn't be excusable. But she has the sense of such things, and *they* were what she loved.' So, by the fire, his hostess explained it, while he wondered the more.

'I thought that last summer you told me just the contrary.'

It seemed, to do her justice, to strike her. 'Did I? Oh, well, how does one know? With Americans one is lost!'